Christmas at Pemberley

D0709167

Christmas at Pemberley

A Pride & Prejudice Christmas Sequel

REGINA JEFFERS

Ulysses Press

Text copyright © 2011 Regina Jeffers. Design copyright © 2011 Ulysses Press and its licensors. All rights reserved. No part of this publication may be reproduced, stored in a retrieval system, or transmitted in any form or by any means, electronic, mechanical, photocopying, recording or otherwise, without the prior written permission of the publisher.

Published in the United States by
ULYSSES PRESS
P.O. Box 3440
Berkeley, CA 94703
www.ulyssespress.com

ISBN: 978-1-56975-991-2
Library of Congress Catalog Number 2011926017

Acquisitions Editor: Keith Riegert
Managing Editor: Claire Chun
Editor: Sunah Cherwin
Proofreader: Elyce Berrigan-Dunlop
Production: Judith Metzener
Cover design: what!design @ whatweb.com
Cover photo: Anonymous, 18th century. Musee des Beaux-Arts, Marseille, France. © Scala/White Images / Art Resources, NY

Printed in the United States by Bang Printing

10 9 8 7 6 5 4 3 2 1

Distributed by Publishers Group West

"An infant is a speck of Heaven that God allowed us to experience." This is the story of a Regency Christmas, one centered on the birth of a child. For me, 2011 offered a special Christmas. In November, my son welcomed his first child into the world—my first grandchild. It is a boy, and I dedicate this book to that "speck of Heaven" we will come to know.

CHAPTER I

❧ ❧ ❧

FROM THE CARRIAGE'S rear-facing seat, Darcy insisted, "Elizabeth, we cannot."

Elizabeth Darcy clung to the coach's strap out of necessity, but despite her husband's reasonableness, she objected to his order. "But, Fitzwilliam, we must be home for Christmas."

"Christmas or not, you're too precious for me to risk your injury under such appalling conditions." He eyed her expanding waistline, but he made no direct reference to the strong possibility that she carried his heir. Darcy gestured to the icy roads they had encountered outside of Harrogate.

With exasperation's deep sigh, she said, "I shall bow to your wishes."

Darcy realized that even after two years of marriage, it still hurt Elizabeth's pride to allow him dominance over her in any way. They had always had a friendly "contention" between them, a well-developed twisting of language and logic. It was this quality that had attracted him to the former Elizabeth Bennet. "Verbal swordplay," he had termed it. He rapped on the roof and gave Mr. Simpson orders to find appropriate lodgings.

Through the trap, his coachman shouted over the elements. "There be a small inn slightly off the main road. Maybe three miles, Sir."

"Take your time, Simpson," Darcy ordered.

❧ ❧ ❧

GREENRUSH PUBLIC LIBRARY

"There is no need, Uncle," Georgiana Darcy assured the Earl of Matlock. "Fitzwilliam and Elizabeth shall be home tomorrow. My brother wouldn't miss Pemberley's Christmas. It's his favorite festivity. Fitzwilliam takes his seasonal duties quite seriously." The girl tried not to flinch at her Aunt Catherine's customary snort. If Georgiana had any inclination that her formidable aunt had called on her brother, the Earl, Georgiana would never have traveled to Matlock on a day trip. Lady Catherine De Bourgh had always frightened the girl, and recently her mother's older sister had all but disowned the Darcy family when Fitzwilliam had chosen Elizabeth Bennet as his wife over Lady Catherine's frail daughter, Anne. In fact, Lady Catherine's condemnation of the new Mrs. Darcy had created a permanent split in the family tree. Darcy had refused to acknowledge the woman he once revered.

"And have we any news of the colonel?" Georgiana's attempted nonchalance sounded contrived even to her. Information regarding Edward Fitzwilliam's inevitable return was the true reason for Georgiana's visit. The colonel had traveled to America nearly a year prior, and she had counted the days, praying for his early return: It was her secret Christmas wish. Along with her brother, Edward served as Georgiana's guardian. It was he to whom she had turned when she felt intimidated by her brother's sense of propriety and her aunt's demoralizing mandates. And Georgiana cherished every moment she had spent with the man. The recent difficulties the army had faced in the Americas had brought her more than one sleepless night.

"We expect Edward's return some time after the New Year," the Countess had shared. "We had hoped he would be able to share the festive days under our roof, but the colonel's last letter indicated otherwise."

Georgiana let out a relief's sigh: He would return soon. "I am pleased, Countess." She had set her teacup on a nearby table. "Fitzwilliam will rejoice in the news."

Lady Catherine had held her tongue longer than anyone could

have expected. Then she spoke, and disdain laced her words. "At least, the colonel's return will force your brother to see to your Come Out. You're nineteen and haven't made your appearance in London's Society. It makes sense that Darcy would need to protect you from his wife's influence," she said with a snarl. "I'm certain that my nephew regrets his choice of mates, but who am I to bring that to his attention?"

Georgiana noted that both the Earl and his Countess rolled their eyes. She wanted to defend her brother's decision, but she would not betray the fact that Pemberley had suffered with Elizabeth's two previous miscarriages. Lady Catherine would see Mrs. Darcy's inability to carry to term proof of Elizabeth Bennet's inferiority. Georgiana's aunt would have no sympathy for the grieving parents. "We've been busy at Pemberley establishing my brother's imprint on the estate," Georgiana lamely offered.

"Nonsense." Lady Catherine ignored her niece's explanation. "Darcy's been the Master of Pemberley since his father's passing."

The Earl interceded. "It takes a young man years to replace his father's legacy. My nephew's marriage has opened new doors for Darcy's separate identity. People considered the late Mr. Darcy one of the best. It's no fault if Darcy has taken his time in creating his own hereditament."

A second contemptuous snort filled the room. "Either way, Child, you should have made your Society entrance. Edward will see that Darcy no longer shirks his duties. The colonel may not have been able to prevent Darcy from denying his familial duty to Anne, but Edward has the legal right to insist upon your presentation. Thank goodness someone in this family understands decency and comportment."

Georgiana wanted to scream that her aunt's narrow view had nothing to do with correctness and everything to do with redress. Instead, Georgiana stood to make her exit. "We hope soon to see you at Pemberley, Your Lordship. My brother always appreciates your pragmatic advice, and I shall look forward to a chess rematch."

The Matlocks followed Georgiana to their feet. Lady Matlock caught Georgiana's hand. "We shall see each other upon Edward's return if not before then. Give Fitzwilliam and Mrs. Darcy our affection."

"Yes, Ma'am." Georgiana turned to Lady Catherine. "As always, Aunt, it's a pleasure to see you. I pray that you have a safe return to Kent." Out of respect, Georgiana dropped a quick curtsy.

"Come," the Countess said. "I am certain that your carriage and Mrs. Annesley await."

∾⊘∾ ∾⊘∾ ∾⊘∾

"It is not much, Fitzwilliam," Elizabeth observed as her husband assisted her from his traveling coach. The small inn on a secondary road obviously lacked the amenities to which they had become accustomed on this journey. No one hustled forward to help Mr. Simpson or Jasper with the coach.

Darcy followed her gaze and tried not to frown. "If the place is clean, dry, and warm, I will be thankful." Icy rain pelted the umbrella he held over their heads. "Let us see what the man has to offer weary travelers."

They entered the building to find a small common room with a full fire in the hearth. Darcy released Elizabeth to the blaze's warmth while he met the jovial innkeeper, who bustled in from the kitchen. "Good-day, Sir," the man called as he approached. Glancing at Elizabeth, he added, "I see that you and yer missus rightly decided to seek shelter from this storm. I be Josiah Washington, and this be Prestwick's Portal."

"An alliterative name." Darcy observed the inn's simplicity.

"Me wife's idea—said it sounded like an expensive painting."

"Would you have a room to let for Mrs. Darcy's and my safe harbor?"

The man laid a registry book upon a tall table. "Darcy?" Mr. Washington smiled merrily. "I know of the Darcys who live in Derbyshire. You be kin to them, Sir?"

Noting the man's age, Darcy said, "Likely my parents."

"It be a great estate. I seen it once for meself," the man said as he handed Darcy a pen and ink.

Darcy smiled, but he preferred not to allow Pemberley to define him. At least, he had not done so since meeting and wooing Elizabeth. His wife had taught him a difficult lesson about pretentiousness.

Elizabeth stepped beside him. "I hope Hannah and Mr. Lucas are not stranded someplace along the road." Darcy had sent his valet and Elizabeth's maid ahead.

"As they left a day before us, I am certain they have missed the storm's worst. I'm sorry that we didn't." He spoke softly to her alone.

"It's five days to Christmas Eve. We shall see Pemberley for the celebration."

Darcy thought of the surprise he had arranged for his wife for her Christmas pleasure. He prayed it wasn't for naught. Although she pretended otherwise, Elizabeth had suffered greatly from her untimely births. The losses had wreaked havoc with his wife's normal playfulness. The first miscarriage had come mere months into their marriage. At the time, Mrs. Reynolds, his housekeeper, had assured Darcy that such lapses were common, and that his wife likely did not even realize her condition until it was over.

The second had occurred nearly a half year later. With that gestation, Pemberley had celebrated Elizabeth's happiness, but some three and a half months into her term, the bleeding began. Darcy had immediately summoned a physician, but the man could do nothing for the child. Saving Elizabeth became the treatment's focus, and although she had recovered physically, he often saw the longing displayed in Elizabeth's eyes. For example, when her sister Jane Bingley mentioned motherhood's joys, his Elizabeth seemed to die a slow, lingering death.

It explained why Elizabeth had refused to acknowledge her current condition. If she didn't form an attachment to the child she carried, its possible loss couldn't bring her pain. So, they—he, his staff, and Georgiana—had participated in a silent dance in which those who attended his wife ordered new dresses, without her approval, for her quickly changing body, and placed footstools close to her favorite chair, and catered to her cravings for chocolate and herring (fortunately not both at the same time). No one mentioned his wife's condition, but they all tended to it.

"If you could do something to brighten Mrs. Darcy's spirits, it would better your wife's chances of carrying to term," Doctor Palmer had suggested less than a month earlier. "The more Mrs. Darcy dwells on her losses, the more likely a repetition will occur."

That very day, Darcy had sent a letter to Longbourn asking the Bennets to join him and Elizabeth for Christmas. His wife hadn't seen her parents since the day she and Darcy had left Hertfordshire for Pemberley. Darcy had refused to allow her to travel following the two prior miscarriages, and then Elizabeth had spent two months with her sister when Jane had had her twins. Her other sister, Kitty Bennet, had visited Pemberley several times, but Elizabeth had bemoaned her father's absence, and even that of her insensible mother. Therefore, he had dispatched the invitation, and the Bennets had readily accepted. He had carefully planned his Christmas surprise, but Darcy hadn't considered the weather.

"If Mr. Parnell hadn't been so obstinate, we might already be at Pemberley," he observed.

In truth, Parnell had snubbed Darcy's offer, claiming it was too generous to Darcy's smaller investors. "You are a fool, Darcy," he had said, "if you think I might involve myself in such a weak scheme. You would give away the cow before you had one drop of milk."

Darcy had refused to do business with such a tight-fisted man. He was all for making a profit, but not at the expense of those less fortunate than he. He had sought out Parnell because Darcy had heard that the man was an astute businessman, and that Parnell understood what was required for success. Instead, he had found a bitter, conniving entrepreneur who spoke venomous words to his employees. Darcy had been glad to leave the negotiations behind.

"I should've left you at Pemberley, but I would have been sore to spend my nights alone or my days without the pleasure of your laughter," he had told Elizabeth as they waited for Mr. Washington to arrange their room. "Quite selfish, but I find myself hopelessly addicted to your closeness."

"I thought you admired me for my impertinence." Darcy relished the fact that she teased him, a welcomed change from Elizabeth's recent melancholy. Perhaps his taking her with him on this journey would promote her healing.

"Impertinence was your estimation," he murmured close to her ear. "I sought the liveliness of your mind." A raised eyebrow lodged her objection. "But I lied," he said huskily. "It was for your skin's creamy satin and that sprinkling of freckles across your nose."

Elizabeth flushed. "Mr. Darcy!" she protested with a gasp.

"Yes, my Elizabeth," he whispered seductively into her hair. "I am here to please you, my love." His smile became positively smug. "You should also know that I admired your easy playfulness, the uncommonly intelligent expression of your beautiful eyes, and your light and pleasing figure."

Although she blushed again, and her voice was tremulous, Elizabeth beamed with joy. She laughed, genuinely and fully, and Darcy's heart opened further to her. Her laugh was the most delightful sound he had ever heard. "Fitzwilliam Darcy," she began, "I cannot fathom how I ever thought you a prig. You are an absolute cad!"

He recognized how Elizabeth had chosen her words to evoke a reaction from him, so Darcy tempered his response. "True, my dear, but I'm your cad," he taunted.

〜◎〜 〜◎〜 〜◎〜

"Welcome to Pemberley," Georgiana greeted Elizabeth's family. A time had existed when the prospect of acting as her brother's hostess would have brought her to tears, but under Elizabeth's tutelage as well as that of her companion, Mrs. Annesley, Georgiana had developed more confidence.

Kitty Bennet boisterously caught Georgiana in a quick embrace.

"I'm so happy to return to Pemberley. Hertfordshire is positively humdrum."

Georgiana smiled warmly. She and Elizabeth's sister had fashioned a companionable relationship over the past two years. Although Kitty didn't share Georgiana's interest in music and art, they both had questions about marriage and love and men, and for Georgiana, sharing their uncertainties had a calming effect. It said that she was not an aberration. Since the weakness she had displayed at age fifteen, she had often questioned her own curiosity. Finding Kitty Bennet equally at a loss for what to do to find love had served as a revelation to the awkwardly demure Georgiana. "It is always a pleasure to see you, Kitty. You've been sorely missed."

Georgiana turned her attention to the Bennets. "Mr. Bennet. Mrs. Bennet. We're pleased you joined us in Derbyshire."

She followed the man's gaze as he said, "The house is all Lizzy said it was." The man sighed deeply. "Where is Lizzy? I expected her to greet us with open arms. It's not like Elizabeth to avoid the cold. Has life at Pemberley made my daughter soft, a real lady of leisure?"

Georgiana blinked away the comment. If she had not heard Elizabeth use a similar teasing tone, she might've believed Mr. Bennet's words held true censure. At first, she had often listened with an astonishment bordering on alarm at Elizabeth's lively, sportive manner of talking to Fitzwilliam, but now Georgiana accepted Elizabeth's sharp wit as the woman's charm. In fact, Georgiana missed Elizabeth's barbed humor. Since Elizabeth's last disappointment, her brother's wife had lost her sparkle. "Fitzwilliam is away on business. He and Elizabeth shan't return until tomorrow. My brother had wanted your presence at Pemberley to be Mrs. Darcy's surprise. You shall have time to settle in before my sister arrives."

Mrs. Bennet caught at her daughter's hand. "Show me Pemberley's grandeur, Kitty. That's all of which you've spoken for months. Although neither Lizzy nor Mr. Darcy saw fit to greet us, we shall persevere. I imagine an estate as grand as Pemberley will have a fair cup of tea to warm my bones and to settle my nerves."

Kitty shrugged good-naturedly as she assisted her suddenly frail mother along the entranceway.

"Miss Darcy," Mr. Bennet interrupted Georgiana's thoughts. "You remember my daughter Mary."

Georgiana curtsied. "Of course, I do. Welcome to Pemberley, Miss Bennet."

"Thank you, Miss Darcy, for your hospitality."

Mr. Bennet cleared his throat. "And this young man is Mary's intended, Mr. Robert Grange. Mr. Grange is a clerk in my brother Philips's law firm."

Georgiana's eyes widened. Mr. Grange was not on Darcy's guest list. "I extend our Pemberley welcome, Mr. Grange."

"Thank you for receiving me, Miss Darcy." The spindly young man with a boyish face bowed stiffly to Georgiana before placing Mary on his arm.

Mr. Bennet bowed formally to Georgiana and then accepted her hand to walk with her. "Mrs. Bennet insisted that Mr. Grange join us. After all, Robert will soon be part of the family. Is that not right, Grange?" Mr. Bennet said jovially over his shoulder. He leaned closer to Georgiana. "I might require something stronger than tea to warm my old bones, Miss Darcy. Besides a fair cup of tea, I pray Mr. Darcy also serves a respectable spot of brandy."

Mr. Bennet grinned conspiratorially at her, and all of Georgiana's apprehension fell to the wayside. "Mr. Bennet, a smooth brandy and my brother's library await you."

~⊚~ ~⊚~ ~⊚~

"Miss Darcy," Jane Bingley apologized. "How do I express my regret for thrusting an uninvited guest upon Mr. Darcy's household? I realize your brother designed this Christmas celebration for Elizabeth's benefit, and my sister Miss Bingley is not among Lizzy's devotees, but I appreciate your accepting Caroline's presence so graciously."

Georgiana had accommodated a second unexpected guest with

as much elegance as she could muster. Although her brother would have relayed his dismay about people imposing on the Pemberley household's goodwill, Georgiana couldn't follow suit. For her, serving as Fitzwilliam's hostess spoke of how far she had come from that girl who had foolishly consented to an elopement. "Miss Bingley has a long-standing relationship with my family. It's not an imposition, Mrs. Bingley." Georgiana motioned a waiting footman forward. "Please show Mrs. Bingley's nurse to the children's rooms and ask Mrs. Reynolds to prepare a room for Miss Bingley."

"You're too kind, Miss Darcy. My husband and family are in the blue drawing room." With a curtsy, Elizabeth's older sister disappeared into the house's interior.

Feeling the agitation of being Pemberley's "mistress," Georgiana let out a slow breath. She would have liked to spend private time at the pianoforte, to secret herself away from the world, but Fitzwilliam had asked her to organize Elizabeth's surprise, and Georgiana would do her best. So, despite wondering whether she was designed to run any man's household, Georgiana straightened her shoulders. She loved Elizabeth, and her sister had suffered enough. Steadying her resolve, she followed Mrs. Bingley toward the room where her brother's guests waited. "Does anyone require fresh tea?" she asked as she swept into the room.

❧ ❧ ❧

"Elizabeth, may I present Sir Jonathan Padget and Mr. Horvak. Gentlemen, my wife, Mrs. Darcy." Both men bowed their greetings. "Sir Jonathan and Horvak are stranded also," Darcy explained as he possessively placed Elizabeth on his arm.

Smiling politely, she said, "I am pleased for the acquaintance, Sir Jonathan. Mr. Horvak." Both men possessed a strong aristocratic look. Besides his clothes' fine cut, Sir Jonathan had chiseled, square jawed features. Horvak, tawny-haired and with roguish good looks, maintained a powerful ease, like that which Elizabeth recognized in her own husband. Wealthy and titled men had many of the same qualities.

"Please join us, Mrs. Darcy." Horvak held her chair.

"Your husband was just explaining his difficult negotiations with Mr. Parnell." Sir Jonathan gestured with an ale glass in his hand. "It is not surprising. Both Horvak and I have tangled with Parnell previously. A man wishing to ship out of Newcastle or Middlesbrough has to go through William Parnell."

"Parnell is as tenacious as they come," Mr. Horvak reported. "But one cannot totally blame the man. Brought himself to prominence with hard work and diligence."

"Does Mr. Parnell have a family?" Elizabeth asked in curiosity. When Darcy had related conversations with the man, Elizabeth had wondered what had made Parnell so negative in his responses.

Horvak shrugged his shoulders. "I couldn't say for certain, Mrs. Darcy. Parnell spends countless hours at his office or down by the docks. The man neglects his wife if he's taken wedding vows; that would be a fact."

"It's also a fact that Parnell is one of the area's richest men. If he's married, Parnell's wife wants for nothing but his company."

～⌒～ ～⌒～ ～⌒～

"And you shall leave me stranded in Derbyshire without family with less than a week before Christmastide?" Lady Catherine argued with her brother.

The Earl expelled a sigh of exasperation; he had tried repeatedly to reason with his sister. "Catherine, the eventual heir to this title is about to be born, and I plan to be with my son when his child comes into this world. Rowland has sent word that it is only a matter of days before Amelia delivers her first child. The Countess insists that we travel to William's Wood. You could always journey with us. I am certain that Rowland would welcome you and Anne."

"But not Mr. and Mrs. Collins," she declared. "I have promised the Collinses return transportation to Kent. Collins visits a cousin in Warrington. In fact, I have asked the Collinses to join me here. I am ever attentive to my duties."

The Earl's jaw set. "You invited your clergyman's family to my home?" His voice increased in volume. "Catherine, sometimes you forget yourself. I had thought that you simply arranged their journey as you commonly do," he said through gritted teeth. "Dear Sister, you may rule Rosings Park in lieu of Lewis De Bourgh, but Matley Manor is under my domain. I invite the guests!"

Lady Catherine's eyebrow rose in disbelief. "You'd deny the Collinses? This was my childhood home, Martin," she asserted.

"The house will be closed while the Countess and I are in Lincolnshire. I had planned to release the staff on Christmas Day anyway. You may choose to accompany me and Her Ladyship to William's Wood, or you may return to Kent." He slammed his fist on a nearby table's edge, sending china and silver to the floor.

"Well, I never!" Lady Catherine sputtered.

The Earl shoved to his feet. "Never what, Catherine?" he accused. "Never considered anyone else's opinions? Never showed true compassion? Never offered your genuine condolences? Never expressed love? There are so many things that you've never done, that I'm at a loss as to which one you mean!" He strode from the room without looking back.

❧   ❧   ❧

"We had planned to wait for Mr. and Mrs. Darcy's return," Charles Bingley announced to those gathered in Pemberley's small dining room, "but I cannot keep a secret." Bingley lovingly reached for his wife's hand. "In June, Mrs. Bingley and I will welcome a new addition to our family."

The Bennets immediately congratulated their eldest, but Georgiana withheld her felicitations. She recognized how this news would "kill" Elizabeth, especially if her brother's wife failed in her own delivery; and even though she desperately wished for her brother and sister's speedy return, Georgiana was happy that Elizabeth didn't have to witness this display.

"Oh, Jane, how smart you are," Mrs. Bennet declared. "You've already given Mr. Bingley an heir and a daughter. "Another child. Another son. I just know it shall be another son."

"I note your lack of enthusiasm," Caroline Bingley whispered conspiratorially. "I thoroughly understand your disdain. My brother has aligned our family with an inferior bloodline, and, unfortunately, so has yours."

Irritated that Miss Bingley had thought her so base as to wish Elizabeth's sister not to know happiness, Georgiana warned, "Be careful, Miss Bingley. Your speech smacks of disappointment." As soon as the words escaped her lips, Georgiana would've taken them back. They were uncharacteristic.

"My," Miss Bingley began, "I see Mrs. Darcy's lack of decorum has permeated your normally amiable nature, Georgiana."

Georgiana stiffened. "If I could have even half of Elizabeth's courage or her intelligence, I'd consider myself a fortunate being." She shot a glance at Mrs. Annesley, who nodded her approval. Needing to escape an embarrassing situation, Georgiana stood. "If the ladies will join me in the music room, the gentlemen may see to their cigars. Miss Bennet has agreed to entertain us this evening. Mr. Grange, I shall charge you with seeing that Mr. Bingley and Mr. Bennet do not tarry."

Her notice brought embarrassment. "Of course, Miss Darcy."

"Ladies," she intoned and led the way from the room.

⟶ ⟶ ⟶

"If you gentlemen will excuse me," Elizabeth said as she stood. The small inn possessed only six rooms to let, and different gentlemen, each driven to seek shelter from the elements, occupied four of them. Two farmers, Mr. Betts and Mr. Dylan—strangers before the storm—had agreed to share the last available room, meaning she remained the single female. Feeling quite conspicuous, Elizabeth had chosen to withdraw to allow the men some freedom. There was no private room where they might take up their cards, cigars, and drink. Instead, the eclectic group shared the common room.

Darcy reached for her hand. "I will accompany you, Mrs. Darcy."

Elizabeth smiled at him. She knew he worried for her health, and she fooled no one regarding her condition, but it was important to her to take control of this pregnancy. She had to deliver on her own terms. Her husband meant well, and she counted herself a lucky woman. What female would deny the company of a highly intelligent and caring man? Besides, Elizabeth considered her husband more than just a bit attractive: Fitzwilliam Darcy was a fine specimen, and she often found herself with unladylike wanton thoughts. In fact, she considered him roguishly beautiful and heart-stoppingly seductive, and even after two years, Darcy's charms—the same charms that she had once adamantly denied—made her vulnerable. "You may, most assuredly, escort me, but I would encourage you to join the gentlemen in cards or talk of sport."

"I will consider it, Mrs. Darcy."

Elizabeth simply nodded her understanding. They had traveled together because Darcy had refused to permit her being out of his care. Her husband had portrayed his business trip as an opportunity for Elizabeth to see a part of England she had never experienced, as well as a means to purchase unique Christmas gifts. He even subtly suggested that she might visit with her sister Lydia when they stayed in Newcastle. And although she appreciated her husband's attentiveness, she wouldn't believe that Darcy was unaware of the fact that Lydia and Mr. Wickham had left Newcastle for Carlisle some three months prior. More than likely, her husband had had a hand in Mr. Wickham's transfer. Darcy had seen to Lydia's marriage when no one else could assist the Bennets in locating Mr. Wickham. Unabashedly aware of her sister Lydia's propensity for profligacy, Elizabeth did what she could to keep her youngest sister from the poorhouse. The Wickhams were extravagant in their wants and heedless of the future. They were always spending more than they ought. By practicing what might be called economy in her own private expenses, Elizabeth had frequently sent her sister additional funds, but it was not enough to prevent the Wickhams from moving from place to place in quest of a cheaper situation.

Darcy stepped into the room with her before gathering Elizabeth into his embrace. Without prelude, he kissed her thoroughly. "I've been wanting to do that for the last two hours." He trailed a line of wet kisses down her neck. "I never tire of touching you," he rasped.

Quickly enticed by his heat, Elizabeth's eyes fluttered closed as she whispered huskily, "For too long, I tried to keep my heart safe."

He teased, "You could not. Not even when you were wretchedly blind to my finer qualities?"

Elizabeth chuckled ironically and pressed herself to him. "I did once gratify my vanity in useless mistrust. I've courted prepossession and ignorance, and I once drove reason away." She felt her husband's deep steadying breath and his instant hardness along her thigh. *I wish I'd known before how gullible men are to words of loyalty*, she thought. "In essentials, my love, you are very much what you ever were."

"And you love me that way?" he rasped as his mouth slid along her collarbone.

"I love you in every way possible, Mr. Darcy." Elizabeth snaked her arms about his neck.

Darcy kissed her deeply before reluctantly releasing her. "I shan't tarry long." He straightened his coat's lines. "I was never a card player." He glanced about the room to see that the maid had stoked the fire as he had instructed. "Keep the door locked. I'll knock upon my return. One never knows how a man will act when he has nothing to do but to drink."

"Do you expect trouble?" she asked with a touch of concern.

Darcy shook his head in the negative. "Just trying to anticipate the possibilities," he mumbled. "Trying to protect my wife."

"You have my permission, Mr. Darcy, to cater to my needs as

often as you please." Elizabeth went on tiptoes to kiss his chin while a slight smile crossed his face.

⌒ஒᏂ ⌒ஒᏂ ⌒ஒᏂ

"Thank you," Kitty whispered as Georgiana passed her in the drawing room.

Georgiana's eyes scanned the room, making sure her brother's guests found adequate refreshments. "I gladly accept your gratitude, Miss Kitty," she mumbled. "But I'm at a loss as to what I've done to earn it."

Kitty observed Georgiana's countenance closely. She had admired Mr. Darcy's sister from the beginning of their acquaintance. With Lydia's speedy marriage, Kitty had been left with no confidante and little confidence in her own ability to attract a man. Fortunately, Jane and Elizabeth had stepped in—had brought Kitty to Pemberley and to Mr. Bingley's estate in neighboring Cheshire. Her elder sisters had introduced Kitty to young women and men of quality. While at Pemberley, Kitty had found a copemate in Georgiana Darcy. "I overheard your conversation with Miss Bingley regarding Lizzy."

Georgiana kept her eyes on the room, but she said softly, "Elizabeth is my sister, and as a Darcy, her name is mine to protect. However, even if it were not so, I would defend Elizabeth. It is the least I could do for all she's given me: acceptance, understanding, compassion, conviction, and you, Kitty." She finally looked at her friend. "Yes, Kitty, Elizabeth's gift of her own sister was one of her greatest. I desperately needed someone with whom to share my childhood musings. Luckily for me, you also sought such consolation. We've done well together, and, for that, I owe Elizabeth my allegiance."

Kitty flushed from the notice. "You honor me, Miss Darcy." Emotions washing through her, Kitty's eyes filled with tears. "Those early days were awkward for us, but our amity pleases me. We've become quite adept at recognizing the best in each other."

"That we have." Georgiana smiled reassuringly. "Therefore, until Elizabeth's return, would you assist me in seeing to everyone's needs? You're familiar with Pemberley's inner workings."

"I'd be pleased...very pleased."

∼⌒∼ ∼⌒∼ ∼⌒∼

"Have you recently spent time in London, Miss Bingley?" Mrs. Bennet had cornered the woman near the pianoforte.

Caroline's eyes hardened in disapproval. "I'm often in London, Mrs. Bennet, as well as Edinburgh. I travel to my friends' country seats when Society is not in Season," she intoned aristocratically.

"I certainly would have no objection to time in London, but Mr. Bennet hates town." Mrs. Bennet announced a bit louder than necessary.

Caroline smiled mockingly. "If you were to spend time in London, Mrs. Bennet, where might you stay? If Mr. Bennet despises London, it's not likely that he maintains a home in the city."

Mrs. Bennet ignored the woman's tone. Although she was well aware of her social abyss, she let nothing dissuade her, so she had succeeded where others had failed. Despite her family's financial situation, she had married off three daughters and a fourth had made a respectable match. Only Kitty remained unattached. Jane and Elizabeth had married well, especially Elizabeth. "My brother and sister Gardiner maintain a London home," Mrs. Bennet declared.

Miss Bingley replied with feigned graciousness. "Oh, yes. That would be the brother in Cheapside, would it not?"

"And you find Cheapside below you, Miss Bingley? If I recall, you once called upon my Jane at my sister Gardiner's home. Did you find it lacking?"

Miss Bingley said through gritted teeth, "It was a most pleasant house for that part of the city, but you must understand, Mrs. Bennet, that the Gardiners' home cannot be compared to those in Mayfair. A man who lives where he might oversee his warehouses wouldn't be accepted in the finest homes."

"As your father earned his money in trade, and your brother maintains those connections, I'm surprised, Miss Bingley, that you receive invitations to *ton* events. Perhaps that's why you cling so tightly to your Pemberley association." Having the upper hand, Mrs. Bennet strode away.

Claiming a cup of tea, she took a chair close to where Mary rifled through sheet music. She would never tell anyone how out of place she had felt as she had taken in Pemberley's splendor: the spacious lobby, the elegantly decorated sitting rooms, the large, well-proportioned dining room, and the family portrait gallery. She'd known from Jane's and Elizabeth's descriptions that Mr. Darcy had extensive wealth, but she hadn't conceived of the disparity between her own existence and that of her least-favorite daughter. She loved Elizabeth, but her second child had defied her at every turn. Elizabeth was Mr. Bennet's daughter: Her husband and Lizzy had shared a love for reading and a fondness for twisting the King's English, neither of which she cared to think on.

Taking a sip of tea, she settled smugly into the chair's cushions. At least, between Jane and Elizabeth, she wouldn't live in poverty when Mr. Bennet passed. It was that particular fear that had driven her to beg Elizabeth to marry Mr. Collins. Longbourn was entailed upon the man, and she'd thought it might remain in her control if the clergyman had chosen one of her daughters. Collins had eventually proposed to Elizabeth, but her daughter had vehemently refused the man—leaving the family in limbo. Mrs. Bennett had cajoled and threatened, but Lizzy had persevered. Now, it seemed that her second child had proven herself most astute in her denial of Collins. "Mr. Darcy holds Elizabeth in deepest regard," her husband had assured her when he had announced their daughter's impending marriage. She hadn't believed it, at first. Elizabeth and Mr. Darcy had appeared to scorn each other. How was she to know that the man possessed a *tendre* for Lizzy? How was she to know any of it when no one thought her worthy of his trust?

The gentlemen joined them in a timely manner, and everyone prepared to enjoy Mary's performance. Yet, before they could begin, Georgiana stepped forward. "By this time tomorrow, Fitzwilliam and Elizabeth shall have returned to Pemberley. My brother wished to surprise his wife with your presence. Our Elizabeth has missed you deeply, and she speaks of her Hertfordshire family with fondness. Traditionally, we decorate Pemberley's halls the evening before Christmas, but I'm hoping that you'll join me tomorrow as I undertake that task a few days early. I wish my family to return to a fully bedecked household—to step into a Christmastide fantasy."

Jane piped up. "I love gathering greenery. Mr. Bingley and I shall join you, Miss Darcy."

"As shall I," Kitty added.

"Miss Bennet and I are at your disposal," Mr. Grange said from his waiting position behind Mary. He would turn the pages for his intended.

Mr. Grange chimed in, "I'm not as young as I would like, but I can still use a saw long enough to cut evergreen branches."

Mrs. Bennet dropped her eyes. Never very athletic nor one to enjoy the outdoors, she didn't want to tramp across the lawns. "Perhaps I might better serve by adding my expertise to your housekeeper's efforts."

"Of course," Georgiana said earnestly. "Mrs. Reynolds shall appreciate your ideas."

Caroline snickered, drawing attention to the fact that she had made no commitment. "What?" she snapped.

"Shall you join us, Caroline?" Jane asked softly.

"I think not," she said with indifference. "I rarely rise before noon, but, more importantly, domesticity is not my forte."

Kitty noted Georgiana's disappointment. "As you wish, Miss Bingley," Kitty said pertly. "Now, Mary, what shall you play for us?" She wouldn't permit Miss Bingley to destroy Georgiana's plans. "Come, Miss Darcy, you're to sit with me. When Mary finishes, we shall make a list of what we need to give Pemberley a festive look."

~⊚~ ~⊚~ ~⊚~

Left alone, Elizabeth instinctively sought her small traveling box. Changing into a night rail and dressing gown, she curled up in a chair before the fire and unwrapped a beribboned bundle of letters. When Darcy spent time away from the estate, she often reread his letters. It was her way of keeping him close. Of course, the bundle held that legendary first letter, the one he had written to Elizabeth after his Hunsford proposal. She had once promised to burn it, but she would fight anyone who thought truly to do so. It was the letter that changed her life—the one which had given her a true understanding of the man so necessary to her existence.

Sitting before the blaze's warmth, Elizabeth easily remembered how with his second proposal, Darcy had mentioned his letter. "Did it," said he, "did it soon make you think better of me? Did you on reading it, give any credit to its contents?"

She had tried to allay his fears. She had explained what its effect had had on her and how gradually all her former prejudices had been removed.

"I knew," said he, "that what I wrote must give you pain, but it was necessary. I hope you have destroyed the letter." Of course, she had not. Elizabeth had read and reread it so often that she could recite it by heart. "There was one part," Darcy had continued, "especially the opening of it, which I should dread your having the power of reading again." It was so typical of her husband to worry that his words had brought her mental suffering. She loved him dearly for his compassion. "I can remember some expressions which might justly make you hate me." As if she could hate a man who had unselfishly saved her family from ruin.

Elizabeth had seized the opportunity to protect him—to let Mr. Darcy know that she welcomed his renewed attentions. "The letter shall certainly be burnt, if you believed it essential to the preservation of my regard; but, though we have reason to think my opinions not entirely unalterable, they are not, I hope, quite so easily changed as that implies." Yet, she had not burnt that first letter or any of the others that had followed. For a man who was abashedly silent at the most social of times, her husband was absolutely eloquent when he put pen to paper. Starting with the morning after their wedding night, Darcy had marked poignant moments with personal notes left on her pillow. She would wake to find what he couldn't say in person. Tonight, she began her reading with that wedding night homage to their love: "My dearest, loveliest Elizabeth," she read aloud.

Chapter 2

〜◦〜 〜◦〜 〜◦〜

My dearest, loveliest Elizabeth,

As I sit at this desk in awe of the most splendid of gifts that you have offered me this night, my heart overflows with love. The loneliness has dissipated, and I do not speak of the physical closeness we shared last evening—as exquisite as it was—I speak of the happiness that you have brought to my life and to Pemberley. From the beginning, you destroyed my hard-earned peace, and many times I found myself spiraling out of control, but I would, willingly, suffer the pain again to know you for but one day—one hour, even. You are everything—firmly planted are my hopes—you are the coming chapters of my life's book.

D

A TEAR SLID DOWN HER CHEEK, but Elizabeth didn't whisk it away. He had rattled her senses that night. Rattled. Shaken. Turned her world upside down in the most tantalizing ways. Her heart had pounded so intensely when she'd looked upon her husband for the first time: It had mimicked the cadence of his as Darcy drew her into his embrace. Unbelievable desire had coursed through her—ricocheted through her body and devoured her soul. Luckily, she'd spoken quite frankly with her Aunt Gardiner prior to the wedding night. If not, his power over her might have frightened Elizabeth. Instead, she'd viewed it as a challenge, and although she'd allowed Darcy to lead, she'd learned to exercise her own power. Elizabeth loved it when he surrendered to her—when he couldn't deny her.

A smile turned up her mouth's corners. They were good to-gether—the absolute best. Her hand instinctively rested on her abdomen. "Please, God," she whispered. "This time…please." She wanted so desperately to prove to Darcy and to the world that she was worthy of being the Mistress of Pemberley—worthy of his love.

For the next hour, Elizabeth thumbed through the various notes and letters. Two of them she'd left folded—letters from Darcy after each miscarriage. Ignoring them didn't mean that she'd never read them—quite the reverse. They were two of her favorites, but she held the strong belief that this gestation would prove successful if she could control all the outside forces—neither too much gaiety nor too much hardness nor too much melancholy. She would keep an evenness—an equable, systematic, methodical order. Maybe then God would see fit to reward her with the child she desper-ately wanted.

"Maybe it's my punishment for the sin of pride. I once thought too highly of my own intelligence and not enough of Fitzwil-liam's inherent goodness." Mr. Darcy's constancy had never ceased to amaze her. She could not think of Darcy without feeling that she had been blind, partial, prejudiced, and absurd. Fixed there by the keenest of all anguish and self-reproach, she could find no interval of ease or forgetfulness. "Punish me, God," she whispered. "Not him. My husband is the best of men."

Swallowing back her tears, Elizabeth put the letters away. A few moments later, Darcy's knock announced his return. He kissed her cheek upon his entrance. "I see you've managed without my serv-ing as your maid," he remarked as he strode past her.

"I didn't realize you wished to assume Hannah's duties, Mr. Darcy," Elizabeth said teasingly as she closed and locked the door behind him.

Darcy turned toward her, a smug smile gracing his lips. "I'm more adept at removal of garments, Mrs. Darcy."

She crossed the room and crawled into the bed. "I'll keep that in mind, Sir, in case you ever need a reference letter."

Darcy watched his wife carefully, trying to take his cue from her. "Did you find something entertaining to do?" He removed his jacket and draped it over a chair's back and then turned his attention to his cravat.

"Just some quiet time," she said as she draped the blanket across her lap.

Darcy continued to undress before stoking the fire again with more coal and kindling. "We may be here a couple of days, Elizabeth," he informed her as he joined her under the wool blankets. "Two more gentlemen have taken shelter. They came north from Manchester. They said the storm was just beginning in the south when they left, but it turned icier the farther north they traveled." He blew out the lone candle.

"How in the world did Mr. Washington accommodate them?" she asked with some surprise.

"Mr. Horvak and Sir Jonathan graciously agreed to double up."

Elizabeth turned into his embrace as Darcy slid his arm under her pillow. She rested her head upon his shoulder. "Then I'm still the only female among Mr. Washington's guests." She could not disguise the tentativeness in her tone.

"I will protect you, Elizabeth."

"I know, Fitzwilliam. I'm just being foolish."

~&~ ~&~ ~&~

"Mother, we cannot," Anne De Bourgh offered her weak protest. She'd have liked to say more, but Anne had never taken a stand with Lady Catherine—with anyone, for that matter. Never rendered formidable by silence, whatever Lady Catherine said was spoken in so authoritative a tone as marked her self-importance. Anne often wished she could replicate even a quarter of her mother's unflappable nature.

"And why not, may I ask? We cannot travel to William's Wood. Observe the roads, Child." Anne peered through the frosty coach window at the sand-like peppering of the ice pellets on the roadside. A sheen of frigid crystals accumulated in every rut and opening. "Mr. Swank's an excellent coachman, for I'd have none without his expertise, but even he's having difficulty keeping the coach on the road. Martin has released the staff at Matley Manor. Where else would you have us seek shelter?"

"An inn," Anne offered.

Lady Catherine chortled. "You wish to spend Christmas in a common inn? Sometimes I wonder if the midwife didn't switch out my child with one of lesser birth, but then I recall Sir Lewis's reticence, and I know you to be his. The poor man nearly had apoplexy when he asked my late father for my hand. As dear of a man as ever walked the earth, but he'd have allowed the lowest laborer to walk away with Rosings Park if I hadn't insisted otherwise."

"Yes, Mother," Anne said obediently.

"*Yes*, you wish to spend your Christmas at an inn or *yes*, your mother is correct about your father's faintheartedness?"

"*Yes* to the dire situation that the roads present," Anne said—the closest she'd ever come to defiance. Her mother's frequent remarks about Anne's father always irritated her. Anne's former world of love and carefree acceptance had died with the late baronet.

Lady Catherine asked smugly, "Then you agree that we should seek Pemberley's shelter?"

"What if Mr. Darcy refuses us admittance?" Anne asked apprehensively.

Lady Catherine sighed deeply. "Were you not listening to Georgiana when she announced that Darcy and that woman he calls his wife were away from Pemberley? Even with that touch of mettle that I noted on this last visit to Matlock, your cousin possesses both civility and good manners. She'll welcome us."

"And when Mr. Darcy returns?"

Lady Catherine smiled knowingly. "The man's a Darcy. Like his father, Fitzwilliam shall snidely deliver a lecture regarding my duty to his wife, and then he'll welcome the inconvenience. He shall wear his triumph over me as honor's badge."

Still seeking a way to change her mother's mind, Anne reasoned, "I wouldn't wish you to feel Mr. Darcy's contempt, Your Ladyship. A stay at a common inn would be better than your losing face within the family."

Lady Catherine laughed softly. "Do you think I'd permit any man dominion over me? All the time Darcy parades his conde-scension, I shall have the knowledge that I managed to walk un-invited into his home, and there was nothing he could do about it, except to allow me the choice of where I wished to spend the festive days. Darcy is bound to receive me by *duty*; I'll stay at Pem-berley by *choice*."

Anne observed, "The Mistress of Pemberley may have other plans."

A wrinkle of her aristocratic nose signaled Lady Catherine's dis-taste. "The former Miss Bennet shall never defy Mr. Darcy." Even as she said the words, Lady Catherine recalled Elizabeth Bennet's obstinacy. "Are you lost to every feeling of propriety and delicacy?" she had argued with the girl. "Have you not heard me say that from his earliest hours he was destined for his cousin?"

And Elizabeth Bennet had stood there, defiant as ever, when she said, "Yes, and I had heard it before. But what is that to me? If there is no other objection to my marrying your nephew, I shall certainly not be kept from it by knowing that his mother and aunt wished him to marry Miss De Bourgh. You both did as much as you could in planning the marriage; its completion depended on others. If Mr. Darcy is neither by honor nor inclination confined to his cousin, why is not he to make another choice? And if I am that choice, why not I accept him?"

"Oh, yes," Lady Catherine thought, "the girl was quite capable of defying Darcy. And what better way to put a chink in their re-ported marital bliss?"

She'd done her best to align Anne with Darcy, but her daughter had always feigned illness rather than interact with Society. In the early days, she had fought her only child, but her efforts brought Anne such physical pain that after a while, she'd abandoned her efforts to bring Anne to heel and had concentrated her administrations on her sister's only son, trying to reason with Darcy, to make him see the match's advantage. However, her nephew foiled the best of Lady Catherine's plans.

"Despite her poor connections, Mrs. Darcy holds social graces. She'll extend her welcome to her husband's family."

Anne wanted to argue further, to convince her mother of how incogitant it was to impose themselves on the Darcys, especially at Christmastide, to speak of Her Ladyship's own poor manners. But Anne could never find her voice when meeting her mother's close inspection. She truly possessed her father's personality, and as much as Anne missed him, missed the feeling of belonging that Sir Lewis had provided his only child, moments existed when she wished more for Mrs. Darcy's ability to thwart Lady Catherine's plans.

Although she desired her own home and family, Anne had understood that her marrying Darcy was never a reality. The man intimidated her. Even as a boy, Darcy had tormented her for her shyness, claiming it a weakness. Despite being more than a bit humiliated, Anne actually found that amusing. Better than anyone else, she recognized diffidence in both Darcy and Georgiana. She'd always thought Darcy amplified her faults in order to disguise his own.

"It'll be agreeable to spend Christ's birthday with family," Anne observed. "To have Mr. Darcy's good favor again. To know an end to this feud. I've truly missed Fitzwilliam and Georgiana."

"Do not fool yourself, Child," Lady Catherine warned. "Mr. Darcy's forgiveness shall be late coming, and if you imagine that I'm of the persuasion to guard my usual frankness in reference to my nephew's marital nearsightedness, you'll be sadly disappointed. Only when Mr. Darcy admits his mistake shall I extend my forbearance."

Silently, Anne groaned. She knew from private moments with Georgiana at Matlock that Mr. Darcy violently loved the former Elizabeth Bennet. When that fact was added to his reluctance to admit any weakness, it wasn't likely that he would give Lady Catherine any satisfaction. They'd intrude on the Darcys' Christmas, ruining the day for everyone.

~ ~ ~

"Do you suppose that Georgiana is safe?" Elizabeth asked as she and Darcy shared breakfast in the inn's limited seating area.

"Georgiana is fine," he assured. "She was to return to Pemberley two days prior, but even if my sister was delayed, my Uncle Matlock would see to her safety."

Elizabeth looked longingly at the snowy landscape through the ice-laced windowpanes. "Might we take a short walk, Fitzwilliam?" she asked, lost in her own world.

Darcy recognized her need for daily exercise. Traveling for two days had left Elizabeth confined to his traveling coach. More often than he should, Darcy recalled how Charles Bingley's sister, Caroline, had criticized Elizabeth for her preference in walking. "To walk three miles, or four miles, or five miles, or whatever it is, above her ankles in dirt, and alone, quite alone! What could she mean by it? It seems to me to show an abominable sort of conceited independence, a most country-town indifference to decorum."

Darcy smiled knowingly. "I would love some time outdoors," he responded genuinely. "Especially with you." He teasingly waggled his eyebrows.

His amusing attempt to ease her qualms spoke of Darcy's love. Elizabeth drew in a deep, determined, definitive breath. "Why is it?" she whispered. "Why, after two years, do I still see you as I did on our wedding night?"

Darcy felt his groin tighten: She had that effect on him. And Elizabeth had just uttered the most provocative thought wrapped in a cloak of sentimentality, something she did with regularity. It kept him off balance—topsy-turvy. He would be going about his duties as Pemberley's master, and his wife would say something inviting, and his thoughts were lost to her. It had been that way from the beginning: Elizabeth would challenge him with a pert curve turning up her mouth's corner. Lord, help him! The woman had no idea how crazy she drove him!

"Because I love you. From the day I met you, I saw *us—Us* as the way life should be," he murmured close to her ear.

He noted the memory of heated sensations in his wife's eyes as his breath's warmth caressed her neck. "I may return to my bed before the walk," she seductively said.

Darcy warmed from the inside out. He stood slowly. "A man should see his wife to their chamber." He held out his hand. Elizabeth placed her fingers into his palm, and his grasp closed tightly about them.

~⌖~ ~⌖~ ~⌖~

"Does everyone have a hat and gloves?" Bingley asked as he surveyed the group gathered in Pemberley's main foyer. "Last evening held an icy mix. Watch your step and stay close together."

"Do not forget the mistletoe," Kitty taunted good-naturedly.

Georgiana motioned toward the house's rear. "If we exit through the upper gardens we can reach the woods in half the time and distance."

"Lead on, Miss Darcy," Mr. Bennet proposed. "You know the best way."

~⌖~ ~⌖~ ~⌖~

Elizabeth waited patiently as Darcy spoke to Mr. Washington about the area surrounding the inn. They had spent the last hour in bed, and now they would walk off the remainder of their "stranded" frustrations. Although the facilities were adequate, Elizabeth would prefer her own home at Christmas. With Mrs. Reynolds's assistance, she'd planned the decorations. Her first Christmastide at Pemberley, she was still a bride, less than two months married, and Elizabeth had bowed to Pemberley's long-time housekeeper's wishes. Having celebrated her second wedding anniversary in November, this was to be her third Christmas as Pemberley's mistress and her first at planning the Tenants' celebration. She'd hate to leave final preparations to Georgiana.

Christmas in this dreary inn would be a sorry excuse for a holiday if the roads didn't clear soon. Looking about the room, Elizabeth's eyes fell on Darcy. She sighed deeply. At least, they were together. Being at Pemberley meant nothing if her husband was elsewhere.

"A copper for your thoughts," Darcy said as he approached.

Elizabeth bestowed a brilliant smile upon him. "I'd just considered how fortunate I am to be your wife. To be at Pemberley would be heavenly, but not without your presence. Though I must admit that sometimes when we're there, I imagine our hearts beating in tandem." Her frankness always appeared to have the oddest effect on Darcy. His eyes devoured her.

"Even when I thought I'd lost you forever, I lived with hope. I am thankful you became my *forever*, Elizabeth," he murmured softly.

"You have me now, Mr. Darcy," she said, keeping her voice light.

His steely grey eyes turned onyx. "And I bless each day because of your love."

As they stared lovingly at each other, the innkeeper's wife hustled toward the kitchen, and Elizabeth impulsively turned to the woman. "Mrs. Washington."

"Yes, Mrs. Darcy?" The pleasingly plump woman brushed a hair's strand from her flushed face.

Elizabeth caught Darcy's hand to pull him along with her as she approached the harrowed-looking woman. "I realize you're terribly busy and probably haven't considered how close Christmas Day might be."

The woman sighed deeply. "Me and Mr. Washington planned a quiet day, but the English weather be having other ideas."

"Would you mind, Ma'am, if Mr. Darcy and I cut some greenery and brought it back to the inn? A bit of the festive days?"

"Are you certain, Elizabeth?" Darcy asked. She knew he worried she might overdo it.

"Please, Fitzwilliam. I want Christmas; I really want Christmas at Pemberley, but if that proves impossible, I want Christmas here. I cannot tolerate bare rooms and nothing recognizing the day's meaning."

Darcy nodded. She noted something secretive passing over his countenance, but Elizabeth assumed he had bought her something expensive, and it awaited her at Pemberley. "I'll see if I can recruit several of the other gentlemen. We'll cut the branches while you supervise. I'm sure Padget and Horvak will want some exercise." He started away to where the men sat playing cards.

"See if any of the gents be interested in some hunting," Mrs. Washington said to Darcy's back.

He turned to her. "Why is that necessary, Ma'am? Is there something we should know?"

"Well, Mr. Washington be unhappy with me mentioning it, but we didn't plan for so many guests for the days before Christmas. Supplies be getting' a bit low. Feeding ten folks, yer help, plus our workers and arn selves takes a bit of doing."

"I will ask," Darcy assured her. "Are there guns available if anyone is interested?"

"I sees to it, Mr. Darcy."

☙ ☙ ☙

"Lady Catherine!" Mr. Nathan blustered as he helped the woman with her cloak. "I was unaware of your arrival, Ma'am."

Lady Catherine ignored Darcy's servant. "Where is my niece? I must speak to Miss Darcy. Is there no one to greet me in this great house?"

A woman Her Ladyship didn't recognize stepped into the hallway from the morning room. "May I be of assistance, Your Ladyship?"

Lady Catherine menacingly asked, "Who might you be, and why are you serving as hostess in my niece's stead?"

Obviously disconcerted by her question, the woman flustered. "Bingley...I am Miss Bingley," she stammered. "Charles Bingley, Mr. Darcy's friend, is my brother. Charles and Mrs. Bingley have joined Miss Darcy in the nearby woods to gather greenery for the holiday decorations."

"I see," Lady Catherine scowled. Although she was well aware that the woman standing before her had once held aspirations of being Mrs. Darcy, Her Ladyship had never met Mr. Darcy's friend. Normally, Lady Catherine would consider making the woman an ally in convincing Darcy to be civil during her intrusion; however, despite Miss Bingley's social graces, Lady Catherine considered the woman below the current Mrs. Darcy. Miss Bingley may have more money and a better education than the former Elizabeth Bennet, but Mr. Bingley's father had dealt in trade. Miss Bingley was a Cit! Disregarding the lady's offer of assistance, Lady Catherine instructed Darcy's staff. "Miss Anne and her companion shall require adjoining suites, and I shall have my usual chambers."

"I have sent word to Mrs. Reynolds, Your Ladyship. Would you care to join Miss Bingley in the morning room?"

Lady Catherine glanced at where Miss Bingley waited patiently. "I think not, Mr. Nathan. We had an early breakfast at my brother Matlock's. Some tea and biscuits shall be sufficient. Anne and I shall await Miss Darcy in the small drawing room."

Mr. Nathan bowed obediently. "I will have someone see to the hearth and send a footman to find Miss Darcy." He led the way to the room. "I will serve the tea myself, Ma'am."

～☙～　～☙～　～☙～

Kitty mischievously scooped a handful of snow into a tight ball. She hid her icy creation under her cloak's flap and waited for Mr. Bingley to step away from Jane. She had thought to hit Mr. Grange, but neither Mary nor the gentleman possessed a sense of humor. "Look," Kitty whispered to Georgiana. "Let's see if Mr. Bingley can protect himself. You make one also, and we shall attack together."

Georgiana smiled easily. Gathering the evergreen branches and holly had gone well. "Do you suppose it would anger Mr. Bingley?" Without waiting for an answer, Georgiana formed a ball from the line of snow sitting on the fence rail.

"Mr. Bingley?" Kitty chuckled. "As amiable as my sister's husband is? Not likely."

Georgiana giggled. "Then let's have some enjoyment."

Mr. Bingley bent to gather an armful of branches, but as he turned his back, two snowy spheres found his right shoulder. Plop! Splat!

Surprised, he turned to see Kitty and Georgiana hugging each other tightly while stifling bursts of laughter. "Ah!" he smiled widely. "So, that's how it's to be. A man labors to please a woman's whims, and then she turns on him," he taunted. As Bingley spoke, he dropped his stack of pine boughs on a horse blanket they had earlier spread on the ground, and then he armed himself. Playfully tossing the icy ball into the air, he teased, "You leave me no other choice, Sisters, but to defend myself."

Jane Bingley stepped between the girls and her husband. "Kitty was just playing, Charles."

"Oh, no, my wife," he continued his banter, "our sisters have declared *war*."

Kitty peered around her eldest sister. "No war, Mr. Bingley. Just men against women."

Bingley's hands flitted in large circles above his head. "Oh, woe! We are beset! Come along, Grange; you're with me, as are you, Father Bennet."

"Charles!" Jane warned.

"No reasoning permitted, Mrs. Bingley," he mocked. "You're now one of them." To prove his point, Bingley lobbed his snowball in his wife's direction.

Laughing, Jane attempted to return his attack, but her icy missile actually fell apart before it made contact.

Totally enjoying the play, Kitty and Georgiana hastily squeezed fist-sized snow sausages and flung them in the direction of the three men. Mary's efforts were less stellar, but even she became caught up in the spontaneous fun.

"Sorry, Papa," Kitty called as one of her efforts slid down her father's neck and into his cravat.

"Careful with my wife," Bingley cautioned the other men. "Remember she's carrying my child."

"Then my eldest shouldn't put herself in the way of my best pitch." Mr. Bennet purposely barreled a loosely packed snowball at Jane.

"Papa!" she protested, but returned a strong lob, landing a solid hit in the middle of his chest.

Laughter filled the frosty morning air. Soon, it was no longer men versus women. Each person fought everyone else, and cloaks and greatcoats were soon drenched in snow. Just as Mr. Bingley caught his wife and planned to dump her in a nearby snowdrift, the clearing of a deep voice brought them all up short.

"Yes, Thomas?" Georgiana fought to catch her breath.

"Pardon, Miss Darcy. Mr. Nathan asked me to fetch you. Your aunt, Lady Catherine, is waiting for you in the small drawing room."

Georgiana gasped, "Lady Catherine?"

"Yes, Miss. She and Miss De Bourgh."

Georgiana swayed in place. "Oh, Lord," she murmured. "What could Her Ladyship mean by her visit?"

"Do you wish me to accompany you, Miss Darcy?" Mrs. Bingley came to stand beside her.

Georgiana shook off the idea. "No, I should see my aunt alone." She took off at a trot in the house's direction.

Mrs. Bingley turned to her husband. "Charles, you and Mr. Grange should oversee bringing the greenery to the house. Papa, could you intercede with my mother until after Miss Darcy has the opportunity to address Lady Catherine's needs."

"I'm on my way, Jane." Mr. Bennet followed Georgiana toward the side door.

"Kitty," Jane continued. "I know Miss Darcy needs to tend to Her Ladyship alone, but you might be available to support her— even if she thinks she doesn't need it."

"Certainly." Kitty rushed to catch up with her father.

"Caroline's at the house," Bingley assured his wife.

Jane glanced quickly to where Mary assisted Mr. Grange. Assured of some privacy, she said, "That's what I fear. Lady Catherine knows nothing of Elizabeth's problems in carrying to term. I would prefer that she didn't learn of Lizzy's anguish from either my mother or your sister. Neither would realize the pain that such knowledge in Lady Catherine's hands would give Mrs. Darcy."

"Then you should speak to Caroline," Bingley observed.

"It might be better coming from you, Charles. Caroline has no true affection for Elizabeth. She would disregard my pleas on Lizzy's behalf."

Bingley accepted the task immediately, as his wife gave orders to the waiting footmen. He certainly didn't look forward to speaking to Caroline about such a private matter, but he would for Darcy. Although, as a man, Darcy hadn't displayed his feeling, Bingley knew that his friend had suffered as much as Mrs. Darcy, and that Darcy would feel compelled to protect Elizabeth—to be strong for his wife. Bingley would do whatever was necessary to divert Caroline's spitefulness.

〜⊙〜　〜⊙〜　〜⊙〜

Georgiana tucked in several wisps of loose hair as she rushed to where Lady Catherine waited. A thousand errant thoughts rushed through her head. She couldn't send Lady Catherine away, but what could she do about having both her aunt and Elizabeth's family under the same roof? "Oh, Fitzwilliam, I wish you were here," she groaned. Opening the room's door, her fears jumped to the forefront: Mrs. Bennet jabbered away, and Lady Catherine didn't look pleased.

∼⦿∽ ∼⦿∽ ∼⦿∽

"Why, Lady Catherine. Imagine my surprise when Mrs. Reynolds and I received word of your arrival." Mrs. Bennet swept into the room. "I immediately made my way to greet you properly. You're aware, I am certain, that Mr. and Mrs. Darcy are away, but they are expected by this evening." She sat without being given leave to do so. "I'm surprised that Miss Darcy didn't mention your arrival, Your Ladyship. What a grand surprise it'll be for Mr. Darcy! Oh! I'm ahead of myself. Certainly, Mr. Darcy must have invited you to Pemberley also."

Lady Catherine bit her words. "My nephew…Mr. Darcy invited you to Pemberley?"

"Of course. You didn't think me here uninvited?" Mrs. Bennet helped herself to tea. "Even with my Elizabeth as mistress of this great household, I'd wait for an invitation." Mrs. Bennet thought of how long she had waited to be a part of Elizabeth's life, but she certainly wouldn't disclose that fact to a woman who had maligned her daughter. Plus, she recalled quite well Lady Catherine's Longbourn visit. She had tried to make the best of an awkward situation, but Her Ladyship had been less than pleasant.

In fact, Mrs. Bennet had thought she'd outshone the great woman. Lady Catherine had arrived at an early hour—one too early in the morning for visitors. Her Ladyship had entered the sitting room with an air more than usually ungracious, had made no other reply to Elizabeth's salutation than a slight inclination of the head, and had sat down without saying a word. Mrs. Bennet admitted to being flattered by having a guest of such high importance and had received Lady Catherine with the utmost politeness, but Her Ladyship had rudely questioned Elizabeth, had criticized Mrs. Bennet's favorite sitting room, and had marked their lack of a proper garden. All she could do was to valiantly defend her home by reminding Lady Catherine that she possessed more than did Sir William Lucas, of whom Her Ladyship openly approved.

Now, the same formidable aristocrat sat before her, and Mrs. Bennet had an opportunity to rise once again above Lady Catherine's censure. However, before Her Ladyship could respond, Miss Darcy rushed into the room. "Lady Catherine," she gushed as she dropped a curtsy. "I was unaware you planned to join us at Pemberley. Had I known, I would've been here to receive you." Georgiana fought the urge to wipe her sweaty palms on her day dress.

"I've seen to Her Ladyship," Mrs. Bennet announced.

"Thank you, Ma'am." Georgiana took a few tentative steps forward. "The others are bringing in the greenery," she improvised. "I heard Mr. Bennet asking for you. I'm afraid we let our mirth carry us away. Your husband needs your assistance to ward off a chill… dry clothes and hot tea." Georgiana realized how she rambled on, but she couldn't seem to stop.

Just then Kitty stepped into the open doorway. "Oh, there you are, Mama," she said as if she had looked for her mother elsewhere. "Papa sent me to find you." Awkwardly, she turned to Georgiana. "Excuse me, Miss Darcy. I didn't mean to interrupt your conversation."

"It is well, Miss Kitty," Georgiana said with a thankful smile.

"Men are so helpless, are they not, Your Ladyship?" Mrs. Bennet stood to make her exit.

Lady Catherine glowered from the familiarity. "I'm certain I would have no notion of such a weakness," she hissed.

"Come along, Mama." Kitty said firmly from the doorway. She offered a respectful curtsy. "Lady Catherine. Miss De Bourgh." Then she led her mother from the room.

Lady Catherine waited to hear the receding footsteps before saying, "Mrs. Jenkinson, would you see to our rooms and our luggage?"

"Certainly, Your Ladyship."

"And close the door on your way out."

Lady Catherine paused until Anne's companion departed, and then she turned her anger on her niece. "Your brother—my nephew—saw fit to invite that woman and her daughters to Pemberley!" she accused. "In my sister's house that witless excuse for a mother presumes to serve as hostess! Lady Anne Darcy must have turned over in her grave. It's bad enough that Darcy places that obstinate, headstrong girl in my dear sister's stead, but to welcome a houseful of people of inferior birth is inconceivable—people of no importance in the world and wholly unallied to the family."

Georgiana flinched, but the litany fell from her shoulders. Her fists clenched, and her cheeks flushed, but she held her composure. She had not learned how to control her aunt's venom, but she had learned how to allow the woman her censure without taking it personally. Elizabeth had taught her. Her sister, in a moment of pure abandon, had once described Lady Catherine's attack—the one leading to Fitzwilliam's renewing his proposal to Elizabeth. Georgiana had experienced one of her numerous diffident moments, which had ended in tears and in Elizabeth's embrace. To highlight her explanation, Georgiana's sister had acted out the scene between her and Darcy's aunt. It brought giggles of disbelief, but it also demonstrated to Georgiana that she should not allow Lady Catherine—or anyone else, for that matter—to define her. Therefore, despite her aunt's reproach, she didn't believe that Fitzwilliam's display of affections would upset their mother. Georgiana had few direct memories of her parents' reported love affair, but every story spoke of their devotion.

"Lady Catherine," she began tentatively, "as Pemberley's master, Fitzwilliam may invite whomever he chooses to his home. My brother wished to share his festive days with his wife's family. It's not for me to criticize." Georgiana left the implication for her aunt to interpret.

Frost dusted Her Ladyship's countenance, and as if she'd not heard her niece, Lady Catherine continued, "To complicate the matter, Darcy has opened his door to that family of Cits."

Georgiana blinked away her confusion. "Do you speak of Mr. Bingley's family, Aunt?"

"Who else, Child?"

Georgiana shot a pleading glance at her cousin, but Anne remained seated with downcast eyes. The rebellious part of Georgiana's mind screamed that she was no longer a child, but one look at her aunt's outraged countenance quashed that urge. "Mr. Bingley and my brother have been acquaintances for several years. The Bingleys have often shared Fitzwilliam's hospitality. I don't understand your sudden objection, Lady Catherine."

"My objection," Her Ladyship snapped, "is that I'm to be subjected to an array of commonness from those who seek positions above their reach by using their dirty hands to throw about their wealth to those who possess airs beyond their low connections!"

Georgiana could no longer accept her aunt's dictatorial attitude without an argument. It was all of a piece with Lady Catherine. "Let me see, Your Ladyship, if I understand. As a *child*, I may lack the capacity to comprehend. You've invited yourself to my brother's home and now object to those with whom Fitzwilliam has chosen to spend the festive days. As it's such a wholly dishonorable situation, I'll ask Mr. Nathan to arrange for your safe passage to Lambton or wherever you choose to seek lodging." Georgiana turned on her heels to leave.

"Have you gone batty, Georgiana?" Lady Catherine charged.

Her aunt's words stung. Hers was a false bravado covering a very fragile self-confidence, and for a fleeting moment, Georgiana wondered if she played dangerously with her brother's good will. Yet, a small voice—Elizabeth's voice—said Fitzwilliam would celebrate his sister's liberation. Her spine stiffened. "Have I omitted some fact, Your Ladyship?"

Lady Catherine chortled. "The abominable roads, Georgiana," she reminded her niece. "If the conditions were acceptable, and I wasn't to meet Mr. and Mrs. Collins, Anne and I could have returned to Kent or London or even have chosen to spend our days with Matlock and Lindale. They await Lindale's heir to the Earldom. Under these horrendous conditions, you cannot mean to send me out on the icy roads."

"I wouldn't have you injured in any way, Your Ladyship." A twinge of guilt ricocheted through Georgiana's resolve. "But neither would I have you subjected to unacceptable company."

"Your Ladyship, maybe we should return to Lambton," Anne ventured. "Surely, Mr. Swank can maneuver the coach safely the five miles to the village."

Lady Catherine glared at her only child. "First, to find appropriate rooms with the current road conditions would prove impossible. Second, there's the issue of Mr. and Mrs. Collins. I sent word to the man yesterday that we would wait for him at Pemberley."

Georgiana felt another surge of seething anger. She presented a calm exterior, but every nerve ending stood on alert. Despite her best efforts, a mulish set locked Georgiana's jaw. "If I understand your current disapprobation, Your Ladyship, you disdain my brother's chosen house guests. Yet, you cannot leave Pemberley because of the road conditions and because *yesterday* you invited Mr. and Mrs. Collins to join you here. Without Fitzwilliam's knowledge!" Georgiana could no longer conceal her frustrations. Her aunt's actions defied comprehension.

Lady Catherine's defiant chin rose another half inch. "That is an accurate summary."

Wishing nothing more than a hasty retreat, Georgiana dropped a curtsy. "I must inform Mrs. Reynolds of the Collinses' arrival. I'll leave it to you, Your Ladyship, to determine whether you can maintain civility under such dire circumstances. Please keep in mind that Fitzwilliam shall require nothing less."

Lady Catherine's upper lip curled in what could only be described as a snarl. "I always thought you a wisp of a girl. You may have a backbone, after all. Although I must admit, I preferred the gentler, more caring Georgiana Darcy."

Chapter 3

∾⊙∾ ∾⊙∾ ∾⊙∾

"DOES BARON BLOOMFIELD hold a special interest, Elizabeth?" His wife's intense absorption in every move Bloomfield made ate away at Darcy's composure.

She blushed. "Lord, no!" She declared self-mockingly. "No one can compare with you, Fitzwilliam."

Darcy had tried to hold some part of himself apart from her, but from the beginning Elizabeth had held his heart in her grasp. The first time he had laid eyes upon her at the Meryton assembly, shock had slammed through him. "She is tolerable, but not handsome enough to tempt me," he had told Charles Bingley, but his mind had shattered to a single thought: shards of desire for Elizabeth Bennet.

And he'd always been jealous—he'd tried desperately not to be, but was most assuredly so. At Netherfield, he'd said things he knew would provoke her just to draw Elizabeth's attention away from Bingley. He wanted her gaze on him. With his cousin Edward, the green-eyed monster had reared his head quite dramatically. There were moments at Rosings Park that he considered calling the good colonel out. He had ached for her—to know the splendor of her love.

On their wedding night, Darcy had remained at her bedchamber's door, watching her brush her raven-touched locks. He knew she was nervous, for he could see her top teeth catch up her bottom lip—a habit Elizabeth had when worried over something. The virginal white gown had only increased his desire. Recognizing his duty to his name, Darcy had always assumed that he'd desire the woman that he wed, but with Elizabeth it was more than the physical contact. He enjoyed her company—his wife's astute, honest opinions—the completeness she brought to his life. She'd turned his world upside down; he was powerless against the control she held over his heart, his body, and his mind. That demure nightgown had stood between him and happiness.

No one can compare with you, Fitzwilliam. Elizabeth's words echoed in his brain and shot straight to his groin. "Then would you care to explain your devotion to the baron?" he asked on a rasp.

Elizabeth chuckled self-consciously. "You'll think me a complete fool." She paused to judge her husband's seriousness and then continued her explanation. "Whenever we're traveling, I watch people to discover who seems content with his lot in life. With gentlemen, such as the baron, I try to guess what equipage they might drive— the color of the crest and livery or what type of horse each man rides. If we're at a coaching inn, I might watch to see if I'm correct."

Darcy smiled lovingly. "And are you accurate in your estimations?"

Elizabeth laughed softly. "Rarely."

He fought to keep the laughter from his response. "I'm all astonishment, my love. You're known for your incisive judgments."

Elizabeth swallowed her mirth. "As you well know, Mr. Darcy, I've experienced moments when I've taken no note of a person's true goodness."

"As when you said, 'I had not known you a month before I felt that you were the last man in the world whom I could ever be prevailed on to marry'?"

Her mouth's corners turned upward in amusement. "I did abuse you so abominably to your face. However, even you, my husband, admitted that you deserved my rebukes. For though my accusations were ill founded, formed on mistaken premises, your behavior to me at the time had merited the severest reproof."

"It was unpardonable," Darcy said seriously. "I cannot think of it without abhorrence."

"We will not quarrel for the greater share of blame annexed to that evening," said Elizabeth. "The conduct of neither, if strictly examined, was irreproachable, but since then we have both, I hope, improved in civility. Instead, let us dwell on the baron's steed. I say that, as a privileged gentleman, the man rides a grey gelding."

Darcy allowed her to turn the subject. They'd analyzed their maddening courtship on more than one occasion. "Just a bit skewed," he said with pleasure. "A roan-colored stallion."

"See, I'm perfectly insensible," she declared.

Darcy countered, "You're perfectly beautiful."

Elizabeth's eyes sparkled—a teary mist. "You're prejudiced on my behalf, Mr. Darcy."

"Until I met you, Elizabeth, I was always moving but ever going nowhere."

"You say the most delicious things, Fitzwilliam." She slid her hand under his. "We brought Christmas to Prestwick's today, Mr. Darcy." She inhaled the pine's calming scent.

Darcy followed her gaze as he tightened his hold on her hand. "You brought Christmas to Prestwick's, Mrs. Darcy. Your handiwork pokes its head from every corner."

"The maid Nan helped," she shared.

"But to your credit, Elizabeth, the Washingtons owe their thanks."

Elizabeth accepted his acknowledgment with grace. She'd learned to give in to his kindness. "And the gentlemen found some game?" After their conversation with Mrs. Washington, Darcy had first organized a hunt for Christmas greenery and then a different type of hunt.

"Padget's an excellent shot," he disclosed. "He, Lord Horvak, Mr. Rennick, and Mr. Livingstone managed to bag several rabbits, a few game birds, and a deer. Mrs. Washington was most appreciative."

Elizabeth guarded their privacy. "The baron didn't participate?"

Darcy whispered, "Mr. Bradley's gout and age kept him from joining the group. Mr. Betts and Mr. Dylan, the farmers who came in early that first night, helped Mr. Washington's man in the stable."

"They've gotten along well for having not known each other previously," Elizabeth observed.

"They have," Darcy continued. "But they're both accustomed to hard work. And Horvak and Padget's friendship has allowed Livingstone and Rennick a room. The baron is the only one who expresses an entitlement."

Elizabeth smirked. "As I assumed. At least, Mr. Darcy, I was correct in one of my estimations."

⁓　⁓　⁓

"Mr. and Mrs. Collins." Georgiana greeted the couple, along with the local vicar, in the main hallway. Kitty stood beside her. "Welcome to Pemberley. I'm Georgiana Darcy."

"Miss Darcy," Mr. Collins bowed stiffly before continuing, "I entreat your pardon for imposing on your family's good will, but I beg to know of Her Ladyship's continued good health."

Georgiana considered the cleric's impertinent freedom beyond the pale, but Kitty had warned her of the man's determined air of following his own inclination. Eyeing Mr. Collins with restrained wonder, Georgiana managed to assure the man that his patron awaited him in the drawing room.

"I'm pleased to hear it, Miss Darcy."

He puffed up to begin again, but Kitty shrewdly said, "Charlotte, you look exhausted. Were the roads horrid?"

"They're passable with great care," Charlotte Collins assured them. "Miss Darcy, allow me to add my gratitude to that of my husband for granting us your hospitality."

Georgiana noted a painful impatience cross Mrs. Collins's countenance. "I'm certain my sister shall be pleased to have you among our guests, Mrs. Collins. Elizabeth speaks often of your long-standing friendship." Turning to the young vicar, Georgiana greeted the man who assisted Mr. Nathan with everyone's wraps. "Mr. Winkler, it was considerate of you to see Mr. and Mrs. Collins to our door, Sir."

"Mr. Collins called at my home when he could secure no one's services because of the road conditions," he said dryly.

"You took upon yourself a great kindness," Georgiana remarked. "You'll dine with us, Mr. Winkler," she ordered. "It's the least we can do."

"Thank you, Miss Darcy," he said politely. "And you, Miss Catherine. It is pleasant to hear of your return to Derbyshire."

When the young vicar bowed over Kitty's hand, Georgiana noticed his apparent nervousness. Something told her that the cleric had chosen to escort the Collinses to Pemberley because of Kitty's return. She would have to ask her friend about the possibility. "We'll join my aunt and the others in the main drawing room."

"Come, Cousin." Kitty took Mr. Collins's arm. "Mr. and Mrs. Darcy are away, but are expected this evening. Mr. Darcy plans a surprise for my sister. We're all part of Elizabeth's Christmas. In addition to Her Ladyship and Miss De Bourgh, the Bingleys are in attendance, as are your family: Mama, Papa, and Mary."

Georgiana walked beside Mrs. Collins and the vicar. They trailed Kitty and her cousin. "Elizabeth is well, I pray," Charlotte whispered.

"Mrs. Darcy is quite well. I cannot imagine Pemberley without her. She brings life to my brother's home."

"I don't doubt it," Charlotte added. "Elizabeth was always the most resourceful of our friends."

They entered the room to find Collins bowing low over Lady Catherine's outstretched hand. "Oh, Your Ladyship, I cannot thank you enough for the benevolence you have shown me and Mrs. Collins."

"And you found your relative well, Mr. Collins?" Lady Catherine intoned royally.

"We did, Your Ladyship. Of course, Mrs. Collins and I steadily resisted the invitation of my Warrington cousin to remain through the festive days."

He bowed again to Miss De Bourgh and a third time to the room as a whole. The man was everything Georgiana had heard: Mr. Collins was not a sensible man, and the deficiency of nature had been but little assisted by education or Society, the greatest part of his life having been spent under the guidance of an illiterate and miserly father; and though he belonged to one of the universities, he had merely kept the necessary terms without forming at it any useful acquaintance. The subjection in which his father had brought him up had given him originally a great humility of manner; but it was now a good deal counteracted by the self-conceit of a weak head, living in retirement, and the consequential feelings of early and unexpected propriety. A fortunate chance had recommended him to Lady Catherine De Bourgh when the living of Hunsford was vacant; and the respect which he felt for her high rank and his veneration for her as his patroness, mingling with a very good opinion of himself, of his authority as a clergyman, and his right as a rector, made him altogether a mixture of pride and obsequiousness, self-importance, and humility.

"It's good you have come, Collins," Lady Catherine declared. "We may need to leave early for Kent."

Georgiana recognized her aunt's manipulation and remained silent, but the others civilly protested Lady Catherine's exit. "You cannot mean to depart, Your Ladyship," Caroline said. "Surely, Mr. Darcy would not approve of such a precipitous change in your travel plans."

"Certainly," Mr. Collins clarified, "we'll do as Your Ladyship directs, but I would encourage you to think upon it, Ma'am. The roads were treacherous, were they not, Mr. Winkler?"

Without even an introduction, Collins had brought the man into the conversation. Mr. Winkler bowed to the room. "The going would be quite slow, Your Ladyship."

Georgiana added quickly, "May I present Mr. Thorne Winkler? Mr. Winkler holds the living at Lambton." She introduced the man to each cluster of guests.

"I'm extremely pleased to make your acquaintance, Mr. Bennet," Mr. Winkler said formally. "It's been a fortuitous occasion to have Miss Catherine among my congregation when she has visited at Pemberley."

Mr. Bennet winked at his daughter. "I gladly bequeath my daughter's religious development to you, young man."

"I assure you, Mr. Bennet, that Miss Catherine doesn't require my guidance. Your daughter brings honor to your household."

When Georgiana shot her a warning glare, Lady Catherine stifled a snort of derision.

Mr. Bennet ignored Lady Catherine's unbecoming behavior. "Of which daughter do you speak, Mr. Winkler? After all, Mrs. Darcy is also my daughter," he said teasingly.

"Papa, stop it!" Kitty protested. "Mr. Winkler's not aware of your propensity to twist people's words."

Mr. Bennet chuckled. "Very well, Kitty. I will spare the gentleman for the time being."

Kitty flushed, but Georgiana would've bet it wasn't from embarrassment. *When had Kitty and Mr. Winkler moved to a more intimate stage?* Georgiana's need to speak to Kitty privately increased.

Mr. Collins explained, "When Mrs. Collins and I could secure no other transportation, I called on Mr. Winkler, and the gentleman was kind enough to escort us to Pemberley personally in his gig."

"His gig?" Mrs. Bingley gasped. "My, Charlotte, you must be chilled through. Come nearer the hearth. Let me pour you some tea. We have not seen you in well over a year." Jane gestured to a cluster of chairs.

Mr. Bingley followed his wife's lead. "You, too, Collins. Winkler. Please join us for tea. Miss Darcy has most graciously provided us with the best of Pemberley's hospitality."

"I believe my niece is capable of welcoming her own guests, Sir," Lady Catherine intoned. Her words stilled the room.

Georgiana blushed, but she managed to say, "In my brother

and sister's absence, I hold no objection to Mr. and Mrs. Bingley's assistance. After all, we're family and close acquaintances."

"Thank you, Miss Darcy," Jane said softly. "As Mr. Collins is a Bennet cousin and Mrs. Collins is a long-time neighbor from Hertfordshire, it seemed only fitting to offer my subvention in Elizabeth's stead, but I would never think to circumvent your position at Pemberley."

Lady Catherine had created a rift in the group's rapport. "Of course not, Mrs. Bingley. I would never criticize anything of your doing."

"This is an excellent room," Mr. Collins observed as he shot a glance at Lady Catherine. "Of course, it is nothing when compared to Rosings Park."

Mr. Bennet chuckled. "Beware, Collins, that you don't offend the man who offers you hospitality despite his absence. Praising Her Ladyship would be advisable only if you cannot offend Mr. Darcy, unless you've a deep desire to be driven into the elements."

Collins blustered, "I meant no offense, Miss Darcy. Both estates are magnificent in their own rights."

Georgiana bit back her retort. To think that anyone might attempt to compare the two was ridiculous. Pemberley's rooms were lofty and handsome, displaying Fitzwilliam's taste; they were neither gaudy nor uselessly fine—with less of splendor and more real elegance than the furniture of Rosings. "No offense taken, Mr. Collins. Rosings Park is a grand estate fitting my aunt's position as an Earl's daughter and a baronet's wife. Pemberley reflects the same noble line on the maternal side, and on my father's, a respectable, honorable, and ancient, though untitled family." With some satisfaction Georgiana noted her aunt's raised brow and her cousin's smirk of amusement.

"I'm certain my husband regrets his wording, Miss Darcy," Charlotte intervened.

Mr. Bennet replied, "I'd assume that Mr. Collins's regrets are numerous, but God offers forgiveness. Does He not, Collins?" The mocking smile returned.

"Our Lord is benevolent," Collins responded in some confusion.

"Then everything is well. You shall ask for forgiveness for your offense, and we'll all go forward."

Mr. Nathan tapped on the door. "Excuse me, Miss Darcy. Mr. and Mrs. Collins's quarters are ready. Meg waits in the main foyer to escort them to their rooms."

"Thank you, Mr. Nathan. Might you also make one of the empty bedchambers available for Mr. Winkler's use?"

"Certainly, Miss Darcy."

⁓ ⁓ ⁓

"Pardon, Mr. Darcy." Mr. Livingstone bowed. "Mr. Rennick mentioned that you planned to depart tomorrow. I thought you should know, Sir, a misty rain has returned. What little thaw we earned today has refrozen. The wet rain is freezing on the slick surfaces."

Darcy had knowledge of this weather's turn, but he'd hoped to keep it from his wife. "Thank you, Livingstone. I suppose Mrs. Darcy and I will have to reevaluate our plans if the rain continues overnight." He noted his wife's fallen countenance.

The gentleman bowed again. "I'm at your service, Mr. Darcy."

Watching him walk away, Darcy returned his attention to Elizabeth. "Livingstone could be in error, my dear. No one can predict the weather."

"I know it's insensible, Fitzwilliam. I'm warm, I want not for shelter or food, but all I desire for Christmas is to be at Pemberley with my family."

Darcy wondered if his wife had discovered his surprise. "Your family is in Hertfordshire."

"You're my family, Fitzwilliam. You and Georgiana and Mrs. Reynolds and the tenants. Pemberley is my home," she insisted.

Darcy felt desire's familiar rush. "Yes, it is. It's as if, before you arrived, Pemberley was only a fine house. Now, it's a home. You have left your imprint on it, my dearest Elizabeth."

Before she could respond, the sound of a carriage before the inn brought everyone to his feet. Scrambling to the windows for a better view, Darcy made a point of shadowing Elizabeth with his body. Using a napkin to wipe away the pane's cold dampness, Darcy peered over Elizabeth's shoulder. "A gentleman," he whispered close to her ear.

"And a lady." Her face turned up to his in anticipation.

Darcy wouldn't tell her there was, literally, "no room at the inn." He recognized his wife's need for female company. At Pemberley, she had spent her days interacting with Georgiana, Mrs. Reynolds, and others from the community. On this trip, as Mr. Parnell had had no wife, Darcy's business had left Elizabeth alone to entertain herself in a strange city. Leaving her behind as he met with the cantankerous Parnell, Darcy had actually wished Elizabeth's youngest sister Lydia Wickham had remained in Newcastle. He had done his wife a disservice by imposing his needs upon her.

As they and several others watched, the man braced the woman's step on the icy path, and within seconds the inn's door swung wide to a couple draped in soaking wet outerwear.

"Greetings," Mr. Washington called as he approached. "Welcome to Prestwick's Portal."

The young man removed his beaver and shook the dampness from his greatcoat. Quickly checking the woman to see to her comfort, he turned to the innkeeper. "We were certainly pleased to see the road markings leading to your inn, Sir." The man helped the lady with her cloak. "I hope you have a room available for Mrs. Joseph and me."

Mr. Washington's face fell. "I fear, Sir, that we're beyond capacity. Even my maid's room is being used for two of the gentlemen's gentlemen." He gestured to those who curiously looked on.

Elizabeth broke away from the group and intervened. "Surely, something can be arranged, Mr. Washington. Obviously, Mrs. Joseph cannot return to the icy roads." She referred to the young woman's physical condition—very much with child. "It's simply too dangerous."

"Where would you have me house the Josephs?" Mr. Washington asked defensively. "Every room's full." He glanced toward where the baron sat alone in the common room. "We have no other options."

The group's gaze followed his to where Baron Bloomfield finished his meal. "What say you, Bloomfield?" Sir Jonathan asked. "Are you willing to relinquish your room to the couple?"

The baron looked up with disdain. "You address me, Padget?"

"Are you of the persuasion, Sir, to consider a room reshuffling to accommodate Mr. and Mrs. Joseph?"

Bloomfield's gaze fell on the waiting couple before a snarl curled his upper lip. "I think not. The prospects of sharing a room with a wheezing and gouty Bradley are impossible. It's bad enough to experience the man's aches and pains through this inn's thin walls. Encountering the man's complaints first hand will not occur."

Darcy, recognizing Elizabeth's building ire, suggested, "Mrs. Darcy, why do you not see Mrs. Joseph closer to the hearth while we sort this out. I'm sure the lady could use some hot tea."

Elizabeth resented being relegated to the role of hostess, but she heard her husband's resolve. He understood her objections to the baron's persistence and would deal with it on her behalf. "Certainly, Mr. Darcy. Come, Mrs. Joseph. You must be chilled quite through."

"Thank you, Ma'am. I'm just that." Mrs. Joseph accepted Elizabeth's arm as support.

Darcy cleared his throat. "Gentlemen, perhaps we can place our heads together and come up with a solution for the Josephs' dilemma." He gestured to a small table, and the other travelers—minus Bloomfield and Bradley—joined him. "Mr. Washington, I'm certain Mr. Joseph could use a tankard of ale."

Elizabeth ordered tea and soup for the lady and settled Mrs. Joseph before the fire. "I'm Elizabeth Darcy," she said as she helped the woman lower her frame into the straight-backed chair. "My husband and I are from Derbyshire."

"I'm pleased to have the acquaintance, Mrs. Darcy." Mrs. Joseph extended her hands to the fire. "I'm Mary Joseph. My husband and I reside in Staffordshire." She expelled a deep sigh as the warmth reached her. "It's been a treacherous few hours."

"You have been traveling long?" Elizabeth asked.

"Three days. Matthew allowed extra time because of my condition." Mrs. Joseph rested her hand comfortably on her expanded abdomen. "We return to Northumberland. Newcastle, actually. We received news recently that my husband's mother has taken seriously ill. Her days may be numbered so we set out to be at her bedside."

Elizabeth waited for Nan to place the tea and soup on a nearby low table before responding. "Mr. Darcy had business in Newcastle. We had hoped to be at Pemberley by Christmas, but now we're unsure."

Mrs. Joseph glanced about the room. "At least, there's a holiday touch about the space. The pine scent is quite comforting."

Elizabeth nodded her agreement. "The men gathered the greenery today, and the inn's proprietress and I organized the arrangements."

Mrs. Joseph sipped the warm tea. "I approve, Mrs. Darcy."

Elizabeth smiled easily. "It was a female whim, but upon Mr. Darcy's insistence, the gentlemen—at least, a few of them—acquiesced." Elizabeth poured herself some tea. "I hope you'll not find my next comment too personal," she said tentatively. "But should you not be in the midst of your confinement, Mrs. Joseph?" Considering her own tenuous condition, Elizabeth added, "A woman cannot be too careful under the circumstances."

Mrs. Joseph's chocolate brown eyes sparkled with the room's warmth. "I suppose I should've taken the weather into consideration; it's late December, after all. But as I'm a month from my delivery, I thought it best to support my husband. Matthew would never forgive himself if he wasn't at his mother's side when her time came, and I wouldn't selfishly demand that he choose between the woman who sacrificed everything for him and me." Mrs.

Joseph nervously giggled. "What if I were not my husband's first choice, Mrs. Darcy? Can you imagine the wedge driven between us if that were so?"

"I have no doubt that Mr. Joseph would realize his duty rested with you, as would the elder Mrs. Joseph," Elizabeth assured.

The woman shot a fleeting look toward her husband. "I wouldn't wish for Mr. Joseph to choose me out of duty, Mrs. Darcy. I'm vain enough to seek the man's love."

Elizabeth observed, "Few of us of any station have the luxury of knowing true love in marriage, Mrs. Joseph. If you are so fortunate, I commend your joining."

The young woman sipped her creamed soup. "Do you count yourself among those fortunate ones, Mrs. Darcy? I know it's truly none of my concern, but as we are, apparently, the only female guests here, I suspect we'll become intimate friends thanks to our circumstance."

Elizabeth didn't turn her head, but she knew Darcy watched her. The thought of his constant attention brought a smile to her lips. "I know Mr. Darcy's affections," she said softly.

"Good," Mrs. Joseph pronounced. "Then you'll understand the necessity of my accompanying Mr. Joseph on this journey." She sighed deeply. "Of course, I had an ulterior motive. My father and I parted with bitter words. I had hoped that if I delivered his first grandchild where he might meet the babe that he would forget what he saw as betrayal."

"A child can resolve many ills. Our Lord sent his son to offer us forgiveness."

"I don't wish to portray my father in a poor light. He placed everything aside to raise a daughter alone after my mother's passing. He worked countless hours to create a successful business, but he provided me both sympathy and encouragement. Through all his trials, he demanded only one thing from me—my loyalty. He had chosen a man who would follow my father's every order, but I had other ideas. Unfortunately, my father couldn't fathom how

I could love another more than I loved him. To complicate the matter, Mr. Joseph accepted a living outside of Stoke-upon-Trent. My father took what he saw as my complete abandonment of him quite hard."

Elizabeth thought of her own father. "I'm one of five daughters, but I suspect that my father feels abandoned by each of us."

"However, he misses you the most, Mrs. Darcy," Mrs. Joseph said with some amusement.

Elizabeth blushed from the obvious. "I flatter myself that Mr. Bennet prefers me over my sisters. I'm terribly vain, you see, Mrs. Joseph. Perhaps you may not wish my acquaintance, after all."

"I wouldn't criticize your pride, Mrs. Darcy," the lady teased.

"My sister Mary once observed that pride is a very common failing. That human nature is particularly prone to it, and that there are very few of us who do not cherish a feeling of self-complacency on the score of some quality or other, real or imaginary. Vanity and pride are different things, though the words are often used synonymously. A person may be proud without being vain. Pride relates more to our opinion of ourselves; vanity to what we would have others think of us."

"Your sister is quite wise, Mrs. Darcy."

Elizabeth smiled happily. Having a lady's company created a relaxed atmosphere. She quite enjoyed the pert Mrs. Joseph's easy-going wit. "Mary has been called several things, but 'wise' isn't among them. She's my most serious sister and the most talented. Mary spends countless hours at her studies and at practicing her music."

"Tell me of your other sisters, Mrs. Darcy."

"Then what would you have me do?" Mr. Joseph asked through gritted teeth.

Mr. Horvak asked, "Could Mr. and Mrs. Joseph stay in the common room?" As a group, they had determined that it would be impossible to move people's rooms. Each occupant was a minor son of the aristocracy or a titled gentleman, except for Mr. Betts and Mr. Dylan. Although they lacked status, the two remained as Mr. Washington had refused to ask them to relinquish their shared chamber. With their hard work about the inn, the men had earned a right to a room.

"I cannot see it," Mr. Washington insisted. "A woman sleeping where men play cards and drink is not appropriate. Mrs. Washington and I have taken pallets before the kitchen hearth and Nan in the storeroom. Every space within the inn is full. If I had a private parlor…"

"We cannot ask Mr. and Mrs. Joseph to resume their journey," Darcy insisted. He had watched his wife's animation with pleasure. She had needed another lady's company, and besides advocating the solution to the Josephs' predicament because it was the charitable thing to do, Darcy wanted Mrs. Joseph's presence to ease Elizabeth's unrest.

"Of course not," Mr. Washington declared. "However, the best I can do is a mattress in the stables. I have drivers and footmen and valets to house in addition to each of your rooms. We would be sorely pressed if some of you gentlemen hadn't pitched in with the chores and hadn't brought us some ready meat to feed everyone. People are sharing the attic and the storage areas. You and Mrs. Joseph might spend your days in the common room and your nights in one of the stalls. We can put your Tilbury coach and maybe a couple of ours under the lean-to. That will free up more space."

"But are there not others sleeping in the barns?" Padget asked.

"Several of yer men have bedded in the loft."

"It doesn't seem proper," Padget continued. "To place a woman in such a position."

Washington sighed heavily. "It be all I can see as proper. Mr. Joseph will see to his wife's safety."

Resigned to the solution offered, Mr. Joseph gathered his gloves. "I cannot place Mary and my child in danger by returning to the roads. We had two close calls today—too close for my mind's peace." He stood reluctantly. "I should speak to Mrs. Joseph. I hope, Washington, that there are additional blankets available."

"I'll see to it, Sir."

Darcy moved ahead of Joseph. Reaching Elizabeth, he extended his hand. "Come, Mrs. Darcy. We'll retire for the evening."

Elizabeth accepted his hand. "May I first give you the acquaintance of Mrs. Joseph?" she asked tentatively.

"Of course, my dear."

"Mrs. Joseph, may I present my husband, Mr. Darcy?"

The lady inclined her head. "I'm pleased for the introduction, Sir. Mrs. Darcy and I have become fast friends."

"That's a most fortunate situation. Mrs. Darcy has had only my poor companionship on this journey," Darcy said teasingly.

Mrs. Joseph smiled knowingly. "Your wife, Sir, would beg to differ. Mrs. Darcy has extolled your fine qualities."

He chuckled lightly. "My wife has the kindest heart." Darcy bowed to the woman. "We'll see you in the morning, Ma'am." He escorted Elizabeth to their shared room.

Inside their quarters, Darcy quickly took Elizabeth into his arms and kissed her hungrily. He smiled with anticipation. His wife's body warmed under his fingers' firm strokes along her collarbone. A loving blush shivered through her, and Darcy deepened the kiss. Elizabeth locked her arms behind his neck and lifted her body to his. Her breasts, hips, and thighs pressed along his front, and Darcy groaned audibly as his manhood hardened.

Her tongue touched his in desire's erotic dance, and Darcy shuddered on a breathy intake. His arms tightened about her, and he bent to lift his wife to carry her to the bed. The fire leapt between them: Desire and need kindled and sparked. His thoughts scattered as delight filled his lungs with her scent. "I love you," he whispered—his breath's heat caressing Elizabeth's neck.

Nearly an hour later, they lay with arms and legs entangled. "I suppose I should see to my ablutions," Elizabeth said sleepily. She stretched lazily against him before burying her nose in Darcy's chest. Then she trailed a light line of kisses along his jaw. "Thank you, Fitzwilliam." Elizabeth paused to nibble behind his ear. "For assisting the Josephs with lodgings. Whose room were they given?"

Darcy shifted her in his embrace. Without looking at her, he said, "No one's room." He knew she wouldn't appreciate the solution taken by Mr. Washington.

She pushed up on one elbow. "Explain, Mr. Darcy." Her voice held her suspicion.

"The baron refused to share with Bradley," he clarified. "Mr. Washington felt Betts and Dylan had earned their room." Elizabeth nodded her encouragement. "In the long and short of it, every available space is in use. The Josephs have bedded down in the stable."

Elizabeth gasped. "Surely you jest, Fitzwilliam. That was the accepted solution. Eight men could offer no better accounting than to place a woman eight months with child in a cold, damp stable?" Elizabeth scampered from the bed before Darcy could catch her. "I shan't have it, Fitzwilliam! Do you hear me? I shan't tolerate such treatment for Mrs. Joseph!" She pulled her chemise over her head.

Darcy swung his long legs over the bed's edge and sat up. "What would you have me do, Elizabeth? Would you have me tell Mr. Washington how to conduct his business? Would you demand that I physically force the baron from his room and give it to the Josephs? Washington and his wife and Nan have taken pallets in the kitchen. You must remember that each guest, except Betts and Dylan, brought servants, such as our Mr. Simpson and Jasper, who are being housed in the barn and attic and storage spaces." He pulled on his small clothes and breeches. "It was a reasonable resolution. The Josephs will spend the day in the common room. It's only for a short while—a day or two—until the weather breaks."

"Why can the Josephs not stay the night in the common room?" Elizabeth demanded.

Darcy sighed heavily. He understood his wife's angst: He had not agreed to Washington's pronouncement, but Darcy had felt his hands tied. "The others are using it for socializing. Even the hostlers and coachmen are sharing time there. Washington wouldn't want to lose the business."

Elizabeth reached for her day dress. "We must do something, Fitzwilliam." Tears misted her eyes. "Of everyone at Prestwick's, we best understand the danger Mrs. Joseph faces."

Darcy moved to embrace her. "The lady seems hardy enough." He stroked Elizabeth's back as she fought for control.

Elizabeth rasped hoarsely. "Most would've said the same of me."

Darcy swallowed hard. For his wife's sake, he had masked his own anguish at losing both their children. Elizabeth needed him to be strong, and so he had only allowed his introspection when riding alone across the estate or in the night's middle when his wife sought the comfort of his arms. Then, he, too, grieved for the children he would never hold. "It's not the same, Elizabeth," he managed to say quietly.

Elizabeth moved slightly to where she could see his face. Silently, she held his gaze before reaching for his hand. His wife placed his splayed fingers upon the swell of her abdomen. "What would you wish for me…for our child, Fitzwilliam?"

Darcy breathed deeply to steady his nerves. Elizabeth had chosen this moment to acknowledge that she carried his child. His fingertip traced a line across her cheek. "I would want someone to move heaven and earth to protect you and our child." His right hand gently cupped the rise where his heir lay. "I would demand it and wouldn't care whose censure I provoked."

"Then let's be the ones to protect Mary Joseph."

"Tell me how you wish to proceed." Darcy pulled Elizabeth to him again. "Whatever you wish, it is yours, Elizabeth. Command me as you will." Unbidden, an image of Elizabeth cradling their child sprung to life.

"We'll share our room with the Josephs. At least, it's warm and dry."

Darcy simply nodded. He would follow Elizabeth's wishes. She had openly accepted her condition, and Darcy recognized in her declaration a step in his wife's healing. "I'll dress and go find the Josephs. You should set your mind to rearranging the room to accommodate four people."

Chapter 4

෨ ෨ ෨

GEORGIANA PLASTERED ON A SMILE as she entered the dining room. Sixteen people would sit to supper—of them, eight had not received invitations. It irritated her that these people had intruded on her brother's quiet family Christmas, and it irritated her that her brother hadn't arrived to resume his position at the table's head.

"I would've thought Lizzy and Mr. Darcy would have arrived by now," Mr. Bennet observed. "I pray they haven't suffered an accident or met other hazards along the road."

Mrs. Bennet's hand fluttered about her face. "Oh, do not pronounce such dire circumstances, Mr. Bennet. Have you no compassion on my poor nerves?"

Mr. Bennet's smile betrayed his amusement. "I have a high respect for your nerves, as you well know, my dear. They are my old friends. I have heard you mention them with consideration these twenty years at least."

"Nerves," Lady Catherine grunted. "I've never understood how some women always fancy themselves beset with nerves."

Mr. Bennet's face lit with amusement. "I assure you, Your Ladyship, that Mrs. Bennet's nerves are quite real. I have witnessed their effect on numerous occasions."

"I am of the opinion that women who seek such attentions possess weak minds."

"Mother!" Anne gasped and looked quickly to Mrs. Jenkinson for support. Swallowing hard, she ventured. "I'm certain Your Ladyship didn't mean to insinuate that Mrs. Bennet suffers from a feebleness."

Lady Catherine sipped her wine. "Of course not," she said grudgingly. "Mrs. Bennet, obviously, does not seek Mr. Bennet's attentions through devious stratagems."

"I suppose that means, my dear, that your stratagems are right-handed by nature." With his wine glass, he saluted his wife across the table before turning his attention to Charlotte Collins. "Sir William seems content with Maria's match. Your sister's young beau has a promising future in London."

"Yes, Papa has written that he hopes to return to St. James when he and Mama travel to London to meet Mr. Richardson's family." Charlotte indicated Mr. Grange. "And Mrs. Bennet appears pleased with Mary's match."

"Yes, our Mary has snatched up a viable candidate. At least, Mrs. Bennet has said such on countless occasions, so I must believe it so. After all, Her Ladyship has deemed my wife to have no mental deficiencies."

Charlotte chuckled lightly before saying softly, "Lady Catherine is perceptive in her evaluations."

Mr. Bennet smiled knowingly. "Lizzy has assured me that nothing is beneath the great lady's attention."

Mrs. Collins tightened the line of her mouth. "Her Ladyship is all kindness. She has taken it upon herself to oversee my domestic concerns familiarly and minutely, offering advice on how everything ought to be regulated."

Georgiana, who sat at the table's head, could easily hear their conversation, and she recognized the extent of her aunt's interference into the Collinses' lives. It didn't surprise her. As a child, she had admired her aunt's steadfastness, especially after Sir Lewis's passing. Few men could run an estate as efficiently as did Lady Catherine. Time, however, had taught Georgiana that Her Ladyship was not in commission for the peace of the area surrounding Rosings Park; instead, Lady Catherine was a most active magistrate in her own parish, the minutest concerns of which were carried to her by Mr. Collins, and before him, Mr. Knight; and whenever any of the cottagers were disposed to be quarrelsome, discontented, or too poor, her aunt sailed forth into the village to settle their differences, silence their complaints, and scold them into harmony and plenty. Lady Catherine bullied people into doing what she said, and although Georgiana understood her aunt, the girl couldn't help but feel sorry for those of whom Her Ladyship took notice. She also felt compassion for the former Lady Catherine Fitzwilliam, who had been thrust by Sir Lewis's death into a man's world.

"Tell me of your Hertfordshire family, Mrs. Collins," Georgiana ventured.

⁀⁀   ⁀⁀   ⁀⁀

"Mr. Darcy!" Mr. Joseph looked up in surprise from where he draped a horse blanket over the stall's slats to protect his family's privacy.

Darcy remained some six feet removed from the enclosure. "Could I speak to you privately, Mr. Joseph?"

The man glanced behind him and then squeezed through the narrow opening between the fence's slats. "How may I serve you, Mr. Darcy?" the man asked warily.

Darcy gestured to the barn's main door. "Over there." When they had secured privacy, Darcy cleared his throat. Uncomfortably, he began, "My wife has taken a liking to Mrs. Joseph." He noted the man's frown. "Therefore, my Elizabeth is greatly concerned for Mrs. Joseph's health and well-being."

"Please express our gratitude to Mrs. Darcy, but I'll see to my wife's safety."

Darcy nodded. This would be embarrassing. "I would expect nothing less, Mr. Joseph. Yet, Mrs. Darcy has charged me with a specific task: My Elizabeth wishes us to share our chamber with you and Mrs. Joseph."

As suspected, the man took the suggestion as criticism. "I may not be as rich as the Darcys of Pemberley," Joseph hissed through gritted teeth. "But I can provide for my wife and child."

Darcy understood Joseph's anger. "I assure you, Sir, that I intend no offense."

"What is it, Matthew?" Mrs. Joseph appeared at her husband's side. She offered Darcy a brief curtsy. "Has something happened to Mrs. Darcy, Sir?"

She wore her cloak and gloves with a blanket draped about her shoulders. "Mrs. Darcy is well, Ma'am, but she worries for you and your child."

Mrs. Joseph glanced at her husband's sullen countenance. "It's not the most comfortable accommodation, but Mr. Joseph will see to our beds."

Darcy sighed deeply. "I have promised my wife that I would extend an invitation to you and Mr. Joseph to share our quarters."

"And I've assured Mr. Darcy that we do not require his benevolence," Mr. Joseph emphatically asserted.

The lady placed her hand gently on her husband's arm. "Matthew, I'm certain Mr. Darcy is as uncomfortable at making his offer as you are at receiving it. May we hear him out before we respond?" Her husband grudgingly nodded. "Finish what you came to say, Mr. Darcy."

"Thank you, Ma'am." He took a deep breath and proceeded with his invitation. "As I said previously, Mrs. Darcy voices her concern for your health, Mrs. Joseph. It is miserably cold outside, and without heat, this situation will only increase. Mrs. Darcy believes it best that we open our door to you." He paused briefly to gauge their reactions. Mr. Joseph still saw Darcy's commission as interference, but the lady puzzled over what Darcy said.

Throwing caution to the side, Darcy continued. "My wife and I have lost two children, and it is likely that Mrs. Darcy is being overly cautious," he explained. "But your comfort and protection, Ma'am, is important to Elizabeth; therefore, it's important to me." He swallowed his qualms. "I shouldn't share additional intimacies, but my Elizabeth has denied her own gestation until an hour ago when she spoke of what she would want for our child if we were in your situation.

"Mrs. Darcy has protected her heart from the pain of losing another child by not accepting our future happiness. Tonight, she has acknowledged our possibilities—our joined life. Through you and Mr. Joseph, Elizabeth has allowed the world to keep spinning. She has promised to keep you safe, Mrs. Joseph, and I have promised the same for her. I'm not offering royal accommodations. You'll still lie upon a pallet, but it will be before a warm hearth. You'll have some privacy. My offer must be superior to a straw bed and sharing this space with more than a dozen drivers, hostlers, and footmen."

Darcy didn't miss the shiver shooting through the woman's body. "Matthew, it would be infinitely better than what we have here," she said softly. "Can you see past your pride to accept Mr. Darcy's kindness?"

Joseph's countenance softened when he looked upon his wife's upturned face. As Darcy loved Elizabeth, this man loved his wife. "Is this what you wish, my dear?"

"I shall accept whatever decision you make."

The man nodded slightly and then turned to Darcy. "How will this work, Sir?"

Darcy smiled in triumph. "In truth, I'm not certain. Mrs. Darcy was rearranging the room's furniture when I left. She has sent for an additional screen to separate the room. I suspect, Mr. Joseph, that we should leave the details to our wives. They are likely more adept than either of us in such matters. It'll be a life experience for us all. Yet, it will pass; within less than eight and forty hours, we'll each be on our way."

"Then should we not go in, Matthew? I must admit that I should love another cup of tea." Mrs. Joseph reached for her husband's hand. "Thank you, my husband."

The man's good humor restored, he said, "Allow Mr. Darcy to see you to the inn. I'll gather our belongings and the blankets Mr. Washington provided and join you there."

Darcy spotted his footman waiting nearby for possible orders. "My man will help you, Joseph." He gestured his servant forward.

"Jasper, would you see to Mr. Joseph's luggage? Show him to Mrs. Darcy's chamber."

"Immediately, Sir." The footman moved to where the Josephs had stored their luggage.

Offering his arm to Mrs. Joseph, Darcy escorted her toward the inn. "Mrs. Darcy will be pleased to have a female companion. I sent her maid ahead, so my wife is quite lonely."

"Was what you said of Mrs. Darcy true, Sir? Has she known untimely pain twice?" She stepped gingerly on the icy surfaces.

Darcy tried to mask his own hurt. "Elizabeth has projected our losses to her current condition. If you have any thoughts of gratitude, Mrs. Joseph, I would ask that you treat my wife well. You'll have no other obligation. I'll be quite content."

⟶ ⟶ ⟶

Without asking Georgiana's permission, Lady Catherine stood to end the meal. "The ladies shall withdraw," she announced to the table.

Everyone's eyes immediately fell upon Georgiana, and she felt her composure falter, but Kitty, who sat on her left, reassuringly touched Georgiana's hand under the table linen. For a brief second, they held each other's gaze, and then Georgiana recovered. "Thank you, Your Ladyship, for reminding me of my duty. I was so enjoying the conversation that I didn't wish it to end." On shaky knees, Georgiana forced herself to her feet. "As my aunt has indicated, the ladies shall take tea in the green drawing room. I've arranged cards and other entertainments for when the gentlemen rejoin us." The other ladies followed her example. "Your Ladyship, might I ask you to lead the way?"

With satisfaction, Georgiana noted her aunt's flustered countenance. The fact that Lady Catherine hadn't expected the light rebuke pleased her. With a huff, her aunt exited the room followed by Georgiana. However, outside the dining room Georgiana paused to speak to each woman as she passed. "Mrs. Bennet, might you and Mrs. Bingley pour the tea?"

"Of course, Miss Darcy." Jane caught her mother's arm to control the woman's predictable response to Lady Catherine. She directed Mrs. Bennet toward the drawing room.

Georgiana continued her instructions. "Miss Bennet, may I impose upon you and Miss Bingley to see to the card tables? I would be most appreciative."

"As you wish, Miss Darcy."

Charlotte paused briefly. "Mrs. Jenkinson and I shall see to the chessboards."

"Thank you, Mrs. Collins. Mrs. Annesley shall assist you."

Although Kitty had tarried outside the closed dining room door for support, Georgiana first felt compelled to address her cousin. "Anne, please tell me Her Ladyship does not plan further acerbic displays."

Anne glanced nervously toward the direction everyone led. "Who can say for certain what Her Ladyship has planned?"

Kitty moved closer, but Georgiana continued, "Why has my aunt come to Pemberley? Does Lady Catherine mean to wreak havoc on Fitzwilliam's celebration? Does she so despise my brother for defying her? Or is Mrs. Darcy her target?"

Anne looked sympathetically at Georgiana. "All I know for certain is the Earl left for William's Wood to attend the birth of Rowland's child. Whether my mother therefore placed her objections aside and returned to Pemberley of her free will, or she truly feared the storm, I cannot say. Her Ladyship used the Collinses as an excuse for not departing for Kent, but, as you know, she managed to send word to Mr. Collins to come to Pemberley rather than to Matley Manor. Of course, that is assuming the Collinses' coming to Matlock was the original intention." Anne moved away to follow the others.

"Do you believe Lady Catherine will intentionally hurt Elizabeth?" Kitty whispered.

Georgiana frowned. "I have no idea. My aunt is quite unpredictable. I do know, however, that it would kill Fitzwilliam to see

Elizabeth injured by Lady Catherine. I must do something to ensure Her Ladyship does not ruin my brother's holiday."

"I shall speak to Charlotte and see what she knows. We need to discover whether Lady Catherine planned to meet the Collinses at Pemberley or at your uncle's estate."

"Thank you, Kitty. I couldn't do this without you."

"We are sisters," Kitty insisted. "Maybe not blood sisters, but sisters, nevertheless."

Georgiana smiled sweetly. It was a comforting thought. "Yes... yes, we are."

~◎~ ~◎~ ~◎~

Darcy directed Mrs. Joseph through the common room and up the narrow stairs leading to the sleeping rooms. He tapped lightly on the door, and it swung wide to admit them.

"Oh, thank Goodness!" Elizabeth reached for Mrs. Joseph's hand. "I feared you might refuse Mr. Darcy. Come in. Please, come in where it's warm. Oh, my. Your hands are icy cold."

"Thank you for your kindness, Mrs. Darcy." Mrs. Joseph's cheeks pinked. She let Elizabeth lead her to the hearth. "In...in the stable...this seemed more reasonable...than it does...does in this room," she said nervously.

Elizabeth flitted from one place to another. "As you see, with Nan's assistance, I have moved the dresser and have added a screen, essentially dividing the room in half."

"Privacy will still be an issue, Mrs. Darcy," her husband said from behind her.

"It's true," Elizabeth turned to him, "but if Mr. Betts and Mr. Dylan—two complete strangers—can share a room, and Mr. Horvak and Sir Jonathan can share, as well as Mr. Rennick and Mr. Livingstone, then surely we might find a way. It's only for a day or two."

Darcy smiled at her enthusiasm—Elizabeth's happiness was infectious. "We've agreed in spirit, Mrs. Darcy. We're simply looking for guidance on how to proceed."

Elizabeth began to pace the small open area in the room's middle. "Well, we'll make pallets for the Josephs before the hearth."

"We all assumed as such, Mrs. Darcy," he teased.

"The gentlemen will sleep in…" Elizabeth gestured wildly with her hands.

Darcy chuckled as she blushed. He had wondered what she might say about the sleeping arrangements. In fact, he had anticipated this moment from the instant that she had "ordered" him to seek out the Josephs. Ideals were one thing, but reality was quite another. However, when Elizabeth turned to him with pleading eyes, Darcy melted. "Let me see." He paused awkwardly. "I suppose the ladies could dress for bed first."

"While the men wait downstairs," Elizabeth interrupted.

"And we'll be completely covered when you return," Mrs. Joseph added.

Elizabeth picked up on the woman's thoughts. "We could leave one candle burning until the men's return. When they rejoin us, they will extinguish the light and prepare for bed in the darkened room."

Mrs. Joseph gestured toward the hearth. "The fireplace and the moonlight should be bright enough for them to complete their preparations."

Elizabeth's countenance brightened. "See, Fitzwilliam. It can work."

"I never doubted it, my dear." He moved to answer Mr. Joseph's knock. "Come in," he said to the man. "While you and Jasper have been retrieving your belongings, Joseph, our ladies have worked out the logistics. I told you our wives were quite sensible."

The man looked suspiciously at Darcy, but his wife showed Darcy's servant where to place their things. "Now, Matthew," she said, taking the extra blankets from his hands, "I want you and Mr. Darcy to go downstairs and enjoy a few drinks with the other men. Do not return for, at least, an hour." She shot a glance at Elizabeth, who nodded her agreement. "Mrs. Darcy and I shall have everything settled by then."

"Are you certain, Mary, that this is what you want?" Mr. Joseph asked seriously.

His wife squeezed his hand. "It's as it should be, Matthew. For reasons we don't understand, we're supposed to be here at this time. At least, my hands are warm." Mrs. Joseph smiled pointedly at him.

"As you wish, Mary," he said softly. Turning quickly on his heels, Mr. Joseph strode from the room. "Come, Mr. Darcy. We must socialize."

The door closed softly behind her husband before Mrs. Joseph dropped her guard. "Tell me, Mrs. Darcy, why you've chosen this path? Why is it imperative that Mr. Joseph and I share these quarters?"

Elizabeth's eyebrows twitched in disbelief. "If you're asking if I see this as an act of charity—one to feather my own list of good deeds, then you'll be sadly disappointed." Trying to discover the words to explain the unexplainable, Elizabeth bit her bottom lip. "I don't know that I can describe my thoughts well enough to satisfy your understanding. I'm searching for order and reason amongst the chaos that would allow a man such as my husband to know the pain of burying both his parents and to experience what seems impossible—that he has had to shoulder the devastation of losing two children before he could hold either in his arms. I am fiercely indignant at the world's injustices, and I'm fighting in my own disjointed way to ease the pain that God has left behind. Maybe by seeing to your needs, I'm healing my own heart and that of Mr. Darcy, as well."

Mrs. Joseph nodded curtly. "Then let's heal the discord—make our own happy endings."

"Blur the line between appearance and truth?" Elizabeth regarded the woman thoughtfully.

"Exactly."

"What do you suppose they're doing up there?" Mr. Joseph grumbled as he and Darcy sipped ale. They had endured the ribbing of the others—some of it quite bawdy in nature.

"As my Elizabeth is a very practical woman, I suspect that she and Mrs. Joseph are arranging the sleeping situation and calculating how best to proceed."

Joseph's smile had a mocking edge. "Mrs. Joseph is as level-headed as they come. I'm blessed by my wife's good sense."

Darcy examined the contents of his glass. "Then we're back to square one: We should trust our wives to do the proper thing in this matter."

～⊚～ ～⊚～ ～⊚～

"Greatness tipped Anne, even as a child," Lady Catherine announced to a shocked room. Instead of praising Mary's performance on the pianoforte, Her Ladyship extolled Anne's non-existent musical ability.

At a nearby table, Mr. Collins reinforced his patron's words. "Absolutely. A woman of distinguished birth. Apparent on first glance. Miss De Bourgh is far superior to the handsomest of her sex."

Mr. Bennet trumped the card Mr. Collins played. "It is happy for you that you possess the talent of flattery with delicacy, Collins." Mr. Bennet winked at Mary.

Collins ignored Bennet's comment. "I thought I might read aloud from *Fordyce's Sermons* after a few card hands if anyone would care to join me in the library."

Georgiana noticed that Anne blushed from her mother's false praise, but she said nothing. Instead, Anne kept her head down and attended to her embroidery. "I'm sorry, Anne," Georgiana whispered as she bent to inspect her cousin's work.

Anne glanced up briefly. "I should be accustomed to it, but the platitudes are hard to bear before so many witnesses."

Georgiana touched the stitching as if to point out an error. Having recalled many nights when she comforted a distraught

Cousin Anne, Georgiana said, "My aunt brings attention to you for reflected glory. If you're everything she claims, Lady Catherine hasn't failed as a mother."

"How did you become so astute?" Anne asked quietly.

Georgiana shrugged. "It's the Darcy blood…always so reasonable. It's the Fitzwilliam family blood that holds the emotional response."

"Play for us, Georgiana," Anne encouraged. "Let us hear the emotions."

Georgiana smiled warmly. "That may be exactly what I need to stay my anxiety."

Mr. Nathan cleared his throat from behind her. "Excuse me, Miss Darcy. A report from the gatehouse indicates visitors on the main entrance."

Georgiana breathed a relief's sigh. "It must be Fitzwilliam and Mrs. Darcy," she whispered. She shot a quick glance to where Lady Catherine continued to play her fish. "I would prefer to inform my brother of the additions to his household before he and Elizabeth make their entrances. Excuse me, Anne." She nodded her departure. "Come with me, Kitty. I may need your support."

"But Elizabeth isn't to know that I'm here," Kitty reminded her.

"We'll think of something." Georgiana tugged Kitty along behind her as they made their way to the main foyer.

༄ ༄ ༄

Darcy tapped lightly on the door to signal his and Mr. Joseph's entrance. "Come in," Elizabeth called from the semidarkness.

Darcy eased the door open and slid into the rearranged room. Nodding to Joseph, he silently made his way to where Elizabeth lay curled under the blanket. A single candle lit the space. He began to remove his jacket and boots.

Mr. Joseph made his way gingerly across the altered space. Mrs. Joseph rested on a mat before the hearth. Two folding screens separated the areas.

"Tell me when I can extinguish the candle," Darcy said aloud.

Joseph didn't answer, but Darcy could hear the man moving about so he assumed that Joseph had heard him. Darcy removed his cravat and waistcoat and draped them over a chair back. Then he waited for Mr. Joseph to finish his undressing. "You can put out the candle, Mr. Darcy," Mr. Joseph's deep voice filled the room.

Obediently, Darcy blew out the flame and then removed his shirt. He slid under the blanket and took his wife in his arms. Darcy spooned Elizabeth's body with his and silently kissed behind her ear. "I love you," he whispered.

Automatically, Elizabeth rolled over to press herself to him. She lightly kissed his chest and breathed the words, "Thank you."

Darcy kept his mouth close to her ear. "You owe me, Mrs. Darcy." He purposely ran his tongue over her ear's folds. "And when we escape this small crisis, I'll have my price."

"Which is?" She smiled against his chest.

Darcy sucked on Elizabeth's ear lobe. "You know as well as I, Elizabeth." Then he kissed her tenderly. Settling her comfortably in his arms, he turned to bury his face in her hair. Inhaling the scent of lavender, he said softly, "Good night, my love."

⤙𝒶⤚ ⤙𝒶⤚ ⤙𝒶⤚

Georgiana and Kitty raced along the passage and down the main staircase. "We'll tell Elizabeth that your parents allowed you to return to Pemberley because you were lonely now that Miss Bennet is engaged."

"Elizabeth will never believe I miss Mary's company," Kitty objected.

Georgiana tutted her disagreement. "We just need for our sister to believe us long enough for her to reach the drawing room to greet your family."

They waited impatiently for the Darcys' arrival, each girl fidgeting with her dress. Then Mr. Nathan opened the door, and instead of Mr. and Mrs. Darcy, three winter-cloaked gentlemen strode through the opening. Both girls stood in awe of the men—all fine specimens of maleness. "Oh, my," Kitty swallowed her words. She clawed at Georgiana's arm.

But Georgiana stood frozen in place. The man in front held her mesmerized. A year—more than a year had passed since she had last seen him, but he remained as before. Solid. Raven haired. Smoky blue eyes. Eyes that appeared to look through her. *See me.* Georgiana willed herself not to say the words. He was not quite as tall as Fitzwilliam, and the man's broad shoulders filled Georgiana's gaze. "Edward!" she called and launched herself into his waiting arms. In his embrace, Georgiana inhaled him deeply. He smelled of cold and leather and sweat and the spicy cologne he always had worn. "Thank God, you've returned to us."

Her cousin picked her up, clutching Georgiana to his chest, and swung her around in a circle. "My, goodness!" he laughed easily. "What happened to my little Georgie?"

"You've been away for a year, Edward," she protested.

"So, I have." He laughed again as he set her on her feet. "Where's that rascally brother of yours?" He glanced toward the main stairs.

"Fitzwilliam and Mrs. Darcy are on their way from Northumberland," she explained.

Edward frowned. "Well, Fitz will be delayed. We barely made it from Liverpool on horseback. Darcy won't chance it in a carriage." The colonel gestured to the men waiting behind him. "Do you have rooms available, Cousin? I don't wish to attempt riding to Matlock."

"Of course." Georgiana nodded to Mr. Nathan, and the man ducked into a servant's passageway to do her bidding.

Edward spotted Kitty waiting patiently. "And is this who I believe it to be?" he asked teasingly.

"You remember Mrs. Darcy's sister Catherine from the wedding, do you not, Edward?"

The colonel bowed to Kitty. "Absolutely. I am pleased to find you at Pemberley, Miss Catherine."

Kitty curtsied to the group. "I'm certain Mr. Darcy and Elizabeth shall be thrilled for your return, Colonel."

Edward placed Georgiana's hand on his arm. "Allow we to introduce my traveling companions, my dear. Miss Darcy. Miss Catherine. May I present Lieutenant Roman Southland? The lieutenant is my assistant."

The officer bowed formally. "Miss Darcy, the colonel has spoken often of his cousin, but his words didn't do you justice." He kissed Georgiana's outstretched hand. "Thank you for accepting our intrusion upon your hospitality."

"Pemberley would never turn away the colonel's associates," Georgiana responded. "Edward is family." She wanted to ask what her cousin had said of her and how often the colonel spoke of her, but instead, Georgiana smiled welcomingly at the man.

"And this gentleman," the colonel indicated the man not wearing a uniform. "This is Mr. Beauford Manneville. Mr. Manneville is from South Carolina in the Americas, but he's come to our 'enemy' shores to do business with our government and to renew his acquaintance with his distant cousin Lord Shelton."

"Welcome to England, Mr. Manneville." Georgiana curtsied and again extended her hand. "I'm sorry that your first experience on British shores brings you icy roads."

The colonel laughed softly. "You don't understand, Georgie. In South Carolina, snow rarely falls. Cold weather doesn't tarry either. Is that not correct, Manneville?"

The man openly shivered. "I've never been so cold, Colonel, and you may leave your levity out of it, Sir."

Colonel Fitzwilliam bowed stiffly. "As you wish, Manneville." He turned to Georgiana with a touch of lightheartedness. "And from what did we pull you ladies?"

Georgiana suddenly remembered the others waiting in the drawing room for her return. "Oh, Edward," she gushed. "I am doubly happy to see you, especially in Fitzwilliam's absence. We've a houseful of guests, including Lady Catherine and Anne."

"Darcy invited our aunt for Christmas?" he asked incredulously.

"No. Her Ladyship invited herself, as well as Mr. and Mrs. Collins. Lady Catherine visited the Earl, but His Lordship and the Countess have traveled east to welcome the arrival of Viscount Lindale's first child."

Edward beamed with the news. "Did you hear, Southland? I'm to be an uncle. My brother Rowland's wife is in her confinement."

The lieutenant removed his gloves and laid them nearby. "Then it is fortuitous that we didn't seek Matlock. It appears your family is scattered between here and Lincolnshire, Sir."

"They are. That they are." He smiled genuinely at Georgiana. "Come, Gentlemen. I'll introduce you to Lady Catherine De Bourgh, my family's paragon of virtue," he said teasingly.

Georgiana fell into step beside him as they climbed the stairs. "In addition to Her Ladyship and Anne, the Bingleys and the Bennets are in residence," she said softly.

"My, you do have a houseful. I thought you exaggerated, Cousin. How many await me in the drawing room?" he directed Georgiana toward the open door. Kitty and the lieutenant followed, and Mr. Manneville brought up the rear. "Counting you three, we number nineteen," she responded. "Fitzwilliam invited the Bennets and Mr. and Mrs. Bingley as a surprise for Mrs. Darcy, but others have sought shelter at Pemberley." Georgiana leaned against him. "Handling so many distinct personalities has been challenging."

His finger stroked her arm. "You've performed well, Georgie. I'm proud of you."

They had reached the open door. Taking a deep breath, Georgiana glided into the room. "Look who's joined us," she announced.

For the length of two heartbeats, no one moved, and then Anne, Lady Catherine, and Mr. Bingley rushed forward to greet the colonel. Anne, who was the closest to the door, reached him first.

"Edward," she gasped. "You've returned to us. Bless the Heavens!"

The colonel embraced her warmly. "I'm well, Anne." He kissed her cheek. "You look lovely."

"My health has improved," she said shyly.

"That pleases me more than you know." Edward then turned to his aunt. He took Lady Catherine's outstretched hand and bowed over it. "Your Ladyship." He offered the obligatory air kiss. "You, too, look well."

"I am as I always am, Edward." She accepted his whispery kiss on her cheek. "You are a fortnight early, Sir. The Earl departed for Lindale's estate less than a day prior."

"So Georgiana has informed me." He glanced about the room taking in familiar and unfamiliar faces. "I pray Lady Lindale has a safe delivery."

Lady Catherine stepped to the side. "We are anticipating Darcy's arrival," she clarified.

The colonel nodded his understanding. "As I have explained to Georgiana, I would not expect Darcy for, at least, another day. We traveled by horseback from Liverpool. The roads remain treacherous. We walked the horses the last seven miles or so."

"That's disappointing," Mr. Bingley observed, "but safety is paramount to speed in such cases."

The colonel blew out a long breath. "It was a difficult journey." He shook Bingley's hand. "If you will allow the impropriety," he said to the group, "my associates and I will freshen our clothes and then rejoin you. With such a large party, introductions will take some time."

"Of course, Colonel," Lady Catherine declared before Georgiana could open her mouth. "I assume my niece can have meals sent in."

Edward interrupted. "Georgiana is a gracious hostess, Aunt. My cousin will see to our needs without error. She's Lady Anne's daughter and understands her duties."

"Come, Gentlemen." Georgiana gestured toward the hall. "Mr. Nathan has indicated that your rooms are ready. I'll show you the way."

The three travelers bowed solemnly to the room and followed her. Georgiana caught Edward's hand. "Thank you for deflecting Her Ladyship's implied censure."

"You don't need rescuing, Georgie," he whispered. "But I'll act your gallant if you prefer."

"You are my gallant, Edward," she said softly. "You always have been." With a coy smile, Georgiana moved away to order food and drink.

ᗞ ᗞ ᗞ

"In late summer, the British won the Battle of Bladensburg and marched into Washington," the lieutenant explained to a captivated audience gathered around the drawing room hearth. He, the colonel, and Manneville had updated the Pemberley household on the action he and Colonel Fitzwilliam had seen in the Americas. "We burned most of the public buildings, and the American President, Madison, fled into the countryside."

"It sounds as if the British have everything in hand," Mr. Collins remarked.

Edward said dryly, "The lieutenant omits the fact that he saved me from a bullet at Bladensburg." His words sent an obvious shiver through his young cousin's body, and he wished he had withheld the information that had brought Georgiana anguish. He still couldn't believe the changes in her. She was absolutely mesmerizing.

"It was my duty, Sir," Southland protested.

"It was an honorable act," Edward corrected.

Manneville chortled. "You hear only the British side."

Mr. Bennet questioned. "Is there another side, Mr. Manneville?"

The man stood closer to the fire than the others. He continued to warm himself. "If you inquire whether my loyalties lie with the Brits or the Yanks, Mr. Bennet, I'd confess to neither passion." The man's words smoothly tripped from his tongue. "My father was British and my mother American. I win either way."

Caroline Bingley, who'd been watching both strangers carefully, ventured, "Have the British suffered losses, Mr. Manneville?"

"The American defense of Fort McHenry turned back the British forces, Ma'am." He continued with the enticing lilt that took tragic events and softened their edges. "In the North, Captain Thomas MacDonough destroyed the British fleet in the Battle of Lake Champlain. The British have retreated into Canada."

"When we departed," Edward explained, "our forces under Wellington's brother in marriage, Sir Edward Pakenham, marched into the city of New Orleans. Some 10,000 troops and fifty ships are involved."

"Shall the British prevail?" Kitty asked innocently.

The lieutenant resumed the telling. "The Americans have a veteran leader in Major General Andrew Jackson."

Mr. Manneville let out a harsh chuckle. "They call Jackson 'Old Hickory' for a reason. He won't bend."

Lady Catherine interrupted, "Well, I have had enough of this unholy war for one evening." She stood to depart. "Edward, we are pleased in your safe return. Matlock will be sorry he missed you."

"I'll send Father word when the weather changes." He bowed to her. "Good evening, Your Ladyship."

"I should've taken my leave some time ago," Mr. Winkler announced to the group.

Georgiana caught Kitty's blush. Mr. Winkler had stood behind Kitty's chair for the last hour. "You cannot leave, Mr. Winkler. I cannot have you hurt after playing the Good Samaritan for Mr. and Mrs. Collins."

"That's too kind, Miss Darcy. But I should not…" Winkler began.

"Nonsense," the colonel declared. "Mr. Darcy can afford a room for your comfort, Winkler."

Georgiana's gaze never wavered. "It's settled, Sir."

～ふ～ ～ふ～ ～ふ～

An hour later, Georgiana and Kitty climbed the main stairs together. "When had you planned to tell me of Mr. Winkler?" Georgiana teased.

"As I did not know myself until this evening, how could I tell anyone?" Kitty's eyebrow kicked up.

Georgiana giggled. "What do you think of the possibilities?"

Kitty clicked her tongue against the roof of her mouth. "Delicious. At least, in some ways. Mr. Winkler is a fine-looking man. But then again, so are Mr. Manneville, Lieutenant Southland, and your cousin."

Georgiana jerked to a stop, her mind rebelling at her friend's words. "Kitty, you're welcome to choose among our guests. Look to Mr. Winkler, to Mr. Manneville, or to the lieutenant. Look to any of them except the colonel."

Kitty wrapped her hand around Georgiana's elbow and smiled sweetly. "Exactly as I supposed. So, that's how the land lies?"

"That's exactly how it is."

CHAPTER 5

❦ ❦ ❦

DARCY'S EYES OPENED to the first streaks of light working their way between the window shutters' slats. He inhaled his wife's sleep-seduced body as she burrowed deeper into him, seeking his heat as her own. Even during the warm summer months, Elizabeth woke in need of the day's heat; and from that first morning when they had awakened in each other's arms, Darcy had willingly provided it. Enjoying her softness along his body's length, he tightened his embrace. Elizabeth had invaded his dreams, haunted them, in fact, from the night of the Meryton assembly, the night he had first laid eyes on her.

He would wake in yearning, thinking of how it would be to fill his lungs with her scent and to know her taste on his tongue. Elizabeth's ardent spirit had ruined his life—the arrogant and presumptuous life he had led before meeting her: the dreadful time when he had simply existed, half-alive and half-dead. Sometimes, he had wished that he could explain how much she had changed everything he had known before her, how much joy Elizabeth brought him each day. He had even considered begging her to forego their having a child. If it meant losing Elizabeth, Darcy would rather not have an heir. Pemberley could pass to Georgiana's children.

A light knocking brought his senses fully alert. Easing Elizabeth away, Darcy unwrapped the blanket and sat on the bed's edge. Standing gingerly and testing his legs, he had taken several steps in the door's direction before he recalled the double occupancy. He reached for his shirt and pulled it over his head and then cinched a robe over that.

Watching his step in the crowded room, Darcy made his way to the door. Opening it, he found Mrs. Washington and Nan holding ewers of hot water. "Morning, Sir," the inn's proprietress whispered. "Brought ye fresh water."

"Thank you, Ma'am," he said huskily. "Put it on the table." He gestured to a small side table along the wall.

"Breakfast be ready in half an hour, Sir," she informed him.

"Mr. Joseph and I will be down soon, the ladies a bit later." Darcy remained by the door. "How does the weather look?"

"Stopped raining. Now if we kin get some sunshine to help with the meltin', things might return to normal." Mrs. Washington brushed a hair wisp under her cap.

Darcy had wanted to depart for Derbyshire. "What are the travel possibilities?"

"Mr. Washington say it'll not happen 'til the morrow, but ye kin sees for yerself when ye come down, Sir." She turned to leave. "It be a good thing, Mr. Darcy. What ye and Mrs. Darcy did." With a quick glance about the room, the woman disappeared into the dark hallway. With a disbelieving look of her own, Nan closely followed.

Darcy hefted one of the ewers and carried it to his side of the room. Pouring some water in a bowl, he undressed to the waist and washed as best he could. Then he lathered his face and finally lit a candle so he might see his reflection in a small mirror. Removing the razor from its case, he ran the edge along the whetstone to sharpen it.

"So handsome," a husky whisper brought his attention to the bed's female figure.

Smiling broadly, Darcy teasingly leaned over her, pretending to want to kiss Elizabeth while spreading the lather from his face to hers. "Morning, Love," he whispered seductively.

"No!" she gasped on an inhalation and shoved hard against his bare chest. "You cannot, Fitzwilliam." She pulled the blanket over her head, further muffling her words of protest.

Darcy gently wrestled the linens from her hands. Leaning over her and pressing his weight across Elizabeth's body, he lovingly caught her hands and brought them to rest above his heart. "I could." He draped himself closer. "But I would not." He paused to give her time to stop squirming. "If you promise me your loyalty." He shielded his words from the Josephs.

Elizabeth quieted before staring deeply into his eyes. "I'm far from devoid of proper feelings where you're concerned, Mr. Darcy. I love you to distraction."

Darcy stroked her cheek. "My heart beats out a love staccato— one bearing your name, Lizzy."

A hushed conversation from the partition's other side told him that the Josephs also stirred. He released Elizabeth and sat on the bed's edge. Taking a steadying breath, Darcy spoke loud enough for all to hear. "Mr. Joseph, if you'll see to the fire, I'll light the candles. Mrs. Washington has brought hot water. I suggest we dress and go down to breakfast. Then the ladies can see to their needs and follow us."

From the screen's other side, he heard the stirrings come to life. "Thank you, Mr. Darcy. I'll inform you when I've completed my ablutions."

"Perhaps we can assess the road conditions ourselves." Darcy reached again for the razor and adjusted the small mirror. Making the first swath, he added, "Mr. Washington doesn't hold out much hope, but I'd prefer to draw my own conclusions."

～☙～ ～☙～ ～☙～

"Good morning, Edward," Georgiana said from her place at the table's head. She'd purposely arisen early because she knew her cousin would be one of the first to breakfast. Her eyes followed his movement. For nearly three years, Georgiana had pined after the man. Edward Fitzwilliam had offered her comfort when she'd foolishly considered an elopement with George Wickham. Along with her brother, the colonel served as her guardian. He had, over the years, read her bedtime stories and tended to childhood injuries.

However, the incident with Mr. Wickham had changed everything. She'd learned, despite her naiveté, some very hard lessons, and Edward had guided her every step. Because of him, she'd allowed her shame to fall away. As proof, Georgiana would offer her ability to converse with Kitty about Lydia Wickham's marriage without fighting the fear of someone else knowing of her earlier insensibility.

"Good morning, my dear." Edward bent to kiss her cheek. "You're up early."

"I keep country hours," she countered.

The colonel began to fill a plate from the covered dishes. "I wanted to inspect the roads to see whether it would be safe to send a messenger to the Earl regarding my return."

Georgiana's gaze followed his shoulder's line to his narrow waist, which the cut of his uniform emphasized. His familiar form looked leaner, but there was nothing wrong with the colonel's appearance. At age one and thirty, he'd now served in the British military for a decade. During those years of service, she'd stood silently cheering his successes as he neared his career's pinnacle. But while the colonel saw to his duty in the American war, Georgiana had taken a vow that if he returned home safely, she'd no longer remain silent.

Edward came to the table with a plate heaped high with eggs, bacon, and kippers. He speared one and inspected it. "Thank God for British food, at last." He took a hefty bite.

"You've lost weight, Edward."

"I plan to allow your brother's generosity to add a few pounds to my frame."

Georgiana breathed easier. She'd worried whether he might rush off to William's Wood. "Then you'll remain with us for a few days? I'd enjoy that very much."

He smiled lovingly at her and reached for her hand. "You

didn't think I'd leave you alone with Lady Catherine in residence? With Darcy away, our aunt will take advantage. Even after Darcy's return, I'll tarry a few days. Your brother isn't likely to be of a mind to accept an invasion of his marital bliss."

She interlaced her fingers with his. "Although I truly welcome your presence in dealing with Her Ladyship's demands, I pray that Pemberley offers other inducements." Georgiana slid her hand up his sleeve. "You were missed, Edward—more than words may express. You were always in my prayers."

Georgiana noted the exact second her cousin's demeanor changed. He said nothing out of the ordinary, but she heard the hitch in Edward's breathing. It matched hers. A frown graced his forehead. As if he were unsure what had just happened, the colonel said, "I thought of you always. Ask the lieutenant. He'll tell you that I've sung your praises on two continents."

She slowly removed her hand and returned it to her lap. "What more could a lady request of a man she admires?" she asked with a bit of amusement when his eyes followed her hand. "To be spoken of…to have her name on his lips."

~ ~ ~

"There you are, Elizabeth." Darcy stood to greet her. He took her hand and brought it to his lips.

"Mrs. Joseph and I took a few moments to reorganize the room. I apologize if we kept you waiting." She smiled glowingly at him.

Darcy wouldn't criticize. Despite a few dark shadows under her eyes, his wife appeared happy. He wondered what it was about Mrs. Joseph that gave Elizabeth a sense of calm. Whatever it was, Darcy would foster the relationship. "We've ordered breakfast." He seated her beside him.

"I'm ready to break my fast," Mrs. Joseph boldly declared. "I kindly tell Mr. Joseph that eating for two is a tiring occupation." The woman accepted her husband's assistance.

Mr. Joseph braced his wife's weight. "This journey's been difficult for you, my dear. We should've thought better of it."

"Mother Joseph is ill," she explained. "We could do nothing else. Our consciences demanded it. I don't regret any discomfort we've experienced." She smiled sweetly at her husband. "We must think of it as an adventure." Mrs. Joseph laughed lightly. "Besides, we've made the acquaintance of the Darcys, and I, for one, cannot imagine how our journey would have been without them. We'd be picking straw from our hair and worse without their charity."

Resigning himself to her logic, Joseph sighed deeply. "I was quite warm last evening—a much better situation than I expected when Mr. Washington announced a lack of rooms."

"Then let's learn of our new friends, Matthew. I want to genuinely call Mr. and Mrs. Darcy by that designation."

❧ ❧ ❧

"Miss De Bourgh." Southland bowed from the library's entrance. "I beg your pardon. Mr. Nathan said I might find the colonel here."

Anne De Bourgh looked up tentatively. "I believe my cousin planned to check the road conditions. He'll return shortly."

The man eyed her with an interest Anne rarely experienced. He actually appeared to seek a conversation with her. "Would I be disturbing you, Miss, if I waited with you for the colonel's return?"

Anne shot a quick glance at her long-time companion, Mrs. Jenkinson, and with a nod, the lady silently agreed. Swallowing her initial shyness, Anne managed, "Certainly, Lieutenant. Would you care for tea?" She gestured to the pot on a nearby serving table. As he slowly approached the chair where she remained seated, Anne fought for composure. She couldn't remember the last time a gentleman had sought her company.

"That would be quite pleasant, Miss De Bourgh." He took the seat across from her. "Dark English tea was one of the things I missed the most while serving in America. People do not brew a proper cup of tea anywhere but on our shores."

Anne nodded to the cream and sugar, but Southland declined with a shake of his head. "Have you traveled extensively, Lieutenant?" she asked. To the best of her memory, this was the first time in over a decade that she had entertained a gentleman without her mother's structuring the conversation, and Anne wondered how she was doing. Silly as it seemed, she hoped Lieutenant Southland didn't find her a complete ninny.

"More than I care to think, Miss. Mostly, I've spent time in the East…at least, until I took on the role as the colonel's aide. America, even with its less civilized circumstances, was a more obliging situation than were Persia and India. The States have a common thread—a very British thread—flowing through the countryside. The Americans may oppose our rule, but they practice our language, our religions, and our system of government."

As indecision crossed her countenance, Anne questioned, "And do not our British colonies offer similar values?"

Southland's gaze appraised her cautiously. "No, Miss De Bourgh. Even though we've colonized other lands, only North America has assumed our culture and made it its own."

Intrigued by his opinions, Anne's eyes narrowed as she seriously considered his words. "Would you consider returning to the Americas, Lieutenant? I mean, after the war. Is there something unique that would impel your return?" Foolishly, she prayed he wouldn't mention another woman.

"Oh, no, Miss De Bourgh," he said emphatically. "I'm more than happy to have my feet planted firmly on British soil." He slanted a quick glance her way. "If I received orders to ship out to America, I'd go, of course, but I'd prefer to finish my duties in England."

"Finish?" Anne returned her cup to its saucer. "Do you plan to leave the service, Sir?"

The lieutenant's grin widened. "As we have Napoleon on Elba, I don't anticipate a need for my role much longer. I'll leave with what salary is due me. At this time, I've not considered a settlement." He said slowly, "My father would prefer that I marry and set up my nursery."

Anne blushed thoroughly. Although her own thoughts had drifted to marriage, she still thought herself doomed to spend her life alone. She needed no reminder of the barrenness of her existence. "A marriage often solves a young man's future," she said softly.

"At five and twenty, it would appear that I should consider my father's advice."

"Where do you call *home*, Lieutenant?" Mrs. Jenkinson finally asked from her position across the room. As Anne's companion, she would normally curtail her intercourse with those her employer entertained, but Anne had sent the woman a pleading glance, and luckily, Mrs. Jenkinson had turned the conversation from the marriage topic.

"Outside of Lewes, on the way to Hailsham, Ma'am." His voice held a familiar inflection. "You must forgive me, Miss De Bourgh. I confess that I hold an acquaintance with Rosings Park. My father's first cousin was Mr. Knight, Mr. Collins's predecessor. Knight often wrote to my father of the comings and goings of Hunsford, and I've seen Rosings Park on several occasions…at least, I'm familiar with the estate's gatehouse."

"Is my cousin, the colonel, aware of your connection to our family?" Anne asked suspiciously.

A mischievous smile expressed his admission even before the lieutenant pronounced the words. "Aye, Miss. The colonel quickly recognized my curiosity regarding the Right Honorable Lady Catherine De Bourgh and Rosings Park, and I confessed the connection, weak as it may be. The good colonel then humored me by regaling me with tales of Hunsford and Her Ladyship. Of you, also, Miss De Bourgh."

Anne frowned with disbelief. "The colonel spoke of me? Surely, you must be mistaken."

"I assure you, Miss De Bourgh, that Colonel Fitzwilliam included you in his retellings. Generally, he spoke of your childhood…of his and Mr. Darcy's tormenting their female cousin and the girl's father taking them to task for their unkindness. The colonel regretted his participation…in hindsight, that is."

Anne said incredulously, "Boys have no compassion."

"I cannot concur, Miss De Bourgh. Boys simply see the world from a narrower scope. They don't consider their actions' consequences," he said smoothly. "Yet, the colonel also spoke of his delicate cousin Anne whose smile could light up a room if she only cared to share it with others."

His words utterly stunned Anne. "You jest, Lieutenant. It's unkind to tease me, Sir. I cannot conceive of Edward verbalizing such thoughts."

"Yet he did, Miss De Bourgh. Your cousin holds you in the highest regard."

Lieutenant Roman Southland knew full well his words' effect on the spinster Miss De Bourgh. He had made it his business to become well versed with the De Bourgh family. As a child, he'd heard his cousin speak of Rosing Park's grandeur, of Sir Lewis's affability, and of the bounty and beneficence the bestowing of a valuable rectory had had on the Southland family.

When the colonel's aide-de-camp's position had become available, Southland had actively pursued it. From the beginning, he'd felt an affinity with the colonel, and even with the past year's dangers on the American continent, Roman hadn't regretted his alliance with the Fitzwilliam and De Bourgh families. Somehow, unconsciously, he felt that he belonged with them.

As Southland was a minor son, some would see his obsession as a means to better his position in life, but that was never the intent. Roman truly believed destiny had claimed him. Finding the De Bourghs at Pemberley provided an unusual opportunity, and he'd do all he could to bring fruition to his hopes.

✎ ✎ ✎

"The second of five sisters," Mrs. Joseph gasped. "How ever did your mother manage?"

"Mrs. Bennet has a tenacious spirit," Darcy growled.

Elizabeth laughed ruefully. "My mother," she explained, "did not consider Mr. Darcy a viable suitor."

"You jest?" Mr. Joseph asked incredulously.

Darcy mockingly smiled. "It seems that Mrs. Darcy's cousin Mr. Collins and his rectory on my aunt's estate tempted my mother in marriage. She sat her sights on the dear clergyman for my wife's mate."

"Be fair, Fitzwilliam," Elizabeth offered a half-hearted reprimand. "My mother thought only of my future. Besides, Mr. Collins shall inherit Longbourn, and Mrs. Bennet wished to preserve the family connection. And even I had no idea of your regard at the time."

Mrs. Joseph squeezed Elizabeth's hand in affection. "How did you ever find your way to Mr. Darcy?"

Darcy responded in Elizabeth's stead. "Thankfully, my wife's own tenacity won out. She refused her cousin's plight and gave me an opportunity to win her hand."

"A true love story," Mrs. Joseph declared. "Just like in the Minerva Press novels of which Mr. Joseph says I shouldn't pollute my mind." She laughed softly. "But I'm of the persuasion that when a man loves a woman he can conceive of no other in her place; and even though men still run the world, it means nothing without that particular woman by his side."

"That's my wife," Joseph chuckled. "The incurable romantic."

❦ ❦ ❦

Mr. Manneville bowed to the Bingleys and to Kitty Bennet. "Might I join you?"

"Certainly." Bingley gestured to a nearby chair. "We're enjoying some early morning tea. Mrs. Bingley must work up her appetite," he said with loving amusement. "Would you care for some?"

The man's nose rose in displeasure. "I would prefer coffee if it's available."

Jane Bingley motioned a footman forward. "Allow me to order

some, Mr. Manneville. I fear neither Mr. Bingley nor I have developed a taste for the beverage."

Manneville straightened his jacket as he sat. "What of you, ladies?" He addressed Caroline and Kitty. "Have either of you taken to the so-called bitter taste of coffee?"

Kitty answered immediately. "Although Mr. Darcy's staff always makes it available, I've not had the nerve to sample the brew. It does have a robust aroma though. Very tempting."

"That it does, Miss Catherine," Manneville agreed.

Caroline sniffed audibly. "The only way I could tolerate the drink would be to weaken it with plenty of cream and sugar."

Manneville challenged, "That's my sentiment when it comes to tea."

Manneville noticed how Bingley squirmed, indicating his discomfort with the conversation's tone. *The man would make an easy mark in a card game*, he thought.

"I hope you found your accommodations adequate, Manneville," Bingley said.

"My unknown host does himself proud, Mr. Bingley. Of course, a ship's onboard accommodation is always lacking unless one captains the vessel; yet, my American home has the best, and I'm accustomed to such luxury."

"Mr. Darcy's home is one of England's finest," Bingley asserted.

However, before the man could finish, Caroline interrupted. "I wouldn't have thought, Sir, that one might find anything as grand as Pemberley in the Americas."

"Then you would assume incorrectly, Miss Bingley. I don't pretend that my own house can rival Mr. Darcy's, but my simple plantation house does boast twenty chambers and a more than adequate ballroom."

"Twenty bedchambers?" Kitty gasped.

"Yes, Miss Catherine," he said proudly. "And of course, I've a home in Charleston, overlooking the bay."

Manneville expected Bingley's caution. "You'll find that in

British society, Manneville, people do not discuss their wealth or lack thereof."

Self-mockingly, Manneville chuckled. "I'm well aware of British norms, Mr. Bingley. My father made certain of my education in such matters. However, I don't plan to tarry in England. I'm in the country to see to family matters and to test the marriage market. And, as far as announcing my wealth in British society, Sir, I'm at a disadvantage. When you or Mr. Darcy or the colonel walks into a room, everyone already knows you and your family history."

"You mean to seek a wife, Mr. Manneville? A British wife in America?" Jane asked with more than a little curiosity.

"It is my wish, Mrs. Bingley. A British wife would rule South Carolina's society, and I'm an ambitious man. Such a wife could bring me glory," Manneville said bluntly.

Bingley sputtered, "You're...you're very direct, Sir."

Manneville's smile widened. "I suppose that I am. It's my American upbringing. I simply never saw any reason to hide the obvious. It would give me no advantage."

"Is having the advantage important, Mr. Manneville?" Caroline asked suspiciously.

"It's an *absolute* in both business and life, Miss Bingley."

～⌒ ～⌒ ～⌒

"Will you, ladies, be well while Mr. Joseph and I examine the road conditions? We thought we might take a walk in the main road's direction," Darcy said as he stood and put on his gloves.

"We'll finish our tea and then return to the room, Fitzwilliam. Nothing ill shall occur during broad daylight." Elizabeth stated the obvious.

Darcy squeezed her hand. "We shan't be long—less than an hour."

Darcy and Mr. Joseph walked along the rural road, scrutinizing the area carefully. Although some thawing had occurred, the icy conditions remained. "This could refreeze overnight and make travel slower." Joseph indicated the water accumulating in the ditches lining the road.

Darcy made his own observations. "But the road is graded well. See how it curves down to allow the runoff. There's little water on the road's surface. Another day should permit our escape. I imagine the main road has already opened to limited service."

"It will be a slow go, nevertheless," Joseph added. "Between the resumed traffic and the storm's remnants."

Darcy turned toward the inn. "I suppose we should start back. I wish to speak to Mr. Simpson regarding his assessment of the dangers before discussing our plans with Mrs. Darcy."

"You seek your wife's opinion, Mr. Darcy?" Joseph's eyebrow rose in disbelief.

"As my wife is very astute, I'd be a fool to ignore her fine mind." Darcy suspected that his marital bliss came not from his seductive prowess but because he treated Elizabeth as his partner rather than as chattel. He was of the mind to believe that she'd never have consented to marry him if he hadn't admitted that she had taught him about selfishness. He remembered well his confession to Elizabeth:

"I have been a selfish being all my life, in practice, though not in principle. As a child I was taught what was right, but I was not taught to correct my temper. I was given good principles, but left to follow them in pride and conceit. Unfortunately an only son, I was spoiled by my parents, who allowed, encouraged, almost taught me to be selfish and overbearing; to care for none beyond my own family circle; to think meanly of their sense and worth compared with my own. Such I was, from eight to eight and twenty; and such I might still have been but for you, dearest, loveliest Elizabeth! What do I not owe you? You taught me a lesson, hard indeed at first, but more advantageous. By you I was properly humbled. I came to you without a doubt of my reception. You showed me how insufficient were all my pretensions to please a woman worthy of being pleased."

"Then it's as Mrs. Joseph asserts? Yours is a love match?" Joseph added smugly.

Darcy walked on in silence for a few minutes. "I would've assumed, Sir, that you, too, cared deeply for your wife. Was I mistaken?"

"You've not erred. My wife holds my highest regard."

"Yet, you refuse to admit to loving your wife," Darcy observed.

Joseph countered, "I do not hear your professions, Sir."

Darcy chuckled. "I see how it is. If I'm man enough to admit to loving Mrs. Darcy, you could follow suit. If that's what it takes, Joseph, I confirm that I'm hopelessly in love with my wife. You now have my permission to admit your own weakness."

The man reddened. "I assure you, Mr. Darcy, that I do not require nor seek your permission for anything."

Darcy's smile widened. "And that's how it should be, Joseph. My affection for my wife—my decisions regarding my estate—my sister's guardianship—are all mine. They're none of your concern unless I choose to share them, as your life belongs to you until you care to speak of it. Do not mimic another man's actions, Joseph. Do what's best for you. That's a lesson which I learned from Mrs. Darcy."

Only the crunch of their boots on the frosty lane broke the silence for several minutes. "I didn't mean to offend, Mr. Darcy."

"You didn't offend, Joseph. I spoke because I observed in you my own tentative nature. We men are not free to express our thoughts. Women strike up instant relationships. Look at our wives as proof. It is how Society deems our roles so we must develop confidence in our choices, and, more importantly, we must guard against accepting outside examples as the norm. The true north is what works for us—what makes us personally satisfied with our lives."

∼◎∼ ∼◎∼ ∼◎∼

"What do you think of Mr. Manneville and the lieutenant?" Mrs. Bennet asked Kitty as they laced the threads of a matted waistcoat they repaired for Mr. Bennet.

Kitty had taken refuge in her mother's room. She had accepted responsibility for monitoring Mrs. Bennet's activities. Kitty, who loved creating fashionable designs, concentrated on the looped stitches forming a monogram. "They're fine-looking gentlemen," she mumbled.

"I'd imagine that one or both would be considering marriage," Mrs. Bennet hinted as she fluttered about the room.

Still involved in the stitching, Kitty absentmindedly responded, "Mr. Manneville said as much earlier today."

"Did he now?" Mrs. Bennet asked with delight. "That's a fine situation."

Kitty's head snapped up in full attention. "Mama, don't even think it! Mr. Manneville will return to America."

"But the man is very rich, is he not?" Mrs. Bennet's tone conveyed the direction of her thoughts.

"If he's to be believed," Kitty confirmed.

Picking up her embroidery hoop, Mrs. Bennet returned to her stitching. "I suppose one might corroborate the man's worth through the colonel or Lieutenant Southland."

Kitty recognized her mother's manipulations. "I've no desire to live in America," she asserted.

"Who says the man cannot be convinced to stay in England?"

Kitty's eyes widened in disbelief. "Mr. Manneville despises English tea!"

Mrs. Bennet chortled. "What does that have to do with anything? I'll speak to him myself to determine his true intentions."

～๛～ ～๛～ ～๛～

"Southland, I've been looking for you." Colonel Fitzwilliam cornered his aide in the library.

The lieutenant scrambled to his feet. "I apologize, Sir. I was unaware of your return to the house."

"Some thirty minutes ago," the colonel offered a mild reprimand. The lieutenant remained at attention. "Again, I apologize,

Colonel. While I was reading, I evidently lost track of time, Sir."

"Relax, Lieutenant." Edward reeled in his temper.

Southland lowered his shoulders. "How may I serve you, Sir?"

"You can tell me what you're about. What's this I hear of your having an intimate conversation with my cousin?"

The lieutenant's glance was so brief that Edward couldn't read the man's true motive. "I assume, Sir, that you refer to my speaking to Miss De Bourgh."

"You had better not have spoken intimately to Miss Darcy," Edward growled.

"As Miss Darcy is so much younger than Miss De Bourgh?" Southland asked uncertainly.

Edward jerked his head up in surprise. "As Miss Darcy is an innocent." Warning rang in Edward's tone.

"And Miss De Bourgh is not?"

That was the wrong thing to say. "I'll not tolerant insolence, Lieutenant!" Edward swallowed his initial anger. "Damn it, Roman! You know that wasn't what I meant. Miss De Bourgh is equally as innocent, but she has a companion with her at all times. At Pemberley, Miss Darcy's companion allows her charge some freedom. I'd not approve of your approaching either cousin."

"Did I say something to offend Miss De Bourgh? If so, I'll apologize immediately, Sir."

"Miss De Bourgh didn't appear offended by your conversation," Edward conceded.

The man appeared puzzled. "Then what brings your ire, Sir?"

"I'll not have my cousin made an object of scorn, Southland."

"Scorn, Sir? Why would you believe I meant to *scorn* Miss De Bourgh?"

Edward's gaze locked on his aide's countenance. "Miss De Bourgh isn't the type men seek out for simple conversation."

"I don't understand why not, Sir. Miss De Bourgh is quite handsome and very literate. She may be a bit shy, but in small gatherings, I imagine the lady shows very well."

Edward narrowed his eyes. "Are we both speaking of the same Anne De Bourgh?"

The lieutenant frowned. "I speak of Lady Catherine's daughter." He paused briefly. "You do recall my brief connection to Rosings Park, do you not, Sir?"

Edward stammered, "Of…of course, Southland." The colonel's brow rose in curiosity. "Then you truly enjoyed your time with my cousin?"

"Absolutely, Colonel, and I'd be honored to join Miss De Bourgh again." The man's honesty rang true, but Edward still questioned whether any man could give Anne his attentions without first considering her dowry. She had cowered under Lady Catherine's reign so long that he was certain that Anne had lost the vibrancy she once possessed. It would probably become his father's province to find Anne a suitable marriage of convenience, one of which his aunt would approve—possibly to a widower who needed a mother for his children. "And I'll avoid Miss Darcy unless her companion is present." Southland's words brought Edward from his thoughts.

The colonel's voice was hesitant. "Allow me to caution you, Lieutenant. I didn't bring you to Pemberley to feather your social connections. You're Mr. Darcy's guest, and you're my assistant. I expect you to perform under those guidelines. I appreciate your earlier kindness to Miss De Bourgh; yet, I cannot condone your laying a liaison's foundation with any of the females under Mr. Darcy's protection. If that's your purpose, you'll know the Earl of Matlock's full power, as well as your commanding officer's, in response."

"I understand, Sir."

~Q~ ~Q~ ~Q~

"Our husbands should be on their way back," Mrs. Joseph remarked. "And the other gentlemen are coming down to breakfast."

Elizabeth said pointedly. "I am grateful for your presence in that regard. If you and Mr. Joseph hadn't joined us, I would have cautiously taken my breakfast in my room. None of the men have been rude, but it's quite intimidating when one is the only woman among so many men. Like an invasion of holy ground."

Mr. Horvak and Sir Jonathan stopped at the table to pay their respects. When Elizabeth and Mrs. Joseph started to rise, Sir Jonathan said, "Please. That's not necessary. We're kindred souls—those waiting for the Christmas spirit to clear a way home."

"Do you suppose we should even attempt a journey today, Sir Jonathan?" Elizabeth asked.

"My coachman came by earlier, and he seemed to think we'd need another day."

Elizabeth frowned. Despite enjoying Mrs. Joseph's company, she wanted to be elsewhere. "Mr. Darcy and Mr. Joseph are completing their own analysis."

"I suspect your husbands will come to the same conclusions," Mr. Horvak said.

As Nan entered with the gentlemen's meals, Elizabeth said, "We'll leave you to your breakfast." Noticing Mary's sudden grimace, she added, "Mrs. Joseph requires a bit more rest."

"Of course, Mrs. Darcy. We'll speak later." The two men bowed out.

Elizabeth supported Mrs. Joseph to her feet. "Is something amiss?"

The woman frowned. "I suddenly feel very light-headed. Probably nothing—especially for a woman eight months with child. Other women would be considering their confinements."

"I suspect that you didn't sleep well last evening," Elizabeth added as they slowly climbed the stairs.

"Better than I would've in the stable," Mary said ironically. "When one is as large with child as I, sleep doesn't come easily."

"Then you'll take the bed and find some required rest. You were very brave to attempt this journey under the circumstances," Elizabeth assured as she held the room's door for her new friend.

However, a second grimace twisted Mary's countenance, and the woman caught the door frame with white knuckles. "I suspect I shouldn't have had so much ham. It is so salty, and it makes my stomach cramp if I don't drink enough water with it."

"Then let's get you to bed and order some fresh drinking water."

"Thank you, Mrs. Darcy. You're proving to be an excellent friend."

Elizabeth insisted that Mary stretch out across the bed. Once she had the lady settled, Elizabeth draped a blanket over her. "I expect you to nap for at least an hour. I shall tolerate nothing less," she politely ordered.

"And what shall you do while I sleep, Mrs. Darcy?" the woman asked with half-closed eyes.

Elizabeth smiled contentedly. "I have some letters to entertain me."

CHAPTER 6

EDWARD SAT ALONE IN THE LIBRARY. He would need to join his young cousin in Georgiana's efforts to entertain a diverse household. "Who would've thought Georgiana capable of handling any of this?" he asked aloud. "Not I. I saw only a child, but Georgiana is no little girl—not even a silly, giggling teen." The realization brought a smile. He had always considered his cousin ethereally beautiful—her golden blonde, nearly white hair framed a heart-shaped face. She fought to keep the curls in place, but Edward had always preferred it when the wisps broke free and draped over his cousin's forehead and cheeks. Gone were the bows and ribbons of a young girl. In their place, Georgiana sported the sleek fashion of a well-dressed lady. With the smile remaining, Edward expelled a deep sigh. "No time to ruminate over more pleasurable ideas. Her Ladyship awaits." He shoved to his feet. "To everything there is a season."

"Miss Catherine," Mr. Winkler bowed as he entered the morning room. "May I join you?"

Kitty had purposely waited at the breakfast table in hopes of speaking to the man. "Of course, Mr. Winkler. I pray you slept well, Sir."

"An excellent bed," he said good-naturedly. "I sorely hated to leave it." He filled his plate and then took the empty place beside her.

"Then you should have remained, Mr. Winkler. We have so few hidden pleasures in which to indulge ourselves." Kitty adjusted her seat, shortening the distance between them.

The clergyman chuckled lightly. "What sort of man lies about all day?"

"Perhaps a man who works hard to see to his parishioners' needs," she countered.

He smiled kindly. "Perhaps a man who takes his duties seriously and who appreciates the living bestowed upon him by Mr. Darcy."

"You believe this your true calling, Mr. Winkler?" Kitty asked as she poured tea for him.

"It's been my life's dream." Winkler's voice grew more passionate as he spoke of his desire to serve. He spoke of when he first knew that he would serve the Lord and how he had discovered pure pleasure in earning Mr. Darcy's approval. "I have such great plans, Miss Catherine. I'd like to see a village school and some sort of organization to meet to the needs of the elderly, especially those with no family to oversee their care."

Kitty sat entranced. She couldn't remember exactly when she'd become physically aware of this man. She suspected it was at Lambton's May Day celebration. As she had watched, Mr. Winkler had joined several other local musicians at an improvisational concert. He'd lent his talent and his beautiful voice to the entertainment, and she couldn't help but see how the music had overtaken his soul. It was what she thought Heaven must resemble. At that moment, she wanted to know him better.

"It sounds as if you've ordered your life, Mr. Winkler."

The man leaned closer. "Everything except my personal needs, Miss Catherine." His voice took on a husky rasp.

Kitty glanced up to find Mr. Winkler's eyes gleaming with emotion. "What else could a man desire?"

"A woman who shares my passion for my work and my life," he said hoarsely.

Kitty swallowed hard. "You mean to take a wife, Mr. Winkler?"

"If the right woman would agree," he said with another smile.

Yet, before Kitty could respond, the Bingleys and Caroline entered the room. Groaning silently in frustration, Kitty returned to her meal, while Mr. Winkler scrambled to his feet.

"Good morning, Mr. Winkler," Jane said as she curtsied. "I hope you slept well. Kitty, how was our mother?" she added quickly.

Thinking of her mother's marriage manipulations, Kitty said, "Planning for a productive day. She's the consummate mother." Kitty shifted away from him as Winkler resumed his seat.

Bingley motioned to a footman. "Would you ask Mrs. Oliver if Mrs. Bingley might have coddled eggs for breakfast?"

"Right away, Sir."

"Charles, that's not necessary," Jane protested.

Bingley escorted his wife to a seat across from Kitty. "It is necessary, my dear. I'll call on the kitchen later to express my gratitude, but I'll cater to your preferences when possible."

Caroline took the empty setting several seats away. Kitty interpreted it as a deliberate act of disapproval. In spite, Kitty said, "Perhaps Miss Bingley would prefer coddled eggs also, Mr. Bingley."

A frown crushed Caroline's countenance. "Heaven forbid. Slimy, half-cooked egg whites." She snarled in disgust.

Jane took a sisterly note of Kitty's remark before saying, "Have Mama and Papa had their breakfasts?"

"Papa was down very early. I'm sure he's holed up in Mr. Darcy's library. He spotted several titles by Sir Walter Scott he hadn't read. Mama was still in her chambers. She joined me to do some embroidery work on Papa's new waistcoat and then returned to her bed." Kitty accepted the tea a footman poured for her. "Mr. Grange shall escort Mary down in a few minutes."

"How long has Miss Bennet been engaged?" Mr. Winkler asked. "I don't recall your saying so, Miss Catherine, when you were at Pemberley during the summer."

Kitty smiled. The man had recalled details of her life, and that pleased her. "Since the first of October. They prepare for a spring wedding."

"Then the banns haven't been called?" Mr. Winkler sliced his ham.

Bingley finally seated himself beside his wife. "They've placed a notice in the paper, but the banns will wait until the first of February. Mr. Grange will assume additional duties in Mr. Philips's office in March. Philips is Mrs. Bennet's brother in marriage," he explained.

Winkler shot a glance at Kitty, and she blushed. "Miss Catherine will be the last Bennet sister to marry," the clergyman summarized.

Bingley laughed lightly. "My wife's mother will concentrate her energies on Kitty soon." He winked at Kitty. "Of course, we assume Kitty hasn't decided on a proper husband previously. For all we know, she plans to marry immediately. It only takes fifteen days to have the banns called three times. Do you have someone in mind, Kitty? Will you beat Mary to the altar?"

Kitty choked on her tea, and Mr. Winkler gently rubbed her back to curtail her coughing. His kindness made her instantly aware of his touch. Between clearing her throat and taking several steadying breaths, Kitty struggled to recover.

"I apologize, Kitty," Bingley said earnestly. "I shouldn't tease."

She swallowed hard. Mr. Winkler's hand remained. Kitty could feel his warmth radiating through her chest and sinking into her lower abdomen. "I swallowed tea rather than taking a breath," she rasped. Realizing his hand still rested on her back, Mr. Winkler jerked it away, and Kitty found herself bereft of his touch. "I've… I've no plans." She stopped to clear her throat. "No plans for a marriage."

"Are you open to new possibilities?" Mr. Bingley's teasing tone returned. "Do you seek a marriage, Sister Dear?"

"Charles! That's enough," Jane reprimanded. "I suspect that as a child you were quite unrelenting with your taunts to Caroline and Louisa."

Bingley casually chuckled. "With two sisters, I had no choice."

Caroline joined the conversation from her self-imposed isolation. "Louisa and I have always had your best interests at heart, Charles."

Kitty thought of the pain Miss Bingley had caused Jane and Mr. Bingley when the lady's manipulations had separated them—exposing Bingley to the censure of the world for caprice and instability and Jane to its derision for disappointed hopes, as well as involving them both in misery of the acutest kind.

Bingley kindly said, "You've devoted your time and your interest to my well-being, Caroline, and I'm forever in your debt; however, I'd cherish the opportunity to see you in your own home. You deserve the best, my dear."

∾ ∾ ∾

Edward tapped softly on Lady Catherine's door and a maid admitted him immediately. Her Ladyship lounged on a chaise. She held toast in one hand and a teacup in the other. He bowed and then motioned the maid's departure. "Thank you for agreeing to see me, Your Ladyship."

"Why would I not, Edward? You're a most beloved nephew. You've brought honor to the Fitzwilliam name." She gestured him to a chair.

Edward took the seat, but he remained alert. Years of dealing with his aunt had taught him to never underestimate the woman. Dressed in a dark purple velvet gown, his aunt was a paragon of determination, and many shrank from her renowned inflexibility. She was dark of eye and hair, much darker than her brother, Edward's father, and the complete opposite of the fair-haired Lady Anne, Darcy's mother. She could convey her arrogance with a lift of her square chin or a glare along her straight, high-bridged nose. "My choice of military service came as the lesser of two evils, but I'm content with my time. I believe God has placed me in this role to save men from death's grip. I'm thankful for that position."

"As you well should be." Lady Catherine pushed her way to a seated position. "Of what did you wish to speak, Colonel?"

Edward frowned deeply. "I'd like to know your true reason for coming to Pemberley uninvited."

"You came to Pemberley uninvited," she accused.

His eyes forcefully demanded that his aunt not fence verbally. "True. However, I've never expressed indignation regarding Darcy's marriage. Neither did I send him language so very abusive, especially of Mrs. Darcy, when he announced his engagement. You've not spoken to Darcy or his wife for over two years, and then suddenly you appear on my cousin's doorstep. I ask myself *why*, but I cannot decipher your way, Aunt."

"Possibly, I had no other recourse," she said slyly.

Edward forced himself to hold her gaze. Years had taught him that Lady Catherine used her dominating stare to quell her dissenters. "I might believe you sought Pemberley's safety if you hadn't sent word to Mr. Collins before you left Matlock."

"Georgiana told you that, did she?" Lady Catherine accused.

Edward struggled for an obliging response. "I'm Georgiana's guardian. It would be natural for her to seek my advice. And I would warn Your Ladyship not to think that I'll fall for your diversionary tactics. Georgiana isn't the issue. Now, let's revisit your motive for returning to Pemberley."

Lady Catherine's mouth tightened in a furious line. "In reality, I have no response." She waited for his retort, but Edward's silence demanded a longer explanation. "Matlock left for Lincolnshire. I'd already promised Collins a means to Kent." She ticked off her reasons on her fingers. "The road conditions deteriorated before I could make other arrangements. I saw my niece in your family home some days prior, and I realized I missed my sister's offspring."

Edward's eyebrow rose in disbelief. "Do you mean to say, Aunt, that you wished for a reconciliation with Darcy?"

"Marriage is forever. I cannot change what's been done. Although I vehemently disagree with Darcy's choice, I've come to realize that my objections are also keeping me from Georgiana. In order for my niece to have a successful Season, Georgiana needs the weight of her connections. Darcy's position gives Georgiana impetus, but Matlock and Lindale's names lend credence to her consequence." His aunt's words didn't sit well with Edward, but he couldn't identify what it was about the image of his cousin's Society Come Out that bothered him most. It was certainly not Georgiana's appearance; his cousin's beauty would awe even the most hardened heart. Possibly, that was it: He couldn't picture Georgiana in another man's embrace. "The De Bourgh connection shall strengthen my niece's suit."

"So, for Georgiana's sake, you'll swallow your distress regarding Darcy's marriage?" he said incredulously.

"Darcy has thrice sent correspondence offering an appeasement. Admittedly, I've ignored his olive branch, but Christmastide seemed a time for forgiveness."

Edward certainly didn't believe her reasons, but he knew from experience that his aunt believed what she said. Therefore, Lady Catherine's frankness penetrated his reserve. "You are an intelligent woman, Your Ladyship, so I'll forego the customary warning. You're aware of Darcy's nature. My cousin will never tolerate your condemnation of his wife or his guests."

Surprised, he watched as Lady Catherine swallowed her temptation to criticize. "I am appalled by the people with whom Darcy surrounds himself, but I can tolerate his acquaintances without considering them my intimates."

"I pray you can, Aunt." Her sincerity rang of possibilities. "It's comforting to think that you've considered Georgiana's future, but you should also make room for Mrs. Darcy's role in your life. You must maintain no delusions of Elizabeth ever being replaced in Darcy's estimation. The man loves his wife, very much in the manner that the late Mr. Darcy loved Lady Anne. You must accept it, or Darcy will limit your access to Georgiana." He hoped she didn't practice some sort of chicanery.

Their conversation at an end, Edward prepared to leave her; however, Lady Catherine reached out to stay him. "Tell me what has transpired with Mrs. Darcy."

"I don't understand, Aunt."

Lady Catherine sighed deeply in exasperation. "As you said,

Colonel, I'm far from lacking my wits. I have overheard bits and pieces of information. Why has Mrs. Darcy not given her husband an heir?"

Edward's suspicions returned. "If you mean to insinuate that Mrs. Darcy hasn't presented my cousin with his first child because of her low connections, I'll warn you of the danger of doing so. Darcy will bring his ire to your doorstep, Ma'am."

"That wouldn't stop me, Edward," she declared. "I've faced a man's dudgeon before. Give me the facts, and I'll decide my actions."

Edward growled. "I will not be a part of your venomous ways, Your Ladyship. A moment ago, you spoke of harmony. You cannot have it both ways, Aunt."

"You make the assumption that I mean Mrs. Darcy harm. I never said I would openly criticize the chit. I simply said that Darcy's ire wouldn't deter me. Would you prefer that I ask Mrs. Darcy's witless mother?"

Edward felt his cheeks flush. "Mrs. Darcy hasn't carried to term previously," he said through gritted teeth. "But the lady's with child. Darcy hopes the pleasure of seeing her family for Christmastide will give Mrs. Darcy comfort. He's surrounded his wife with those who love her."

"Except for uninvited guests," she observed.

"That's more than half of those in attendance," Edward responded. "Darcy isn't likely to be happy with the alteration in his plans."

"I suppose that means me."

Dismay tightened Edward's jaw. "Your presence will truly be a Christmastide surprise, Your Ladyship."

❧ ❧ ❧

Caroline Bingley tarried at the morning table. Her brother and Winkler sought the billiard room, while Jane and Kitty planned to assist Mrs. Reynolds with the Christmastide decorations. Along with her fiancé, Mary Bennet, to whom Caroline had barely spoken, had come and gone. Mrs. Bennet had taken her breakfast in her room, as had Lady Catherine. Caroline would have liked to converse with the latter, but was thankful not to encounter the former.

Caroline hated being in this situation again. At four and twenty, she was close to being on the shelf, and she wondered if this would be her existence: the uninvited guest at a house party her brother attended. Her parents had always thought her the pretty one, the one who would easily win a husband. Instead, Louisa had won Mr. Hurst's attention within six months of making her Come Out. Soon, Caroline thought, she'd be expected to chaperone the younger people in attendance. Eventually, Charles's growing brood would be referring to her as *Aunt Caroline*. She didn't think that she could bear it. Tending to her own child had once been her girlish dream, but dealing with other people's children would prove tiresome. For a split second, she considered burying her face in her hands and having a good cry, but the sound of approaching footsteps shoved Caroline's shoulders back and her chin upward. She would let no one know her frustration.

"Miss Bingley, I didn't expect to find you here. I went out to have a look at the grounds. Even coated in an icy glaze, Mr. Darcy's home is quite impressive. I'd thought you had joined your family."

"I did, Mr. Manneville." Caroline gestured to a place setting across from hers. "But they had others with whom to converse, and I preferred my own company."

Manneville's step faltered. "I apologize, Miss Bingley. If I'm disturbing your solitude, I'll take my meal in my room."

"Of course not, Mr. Manneville." Caroline motioned him forward. "The festive days often make me maudlin. I didn't mean to offend."

"Is it not peculiar that such a joyous celebration can leave many to question the values they find in their lives? We miss those who've gone before, and we reevaluate the choices that we've made." He allowed a footman to choose his breakfast meats.

"You've captured my thoughts, Mr. Manneville. I was missing

my dear mother and bemoaning my choice of coming to Pemberley rather than joining my older sister Mrs. Hurst and her husband in Devon."

Manneville raised a brow. "Well, I, for one, am appreciative of your presence at Pemberley."

Caroline blushed. She couldn't remember the last time a man openly flirted with her. "When you took to the frozen grounds, did you not risk the chill's return?" she taunted.

"It was the coffee, Miss Bingley." Manneville looked her over with an assessing eye. "It warms a man *properly*."

"Can a person find a *proper* cup of tea in America, Mr. Manneville?" she asked, her lashes lowered.

He laughed lightly and leaned back casually in his chair. "I imagine it possible. Afternoon tea is still quite popular in Charleston's finest homes, and if that doesn't please you, I understand Boston Harbor still reeks of the brew."

The soft roll of his words enticed her. "Would you tell me something of your home, Mr. Manneville?"

"With pleasure." He smiled easily. "Now what would a beautiful woman wish to know?" He dragged out the words in a teasing manner.

"How large?" Caroline interrupted. "How large is the city?"

He tilted his head in a razzing manner, but Manneville spoke with pride. "Somewhere between twenty and five and twenty thousand. Charleston's the wealthiest and largest city south of Philadelphia. It's truly a bustling trade center, with rice and cotton and naval products. It is the center of law in the area. For example, at the Broad and Meeting Streets' intersection, one finds the Four Corners of Law, which is a large civil square surrounded by governmental and religious buildings. St. Michael's Episcopalian can rival many churches in England, and the elegance of the capital conveys its architectural superiority. Churches and banks and civic destiny abound," he said with a touch of conceit. "It's truly a great city."

"It's my hope, Miss Bingley, to place my hat into the political ring. I hold with the belief that the United States' government shouldn't be supporting itself with state governments' hands."

Caroline leaned forward with interest. "And your home, Mr. Manneville?"

"In Charleston, a stately house overlooking the Battery. We raise cotton rather than rice on my plantation. Mr. Whitney's cotton gin has revolutionized how quickly we can process the crop."

"Cotton?" Caroline puzzled. "I don't believe I have ever seen the crop. Nor do I know anyone who wears cotton clothing. Can it truly be profitable?"

His forehead wrinkled in exasperation, and the man ignored her question. Instead, he concentrated on describing the land he loved. "Imagine rows and rows of fist-sized clouds bursting from dark cocoons." He held Caroline's gaze, and the melodic rhythm of his speech mesmerized her. Manneville paused, and she nearly begged to hear more. "It's my hope that if I marry that my wife will agree to a small vacation home in Hickory Valley."

The tone of his voice called to something deep inside her. "Hickory Valley?" she asked with interest.

"About halfway between Charleston and Savannah. Much cooler in the summer months than the cities. It's so beautiful there. I've my eye on the perfect house—a large wrap-around porch where a person might enjoy the night breeze—moss-draped oak trees. The community has plans for a library and a school. Also, rolling hills with pine and hickory trees surround the town."

"It sounds heavenly, Mr. Manneville. A woman would be a fool to reject such a house." Caroline sighed deeply. She'd always wanted her own home; several, in fact. A summerhouse, like in the English countryside, not just a town house.

"Now, it's your turn, Miss Bingley. I want to know of your life."

Caroline flushed. "I have no idea what might interest you, Mr. Manneville."

He sat forward, bracing his weight on the table. "Well, I know of your brother and sister already. Perhaps you would care to speak of your parents. That is, if it's not too painful. From where do you hail? Is your brother's estate your family's heritage?"

Caroline stammered, "I…I fear…I fear, Mr. Manneville, that you misunderstand. My father lacked both a title and land. Our wealth is not old money, and because of it, some of a particular ilk would deny our presence in Society. My brother Charles owns an estate in Cheshire and a house in town, but he didn't inherit either. We're not of Lord Shelton's station."

The man's eyebrow rose sharply. "If you think that a deterrent, Miss Bingley, you'll find me of a sterner disposition than that. Now, I ask again to know of your family."

For a brief moment, she paused to assess his sincerity, and then she said, "My parents came from Manchester, and my father earned his wealth dealing in silks and spices and many of the riches of the East India Company. He had an uncle who brought him along in the trade…"

ᔫᕽᐤ ᔫᕽᐤ ᔫᕽᐤ

She kept an eye on Mrs. Joseph's restless slumber. Elizabeth didn't remember her sister Jane having such a fretful time, and Jane had carried twins. Yet, Mrs. Joseph was quite large, and Elizabeth supposed it affected the woman's sleep.

Having sent Darcy and Mr. Joseph away so Mary could rest, Elizabeth had spent some time reading a collection of poetry she'd bought at a small bookstore in Newcastle. Now, she returned to the stack of letters. The other evening she hadn't read the two that Darcy had composed upon the loss of their children, but today, she felt compelled to revisit them. She'd acknowledged her pregnancy to Darcy. Obviously, her husband knew of her condition, but he'd accepted Elizabeth's fears and made them his own. Somehow, Mrs. Joseph's appearance at Prestwick's had changed everything. As nonsensical as it sounded, Elizabeth no longer dreaded what might happen. If she lost this child, she would try again and again until she delivered a healthy Darcy heir. She possessed no other alternative:

Because of Darcy, she could smile; her life was worthwhile, and she owed him her constant devotion.

First checking Mrs. Joseph's blankets, Elizabeth settled in a chair near the window. Outside, she could hear the water's steady drip from the roof to the ground. The rhythmic pattern made her think of the Maelzel's metronome model, which sat on Georgiana's pianoforte. Hopefully, by tomorrow, she and Darcy would be on their way to Pemberley.

Untying the ribbon, Elizabeth removed the two letters on the bottom. She normally kept the notes in order by the date Darcy had written them, but she had shuffled these two special letters to the stack's bottom when she had read from the missives two nights prior.

She removed the one her husband had composed after the first disaster and unfolded the pages. Shifting her weight so she might see better, Elizabeth read…

2 February
My dearest, darling Elizabeth,

I sit in this semidarkness watching the rise and fall of your shoulders. I recognize your pain and am helpless to drive it away. You pretend not to know that I write this note, and I pretend that you sleep at last. I will not minimize your loss by repeating what you have already heard. What I will say is that although it may seem that you face this loss alone, please remember that I am here—standing beside you. Love—the truth of love—lies between us. I live only for the honor and the love you have given me.

Inside each of us grows a faith in a new day. So, put away the rage. From this we will learn how precious life can be—something I would not freely recognize if I had never held you in my arms.

All my love and devotion,

D

Her poor husband had suffered as much as she; but for her sake, Darcy had hidden his misery. Elizabeth had seen the lines deepen around his eyes and across his forehead. Had Darcy shed tears? She was certain that he had. Elizabeth knew his anguish—how the sunshine had disappeared from his smile.

Carefully, she refolded the first letter and replaced it where the note belonged within the bundle and then removed the second one. It held more tender memories than did the first. She had grieved briefly after the initial incident, but hadn't felt the full loss until the second. Actually, Elizabeth prefaced that. She had experienced the total impact when her sister Jane cradled a small babe in each arm. Her most beloved sister had delivered twins when she could not give Darcy even one child. She had thought herself a failure and had refused to go through that emptiness again.

Elizabeth shot a glance at the resting Mary Joseph. The woman's face betrayed the essence of her dreams—as if an angel had kissed the woman's cheek. *Allow me to reach eight full months*, she thought. *Even with my own imminent mortality*, she prayed, *give Mr. Darcy his child.*

Unfolding the letter she read her favorite part first.

> *Had I never known you, my Elizabeth, I would have never realized what was missing from my life. I am no longer lost: I can emerge from the rain. Living outside your love is not living at all. You are the light in my darkness.*

"What do you read, Mrs. Darcy?" a sleepy voice broke through Elizabeth's thoughts.

Elizabeth blushed and refolded the letter. "Nothing important. Only some letters."

With difficulty, Mrs. Joseph rolled onto her side, "From Mr. Darcy, I suspect," she said teasingly.

Elizabeth's color deepened. "I shall admit to nothing except that they came from a most handsome gentleman."

Mrs. Joseph smiled indulgently. "Mr. Darcy then. He's an intriguing-looking man. Was your husband the most exciting man of your acquaintance, Mrs. Darcy?"

Elizabeth thought immediately of her first impression of George Wickham, whose appearance was greatly in his favor; he had all the best parts of beauty—a fine countenance, a good figure, and a pleasing address. "A pleasing face doesn't define a man's true character, but I admit to preferring Mr. Darcy's countenance above all others." Elizabeth scrambled to her feet. "Let me put these away, and I'll help you to straighten your dress. Perhaps we could go below and join our husbands for tea."

Elizabeth dutifully replaced the letter and retied the outside ribbon. Then she carefully placed the bundle in the bottom of her portmanteau. "Now," she moved to the bed, "allow me to support your stance. You really must exercise more caution, Mrs. Joseph. You have God's most priceless gift to attend."

The woman swung her legs over the bed's edge and sat with Elizabeth's assistance. "I don't understand it," she observed. "When we departed Stoke-upon-Trent, I was quite a bit smaller. I feel as if I've gained weight each day we were on the road. I imagine myself quite heavy." She gently massaged her enlarged abdomen.

"Women, generally, gain their most weight during the last six weeks of their gestation," Elizabeth said absentmindedly as she braced Mrs. Joseph's weight with her own.

Taking several deep breaths, the lady rose slowly. "And how would a gentlewoman know such details?" Mrs. Joseph lightly taunted.

"This gentlewoman's sister's weight doubled with her confinement."

Mrs. Joseph countered, "Maybe that was because your sister delivered twins."

Elizabeth laughed lightly. "There's that possibility." She stepped away from the woman. "I sent Mr. Joseph and Mr. Darcy away so you might rest." She checked her own appearance in the mirror.

Mrs. Joseph shook out her skirts. "How long did I sleep?"

Elizabeth glanced at the small clock on the mantelpiece. "Nearly two hours."

"Two hours!" Mrs. Joseph gasped. "I never sleep so long."

"Your body must have needed the rest," Elizabeth asserted.

Mrs. Joseph began to repair her chignon. "Mr. Joseph must be terribly worried. We definitely should join the gentlemen, or Matthew will storm the door shortly." She pinched her cheeks. "I look so pale." She straightened her shoulders and turned to Elizabeth. "And don't tell me being pale is part of being with child," she warned.

Elizabeth smiled widely. "I shan't speak of it as you know the obvious." She reached for the door, but a grunt of discomfort from behind her brought Elizabeth up short. As she pivoted to the sound, Mrs. Joseph's grimace spoke Elizabeth's worst nightmares. "What is it?" she demanded as she rushed to the woman's side.

Mrs. Joseph swayed in place. Complete fear crossed her countenance. "I…I," she stammered. Then she raised her skirt's hem, and Elizabeth could see the woman's underskirt's dampness.

"Oh, my, you poor dear," Elizabeth sympathized. "Let's get you out of those soiled garments. I'll order some warm water so you might wash, and we'll soak the items afterwards." Elizabeth guided Mrs. Joseph to a plain wooden chair. "I should have considered your personal needs." Elizabeth flushed with embarrassment.

Mrs. Joseph sank heavily to the chair. "No!" she rasped. "You don't understand. The baby…the baby's coming."

CHAPTER 7

ल‍৸ ल‍৸ ल‍৸

"OF WHAT DO YOU GENTLEMEN SPEAK, Colonel?" Lady Catherine demanded from her end of the table. "What are you telling my niece? Let me hear what it is."

Edward looked up with a frown. "Actually, it's Georgiana who holds court, Aunt. My girl has amazed us with her knowledge." He smiled with delight.

"Miss Darcy was explaining the investments Mr. Darcy has made in her name," Mr. Bingley added.

Lady Catherine's eyebrow rose sharply. "I would think, Georgiana, that a lady would allow her guardian to oversee such issues. It's not in a lady's realm to involve herself in wealth's creation."

Edward smiled obligingly, but his tone spoke another language. "You are quite adept in the business world, Aunt."

"I've had no other recourse, Colonel," she said in a snit. "Sir Lewis's passing designed for me a role I never desired. It was why I sought your counsel and Darcy's."

"I meant no offense, Your Ladyship," he said contritely. "But I'll not hear of Georgiana being criticized for having an interest in her own future. The world is changing, Lady Catherine, and I admire my cousin for her initiative."

Georgiana glowed with his praise. "It's Fitzwilliam's doing. My brother insists that I be aware of my fortune. He's set part of it aside—separate from my dowry."

"It's very prudent of Fitz," Edward observed. "Your settlement shouldn't be your only means of support. Unfortunately, even some gentlemen with titles are unscrupulous in the handling of their family wealth."

Southland remarked, "You have our attention, Miss Darcy. Would you share your thoughts with the entire table?"

Mr. Bennet encouraged, "We could all benefit from Mr. Darcy's insights. Despite enjoying Mrs. Bennet and Mrs. Bingley's thorough discussion of Mary's trousseau, I would attend to news of investments. Perhaps the rest of us could consider following my son's advice."

Georgiana pinked, but she launched into her explanation. "Fitzwilliam is most concerned with the men's migration from estates to the cities, but rather than bemoan his losses, my brother has embraced the changes. He has sought out ways to make the lives of those who remain more profitable, and he has followed our father's example and invested in textile manufacturing, purified coals, construction of improved roads and man-made waterways, as well as steam-powered engines."

"Advancements such as what Mr. Manneville described to me earlier—the one you use for cotton," Caroline interjected.

"Yes, Miss Bingley," Manneville answered. "The cotton gin. It's revolutionized how we process the cotton plants."

Georgiana rejoined the conversation. "When I was a child, my father invested in James Watt's steam engines. Papa had holdings in Scotland and became aware of Mr. Watt's improvements in coal mining. I'm proud to say my father was one of the first to become interested in a steam engine's use in hauling supplies. He supported Richard Trevithick's efforts. I suppose it was from him that my brother developed his own connections."

"So, Darcy's invested in this proposed railway system?" Lady Catherine said skeptically.

Georgiana ignored her aunt's censure. Her own enthusiasm bubbled. "He has, Your Ladyship, and the outlay is proving true. Earlier this year, Mr. George Stephenson built the *Locomotion* for the Stockton and Darlington Railway Line."

Bingley confirmed Georgiana's disclosure. "I saw Stephenson's early efforts at the Killingworth Colliery near Durham. I shan't bore the ladies with the design details, but the July demonstration had the engine pulling eight loaded wagons."

"How much weight?" Southland asked with interest.

"Reportedly over thirty tons."

"And the speed?" Manneville inquired.

"Between four and five miles per hour. It's my understanding that the man was working on another geared locomotive, which he's named *Bülcher*."

Edward asked, "After the Prussian commander?"

Bingley laughed lightly. "I wondered if it was a metaphorical remark on the gentleman's fighting style."

Lady Catherine's disapproval showed when she said, "I cannot imagine a titled gentleman soiling his hands with such matters."

Her remark struck a blow to Georgiana's enthusiasm, and Edward wouldn't have it. He had been enjoying the sparkle in his cousin's eyes and her complexion's brightness. He'd found a different Georgiana upon his return to his homeland. His cousin had transformed into a beguiling young lady. Therefore, he directed a subtle set down in his aunt's direction. "Yet, it was my understanding that both Sir Thomas Liddle and Lord Strathmore were financial partners in the endeavor."

Ignoring Lady Catherine's glare, Manneville said, "Your reports of Mr. Stephenson's efforts parallel what Oliver Evans has been doing in America. As a young man in Philadelphia, I was among the crowd gathered on the riverfront to view Evans's *Oruktor Amphibolos*. Evans designed the machine to dredge and clean the city's docks. Yet, he failed to convince the Lancaster Turnpike Company to allow him to replace their six-horse Conestoga wagons with his steam engine."

"Do you suggest the Americans can outdo the British in this matter?" Southland challenged. "Even your famous Robert Fulton's *Clermont* used British components for its engine."

Quietly self-assured, Manneville responded, "Have we returned to that old issue, Southland? I've no particular allegiance to either side in this maddening separation. I'm loyal to South Carolina and to the people who depend on my plantation for their daily survival." He held the lieutenant's gaze before adding, "John Stevens's *Phoenix* was a superior machine, and it was made of inferior American parts—so inferior, in fact, it was the first to navigate an ocean voyage."

Edward laughed, "He has you there, Southland." He gave his aide a warning look. It seemed that there was a constant competition between the two.

"Well, I know one idea that is purely British," Georgiana interjected. With pleasure, Edward returned to his study of her beautiful face. Her eyes widened, and a warm feeling spread through the colonel's chest. "You Americans cannot build a tunnel under the Thames, Mr. Manneville."

A collective gasp passed among those at the table. "A tunnel beneath the Thames?" Miss Bingley asked incredulously. "Whatever for?"

"To be fair, Caroline," Bingley began, "such a passage would make trade more efficient on both sides of the river."

"Did they not try something similar between Tilbury and Gravesend in '99?" Mr. Bennet asked.

"And between Rotherhithe and Wapping some five years ago?" Southland added.

"But have you not heard?" Georgiana ignored both men's questions. She glowed with this new attention, and Edward felt his breathing tighten. "Mr. Marc Brunel's proposed a tunnel under the river Neva in St. Petersburg. Think of the possibilities. Would it not be wonderful?"

Edward's gaze held Georgiana's. "If you find the concept fascinating, I embrace the possibilities also."

"I have never heard of such folly," Lady Catherine declared.

"Maybe not so foolish, Aunt. It's rumored that the Duke of

Wellington is considering investing in the project if Brunel can be brought on board," Georgiana countered.

Lady Catherine snorted derisively. "The Duke should know better. My estimation of His Grace's intelligence is in question."

His voice distant and devoid of all expression, Edward turned the conversation. "I'll not criticize the Duke on or off the battle-field. We've monopolized the conversation long enough. I believe it's time to think more on Pemberley's Christmastide celebration. Please tell me, Cousin, that Darcy will host his annual Boxing Day Tenants' Ball."

"It is far from a ball," Lady Catherine declared.

"A matter of semantics, Your Ladyship," Edward responded blandly. He was well aware that Lady Catherine liked to stir up emotions. The best defense remained to not rise to his aunt's censure. "I prefer Darcy's foray to some of the Season's finer offerings. None of that silly ritual of dance cards and only being able to dance with a lady twice. Nor are there any manipulating mamas trying to shove some debutante into a man's arms."

"Mr. Darcy treats his cottagers well," Winkler remarked with authority. "They sing his praises freely."

Edward smiled reassuringly. "We'll await your commands, Cousin. I'm at your exclusive disposal in settling the event's details. Hopefully, Darcy's coach will make an appearance by this evening."

"I shall ask Mrs. Reynolds to meet with us, Colonel," Georgiana said sweetly. "We shall discover what the good lady has planned and share it with the others."

Edward's heart flipped. She had masterfully handled what could have been a stressful meal. Between the two of them, they had fended off their aunt, and Georgiana had shown great maturity in how she conversed with the other men and how she commanded their respect. He saw no other woman at the table able to do so. It was an astounding discovery for a man accustomed to command-ing his own deference.

～இ～ ～இ～ ～இ～

"What do you mean? The baby's coming?" Dread shook Elizabeth's core. "It's too early," she protested. "You cannot have this child now…in this inn…there's no doctor or midwife."

With white knuckles, Mrs. Joseph grasped the chair arm. "Despite all that, I am quite certain this child is making an appearance today," she rasped.

Elizabeth took several deep breaths to steady her composure. Kneeling before the woman, she reached for Mrs. Joseph's hand. "Do not worry," she managed as she softened her expression. "We can do this together."

Mrs. Joseph smiled weakly. "Of course, we can. That's why God brought us both to this inn at this time. I need someone with sagacity, and God has given me you."

Elizabeth teared with the woman's words. She didn't believe herself capable of delivering Mrs. Joseph's child, and she certainly didn't think herself part of God's plan for this woman; yet, she said, "It's the Christmas season, and if a child can be blessed by God at any time of the year, it's now. Let me aid your change of clothes, and then we'll get you straight to bed. Then I'll seek out Mrs. Washington's help. We'll need extra linens, and I'll require the good lady's assistance."

Mrs. Joseph stood on shaky legs. "I need to tell Matthew."

"First, the clothes and then to bed," Elizabeth said as she supported the woman's weight. "After that, I'll find Mr. Joseph and send him to you."

"I apologize, Mrs. Darcy. You certainly never expected to forfeit your bed when you extended your benevolence to my family."

Elizabeth began to unlace the back of Mrs. Joseph's gown. "Mr. Darcy and I shall adapt; your child's safety is paramount. Fitzwilliam will agree, Mrs. Joseph."

"I believe under the circumstances that you should call me Mary," the woman said. "Mrs. Joseph seems so formal for what lies ahead."

Elizabeth smiled through a false confidence. "Then I am Elizabeth."

❧ ❧ ❧

Georgiana had left Kitty in charge of hanging mistletoe in the downstairs rooms and had sent Mr. Bennet, Mr. Grange, Mary Bennet, and Jane Bingley to oversee the decoration of the barn for the Tenants' Ball. Finally alone, she sneaked into her brother's study and closed the door for a few minutes of silence. She needed time to hear herself think and to relive what Edward had said earlier. He'd referred to her as "my girl," and he'd deflected their aunt's criticisms. It felt wonderful to have Edward's recognition. With a shove, she waltzed across the room, an imaginary partner twirling her with wild abandon. In her mind, Edward's arm tightened about her as she smiled up at him. *It could happen*, she thought. Edward could finally find her appealing.

"Very nice, my dear," a deep voice said from a darkened corner, and Georgiana stumbled to a halt.

"Oh, my," she gasped. Straightening her gown's lines, Georgiana pinked. "I didn't realize you were here. No one," she stammered, "no one was to see my girlish display."

The colonel stepped from the shadows. "I should've said something when you first entered. I apologize if my presence alarmed you, Georgiana; however, I'll selfishly admit that I enjoyed watching you and wouldn't have missed it for a sultan's riches. Your face glowed with the purest joy."

Georgiana dropped her eyes. "I allowed my feminine side to overcome my good reason."

Edward now stood before her. Gently, he cupped her chin and raised it. "I'll not permit your self-censure. I've never seen you more beautiful, Georgiana. From the moment I beheld you on Pemberley's steps, I've been astonished by the changes in you. I admit to having difficulty accepting how much your transformation offers: I'm your guardian, but I wish I was nothing more than an ordinary man."

Innocently, she asked, "Can you not be both, Edward?"

"I'm not certain," he whispered huskily. "It would seem I must decide what role I wish to play."

"Would you dance with me?" Georgiana's gaze traced his face's lines.

Edward smiled easily. "I can think of nothing I'd enjoy more." Sliding his arm about her waist, he edged Georgiana into his embrace.

Their eyes never left one another. "We have no music," she whispered.

"We'll make our own." Edward stepped into the dance by bringing Georgiana next to him. They ignored the required distance between them. Instead, their bodies flowed about the small open area.

Edward concentrated on her face, and Georgiana experienced a change she'd never expected. A flush spread, but it wasn't from embarrassment. The warmth came from her heart and somewhere in her lower stomach. She allowed Edward to direct their steps about the furniture. To guide her through the waltz's intricacies. It was the most exquisite moment she'd ever known. "This is lovely," she said softly.

Edward couldn't dispense with the volatility permeating his body's every pore. Of late, he'd found that nothing or no one could satisfy the deep sense of loneliness that followed him through his daily routine. Nearly a decade of serving his country had proved beneficial for his career and for his purse, but the war's bloodshed and carnage had taught him that life held precious moments; and he should embrace them when they occurred. This was definitely a special moment. He was in a private, darkened room with a very beautiful woman; however, that woman was Georgiana. His sweetly precocious Georgiana. That same girl he'd taught to swim. Whose many cuts and scrapes he'd bandaged. Who always inserted herself into his and Darcy's most private moments. Over whom he had once considered abandoning his honor and killing a man in cold blood. That was the girl in his arms, but Georgiana was no longer a girl. Her very feminine curves fit the planes of his chest and his thigh. He needed to release her and place his cousin away from him. This was madness; yet, it felt so perfect.

"This is lovely," she said softly.

"You are lovely," he murmured. And she was. The look he witnessed earlier graced Georgiana's face again, and Edward realized it was meant for him. He brought that joyous response to her countenance. His heart sang of possibilities, but his head told him to slow down. This was Georgiana, and he'd not hurt her. He needed time to decide how best to proceed.

Reluctantly, Edward slowed their pace. Spinning Georgiana one last time, he brought her to a halt. Making his legs step away, Edward bowed over her hand. "I don't know when I've held a lovelier woman in my arms. Thank you, Sweetest, for reminding me for what I fight."

He watched as Georgiana composed herself. Surely, something had passed between them, but was it "something" he wanted to pursue? He'd spent so much time on the battlefront and in diplomacy that his personal skills skewed toward the negative.

Georgiana recovered well enough to dip a quick curtsy. "I pray you see no more battles, Edward. I worry so when you're away." Her demeanor remained cautious, and Edward noted mystification on her pretty countenance.

"Perhaps we should join the others," he said softly while offering his arm.

Georgiana glanced away. "As you wish, Colonel." She placed her hand lightly on his. "I suppose our guests must wonder at my defection. It would disappoint Fitzwilliam to know of my selfishness."

"Neither your brother nor I would criticize your need for privacy. It must be a family trait. Often I wish for the ability to send everyone else away."

Georgiana paused before exiting through the now-open door. "Does that include me, Edward? Would you have me elsewhere?"

"Never in this lifetime, Sweetheart."

✥ ✥ ✥

"Oh, please beware, Miss Catherine." Winkler rushed forward to steady the ladder on which she stood. "Why are you hanging that ornament? Shouldn't a footman be doing so?" Winkler reached for her as Kitty backed down the ladder's rungs.

"I sent Thomas to find additional ribbon. This string keeps breaking," she said in frustration. Actually touching her leg and hip through her gown, Winkler braced her steps, and Kitty warmed beneath his touch. She hadn't considered the ramifications of climbing on the ladder when the string around the mistletoe ball had broken, leaving the seasonal ornament to hang precariously over the room's center. At Longbourn, she and her sisters had often scaled the ladder to the attic and the one to the hayloft.

"Allow me to assist your descent," Winkler pleaded; real concern laced his voice. His hands came about Kitty's waist, and he lifted her from the ladder. Gently, Winkler placed her on the floor before him.

Turning quickly to face him, Kitty leaned into Winkler. "My," she cooed, "I'd not realized the dangers of such a simple task. Thank you for protecting me, Sir." She noted that the rapid increase of her own breathing had matched his.

"I'd have nothing cause you harm, Miss Catherine. You must know that," Winkler said huskily.

Kitty smiled brightly. "You wish to protect me, Mr. Winkler?"

"With my life." Obviously embarrassed, he stepped back, placing distance between them. Yet, he immediately captured Kitty's hand. "I would pay my addresses to you, Miss Catherine, if you'll accept them."

Although her heart pounded out a loud staccato, Kitty coolly asked, "You mean to court me, Sir?"

Winkler quickly released Kitty's hand. "It would be my wish. Unless, of course, you find my suit repugnant."

Kitty laughed lightly. One of the few things her younger

sister Lydia had shared regarding men was the male's lack of self-confidence. "Never," she said and turned to the ladder.

Behind her, she heard Winkler's frustrated sigh. "Please, Miss Catherine," he said uneasily. "Dispel my misery. Never what? I cannot bear the idea that you'd never love me."

Nearly knocking over the ladder, Kitty spun around in haste. "Love?" she gasped. "You wish me to love you?"

"A marriage based on anything less than love does not interest me. I might tolerate one based on strong affection; but my parents loved each other dearly, and I wish a similar joining."

Kitty thought immediately of her own parents, and she could not form a very pleasing picture of conjugal felicity or domestic comfort. Her mother had, obviously, offered an attraction for her father, but that early affection had gone by the wayside. She knew of no couple's marriage—at least, one of any duration—that maintained that early rush of happiness. Maria Lucas's parents were quite staid. Rumors existed of Sir William Lucas's trips to London. Her Uncle Philips barely tolerated her aunt. But, possibly, Aunt Gardiner had found happiness. Lizzy and Mr. Darcy easily exchanged affection's soft smile, as did Jane and Mr. Bingley, but would their marriages remain so blissful?

As her sister Elizabeth had recently pointed out, their father's behavior as a husband bordered on impropriety. Kitty had reluctantly agreed. She had always seen it with pain; but, respecting her father's abilities, and grateful for his affectionate treatment of herself, Kitty had endeavored to forget what she could no longer overlook and to banish from her thoughts that continual breach of conjugal obligation of decorum, which, in exposing his wife to the contempt of her own children, was so highly reprehensible.

"I'm afraid, Mr. Winkler," she managed, "that until Jane joined with Mr. Bingley and Elizabeth with Mr. Darcy, I possessed no marriage models based on love." Kitty made her decision quickly and reached for his hand. "I'm not sure what to do to make you love me, Sir, but I'll strive to make it so."

Winkler cupped her cheek in his large palm. "You need do nothing special. Just be Catherine. You already hold sway over my affections."

Kitty breathed easier: She'd said the correct thing. "If we're to spend time together, Mr. Winkler, might you call me 'Kitty'?"

The man's countenance lit with happiness. "And you'll call me 'Thorne.'"

"A unique name," she teased.

Winkler's smile grew. "I'll tell you the whole horrid story some day. It'll be part of our courtship."

"I've no such tales," she asserted.

"We'll see about that." Winkler kissed her knuckles. "I'm very adept at discovering others' confidences. Something about the profession makes people free with their confessions."

Kitty caressed his cheek. "You'll be sadly mistaken, Sir." She laughed lightly. "I'm not likely to share my darkest secrets." Hearing noises in the hall, she sobered quickly. "How shall we proceed?"

"How long will your family remain at Pemberley?"

Kitty puzzled. "No one has said for certain, but as Mr. Grange has responsibilities in Meryton, I'd imagine no longer than Twelfth Night."

"Might you remain at Pemberley when your parents depart?"

Kitty thought that her mother would gladly spare her if she knew that Mr. Winkler wished to pay his addresses. "It could be arranged."

"I'd thought we should spend time together," Winkler explained. "I have many and varied duties associated with my living. If we decide to marry, you'll be expected to join me in my mission. I wish you to be fully aware of the responsibilities of being a clergyman's wife before you accept my proposal."

"Then we'll not tell the others?"

Winkler continued, "I'll speak to your father while he's at Pemberley. I thought when the Darcys returned that we could let it be known that we have an understanding. I would speak to Mr. Darcy also. He's my benefactor, and you're Mrs. Darcy's sister. I would want his approval."

"You have this well thought out," Kitty teased.

"I've had longer to consider it—since last summer when you were at Pemberley." This time he kissed the inside of her wrist. "I've thought of little else for months."

Surprise rested on Kitty's lips. "Truly?"

"Truly," he confessed. "I'd heard of your return from Mrs. Oliver when she came into the village to order extra supplies. Thankfully, the Collinses required assistance in reaching the estate. It gave me a good excuse to see you again."

"You shouldn't have risked your safety for the likes of Mr. Collins," she said.

"For the pleasure of your company, I'd risk more than that," he assured.

Hearing more people in the hallway, Kitty said, "I suppose we should finish hanging this ornament before the others catch us alone together, and all your plans go to naught."

Winkler's smile broadened. "Not such a terrible fate. Come, my dear. This time I'll climb the ladder, and you'll steady it." He paused before he took the first step. Slowly, he leaned toward her, and Kitty thought he might kiss her, but, instead, he said, "On Christmas, we might sneak in here alone for a few minutes." Kitty's breath caught in her throat. "Of course, I must finagle an invitation from Mr. Darcy to join the family in order for that to happen. Surely, the roads will be clear before the holiday."

Kitty said with a grin. "I'll see to the invitation." She handed him the beribboned ball.

"Lots of berries on this particular mistletoe," he taunted as he looked down upon her.

"What shall you do with the berries, Thorne?" she asked in a breathy response. Suddenly, the man's presence towered over Kitty in ways having nothing to do with the ladder.

"As is traditional, I'll find a pretty girl lurking beneath the mistletoe. Then I'll steal a berry and claim my kiss."

✧ ✧ ✧

Even over the noise of the common room, Darcy recognized Elizabeth's light tread on the stairs. He had anticipated her joining him for over an hour. The men's posturing had quickly grown old, and he desperately needed a few minutes alone with his wife. With Elizabeth, Darcy had realized that he could be more than an echo of his father, and he no longer searched for what these men didn't know. He had earned the love of a remarkable woman—a woman of exceptional strength. Darcy needed only her for his happiness.

Then he saw her. Elizabeth swayed on the steps, her face pale with worry, and Darcy was immediately on his feet and moving in her direction. He caught her just as she lurched forward. "I have you," he whispered close to her ear, and she sank into his embrace. "What is it?" He braced her stance with his body.

"I cannot do it," she rasped.

"Do what?" he demanded. Elizabeth buried her face in his chest. "Tell me," he said authoritatively.

Elizabeth looked at him, and Darcy recognized her fear. "Mrs. Joseph's baby…I cannot deliver her baby."

"Of course not," Darcy began, but then what his wife really meant became clearer. "Do you mean to say that Mrs. Joseph is…?" He couldn't say the words.

"Yes." Elizabeth disengaged herself from his embrace. "I was in the room with Jane, but I know nothing beyond comforting my sister."

Darcy took a deep breath. "First, let's send Joseph to sit with his wife, and then you and I will speak to the Washingtons. Surely, there's someone in the area who can serve as a midwife."

"Do you think so?"

Elizabeth's voice asked for reassurance, but Darcy held his own doubts. The nearest village was some fifteen miles away. "One thing at a time. Mrs. Joseph needs her husband. Stay here, and let me bring the man to us."

Darcy left her on the steps and returned to the common room. No one below could observe her at the bend in the stairs. Leaning over Mr. Joseph, Darcy whispered, "Come with me."

Joseph looked up in surprise. "Is something astray?" the man hissed.

"Just come," Darcy insisted and turned to leave. He didn't look back to see Joseph scramble to his feet.

Darcy returned to where Elizabeth waited. Turning, he braced her as Mr. Joseph joined them. "What has happened? Where is Mary?" Joseph demanded.

"You should go to her," Elizabeth said softly. "Your child shall make an appearance in a few hours."

Joseph looked like he might faint, but he bolted up the stairs, taking the last six steps two at a time.

~⊚~ ~⊚~ ~⊚~

"Southland, just the man I wanted to find," Edward declared as he entered the library. Neither of them addressed their previous conversation. The colonel knew the man would act professionally. He didn't have to guard against Southland's maneuverings.

The lieutenant scrambled to his feet and came to attention. "I apologize, Sir. I should've informed you of my whereabouts."

"We're not on the front, Lieutenant," Edward assured. "I simply require your assistance in arranging an entertainment."

"I'm at your disposal, Sir." The man remained in formal stance.

Edward's eyebrow rose in amusement. "Then I can count on you to coordinate filling the bird bath."

Southland flustered, "If that…if that's what you require, Sir."

Edward fought the desire to smile. "We should recruit Mr. Manneville to our efforts."

"I assure you, Colonel, I need no assistance in filling a birdbath."

Edward laughed easily. "Wait until you see it, Southland. You may have second thoughts.

~⊚~ ~⊚~ ~⊚~

"That cannot be," Darcy protested.

"We're fifteen miles south of Harrogate. Not close to Skipton or Bradford—at least, not under these conditions," Mr. Washington explained. "The few area farms depend on each other for these needs."

Elizabeth's concern rose quickly. "What is Mrs. Joseph to do? Surely, someone in the neighborhood could assist us."

"We've had no need of such services," Mrs. Washington admitted sheepishly. "God never saw fit to bless Mr. Washington and me with our own children, and Nan be too young to be having her own brood. The girl need be taking a husband first."

"But you know something of what a woman must go through. You can assist Mrs. Joseph with the delivery?" Elizabeth pleaded.

"I'm afraid not, Mrs. Darcy. I know nothing of birthing babies."

CHAPTER 8

❧ ❧ ❧

"SO THIS IS THE BIRDBATH." Manneville smirked.

Edward laughed lightly. "Does it not resemble one? A gigantic birdbath?"

Southland looked on from the structure's edge. "What the hell is it?"

Inspecting for any damage, Edward strolled leisurely about the circle. "When Darcy and I were boys, we believed it had been left behind by an ancient civilization—like the monoliths. As a young lad, my cousin envisioned it the creation of some visitor from the stars. It was Darcy's mother who gave it the affectionate name of 'The Birdbath.' It's made for great adventures," he said in reminiscence. "Yet, in truth, no one knows for sure. The area is perfectly round and lined with flat rocks. Darcy's father brought in engineers and covered the area with Parker's cement. In the summer, the rain creates a shady place for a cooling splash. In the winter, we supplement the rain with water from the well over there." He pointed to a small, bricked structure. "Then we let nature take its course. The birdbath makes a wonderful skating pond. Notice how the rain from the last two days has formed a solid base." He gestured to the frozen surface. "We could add a coating or two today, and tomorrow we could skate upon the bowl."

Southland analyzed the situation. "We should add a few buckets at a time. The surface would refreeze faster that way."

"An apt evaluation," the colonel summarized. "That means you would need to come out here every few hours to check on its progress. Can I entrust this project to you, Southland?"

The lieutenant bowed. "It's a way to repay the Darcys for their generous welcome. It would be my honor, Sir."

Manneville groaned. "I'm not looking forward to the cold, but I'm not afraid of a bit of hard labor. I'll join you, Southland. Especially, if it's a debt of honor."

"Thank you, Gentlemen. I'll send some footmen to help carry the water. We need another three to four inches of ice."

⟿ ⟿ ⟿

"Elizabeth, I don't want you to do this," Darcy whispered sharply. They remained in the darkened hallway outside their bedroom. "It's not proper. No one can expect it of you." Darcy feared that his wife's assisting Mrs. Joseph during the woman's delivery would send Elizabeth further into depression, especially if Mrs. Joseph lost the child despite Elizabeth's best efforts. "I forbid it, Elizabeth."

There had been a time that those words from him would have guaranteed that Elizabeth would've ignored his orders, but with a better understanding between them, she'd come to believe he meant well—meant to protect her. "Fitzwilliam, you know above all others that I've no choice. We're the only ones who stand between disaster and hope for the Josephs."

"What if we cannot give the Josephs what they seek?" He caressed her cheek. "I cannot bear to see you distraught. You're my life, Elizabeth. I'd remain lost forever without you."

Elizabeth walked into his embrace. "My love," she murmured as she buried her face in his chest. She remained in his arms for several elongated moments before raising her eyes to his. "I shan't return to my mind's dark corners. Your love has healed me, Fitzwilliam. So even if I cannot bring Mrs. Joseph's dreams to fruition, I'll not retreat to the Elizabeth of late."

"Are you certain, Elizabeth? This is what you mean to do?"

"Yes, Fitzwilliam. This is what God has placed in my path."

Darcy kissed her forehead and pulled her closer. "You are an angel—a Christmas angel come to life."

Elizabeth laughed lightly. "A non-heavenly being is more likely."

Darcy smiled easily. "You do know how to bedevil a man's sanity."

"You deserved every moment of my disdain," she asserted.

"Deserved is debatable," he argued, "but I'd go through it all again to earn your love."

Elizabeth's hands fisted at her waist as she stepped away from him. "You do not fight fairly, Fitzwilliam Darcy. How can a woman argue against such statements?"

Darcy smiled broadly. "Fighting requires the asking of forgiveness afterwards by one or both of the opponents. As our bedchamber is currently occupied, that's not a possibility."

"See. That's what I mean. Always the most rational of men." She went on her tiptoes to kiss his lips. "Let's rejoin the Josephs for now. We may argue at our leisure after we deal with this crisis."

Darcy caught her hand. "I'll add an upcoming argument and a bout of forgiveness to my agenda book." He bent to kiss her forehead. "I may be rational, but I'm still a man in love."

～⌒ ～⌒ ～⌒

"Miss Darcy, do you have a few minutes in which we might speak privately?" Mr. Bennet stood by the music room's door.

"Certainly, Mr. Bennet. Please come in, and close the door. I just finished my practice."

He smiled easily. "I waited patiently and enjoyed the music. Your expertise on the pianoforte is as exquisite as Kitty has led me to believe. I wish my daughters possessed such talent, but other than Mary, none of them has showed the discipline for practice."

Georgiana left the instrument bench. "Join me before the hearth, Mr. Bennet. Should I send for tea?"

"That's not necessary, Miss Darcy. I'll not take much of your time."

Georgiana settled herself on one of the settees. "Hopefully, you've not found Pemberley's hospitality lacking."

"Far from it. Of course, I'm a man of simple needs: country rather than city living and a bountiful library. Of what I wish to speak is Lizzy's health. Upon our arrival, I'd planned to address my concerns to Mr. Darcy, but as he's not available, I'm pleading with you for information. Plus, I'm uneasy with your aunt's appearance at Pemberley—whether she would attack Lizzy. I tell you, Miss Darcy, I'll not have it. I love all my daughters, but Elizabeth is the one most like the Bennet family. The rest are very much Gardiners, displaying characteristics of my wife's relatives."

"What do you require of me, Mr. Bennet?" His request made her uncomfortable. No one at Pemberley discussed Elizabeth's gestation.

"Mr. Darcy's letter described Lizzy's mental withdrawal. Your brother expressed his anxiety for Elizabeth, and in her letters, my daughter's innate wit and sauciness is missing. How bad has it been for Elizabeth?"

Georgiana took a deep breath as she composed her response. "I agree Elizabeth has lost that special something that makes her unique. She laughs; she cries; but my sister's singularity has disappeared. Having to serve Mrs. Bingley during your eldest daughter's delivery was a double-edged sword. Elizabeth loves Jane and would never wish her sister ill, but Mrs. Bingley's success greatened Elizabeth's failures. In fact, I was thankful Elizabeth was not present for Mr. Bingley's announcement of another child."

Mr. Bennet nodded his understanding. "And Elizabeth is currently with child?"

"So says Hannah. Early on, Elizabeth's maid noted her mistress's condition, but my sister has refused to acknowledge her gravidity. Fitzwilliam has insisted that we accept her reluctance. He has consulted the doctor, and Doctor Palmer advises us to allow Elizabeth to handle this gestation without outside criticism." Speaking so frankly on this personal subject was both liberating and embarrassing.

Mr. Bennet sighed deeply. "I've always known that Elizabeth would find such failures to be pure tragedies. She prides herself on perfection." He paused and cleared his throat. "Should I anticipate Lady Catherine's censure, Miss Darcy?"

"I wish I knew for certain, Mr. Bennet. If so, Fitzwilliam shall never forgive Her Ladyship. My brother would banish our aunt from his home, but the damage could already have been inflicted. Kitty is trying to determine if it was truly by necessity that my aunt sought Pemberley's refuge. Our unease comes from the fact that Lady Catherine sent word to the Collinses the evening before she ordered her coach to Lambton. Kitty hopes Mrs. Collins might share what she knows of Her Ladyship's motives."

"Do you think it possible that Lady Catherine will speak openly of Lizzy's losses?"

Worry misted Georgiana's eyes. "If she does, it'll only confirm Elizabeth's fears of being found wanting."

~◎~ ~◎~ ~◎~

"I object to Mr. Darcy's presence during my wife's delivery," Mr. Joseph declared.

"Matthew, that's not necessary," Mary said softly.

Elizabeth ignored the man's objection. "Why do you not read to Mrs. Joseph?" she suggested calmly.

Joseph rose to his feet. "I'll not read any book until your husband excuses himself from this room," he demanded.

Elizabeth rolled her eyes in exasperation. "Mr. Joseph, I'll remind you that the room belongs to Mr. Darcy. You're here as my husband's guest."

"Oh, I see how it is!" His voice rose in indignation. "Your rescue is limited in its scope. Then never fear, Mrs. Darcy. Mary and I will be out of your way momentarily."

He shoved past her, and Darcy was immediately on his feet. "Now see here, Joseph. You will take care of my wife's safety, and you'll speak to Mrs. Darcy in a civilized tone."

"Matthew," Mary pleaded. "We need Mrs. Darcy's assistance. I need her. Your child needs her."

Elizabeth watched the color drain from the man's face. "I understand," he said through gritted teeth, "but I'll not see you subjected to censure."

"Wouldn't abandoning this room for a stable be seen as foolish?" his wife reasoned.

"Fine," Joseph said grudgingly. "Give me the book." He quickly reseated himself beside the bed.

Elizabeth smiled at her husband, who seated himself on the bed's other side. "I've a better idea. Mr. Joseph, I want you to hold your wife's hand. Whenever Mary has a pain, I want you to take note of the time. Only when Mrs. Joseph's pains are close together will the baby make its appearance."

"And what will Mr. Darcy be doing during this wait?" Joseph asked suspiciously.

Elizabeth picked up the book and handed it to Darcy. She saw his eyebrow rise in amusement when he read the title. "Reading aloud."

"And why is Mr. Darcy the one to read to us?"

Elizabeth smiled knowingly. "For several reasons: First, Mr. Darcy has secretly wondered about *The Heroine* since its release last year, and now he shall understand the book's parody." She squeezed Darcy's hand as she passed over the book. "Secondly, I find my husband's voice quite soothing, and as I plan to find my own rest while I may still do so, Mr. Darcy's reading shall allow me to take moments to recover my energies. With my sister Mrs. Bingley, it was well into the night before she delivered her children."

"Thank you for considering your own health, Mrs. Darcy," her husband said softly.

Elizabeth squeezed his shoulders as she moved to stand behind him. "Mary, enjoy the novel, and relax as much as possible. Trust each of us to do what is necessary."

"I'm not afraid, Mrs. Darcy. God has sent us your good sense."

❧ ❧ ❧

"Another trip into the cold?" Caroline asked as the gentlemen excused themselves from the gathering. "What's so fascinating about Mr. Darcy's gardens dripping in ice?"

Manneville gestured toward Southland. "Just helping the lieutenant with a task." He grinned insolently.

"And that task would be?" Caroline drew out the words.

"Filling a birdbath, Miss Bingley," Southland announced a bit tersely.

"The birdbath?" Georgiana squealed. "What a wonderful idea, but how did you know?"

"The colonel, Miss Darcy. It was his idea," Southland explained.

Mrs. Bennet asked, "What is special about a birdbath?"

"It's very much like a small pond, Mama," Kitty said. "Miss Darcy and I sat beside the water last summer and enjoyed the coolness."

"Then why must it be filled if it's a pond? I don't understand," Mrs. Bennet puzzled.

Georgiana answered, "My father took an earlier structure and created a man-made pool just right for a lady to go wading or for small children to play in the water. During the winter months it's perfect for ice skating."

Kitty became more excited. "Ice skating. I love to skate, but we've so few opportunities in Hertfordshire. Please say we'll skate soon."

"I assume that was the colonel's thought—an afternoon of skating—but it'll be tomorrow before the water's frozen solid enough to support our weight."

"At least, with the birdbath's shallowness, no one shall take a dunking," Georgiana assured. "We shan't keep you gentlemen any longer. I appreciate your efforts on our behalf." She smiled happily at them. "I'll seek my cousin and express my gratitude for his thoughtfulness."

～⌒～　～⌒～　～⌒～

As he began another chapter of the novel, Darcy kept an eye on his wife. Elizabeth had constructed a makeshift bed, using the two mats given last evening to the Josephs. He knew from the tightness in her shoulder muscles that she didn't sleep, but he was happy that she'd considered the child she carried—their child—in her decisions.

Every nerve in his body remained alert—the need to protect her always paramount. Darcy wondered if this time God would answer their prayers. He needed an heir, but he would welcome a daughter, especially if she resembled her mother. More importantly, he sensed that Elizabeth wouldn't feel complete without the child, and she would never achieve the satisfaction he'd found in their marriage.

He didn't know how long he'd been reading aloud—long enough for his throat to feel raspy—long enough for Mr. Joseph to doze off. At least, one of the Josephs had found a peaceful repose. Between Mrs. Joseph's repetitive labor pains and her excitement over the story, she was quite active.

"Is this not the most intriguing story you've ever heard, Mr. Darcy?" Mrs. Joseph asked in a stage whisper. Fluffing her own pillows, she adjusted her position.

Darcy smiled easily. "It is quite different from my usual fare," he said softly. "Yet, I find myself wondering of the heroine's fate, as surely as I might when reading Shakespeare or other great writers."

"You're a poor liar," Mary continued to whisper. "You, Sir, are a literature snob. I've seen your type before," she teasingly challenged.

Darcy thought it amusing that Mrs. Joseph possessed a sharp wit while her husband seemed so solemn and prideful. In some ways, they reflected what people would say about him and Elizabeth. With their mates both resting, Darcy kept his voice low. "I am no such thing," he protested. "I'm a very eclectic reader."

"Have you read many female writers?"

"Unfortunately, I've not, but that's not because of their lack of ability, which is what you wish to imply, Mrs. Joseph. Women have been denied a voice until recently. I've read several works by Charlotte Smith, as well as her male counterparts. My late father thought it important that I become aware of political views. Smith, for example, speaks to the renewal of the land in her *Old*

Manor House and the bleakness of England's history in *Marchmont.*"

"I'm impressed, Mr. Darcy," the lady said mockingly.

Darcy laughed lightly. "I've also read my share of books dealing with individual ambition and social gratification; but I prefer Defoe's ideas on trade in *The Complete English Tradesman* or even his *The True-Born Englishman.*"

"Give it up, Mrs. Joseph." Elizabeth appeared beside her husband. "You shan't find a man more well read than my husband. I'd thought when I left my father's house for my husband's that I might leave behind the man who'd hold that title. Little did I know of Pemberley's extensive library." She rested her hand on Darcy's shoulder, and he reached for her fingers.

"Is it truly delightful, Mrs. Darcy?" Mary's eyebrow rose in interest.

"It ought to be good," Darcy replied; "It has been the work of many generations."

Elizabeth added, "And then you have added so much to it yourself—you are always buying books." They spoke softly so as not to wake Mr. Joseph, but they no longer whispered.

"I cannot comprehend the neglect of a family library in such days as these." Darcy easily imagined the aforementioned Mr. Bennet ensconced in the Pemberley library as they spoke.

Before they could continue their conversation, Mary grimaced and tightened her grip on the bed linens. Elizabeth coaxed, "Breathe through it. Do not hold your breath." She watched the woman's posture relax as the pain passed. "How close are the spasms?"

A bit breathless, Mary gasped, "I've no idea."

"Six minutes," Darcy said flatly.

Elizabeth smiled sweetly at she dabbed Mary's face with a cool, damp cloth. "Thank you, Fitzwilliam. I knew you wouldn't fail to take note."

He said in justification, "You said it was important, Elizabeth." He would understand what Mrs. Joseph suffered in order to better attend Elizabeth later on.

"As it is, Mr. Darcy." She pursed her lips in an air kiss that instantly eased his defenses. "We're getting close." Elizabeth noted Mr. Joseph's stirring from his nap. "No more holding back, Mary: Your husband's composure is no longer your concern. I want you to concentrate on nothing but the safe delivery of your child. If you wish to scream, then do so. If you wish to bury your face in a pillow, it's your prerogative. We'll forgive any of your shortcomings."

"What if I've no shortcomings, Mrs. Darcy?" Mary taunted.

"Then you've no need of me," Elizabeth declared.

∽᷈᷍ ∽᷈᷍ ∽᷈᷍

"You expect me to go over Darcy's head and arrange a Season for Georgiana?" the colonel asked incredulously. He had retreated to Darcy's study to write and frank letters to his parents and to his commanding officer. In reality, Edward had purposely withdrawn not only to complete his correspondence, but also to have a few minutes to consider the many questions that plagued him. First, he didn't understand why he'd received orders to escort Manneville to London. Something didn't add up, and despite doing as instructed, Edward couldn't help but wonder if the American was all he claimed to be. In the war's midst, it didn't make sense to cater to a lone American and to grant the man immunity. Of course, it wasn't his realm to question his superiors, but as he was to ease Manneville's way into polite society, it bothered Edward exceedingly. Plus, he had now introduced Manneville to his family and acquaintances, and the colonel didn't appreciate putting his loved ones in the American's notice. Nothing about the mission had permitted him a solid night's sleep. He simply had to trust that the British government truly understood what they had asked of him.

Edward had thought that once he had returned to England, and specifically to Derbyshire, that the uneasy feeling would dissipate, and in some ways it had, but only to be replaced by a new wariness. Or maybe he should say a new awareness: one of his cousin.

True, it had been a long while since he'd spent time with any woman, and, obviously, more than a year since he'd known an English woman. It was also true that he'd anticipated this homecoming when he'd learned that they'd make shore at Liverpool. And just as truthfully, Georgiana had blossomed into a full-fledged beauty, the type any man would desire, which was another truth that he didn't wish to acknowledge. The thought of Georgiana's beauty being another man's privilege had kept him awake last evening, and that exquisite moment in the library earlier had set his emotions akilter. Now, his imperious aunt had cornered him, invading his private thoughts, and had demanded that he take action on Georgiana's behalf.

"I not only expect it, Colonel, I insist upon it," Lady Catherine said.

Edward bristled. "It would seem to me that if Darcy were deficient in his duty that the Earl, as the family's head, would address his concern to my cousin."

As was typical with Lady Catherine, she ignored everything but her own scheme. "I shall sponsor my niece's Come Out," she announced.

Edward blustered, "You…why would you believe after your recent tiff with Darcy that he'd allow you to present his sister to Society? It would appear that my mother, as the family patroness, would be a more likely candidate, as would Mrs. Darcy. I would imagine that in Fitz's opinion, both would take precedence over your claim."

"The Countess has no desire to spend another Season in London. Your mother prefers her country associations, and Mrs. Darcy possesses no concept of Society's nuances. The lady has limited musical training and knows nothing of art. Mrs. Bennet should have taken her daughters to town every spring for the benefit of the masters. It's incontestable. Five daughters brought up at home without a governess! I have never heard of such a thing. I always say that nothing is to be done in education without steady and regular instruction, and nobody but a governess can give it. And

Mrs. Bennet's lack of decorum! All five sisters out at once! Very odd! Therefore, what could Mrs. Darcy know of the peerage and the *beau monde*?"

The colonel recognized some truth in his aunt's words. Part of Darcy's initial wavering in his pursuit of Elizabeth had been the lady's low connections, but Edward couldn't allow Her Ladyship free reign. "If you expect to win Darcy's favor, you must curb your tongue, Your Ladyship." Impulsively he added, "What makes you believe you'd be more successful with Georgiana than you were with Anne?" Edward watched with pleasure as his aunt paled. "I don't mean to speak cruelly, but surely Darcy will ask something similar. As you are thrusting me into my cousin's place, it seems only prudent that you satisfy my curiosity on the matter. I love Anne, but your daughter was never of the nature to excel in such a setting; yet, you insisted on placing her so."

Lady Catherine's haughtiness spoke volumes. "Anne's health prevented her success."

"We both know, Aunt, that Anne is extremely shy. Timidity is not an illness," he declared.

Lady Catherine snarled, "The military has sharpened your bitterness. I'm certain the Earl would find such qualities less than stellar."

Edward shrugged away her objection. "I would counter that what you see as bitterness is actually reality. That's what a decade of war has taught me, Your Ladyship. Reality cannot be dressed up in ball gowns nor masked by polite chatter. The reality is that you should have found a country gentleman for Anne, but you wanted a titled peer." With those words, Edward made a silent commitment to see Anne settled properly. He'd not have her waste away under Lady Catherine's censure. Immediately, he thought of Southland, and although he'd warned his aide away from Anne earlier, he would now encourage the relationship. A flirtation might be exactly what Anne needed.

"She has my husband's nature," Lady Catherine said with some sadness.

"Then you should not have forced Anne to be something she's not." Edward paused to choose his words carefully. "Allow Anne some freedom, Aunt, or you'll lose her forever. You'll spend your days alone instead of being surrounded by your daughter's family." Edward softened his tone. "As much as I respect you, Your Ladyship, I don't believe you're the person to guide Georgiana's entrance into Society. Like Anne's, Georgiana's delicate nature needs tending—needs a chance to bloom. I've often heard my cousin speak of her deep respect for your ability to thrive in a world dominated by men. Rosings Park has flourished under your hand, but the hardness you needed to survive under such terms intimidates Georgiana. Instead of budding, my young cousin would wither away. I cannot condone nor encourage your plight to bring Georgiana under your auspices."

Lady Catherine snorted. "I see. You would have my niece—my sister's only daughter—brought into Society by Mrs. Darcy."

"If her brother has no objection, I wouldn't interfere in Mrs. Darcy assuming that role. Darcy has always done everything within his power to give Georgiana pleasure. He'll not shirk his duty in such an important matter."

"Would Darcy offend his wife to protect his sister?" Lady Catherine asked sharply.

"I don't believe it would come to that. Mrs. Darcy will bring no shame on Georgiana. She's of the nature to admit her shortcomings and to seek the expertise of others. Who knows? If you resolve your differences with Darcy, it's highly possible that he and Mrs. Darcy will ask your sponsorship for Georgiana." *It's also possible that pigs will sprout wings to take flight.* Edward knew that Darcy would never forgive Lady Catherine's attack on Mrs. Darcy. For family harmony, his cousin might *tolerate* their aunt's presence, but Darcy would not forget the offense.

Edward also realized that he didn't want Georgiana subjected to the attentions of this year's eligible bachelors. In fact, if Darcy insisted on Georgiana's presentation, Edward would take an extended stay in London. A change of posts could be easily arranged. That way he could watch over Georgiana and fend off unscrupulous offers. The image of his waltzing Georgiana across a crowded dance floor brought a smile.

"What do you find so amusing, Colonel?" Lady Catherine's sour tone cut through the beautiful image.

"Just the pleasure of seeing Georgiana well situated, Your Ladyship."

⚬⚬⚬ ⚬⚬⚬ ⚬⚬⚬

"The razor is sharp," Darcy told Elizabeth privately as he prepared to leave. Mrs. Joseph's delivery had progressed quickly, and his wife had determined it was time to excuse him from the room.

Checking off items from the mental list she had constructed while resting on the mat, Elizabeth asked, "You used the strop?"

Darcy moved a step closer. "It's as you wished," he said softly. Then shooting a quick glance at where Mr. Joseph tended his wife, he added. "Are you certain, Elizabeth? This is the course you wish to undertake?"

"It's not what I would choose, Fitzwilliam, but it is what must be done."

"Should I again implore Mrs. Washington to assist you?"

"She'll not agree. Mrs. Washington doesn't wish to suffer the blame if Mrs. Joseph experiences difficulty. Plus, the proprietress cannot leave her inn duties."

"But what if…" Darcy broke off when her fingers touched his mouth.

Elizabeth easily traced his upper lip. "No, *what ifs*, Fitzwilliam. We'll all say our prayers and then leave the rest in God's hands."

Predictably, Darcy bit back his response. Elizabeth smiled knowingly. Her husband objected to her involvement, but he'd allow her to make her own decisions, as well as her own mistakes. It was one of the qualities for which she most admired him. It was how Elizabeth knew her husband would be an excellent father. Their children would know love with no censure. "I'll be close. Please take care." He bent to kiss her temple. "I love you."

"And I you." Then he was gone. Taking a deep breath, Elizabeth turned to face the Josephs. "Let's place you in a position to deliver this child."

Mr. Joseph looked perplexed. "What do you mean, 'position'?"

Elizabeth laughed lightly. "Men are so incompetent in these matters," she said with a wink. "Did you think Mrs. Joseph would simply leisurely lie in this bed and your child would make an appearance in its own good time?"

Mr. Joseph stammered, "I…I'd not thought…thought much on it. What must Mary and I do?"

"You're about to learn that men are not truly the stronger sex," Elizabeth teased.

"Absolutely," Mary added. "No man would tolerate such changes to his body." She lovingly spread her fingers across her abdomen's expanse.

The ladies would've continued their teasing, but when another pain racked Mary, Elizabeth moved everything to the floor before the hearth. She placed bowls of water, soap, several piles of clean rags, Darcy's razor, and two leather cords nearby. On the table, she'd positioned more water, cloths, and towels.

"What do you require of me, Mrs. Darcy?" Joseph asked anxiously.

"First, I need for you to remove your boots, coat, waistcoat, and cravat. If you wish to change your clothes, this would be the time. Likely, anything you have on shall be ruined by the time we finish."

Joseph nodded and disappeared behind the screens. Looking very relaxed, a few minutes later, he reappeared. "I'm at your disposal, Mrs. Darcy," he said with an embarrassed shrug.

"Let's assist Mary to a place before the fire."

The man easily lifted his wife from the bed. "Then what?" he asked as he placed Mary on the feather-stuffed mattress.

"You will sit on the floor and place Mary on your lap."

The woman looked up suddenly. "Are you certain, Mrs. Darcy?"

Elizabeth laughed nervously. "Not really. But one cannot exist in a house with four sisters and numerous aunts without hearing stories of delivering children. I assisted my sister Jane recently, but Mrs. Bingley had a birthing chair available. We've no such convenience so I am relying on instinct and on bits of information I learned when I eavesdropped on my mother and Aunt Philips, as well as my Biblical studies."

Elizabeth's words stunned Joseph. "The *Bible?*"

"Saying she delivered Jane on her knees, my mother once complained about the pampering of women today. So, I assumed it's possible for a woman to deliver upon her knees. Then I thought of Rachel in *Genesis*," Elizabeth explained.

Mr. Joseph nodded. "When Rachel plans to have a child through her maid, she is desperate. She would use Biliah as a surrogate. 'Here is my maid Biliah,'" he recited the words. "'Go into her that she may bear upon my knees, and even I may have children through her.'"

"We cannot expect Mary to suffer childbirth's pains on her knees, but we need to elevate her. So, Mr. Joseph, you will be our *Rachel* and hold your wife on your lap. Mary, you will be our *Biliah* and bring forth our Christmas baby."

As Elizabeth finished her explanation, Mary contracted in pain, clawing at her husband's arm. Without another word, Mr. Joseph lifted her to his lap, placing her back along his chest. "I have you," he cooed and eased her head to rest on his shoulder. "Our child is coming, Mary. We will see it through together."

Unceremoniously, Elizabeth eased Mary's legs apart. "This shan't be comfortable, but we're not the first women to deliver a child under less than pristine conditions," she said as much to herself as to Mrs. Joseph.

"How much longer?" Mary gasped as she fought for breath.

"An hour. Maybe two," Elizabeth said with more confidence than she actually possessed. Reaching for the hem of Mary's gown, Elizabeth said tentatively, "This shall be the first of the uncomfortable situations. I must take a look to see if the child is prepared for his entrance into the world."

Closing her eyes tightly in apparent embarrassment, Mary nodded her agreement, and Elizabeth did what she thought never to do: look upon another woman's nakedness. Surprisingly, it wasn't as repulsive as she had expected. She couldn't say she felt comfortable with the experience, but she no longer saw life through the eyes of a naive girl. Elizabeth knew the marriage bed's pleasures, and she realized God had made women for this purpose. The Lord had designed a woman's body to carry a child to term. Mary was the vessel. That's how Elizabeth would view this experience. "You've begun to open for the child," she said matter-of-factly.

Mr. Joseph stroked his wife's hair. "I'm so proud of you, Mary. You've not complained or fussed through this. I'd have you safe. Earlier, Mrs. Darcy told you to vent your pain. From now on, I expect you to scream your beautiful head off. No more holding it in. I'm capable of loving a woman who sheds a few tears. You don't need to be strong for me." He rocked her easily.

Mrs. Joseph squeezed his hand. "They'll hear me in Newcastle." Turning to Elizabeth, who sat relaxed at her feet, Mary said, "Tell me about your Mr. Darcy. What type of man has won your heart, Elizabeth?"

CHAPTER 9

❧∾ ❧∾ ❧∾

"DID I SEE LADY CATHERINE leaving my brother's study?" Georgiana asked Edward when she cornered him in the upper hall.

Edward's eyes narrowed. "Yes, Her Ladyship sought me out as I used Fitz's desk to write and frank my letter to the Earl and my report to the general."

Georgiana frowned back. "May I ask Her Ladyship's purpose? I worry our aunt intends some mischief."

"I cannot speak to Lady Catherine's Pemberley mission. I've spoken to her firmly regarding her family responsibility, but no one can hope to know Her Ladyship's frame of mind." Edward sighed in exasperation. "That wasn't our aunt's objective today," he continued. "Today, Lady Catherine expressed her concern regarding your presentation."

"You've been on English soil for less than six and thirty hours, and our aunt bothers you with such details," Georgiana said incredulously. "Sometimes…" she groaned.

Edward caressed her cheek. "Sometimes what, Love?"

"Sometimes, I wish people would allow me to choose my own future." Georgiana resisted the urge to stomp her foot in frustration. "At the moment, I wish Lady Catherine had never come to Derby for the festive days."

Edward scowled deeply. "I wouldn't have you upset, Georgie. I've informed Her Ladyship that Darcy will address your needs when the time proves necessary. Either Mrs. Darcy or my mother will serve as your sponsor."

She knew she should express her gratitude for his advocacy, but Georgiana had never wanted a Season. She wanted the man standing before her. Tears misted her eyes. "I thank you for your attempt to stifle our aunt's maneuverings."

"Then how have I unhinged your composure?" Edward pressed, his mouth's corners turned down. "Tell me what you truly want, Georgiana. Whatever it is, I'll move the heavens to make it so."

She gave him a chagrined smile. "If anyone could fulfill my dreams, it would be you; but I'm no longer a little girl. A new doll shan't satisfy me." She gave herself a good firm shake. Impulsively, Georgiana rose on her tiptoes to kiss his cheek. "I came to offer my gratitude for your arrangements for the skating party. It'll be a grand entertainment." With that, Georgiana scurried away, making a point of adding a sway to her hips. After all, Edward was watching.

~ ~ ~

Elizabeth briefly closed her eyes and brought forth her husband's image. "You may question my intelligence when I tell you that it took Mr. Darcy some six months to make inroads into my prejudice against him." As she spoke, Elizabeth kept an eye on the mantel's clock. Spotting the curious rise of Mary's eyebrow, Elizabeth nodded. "It's true: I tried desperately to dislike the man."

"A man of Mr. Darcy's consequence?" Mr. Joseph asked as he adjusted his wife's position.

"Oh, quite so," Elizabeth said playfully. "My father's a gentleman; I'm a gentleman's daughter; in that respect, Mr. Darcy and I are equals. But where the late Lady Anne Darcy was an Earl's youngest child, my maternal aunts and uncles are country lawyers and clergymen. Our consequence is quite below that of Mr. Darcy's family, and I allowed my own insecurities to blind me to my husband's goodness. In those early days, with conceit, I thought my judgment impeccable." Elizabeth paused to observe Mary's reaction to her latest contractions.

"Go on," the woman gasped and clung tightly to her husband's hand. "Tell us more."

Elizabeth bit her bottom lip and went through a mental list of what to expect next. She tried to remember all the details of Jane's delivery. "I shan't bore you with the specifics of our coming together," she began before adjusting Mary's position again. "Let's say there was a great deal of drama, as well as some laughable moments." Elizabeth continued her recitation to distract Mary from the current situation's dire possibilities. "But you didn't ask how we found each other. You asked how I knew that Mr. Darcy owned my heart. It was my husband's sense of honor that solidified my admiration."

"I would expect nothing less," Joseph said breathily as his wife jabbed him in the ribs.

Elizabeth thought this the most bizarre conversation of her memory, but she did not hesitate to keep it going. "Please don't confuse honor with respect. Respect is given because we like a person, and we can withhold it from someone who displeases us, but that's not what the *Bible* teaches us of honor."

"Honor thy mother and thy father," Mr. Joseph stated.

"Exactly," Elizabeth declared. "That's how I knew Mr. Darcy would be a wonderful husband and father. I witnessed how my dear Fitzwilliam has devoted his life to honoring his own parents." She shot a quick glance toward the room's door. She had no doubt that Darcy remained outside in the darkened hallway. He considered it his province to protect those he loved. "And Mr. Darcy has served as his sister's guardian for the last eight years. Miss Darcy blossoms under her brother's administrations. You should hear him praise Georgiana's potential."

Mary grimaced, but she managed to say, "Honor has a…a language all its own."

They all paused to allow Mary to work her way through another spasm. "That's good, Mary," Elizabeth encouraged. She handed Mr. Joseph a damp cloth to wipe his wife's face. With everything settled again, Elizabeth returned to her story. Everything was coming together. From the beginning, she had found Mary to be a woman who loved a good tale. That's why Elizabeth had asked her husband to read to the woman earlier. During that time, Mrs. Joseph had progressed through the stages of her delivery in a relaxed atmosphere. Now, this discussion on honor served the same purpose. Instead of fighting the pain, Mary embraced it. Elizabeth actually began to believe that together they would see this child to a healthy entrance.

"When Mr. Darcy speaks, my husband speaks honorably. His servants and his tenants accept the honor he freely gives them, and they respond with a sincere desire to help Mr. Darcy achieve his vision. My husband is the type of man who speaks *with* a person rather than *to* him, and when he speaks of someone of his acquaintance, he does so to the person's face. Therefore, those who know him serve Mr. Darcy with passion."

"Honor is God's greatest gift," Mr. Joseph observed.

"Honor elevates," Elizabeth whispered as she turned her gaze toward the door. "It speaks with affection."

～⊗～ ～⊗～ ～⊗～

"Lieutenant, do you have a moment?" The colonel had found his aide in the billiards room playing a solitary game.

The officer had come to attention. "I'm at your service, Sir."

"No need for military protocol, Southland." Edward chose a cue stick from those displayed. "How about a game?"

"Of course, Sir." The lieutenant gathered the balls and placed them in the rack. "Have I done something to displease you, Sir? Your expression says you're troubled."

Edward laughed uncomfortably. "I'm not a man who easily expresses his chagrin." He chalked his stick. Taking a deep breath to steady his strike and his resolve, he said, "I came to apologize for my earlier remarks." The balls scattered to the table's four corners, and Edward moved to line up his second shot.

"There's no need, Colonel." Southland waited patiently for his commanding officer to miss. "You spoke from regard for your family. I cannot fault that notion. I should've practiced more restraint. Call it my overwhelming joy at being home again. There was nothing about America that I found comfortable: not the society, and not the conflict. I've thought of England and Lewes every day for over a year; then we arrived in Liverpool, and within hours I was speaking to someone who held similar experiences. It's a poor excuse, Colonel, and I'll refrain from anything beyond polite conversation with Miss De Bourgh."

Edward finished his third shot. "So you don't find my cousin attractive?" he asked tentatively.

The lieutenant leaned against the wall. "That's a loaded question, Colonel." His voice held his suspicion. "If I say that Miss De Bourgh offers no allure, you'll wonder how a man could fail to see your cousin's merits. And if I speak openly of Miss De Bourgh's appeal, then you'll choose another reprimand."

Edward straightened and took a close look at his subordinate. "You have good reason to be cautious, Southland. I'm unsure of my own motives." The colonel paused to gather his thoughts. "I'd take it as a personal offense if someone trifled with Anne's affections, but a part of me would like to see my cousin know a flirtation's pleasure. However, a person participating in such a dalliance must be aware that my aunt has denied Anne many of the events in which my cousin could develop into a sophisticated young woman. Does any of this make sense, Lieutenant?"

Southland stepped away from the wall. "Admittedly, Sir, your message is garbled. It appears you're extending your permission for me to further a relationship with Miss De Bourgh."

"But I'm not encouraging you to give Anne false hopes," Edward clarified. "I'll be brutally honest, Southland. Anne is of a gentle nature, and I suspect she'll take the slightest of attentions as a serious plight, which means my cousin is very susceptible to heartbreak. Therefore, although I truly believe Anne needs to know a man's regard, I wouldn't wish her to suffer. My feelings in this matter are mixed."

The lieutenant placed his stick on the table. "I'd enjoy the opportunity to know Miss De Bourgh better." His gaze met Edward's. "You do realize, Sir, that I've no title and no profession beyond my service to my country."

"I understand perfectly, Southland." Edward squeezed the man's shoulder. "You must decide whether to pursue the connection. It'll not affect our relationship unless you purposely hurt Anne."

ᨒ ᨒ ᨒ

"Mr. Bennet, might I request a few moments of your time?" Winkler asked as the guests gathered for afternoon tea. When Mr. Bennet's eyebrow rose in curiosity, Winkler quickly added, "Privately."

Mr. Bennet nodded his agreement. "This way, Winkler." He led the clergyman across the hall. "Will this do?" They had stepped into an empty drawing room.

The man glanced about nervously. "Yes, thank you, Sir." He paused awkwardly. "Perhaps we might sit."

"Of course." Mr. Bennet led the way to a cluster of chairs. Once they settled themselves comfortably, Bennet asked, "What might I do for you, young man?"

Winkler nervously cleared his throat. "I wished to speak to you, Sir, regarding your daughter Catherine. Miss Catherine and I have become acquainted over the past two years; with each of her Pemberley visits, I've found my affections for your daughter have increased. I'd like your permission, Sir, to court Miss Catherine with the hopes of making her my wife."

"You hold a *tendre* for Kitty?" Mr. Bennet asked with amusement.

"Yes, Sir."

"You will excuse my surprise, Mr. Winkler. Although Kitty has her merits, I have never considered her as a woman who might engender the regard of a sensible young man. I mean, your wife must have additional responsibilities beyond her role as mistress of your household."

"She would," Winkler acknowledged.

Mr. Bennet shook his head in disbelief. "It wasn't so long ago that Mrs. Bennet allowed Kitty and my youngest Lydia to be given up to nothing but amusement and vanity. My wife permitted our daughters to dispose of their time in the most idle and frivolous manner and to adopt any opinions that came their way. Love, flirtation, and officers filled their heads."

Mr. Winkler frowned. "But was that before any of your daughters married? If I recall, Mrs. Wickham took her vows over two years ago."

Mr. Bennet laughed lightly. "I suppose it was. At Longbourn, it seems we're always preparing for a wedding. The time goes too quickly for an old man."

Winkler smiled at last. "My father refuses to realize that my sister is two and twenty. To him, Rose is a willowy girl of twelve."

Mr. Bennet sat back into his chair. "Then I must reconsider how I see Kitty," he said easily. "It'll be an effort, but I'm willing to broaden my opinions."

Winkler appeared confused by Mr. Bennet's witticism. "I'm certain that Miss Catherine would easily fill the role of wife."

"I need no convincing, Winkler," Mr. Bennet said. "I concede my earlier error."

Again, Winkler was flustered. "I have…I've spoken to Miss Catherine, and we've agreed to a time when I might court her. This will allow Miss Catherine time to observe what will be required of her as my wife. I've plans to educate the village children and wish to organize a charity for our elderly. I'd expect your daughter to embrace those initiatives and add her own special insights. Of course, I wish to speak to Mr. Darcy also. As Mrs. Darcy's sister, Miss Catherine could hold great sway in the neighborhood."

"It would appear that you've thought this through thoroughly. Mrs. Bennet and I would like to see Kitty well settled, and having her close to Jane and Elizabeth would be to Kitty's advantage. I've no objection to your suit, Winkler. It'll please Mrs. Bennet, as well."

"We would wait for Mr. Darcy's approval before announcing our understanding," Winkler said.

"Then I'll refrain from informing Mrs. Bennet of this fortuitous event. My wife dotes on her daughters' successes," Mr. Bennet said in renewed amusement.

Mr. Winkler stood and extended his hand. "Thank you, Sir. Perhaps we might carve out time during your stay to speak of possible marriage settlements. With your permission I'd ask for Mr. Darcy's participation in that interview. He prefers to be made aware of anything affecting his position as Pemberley's master, and he's my patron."

"Count yourself lucky, Sir, that the great man's aunt is not the one from whom you must seek favor."

~∞~ ~∞~ ~∞~

"Miss Darcy and I have made arrangements for our Christmastide celebrations in lieu of Mr. Darcy's presence," Edward explained to the group gathered for afternoon tea. "Of course, we'll join Mr. Winkler for services, and then return to Pemberley for an abundant meal. Knowing Mr. Darcy, there'll be plenty of wassail and appropriate trinkets."

"How about the Christmas pudding?" Mrs. Bennet asked.

"Elizabeth, Mrs. Reynolds, and I spent much of the Stir Up Sunday creating Mrs. Oliver's special recipe," Georgiana explained.

Kitty enjoyed a party, so she added, "Shall there be snapdragon and charades?"

"Between now and Twelfth Night, there'll be plenty of games and music," Edward assured.

"Roast goose?" Mr. Bennet asked.

"Absolutely," Georgiana said. "And if anyone has a special request, I'll ask Mrs. Oliver to do her best to meet it."

Mr. Manneville chuckled. "Even very American delicacies, Miss Darcy?" he taunted.

"Within reason, Mr. Manneville," Georgiana said tartly.

Edward added, "Tomorrow, we should be able to skate, and on Christmas Eve, we'll hang the holly and other greenery."

Georgiana left her position near the open door and joined Edward before the hearth. She slid her hand into the crook of his arm, and Edward automatically cupped her hand with his free one. "Of course, the Tenants' Ball is set for Boxing Day. My brother and Mrs. Darcy shall entertain his cottagers and many from the village. It's great fun—very much like a country assembly," Georgiana declared.

"Without even the possibility of the local gentry," Lady Catherine grumbled.

"Very true, Aunt," Edward interrupted her possible tirade. "But that's what makes the Pemberley Tenants' Ball so enjoyable. No one has to worry about the *ton*'s arbitrary rules. A young man can show his intended his attentions without the two-set rule coming into play."

Lady Catherine scowled, "Commonness."

Tightening her hold on Edward's arm, Georgiana clarified, "It's not necessary that you make an appearance. Although Fitzwilliam would welcome your presence, there'll be plenty of food and entertainment at the main house. However, your attendance would bring my brother a great honor in his tenants' eyes."

"The Bennets will be happy to partake of Mr. Darcy's hospitality," Mr. Bennet declared.

"As will the Bingleys," Charles announced.

"I'd like to attend," Anne's quiet voice stayed the room.

"You most certainly shall not!" Lady Catherine roared. "Who shall protect you from the riff-raff?"

Edward smiled secretly. "If that's your worry, Your Ladyship,

I'll ask Lieutenant Southland to escort Anne. You wouldn't mind, would you, Lieutenant?"

Southland bowed to Anne. "It would be my honor, Miss De Bourgh."

"See, Aunt, that was easy to resolve. The lieutenant will guard Anne from ordinary connections," Edward said cynically.

"Everyone is welcome, but no one must decide tonight," Georgiana said judiciously. "What the colonel and I wish to convey is the Darcys' wish for an enjoyable Christmastide."

❧ ❧ ❧

"I didn't hear you express an opinion of Mr. Darcy's Tenants' Ball, Miss Bingley." Everyone had dispersed to late afternoon activities; Manneville had joined Caroline on a settee opposite the hearth.

"I thought you'd joined the lieutenant, Mr. Manneville." Caroline said in feigned indifference.

"I begged a reprieve from the cold," he confessed. "And you didn't answer my query. That seems to be a pattern," he teased. "Do you hold no interest in Mr. Darcy's Tenants' celebration?"

Miss Bingley shook her head. "It's not my preference, but I'm sure my brother and Mrs. Bingley shall insist that we participate; therefore, I'll be committed to make an appearance."

"Why is the event repugnant?" Manneville probed.

Her brow lowered in a frown. "I don't know how to explain without sounding extremely prejudiced." Miss Bingley paused briefly. "And, of course, I don't know why I might choose to share such intimate thoughts with you, Sir."

"Maybe because you know that I'll not judge you," Manneville said quietly. "We Americans see issues differently from our British counterparts."

As if embarrassed, Miss Bingley shifted. "You must understand, Sir, that my father sacrificed much to build his fortune—the fortune Charles inherited. He worked countless hours and dealt with scrupulous as well as unscrupulous clients, all to give his wife and children a better life. There was a time when all any of us could hope for was to live on Society's fringe. All our wealth could not open doors, but slowly that has changed.

"To aid our transitions, my father sent Charles to university and my sister and me to a private seminary in London. We learned to associate with people of rank. It may sound petty, but to attend Tenants' celebrations and to associate with those of lesser connections seems a betrayal to all my father wished for us."

Manneville maintained his teasing tone. "I'm thankful to hear your explanation, Miss Bingley. I feared that jealousy precipitated your objections."

"Jealousy!" she gasped. "To whom would I direct my disdain?"

"I'd heard," Manneville said softly, "that you'd once set your sights on Mr. Darcy."

She demanded, "Who speaks of my private life?"

Manneville chuckled. "Mrs. Bennet is only too happy to elevate her daughters' virtues at the expense of others."

"Vile, disgusting woman," Caroline growled.

"Yes," Manneville said, "the good lady regaled me with tales of your deceit in matters most personal—of your separating the former Miss Bennet from your brother and of your unsuccessful manipulations to land our host."

Caroline turned red with anger. "That old tabby," she spit out the words. "With such apparent connections, could anyone criticize me for dividing Charles from Miss Bennet?"

Manneville scoffed. "Then you don't deny the rumors, Miss Bingley?"

Realizing she'd said too much, Caroline calmed her expression. With a deep sigh of exasperation, she confessed, "I have no wish of denying that I attempted to separate my brother from Miss Bennet. My only regret is that Charles spent several months suffering from disappointed hopes. I never wanted that for him." She raised her chin in defiance.

Manneville tilted his head back and laughed soundly. "Good

for you, Miss Bingley. I admire a plucky woman—one who knows what she wants and is willing to do whatever is necessary to achieve it. Too many women bemoan their fates."

Obviously shocked by his response, Caroline stammered, "But I was…I was unsuccessful…unsuccessful in both cases."

"We know disappointments," he said as he stood and extended his hand. "What I want to know, Miss Bingley, is whether you're the type of person who can focus her energies elsewhere and earn different fortunes." He held her gaze for a few seconds before adding, "I thought I might take in the splendor of Mr. Darcy's conservatory. Would you care to join me?"

She slid her hand into his. Manneville helped her to her feet. "Different fortunes? Of what type of fortunes do we speak, Sir?" She hooked her arm through his.

"Not houses or land or tenants," he said as they strolled toward the door. "Connections and manipulations. Those are the real assets."

ᵔᵃᵔ ᵔᵃᵔ ᵔᵃᵔ

"Lieutenant," Mrs. Jenkinson said as she stepped up behind him. "May we speak privately?"

"Of course, Ma'am." He glanced about the open foyer. "Why do we not step into the music room? At this time of day, the ladies are likely finished with their lessons."

Mrs. Jenkinson gave a curt nod and turned toward the room. Southland watched her go before removing his outer garments. He'd just returned to the main house after adding a few inches of water to the ice pond. The cold had seeped into his bones, and he desperately needed a drink, but the lieutenant would speak to Miss De Bourgh's companion first. All through the afternoon, he had recalled the colonel's conversation, as well as the easy machination of his commanding officer. It seemed so perfect that Roman suspected a gambit. He'd considered Rosings Park and the De Bourgh family his own personal Holy Grail, and now that the proverbial carrot dangled before his eyes, he could see all too clearly how faded were reality's edges: The De Bourghs did not lead an ideal life. Handing the Pemberley butler his gloves, Roman followed the matronly Mrs. Jenkinson toward the empty room.

Entering the well-appointed room, Roman walked leisurely toward the hearth. His instinct told him that Lady Catherine had sent her servant to warn him away from her daughter. Warming himself by the dying fire, he turned to the waiting gentlewoman. "How might I serve you, Mrs. Jenkinson? I hope your appearance doesn't indicate that Miss De Bourgh is feeling poorly."

Mrs. Jenkinson sat primly in her chair, but Southland noted her nervousness. "Miss De Bourgh is quite well, Lieutenant," she said tentatively.

"I'm pleased to hear it, Ma'am." Southland casually propped his forearm on the mantel. "I suppose we should proceed straight to the crux of what you were sent to say to me: Her Ladyship wishes me to stay away from Miss De Bourgh. Am I correct, Ma'am?"

Mrs. Jenkinson blustered. "I've no…no knowledge of Lady Catherine's disapproval, Lieutenant. I…I wished to speak to you of my own accord."

"Your own accord, Ma'am? I fear I don't understand." Southland abandoned his attempt at indifference. He came to sit beside the woman.

"I've but a few minutes before I must return to my duties," the lady said. "Therefore, I pray you'll forgive my abruptness." Mrs. Jenkinson nervously ran a handkerchief through her fingers.

"I'm accustomed to plain speaking, Ma'am," he assured her.

The lady swallowed hard and then brought her gaze to meet his. "I've served as Miss De Bourgh's companion for more than a dozen years. She's as dear to me as my own daughter." She paused briefly. "Therefore, I wish to protect her from those who would practice a deception."

"And you think me a bounder?"

Again, Mrs. Jenkinson's back stiffened. "I don't wish to make assumptions, Lieutenant, but your recent attention to Miss De Bourgh hasn't gone unnoticed."

"I'm well aware of Colonel Fitzwilliam's initial objection to my conversations with his cousin, but he's assured me that he's withdrawn his opposition. Has the colonel returned to his earlier estimation?" Southland, too, held himself in ready alert.

Mrs. Jenkinson's frown lines met. "I have no knowledge of Colonel Fitzwilliam's opinions. He's not spoken them before me."

"If not Lady Catherine or Colonel Fitzwilliam, does Miss De Bourgh wish me to withdraw from our acquaintance?"

"It's not my dear Anne's wish either," the lady confessed. "And before you ask, I would express no opposition of my own if your friendship is true."

Southland smiled knowingly. "You wish to determine whether I offer Miss De Bourgh a false face."

"I do, Lieutenant. Despite Miss De Bourgh's handsome features, my dearest Anne has had few male companions. She is untested, and I wish to know your nature, Lieutenant Southland."

"May I speak honestly, Ma'am?" The lieutenant sat forward to assure intimacy.

"I demand that you do, Sir."

Southland nodded his agreement. "I've heard of Rosings Park and the De Bourghs all my life, and I wish to know more of each. Beyond that, I have no plans. Call it curiosity. Call it idiosyncrasy. I cannot truly explain my interest beyond those facts. For years, the Rosings' family has held a certain mystery, but to be truthful, I never anticipated finding Miss De Bourgh so attractive, nor did I expect to enjoy thoroughly my few brief conversations with the lady."

"The De Bourghs have their faults, Lieutenant. It wouldn't be wise to idealize the life found at Rosings Park," she warned.

"I'm aware of that folly," the lieutenant conceded. "What I'd hoped was to spend time with Miss De Bourgh—to leave the ideal behind and to embrace reality. If the acquaintance proves to the lady's liking, then we'll see where to go from there."

Mrs. Jenkinson's mouth set in a firm line. "That may be difficult, Sir. It's my understanding that you have no title. Lady Catherine isn't likely to approve."

The lieutenant sat back into the chair's cushions. "If things were to progress to that point, I would remind Miss De Bourgh that she's of age. Yet, it's too soon to speak of these matters. While at Pemberley, I would prefer to cultivate the acquaintance. If that's acceptable to you, Ma'am?" He grinned largely.

"I'll be watching you, Lieutenant Southland," Mrs. Jenkinson cautioned. "I'll allow no one to injure Anne."

"I'd expect nothing less, Mrs. Jenkinson."

✎ ✎ ✎

"I need for you to lean back a bit more, Mr. Joseph," Elizabeth instructed. She bumped Mary's knee to open the lady's legs further. "I can see the head. Your child has dark hair," she said nervously. Over the last hour, Elizabeth had questioned God's reason more than once. How could He place her in such a situation? She knew nothing about delivering a healthy child. But here she was, offering advice to both mother and father. *God possesses a unique sense of humor,* she thought.

Mary let out a toe-curling scream. Her stoicism had faded with the pain's intensity. Now, she cried out freely. The spasms were only seconds apart. Less than ten minutes earlier, Mary's press had sent a bloody liquid into a waiting bowl. Elizabeth had quickly changed out the bowls and returned to her position on the floor. "Mary, listen to me," she demanded. "With the next pain, instead of screaming, I want you to lock your jaw and hold in your breath. Concentrate on pushing with your stomach muscles. You might even lean forward."

"Are you certain, Mrs. Darcy?" a very ragged-looking Mr. Joseph asked.

"It is paramount to bringing the child into the world." Elizabeth double-checked the proximity of the razor and the towels she had placed in waiting. "A few more times, Mary, and your child shall be in your arms."

Elizabeth watched the exhausted expression leave the woman's face, and paroxysms of pain take its place. Mary bit down on her bottom lip and pressed hard. "It's coming," Elizabeth coaxed. "You may let out your breath," she instructed. What followed was an explosion of air preceding a long wail of release.

"Very good, Mary." Elizabeth touched the child's matted hair with her fingertips. "Catch your breath, for you must do it again." Mary nodded weakly and gulped for air.

Soon, the next pain and then the next and the next arrived. Each brought further enervation on Mary's part, as well as bringing more of the child into view. "The shoulders are clear," Elizabeth reported as she supported the baby's body. "Once more," she encouraged. "Once more should do it, Mary. We're almost there."

"It is dark outside," Mr. Joseph said out of nowhere.

His wife moaned, "What does it matter?"

Mr. Joseph laughed heartily. "It doesn't, my dear. It was a bizarre attempt to draw your mind away and to give you strength to do the most miraculous thing a woman can do." He kissed the top of his wife's head.

Mary stiffened and pressed her hips upward. With a surge, the child slid into Elizabeth's waiting hands. "Oh, my," Elizabeth blurted and quickly turned the child over. Placing it on the clean cloths she had prepared, she began to wipe the blood and mucus from its body.

"Is it well?" Mr. Joseph demanded. "The child?"

Elizabeth ignored his question. "Stay," she ordered when he started to move. "Mary's body still has a job to complete." All the time her fingers pried at the child's small crevices with the soft cloths. "Come on, Little One," she cajoled.

She lifted the child away from Mary's body as far as the umbilical cord would allow. "I need help," she mumbled.

"I will…" Mr. Joseph began again.

"No!" Elizabeth snapped. "Hold Mary. She has more pain to endure." She turned her head toward the door. "Fitzwilliam," she called. "I need you." Immediately, the door opened. Her magnificent husband was where she expected him to be.

"What do you require? Is the child well?"

With her gaze, she indicated to Mr. Joseph to drop the sheet over his wife's body. Then Elizabeth ordered, "You must help me cut the cord."

In the next second, Darcy was across the room and kneeling at her side. "Tell me what to do."

She stretched out the cord again. "Tie off the cord twice; once to stop the blood from Mrs. Joseph; once to stop the blood to the child. Then cut the cord between the two. Quickly, Fitzwilliam, so I can tend the baby." Darcy did as she had instructed. Meanwhile, Elizabeth held the child close and began to urge the baby to take its first breath. "Come on, Sweet One." She rubbed its back and pressed harder.

Completing the cut, Darcy whispered, "I have the child." Darcy took the baby from her grasp. "See to Mrs. Joseph." Then her husband walked away, the infant close to his chest. With an air of confidence, he swung the child around and laid it on the bed. "You can do this," he said softly as he blew in the stone-still face. As she looked on, Darcy massaged the baby's chest, placed a finger in its mouth to open it, and blew again. He bent closer and blew a third time. Finally, the Lord rewarded his effort. A twittering chirp escaped. "That's right," he whispered gravelly. "Once more." He blew gently into the radish-red face. Finally, the infant opened its mouth and let out its own cry.

Darcy picked it up and turned to those on the other side of the room—only to discover a strange tableau staring intently at him. The picture of the three weary adults struck him as amusing. He laughed easily. "I assume you would like to meet Mr. Joseph's son."

Chapter 10

≈ ≈ ≈

ELIZABETH RUSHED FORWARD to take the child from his arms. "My Goodness, what a miracle," she said as she loosely wrapped the baby in a large cloth. "Come, Little One, and meet your parents."

Behind her, Mr. Joseph rearranged his wife in his arms to better support her. "Our son, Mary," he whispered hoarsely. "We have a son."

When Elizabeth turned, she was startled to witness the pure love between a man and a woman, and for a moment, she wondered if her love for Darcy was as evident. Mr. Joseph caressed Mary's cheek and stroked the damp hair from her face. His gentleness spoke volumes, and even though she knew Darcy loved her equally as well, Elizabeth drew the painful conclusion that without a child, something would always be missing. Swallowing back the loneliness, she hurried to deposit the child in Mrs. Joseph's outstretched arms. "Master Joseph," she said softly and kissed the screeching child's forehead.

His mother's finger stroking the boy's cheek brought him the protection he had expected, and immediately, the child silenced. "He's beautiful, Matthew," she cooed.

Mr. Joseph reached around her and gently touched the baby's tiny fingers. "The most beautiful child God ever created," he rasped.

As Elizabeth looked on, the child's fingers wrapped around Mr. Joseph's pinky. Despite her happiness, she swayed in place, emotions overwhelming her. Immediately, Darcy was behind her. His comforting embrace encircled her, and Elizabeth allowed her husband to gently pull her against him. Darcy kissed the side of her neck. "If I've not told you recently," he whispered close to her ear, "let me say how utterly amazing I find you."

Elizabeth turned in his arms and collapsed against him, the adrenaline draining from her composure. Darcy held her tightly. "I'm frightened," she murmured into his shoulder.

Darcy chuckled. "At least, you overcame the fear until the Josephs had their son."

Elizabeth raised her chin to stare into his countenance. It was the face that she most trusted—the face of one who would never judge her—of one who accepted her foibles. "I did it," she said in a gush of air. "Can you believe it, Fitzwilliam?"

"I always believed it," he whispered. Darcy caressed her chin. "If anyone could save Mrs. Joseph's life, it would be you." Her husband glanced over her shoulder at where the Josephs still cuddled their child. "Let us step away and give Mr. and Mrs. Joseph a moment alone with their son."

Elizabeth's first instinct was to return to the woman, but seeing the Madonna-like look upon Mary's face stilled her. She nodded and permitted Darcy to lead her to the other side of the room. They sequestered themselves behind the screen, and Darcy brought his wife into his arms. For Elizabeth, the exquisite feel of his strength bolstered her own. Instinctively, she raised her chin and accepted Darcy's kiss. Gentle and loving, her husband's embrace spoke of his devotion. "I love you," she said as he released her mouth.

"And I you," he said softly. They continued to speak in whispers. He cupped her chin in his palm and slid his hand down her slender neck. "How did you know I waited outside the door?" He smiled lovingly at her.

Elizabeth shrugged nonchalantly. "You're not the type to spend your time drinking away the hours. Nor are you of the nature to desert a person for whom you care," she declared. Elizabeth traced his mouth with her fingertips. "And I'm vain enough to believe I claim your affections."

"Not vanity, my love." Darcy kissed her fingertips.

Elizabeth smiled easily. "I knew you'd be near if I needed you." She went on her tiptoes to brush his lips with hers. "How did you know what to do to start the baby's breathing? When I attended Jane, the midwife rubbed the twins' backs."

"Do you not recall that Georgiana came early?"

"Now, I do, but I don't understand the significance. Surely, no one permitted you access to the birthing room."

"Although I wasn't there, my parents often reminisced over Georgiana's worldly entrance. Despite warnings from the previous Countess about his inappropriate actions, my father insisted on being with Mother. The midwife threatened to do away with him." This story was a pleasant memory for her husband, and Elizabeth delighted in his relaxed countenance.

"With Georgiana's early entrance, they were all caught unawares. My sister's delivery was reputedly a speedy one. Small and lithe as she is, Georgiana's only complication was her resistance to taking her first breath. The midwife pronounced her dead, but father would hear none of it. He willed Georgiana to life. He rubbed her chest and, literally, blew into her mouth and nose—saying later that her first breath smelled of the brandy he had downed to shore up his nerves."

"Amazing," Elizabeth said.

"Anyway, I've heard the tale over and over. Georgiana loved to hear Father tell it, and he embellished the fact to his daughter's delight; but, when I took Joseph's child in my hands, I did what my father had done. It seemed the most prudent action."

"God works in the oddest ways," Elizabeth declared. "If not for my ready acquaintance with Mrs. Joseph, she'd have been on her knees giving birth in a stable. If not for your family history, the Josephs' son might have followed the way of so many children born too early."

Darcy caught her hand and brought it to rest over his heart. "I cannot conceive of another angel as beautiful as you, my love."

"Would you see to the boy while I help Mrs. Joseph? She has yet to pass the birth." It was not a conversation women normally had with men, but somehow for Elizabeth, it seemed right. When she delivered their child, Darcy would be by her side. As his father had attended Lady Anne, Darcy would attend her. She had no doubt of that fact. Unlike other men who waited downstairs, smoking cigars and drinking toasts, Darcy would be her partner, and if their child suffered, it was his able hands she wanted caressing the baby.

"As you wish. I'll wait here." Elizabeth nodded and started away, but Darcy caught her arm. "What of the cord?" he whispered.

Elizabeth patted his hand. It was reassuring to know that even her confident husband held the occasional doubt. "The blood has likely drained from the opening. Cut it again to three to four inches in length. Leave the tie in place. It will dry up and fall away in a few days. This is normal."

"And the part attached to the mother?" he asked with curious embarrassment.

"Mrs. Joseph's body shall expel what remains of the child's sack within the next hour, and then she can begin to heal."

Elizabeth watched as he puzzled over what she had said. "Really? I never knew. This is not part of a university education," he mused.

"Neither is it conversation unmarried women share." Her eyes danced in amusement. "I'm sure none would consider marriage such a delightful solution if she possessed knowledge of childbirth's physical pain."

Darcy's eyebrow rose in question. "I imagine it might make it more difficult to convince some women," he taunted. "Luckily, you're not of the nature to refuse a man's suit nor to shrug away a challenge."

"Of course, not, Mr. Darcy." She offered a soft smirk. "I'm of the most amiable nature."

"And I'm blessed for it. Blessed indeed."

~ᴏᴏ~ ~ᴏᴏ~ ~ᴏᴏ~

Anne looked up as Southland entered the room. She had heard the rumors. The servants knew everything. Her companion and her cousin had each spoken to the lieutenant about their brief encounter yesterday. Anne didn't know the content of those conversations, but she suspected that her loved ones had warned the lieutenant from her. Men of lesser connections had been sent packing, and she knew the procedure. Unfortunately, her few suitors had abandoned her early on. Now, at the age of seven and twenty, she was quite clearly on the shelf. But Anne had resolved that if Southland showed any interest, she would seize the opportunity.

"Lieutenant," she smiled brightly. "It's delightful to have your company. Come and join me for tea."

The man bowed and came forward. "Thank you, Miss De Bourgh." He glanced about the room. "Should I send for a maid or your companion?"

Anne narrowed her eyes. "That won't be necessary, Lieutenant. I'd hate to worry Mrs. Jenkinson. The weather has taken her energy. Besides, the door remains open."

"If you're certain, Miss De Bourgh." He seated himself across from her, but he remained uncomfortable.

Anne spoke with the barest bit of irony in her tone. "I'm far from being a green girl, Lieutenant. I may converse with a gentleman without causing a scandal." She took a closer look at the man: Broad shoulders. Muscular chest. Several inches shorter than her cousin—an important fact for a woman of her height. Slim hips and firm thighs. Strong chin. Nose a bit too large. Dark lashes. Hairline high on his forehead. Dark hair with flecks of gold from sun exposure. Not handsome, but a most captivating countenance. An infectious, cheeky grin. Anne forced herself to smile as she handed him the teacup.

The lieutenant blinked quickly. "I never meant an offense, Miss De Bourgh. I recognize you're a lady of quality. I'd want no mark on your reputation."

"No offense taken, Lieutenant, but a reputation requires a certain amount of popular favor and influence. Admittedly, my family's good name gives me an unearned distinction; yet, we both are aware of my insignificance. Please, Sir. I don't wish to speak crudely, but I'd ask for honesty between us." Anne felt her lower lip tremble and her eyes mist with tears, but she continued on. It had been more than five years since any man had sought her company and more than eight since a man had proclaimed his affection for her. If by any chance the lieutenant found her interesting, Anne wouldn't shun his attentions, but she would instead embrace them on her terms. Her mother had sequestered her away, so the lieutenant was likely her last prospect. "I'd like to have your acquaintance, Sir. Is that what you wish also?" Having said the words she had practiced all morning, Anne immediately dropped her eyes. The effort to be bold had taken its toll on her. Her hands shook, and greyness crowded her vision. She fought for a calming breath.

"Miss De Bourgh?" The lieutenant's voice expressed his concern. When she did not look at him, the man was on his knees before her. Gently, he took the cup and saucer from her grasp. "Let me assist you," he said softly. "Please, Miss De Bourgh." Urgency laced his words as he caught her hand in his. "If my presence upsets you, I'll make my departure, but I'd see you well first."

Anne gulped for air. "I…I don't want you to depart."

His large hands held hers tightly. The gentleman leaned in and whispered in her ear. "I would remain if that's your wish."

Slowly, she made herself look at him. His closeness warmed her in ways she'd never experienced. "Then I wasn't mistaken. You wish my acquaintance?"

Southland's lips twitched. "I suspect either the colonel or your companion has spoken of their objections."

"Neither," she said quickly.

Disbelief shaped his lips. "I'd have difficulty believing that no one has warned you from me. I've no title, and I'm likely never to earn one."

"No, truly," she protested. "I overheard the servants speak of your heated discussion with my cousin." Their faces were but inches apart, and Anne's breath caught in her throat. The fact that his also hitched gave her encouragement.

Southland chuckled. "I'd forgotten the efficiency of the English serving class. It seems my approaching you yesterday has brought some notice."

"May I ask a question, Lieutenant?" she asked impulsively.

"Certainly, Miss De Bourgh."

"Why have you sought me out? Why me? Why now?" Anne took calming breaths to steady her nerves.

Southland released her hand and returned to his chair. "It's a complicated issue, and I'm not certain I can explain it. I've always desired the connection to your family—but not for the renown or the wealth. My cousin repeatedly extolled Sir Lewis's merits, and I've found the same excellence in the colonel's side of the family."

Anne frowned. "Would you expect excellence on my part?" The thought of her obvious deficiencies frightened her.

"Again, that's not exactly what I meant, Miss De Bourgh. My words may make you believe that I'm a bounder who seeks the connection, but it's much deeper than that." He paused. "As strange as it sounds," he said with a deep sigh, "it's been my belief since my childhood that I'd some day call Rosings Park home."

Anne counted to ten in her head and reversed the numbers before she answered. "Many might think yours a case for Bedlam, Lieutenant."

He smiled easily. "I suppose they would." Again, he paused briefly. "My only concern is whether you find my words crazy."

Her eyebrow rose in curiosity. "I'll have to consider the rationality of such a remark. Or the lack thereof." But Anne actually smiled at him. "When I asked for honesty…"

"You didn't expect what I offered," he finished her thought. Taking a deep breath of resignation, the lieutenant stood to make his departure. "Thank you, Miss De Bourgh, for sharing your tea and your caution. I'll take my leave." He bowed stiffly.

"Lieutenant." Ann made her decision without considering the consequences. "I'd thought to explore Mr. Darcy's library. I wonder if you might also be in need of a book?" She stood and straightened her dress's seams. "If so, we might discuss our favorites." Her heart pounded like that of a racehorse.

Southland let out relief's sigh. "Or the weather."

Anne glanced toward the lace-draped windows. "Oh, the weather is abominable. Could we not seek another more pleasant subject?"

"Absolutely, Miss De Bourgh. I'm your captive audience." Southland extended his arm, and Anne slid her hand into his elbow's crook. His muscles flexed, and she felt the anticipation of a new adventure.

~ぐ~ ~ぐ~ ~ぐ~

Roman couldn't believe his luck: Anne De Bourgh had accepted his arm. They would spend additional time together. *One wouldn't call the woman beautiful,* he thought, *but she was quite handsome in a fragile, delicate way. She was very pale—something a brisk walk in the country on a summer day would easily solve.*

But, on closer inspection, Roman realized that her paleness meant china-white skin—creamy, actually; soft and inviting to a man's touch. She had a pert little upturned nose, wide, doe-like eyes with elegantly long lashes, and her full lips, set too often in a firm line, were inviting when she smiled. Her long, slender neck led to soft shoulders and the delicious swell of her dress above her neckline. She was taller than he had expected, but still the lady's head only came to his shoulder.

It was with a great deal of pride that he escorted Miss De Bourgh through Pemberley's hall. It felt right—as if she belonged by his side. It was an unreasonable conclusion. In reality, they held less than a four and twenty hours' acquaintance, but that didn't matter.

For the first time in his life—since the time he first had heard his cousin speak of life at Hunsford Cottage—Roman breathed freely: This was where God had always wanted him to be.

∾ ∾ ∾

"A small gift from Nan," Elizabeth said as she handed the hastily made child's dressing gown to Mary. The woman had dutifully completed the delivery, and with Mrs. Washington's assistance, Elizabeth had helped to freshen Mary's clothing. Now, the new mother rested once again in the bed. She held the sleeping child in the bend of her arm.

"I'll thank the girl properly," Mrs. Joseph mumbled.

Elizabeth patted the lady's hand. "Why do you not rest?"

"You need rest also," Mrs. Joseph sleepily protested.

"First, I believe I'll go downstairs and have a proper supper with Mr. Darcy. I need time to rest my back." She stretched out her arms. "I'll send Mr. Joseph to sit with you."

"Let Matthew be. No one needs to watch me sleep." Mary's eyelids closed slowly, but then sprung open again. "That's unless you require private time with Mr. Darcy."

Elizabeth smiled easily. "I never tire of the man's company. Even after two years."

"Then by all means send Mr. Joseph up. A woman of your infinite powers should have her every wish." She caught Elizabeth's hand in a tight grip.

Elizabeth's finger gently touched the sleeping child's hair. "My wish is to have what you have, Mary," she whispered.

"You will, Elizabeth." Mrs. Joseph assured. "You'll have your own happiness…you and Mr. Darcy." She paused and took a deep breath. "My child's birth…I was never afraid, because God placed the incomparable Elizabeth Darcy in my life. My prayers…those I recited before Matthew and I left Stoke-on-Trent—they were for God to send an angel to protect my child, and on the third day of travel, I walked into this out-of-the-way inn; and there you were. My own angel."

Elizabeth snorted. "I've been called many things, but 'angel' has rarely been one of them."

"That's where the world's in error, Elizabeth. They see those defenses you show to anyone who barely knows you. They don't see your magnificent heart—your indomitable spirit—the purity of your soul."

Elizabeth laughed self-consciously. "Do not bestow upon me too many exemplary qualities. If so, I'll have to find something good to say of Miss Bingley."

Mary's eyebrow rose in curiosity. "Miss Bingley?"

Elizabeth chuckled lightly. "The younger sister of my sister Jane's husband. She did poor Jane a disservice, and Miss Bingley also had once set her sights on Mr. Darcy."

"Angels can feel jealousy, Elizabeth." Mary squeezed Elizabeth's hand.

"So, there are shades of angelic behavior?" Elizabeth's voice rose in amusement.

Mary laughed also. "Absolutely. God's love is the purest, but mankind can possess levels of the benevolent spirit."

"Then, in your opinion, I have God's attention." Elizabeth puzzled over that concept.

"We all have God's attention, but I believe that He's chosen you among His favorites."

Before she could stifle her words, Elizabeth defensively asked, "Then how could God allow my children to die before I knew them? Before I could tell them of my love?" Tears trickled from her eyes.

Mrs. Joseph swallowed hard. "That's the question which most frightens you, is it not, Elizabeth? You wonder how, if you serve God, He could not honor you with a child of your own. How the rest of the world can know such happiness? How no one, except Mr. Darcy, understands the depth of your fear?"

"Yes," Elizabeth murmured.

"I've no answer that would satisfy your heart: God gives us what we need when we need it. Matthew holds different ideas on such matters, but I believe that when the Bible says that God created man in His own image, that means God has His own foibles. He's a bit selfish. God wished to surround Himself with the laughter of children—the most magical sound in the world. Therefore, sometimes He does the selfish thing and calls the child home early. It's the only explanation that makes any sense."

Elizabeth brushed away her tears. "I'll endeavor to accept your explanation, Mary. It serves as well as any other."

"You cannot argue with a woman named Mary so close to the celebration of our Lord's birth," Mrs. Joseph teasingly reasoned.

Elizabeth smiled easily. "No, I suppose, I cannot."

~~~ ~~~ ~~~

"Mr. Manneville. There you are, Sir." Mrs. Bennet had carefully watched for Caroline Bingley to return to her room to freshen her clothes for supper. Then she approached the American. From her observations, Mrs. Bennet had determined that within the household only Miss Bingley stood a better chance of attracting Mr. Manneville than did Kitty. She planned to emphasize Kitty's assets.

Manneville rose to acknowledge the lady's entrance. "Forgive me, Mrs. Bennet. I was unaware of your seeking me. How may I serve you, Ma'am?"

Mrs. Bennet breezed past him and seated herself on the same settee Manneville occupied. "I've no great need of you, Sir, other than to satisfy my curiosity about your home. You've piqued my interest, Mr. Manneville. I might even implore Mr. Bennet to take the family on an extended holiday once this crazy war ends."

Manneville shrugged uncomfortably, but he politely said, "America's not for the faint of heart. Luxuries are not spread consistently among our citizens. You may find the conditions quite rustic, Ma'am."

"Naturally, you'd assume with my having two daughters so highly placed, that we Bennets are used to only the best, but I assure you, Mr. Manneville, my girls and I can do with much less. My youngest, Lydia, has but a let place, as Mr. Wickham is a lieutenant, very much like Mr. Southland, and, of course, you met my Mary's betrothed. It'll be several years of service before Mr. Grange knows a settled income."

"I see," Mr. Manneville said softly.

But Mrs. Bennet barely allowed the man time for those two simple words. "We're far from poor, Mr. Manneville. I wouldn't wish to leave you with that impression. Mr. Bennet has a fine property in Hertfordshire. What I mean to convey is that some women can adjust quite easily to less than pristine conditions, while others cannot. I brought my girls up with a sense of responsibility. Miss Darcy, for example, is a prime example. A girl raised under these auspicious conditions would never adjust to anything less. Neither could Miss De Bourgh. She is frail. Can one imagine her sailing across the ocean? The woman would never survive. Plus, she is seven and twenty. Quite on the shelf."

"What of…" he began, but again the lady snatched his words away.

"What of Miss Bingley? I suppose that's what you ask, is it not, Mr. Manneville? A man should inspect all the choices. Lord knows, that's the way of the world. It's quite smart of you to have sought my opinion on this matter. With five daughters, I'm quite fluent on a young lady's ability to make a good wife, and you must believe me, Sir, that Miss Bingley isn't the type to please any man. The lady is self-consumed. She caused my dear Jane much grief. A man like you needs a loving wife—an intelligent, unambitious girl, who could give you strong sons and daughters. Miss Bingley is four and twenty, nearly of the same age as Miss De Bourgh. You need someone younger."

"Such as Miss Catherine," Manneville said dryly.

"Kitty!" Mrs. Bennet gasped as if surprised. "I'd never thought of Kitty as a possible mate for a man such as you. I mean—obviously, Kitty has youth to her advantage, and she's by far one of the most sensible girls a man might find. Mrs. Darcy and Mrs. Bingley have introduced Kitty to the best that life has to offer. She could manage any house. In fact, she and Miss Darcy are sharing duties until my Elizabeth returns."

Manneville stood. "You've given me much upon which to think, Mrs. Bennet." He bowed over her extended hand. "I thank you for your concern for my future marital happiness, Ma'am. Now, if you'll excuse me?"

Mrs. Bennet preened under his attentions. She had accomplished what she'd planned. She'd planted the idea's seed. Now, she'd place Kitty in the man's way, starting at supper. While the others dressed for the evening meal, she would change the name cards so Kitty would have the opportunity to converse with Mr. Manneville this evening.

∼⊗∼ ∼⊗∼ ∼⊗∼

To Kitty's horror, for the evening meal, she found herself between Mr. Manneville and Mr. Collins. The look of surprise on Georgiana's face and the one of triumph on her mother's told Kitty exactly what had happened.

"Miss Catherine," Manneville acknowledged her as he took his place.

"Mr. Manneville," she murmured. She shot a glance about the table. Her mother had certainly scrambled the seating arrangement. Poor Mr. Winkler was at the table's other end between Miss Bingley and Mary. Mr. Grange was seated beside Miss De Bourgh. At her end of the table, she and Georgiana held court: the colonel, her father, Lieutenant Southland, Mr. Manneville, Mr. Collins, and Mr. Bingley made up their supper partners.

"It appears an imbalance in the seating has occurred," Manneville said sardonically.

Kitty smiled purposely. "I'd not noticed, Mr. Manneville."

"Had you not, Miss Catherine?" Irony played through his words. Kitty didn't appreciate the man's attitude. She hissed, "If you find the situation disagreeable, Sir, I'm certain that Miss Darcy shall gladly permit you to change with any of her other guests. You'll find either of my sisters or Mrs. Collins most cooperative."

"Not your mother, Miss Catherine? Is she not cooperative also?" he insinuated.

Kitty kept her tone light so others wouldn't see her anger, but her words spoke her true feelings. "I don't know why, Sir, you believe yourself such a desirable supper partner that you'd imply some manipulation on my part to make your further acquaintance, but you are sadly mistaken. I'd happily relinquish my seat to another. Choose your partner, Mr. Manneville, and I'll execute the exchange." She felt a flush of color flood her face.

Manneville leaned closer. "I'm pleased that you possess a backbone, Miss Catherine. I feared a girl of tender years mightn't express her mind. Tell Mrs. Bennet that I'll keep you in mind when I make my decision for a wife."

"You should shorten your list, Mr. Manneville. I assure you that I have no desire to see America." Kitty turned her head to smile at Mr. Bingley, who sat across from her. Out of the corner of her mouth she murmured, "I hope that makes my position clear."

"And if I made you an offer? You would turn it down," he taunted.

Kitty leaned closer to whisper. "We Bennet sisters don't jump at the first offer. Although my cousin will inherit our family home upon my father's passing, my sister Elizabeth turned down Mr. Collins. And believe it or not, my father supported Lizzy's decision. We accept only those offers which most please us."

"Obviously, your older sister chose the superior offer." Manneville nodded to the elaborate surroundings.

"Elizabeth did choose the superior man. Yet, her decision had nothing to do with Mr. Darcy's consequence." She noted the man's disbelief. "In fact, despite the possibility of my mother and sisters losing Longbourn, Lizzy refused Mr. Darcy's first proposal. Only when the man pleased her did Elizabeth change her mind. I have three married sisters, Mr. Manneville, and each has chosen the man she loves." Kitty immediately thought of poor Lydia, who loved a man who didn't return Lydia's devotion, but Kitty hadn't lied to the American.

Manneville frowned. "We'll see if you're a lady who speaks the truth, Miss Catherine." When the man smiled at her, Kitty experienced a flash of dread shooting up her spine.

⌒ ⌒ ⌒

"Pardon, Miss Darcy," Mr. Nathan stepped closer to whisper in Georgiana's ear. "There's one of the tenants at the kitchen door. He heard that Mr. Winkler dined with us this evening."

"Is there a problem?" Edward asked softly.

Mr. Nathan turned his back to the other guests. "Old Mrs. Foxmour, Colonel. The lady is reportedly in a bad way. The doctor gave her but a few days nearly a week ago. The woman has requested to speak to a clergyman, and her son, Artie, asks that Mr. Winkler come and see to his mother's spiritual needs."

"How can we get Winkler to the Foxmour cottage safely?" Georgiana asked.

Mr. Nathan gave the girl a look of approval. "I was thinking of one of the sleighs, Miss Darcy."

"Send Jarvis with Mr. Winkler to help with the horses, and add a basket of staples for the family," Georgiana instructed. "Tell Mr. Arden to have a groom harness the sleigh."

"I will see to it, Miss Darcy." Mr. Nathan bowed out.

Edward briefly squeezed Georgiana's hand. "I'll speak privately to Winkler."

"Thank you, Edward."

The colonel nodded and crossed the room to where Winkler spoke to Kitty, Mary, and Mr. Bennet. "Excuse me, Winkler." He asked privately, "Can I have a moment?" With confidence, the colonel stepped away from the others.

Kitty watched with concern as Colonel Fitzwilliam spoke personally to Mr. Winkler. She noted the empathy cross Mr. Winkler's face. "Something is wrong," she said to herself.

Georgiana, on the room's other side, cleared her voice. "I hope you'll join me and the colonel in some of our favorite parlor games. We thought we might begin with charades, but with a twist. You'll need a partner for this version of the game."

Everyone began to pair up, but Kitty's eyes remained on Winkler and the colonel. When the clergyman hurried toward the drawing room door, she moved also, trailing the man; but before she reached the door, Mr. Manneville blocked her way. "Miss Catherine." He bowed to her. "Would you do me the honor of partnering me in the game?"

Trying to see past him to where Winkler had gone, Kitty mumbled, "I think not, Sir. Now, if you'll excuse me." She started around the man only to be confronted by her mother.

"Of course, Kitty shall partner you, Sir. It's most gracious of you to ask." Mrs. Bennet turned Kitty's shoulders to face the man. "Give Mr. Manneville your assent, Kitty," her mother insisted.

Kitty let out exasperation's sigh. "Mr. Manneville has my answer, Mama."

CHAPTER 11

❧ ❧ ❧

"WHAT ARE THE SLEEPING arrangements tonight?" Darcy asked softly. He and Elizabeth tarried in the common room. The Josephs tended their child in the room the couple shared with the Darcys.

Elizabeth glanced toward the stairs. "It seems that Mrs. Joseph should have the bed."

Darcy frowned. "In principle, I agree, but my concern for your health outweighs my reason. You, too, should share the bed with Mrs. Joseph. The lady's husband and I can make do with the bedding."

Elizabeth slid her hand into his. "I no longer believe that I can sleep without your arms about me, Fitzwilliam. It's one of the reasons I chose to travel to Northumberland. The prospect of more than a week alone at Pemberley would have never done."

Darcy thought of how long it had taken to convince his wife to accompany him, but he said nothing to contradict her. "I'm bereft of your closeness when you're not within my sight." He stroked her palm with his fingertips.

"Then allow me to lie beside the man I love," Elizabeth whispered.

When she said such things, his wife enflamed his desire, but nothing would happen this evening. "As you wish," he said quietly. "I spoke to Mr. Simpson earlier. He believes we can depart on the morrow. Will you be comfortable doing so?"

Elizabeth's dual contradiction crossed her countenance. "Mrs. Joseph must remain a few more days," she thought aloud. "But I do so need to be home. To be with Georgiana."

"Unless Mrs. Joseph has difficulty overnight, I imagine the lady's husband can see to her care. You've served her well, my dear." Darcy brought the back of her hand to his lips. "These fingers—these capable hands have done God's work. Now, it's time to rest. Time to return to our home."

Elizabeth chuckled. "*Rest* and *Pemberley* are not synonymous words."

"True. It's a constant battle to keep such a large estate sound—but it's a glorious battle," he said with pride.

"Some battles are worth fighting," she said softly.

Realizing his wife felt the same as he, Darcy smiled. "On that fact, we can agree. It was a point upon which I suspected we would find congress."

⁓ᴑᴇ ⁓ᴑᴇ ⁓ᴑᴇ

"Mr. Bennet," his wife caught at his arm, "you must make Kitty see reason," she beseeched. "Mr. Manneville has asked Kitty to be his partner, but your daughter insists on leaving the room."

Mr. Bennet, who despised being dragged into these family dramas, sighed deeply. "Is this true, Kitty?"

"Papa, I've no time to explain. Mr. Winkler has rushed away." Pulling free from her mother's grasp, Kitty started forward again.

Mr. Bennet's eyebrow rose sharply. "Mr. Winkler?"

"Yes, Papa. I fear the man needs my help," she said pleadingly.

Mr. Bennet smiled secretly. "Then go on, Girl. Mr. Darcy would know offense if we allowed Winkler to struggle alone."

Impulsively, Kitty kissed her father's cheek. "Thank you, Papa."

Watching his daughter scurrying from the room, Mr. Bennet turned to the American. "I'm afraid, Manneville, that you must find another partner. I've two other daughters in the room who would make comparable copemates. The smartest of my daughters is Mrs.

Darcy, but the others are equally well read," he said jovially. "Then, perhaps, Mrs. Bennet is more to your liking. Or you could prefer cards as your entertainment. I believe Lady Catherine and Mr. Collins plan to play."

Manneville glanced toward the card tables. "I think not, Mr. Bennet. I'll seek another partner. Thank you, Sir."

Kitty rushed through the servants' halls toward the kitchen. A maid reported seeing Winkler headed that way with Jarvis. Kitty burst into the room to find the clergyman conferring with one of the tenants near the back door and Mrs. Oliver filling a large basket with baked goods and cold meat.

"What is it?" she asked as she stepped beside Mr. Winkler.

Despite his countenance's gravity, his eyes welcomed her. "Miss Catherine," he said softly and reached for her hand. "This is Mr. Foxmour. Foxmour, this is Mrs. Darcy's sister, Miss Catherine Bennet."

"I be honored, Miss." The man quickly removed his hat and offered a bow. "I remains most sorry for disturbin' your entertainment."

"Mr. Foxmour's mother is very ill, Miss Catherine. She's in need of a clergyman," he whispered close to her ear. "I will accompany Mr. Foxmour. I don't know how long I'll be away."

"I'm going with you," she asserted.

"Miss Catherine, this is a long, slow process," Winkler reasoned.

Kitty held his gaze. "I wish to be of assistance, Mr. Winkler. My father's aware that I shall accompany you." She hoped he understood. She had no idea what was expected of her as his choice, but she was prepared to learn.

Winkler's smile widened. "Send for your cloak and muff. Mr. Arden prepares a sleigh with blankets, but I would have you properly attired for the weather. I'm sure the Foxmours could use some assistance with the children." The clergyman turned toward the waiting cottager. "How many is it you have, Foxmour?"

"Four wee ones, Sir."

"May I bring some paper and crayons for the children?" she asked quickly.

"You might show them your sketches, Miss Catherine. Your work is remarkable."

Kitty glowed with his compliment. "I'll be only a minute." She gave a quick curtsy and disappeared into the servants' hall leading to her room. She had pleased him; she'd made Thorne Winkler happy with her actions.

A quarter hour later, Winkler lifted her to the sleigh and draped a blanket across Kitty's lap. "Stay warm," he instructed as he climbed up beside her. Jarvis and Mr. Foxmour climbed onto the back as the groomsman gave the horses a touch of the whip to start them along the path to the hedgerows.

Winkler moved closer to shield Kitty from the wind. "Thank you," he whispered. "This will mean much to the Foxmours. You truly do them an honor."

"I'm not certain how much assistance I might be. I've never tended someone who is near death," she said tentatively. "I pray I'll not disappoint."

"You could never disappoint, Miss Catherine." He slid his hand under the blanket and touched the skin exposed above her glove. Automatically, Kitty placed her hand into his. Even through the leather covering their entwined fingers, warmth spread up her arm in a familiar manner.

✑ ✑ ✑

"Mr. Darcy and I shall depart on the morrow," Elizabeth explained as she helped adjust the baby in Mrs. Joseph's arms. Without a wet nurse, the woman fed the child at her breast.

Mary's eyes remained on her son, but she nodded her understanding. "Matthew and I shall be sorry to see you go."

Elizabeth laughed lightly. "You'll have the room to yourselves."

"Yet, it shan't be the same. You've quickly become one of my dearest friends; I'll grieve for the lack of your company."

Elizabeth smiled broadly. "It's been something of an adventure. A story to tell our children and grandchildren—of our Christmas in Harrogate."

"You should know that Matthew and I have chosen to name our son *William,* after your esteemed husband. Shall it please Mr. Darcy?" she asked shyly.

"Oh, yes, Mary. It'll please Fitzwilliam greatly." Elizabeth's brilliant smile grew.

Mary said impishly, "We considered Mr. Darcy's full name, but we thought that you would be choosing *Fitzwilliam* for your first son. And as I plan for our children to know one another two *Fitzwilliams* may be more than either of us can tolerate."

"You may be correct," Elizabeth declared fondly.

"It's a grand name," Mary insisted. "For a man of great consequence."

"For a man of honor," Elizabeth corrected.

～⊘～ ～⊘～ ～⊘～

"I have it!" Edward nearly shouted as he and Georgiana competed against Bingley and Jane. "The answer is the letter 'L.'"

Jane laughed infectiously. "I thought we had you that time, Colonel." Through a process of elimination, only those two couples remained in the game. The others had clustered their chairs in a large circle to cheer on the duos.

"That was quite clever, Mrs. Bingley," Georgiana declared. "You riddle dark, disclose my name. No doubt you will descry it. Or dillydally about the centre until I deliver."

"I thought it the letter 'D,'" Mr. Grange said, "but that was too obvious."

"Too obvious indeed," Mr. Bennet said from where he observed the goings-on. Mrs. Bennet, the Collinses, Lady Catherine, Mrs. Jenkinson, and Mrs. Annesley had retired some time earlier. He had promised to keep an eye on the couples and to wait for Kitty's return. Although his wife hadn't understood why he had allowed Kitty to accompany the clergyman, Mr. Bennet had convinced her that if Kitty proved useful that Elizabeth's husband might sponsor Kitty as Miss Darcy's companion during the Season.

Mr. Bennet despised his wife's manipulations in these matters, especially where Mr. Manneville was concerned. The man was too mature, too diligent toward his own agenda, too sophisticated in an uncivilized manner, too American for his daughter. He wanted Kitty safe and well settled. If he had done his duty in that respect with Lydia, he wouldn't have been indebted to Mr. Darcy for whatever of honor or credit was purchased for his youngest daughter. The satisfaction of prevailing on one the most worthless men in Great Britain, in the form of Mr. Wickham, to be Lydia's husband might then have rested in its proper place. After Lydia's folly, Mr. Bennet had at last learned to be cautious. So, tonight he'd encouraged Kitty's association with Mr. Winkler.

The young man had approached him regarding his growing affections for Kitty and had spoken of his desire for Kitty to serve by his side. "This will be a good test of Kitty's mettle," he had told himself. "Kitty will decide tonight how she truly feels about the man."

～∞ ～∞ ～∞

"This be Mrs. Darcy's sister," Mr. Foxmour explained to his wife. "And ye know Mr. Winkler."

"Please come in." Mrs. Foxmour ushered them forward. Even Jarvis and the groomsman received a hearty welcome.

Mr. Winkler helped Kitty with her cloak. "Miss Catherine came to assist with the children," he said.

"That be wonderful, Miss." Mrs. Foxmour guided them closer to the fire.

"I brought some paper and crayons," Kitty gushed.

"A real treat," Mr. Foxmour said.

Mr. Winkler placed the basket on a nearby table. "And the Darcys sent over this offering."

The thoughtfulness deeply moved Mrs. Foxmour. Tears misted her eyes, and she reached for the handkerchief tucked inside her cuff. "Mr. Darcy be a good master."

Mr. Winkler took the lady's hand. "Why do you not take me to see your husband's mother?"

"This way, Sir." She gestured to a small room marked by a curtained doorway.

Winkler squeezed Kitty's hand and followed the woman to where the elder Mrs. Foxmour lay. Kitty glanced around the small cottage. There were but three rooms: the one where she currently stood and two smaller ones. Evidently, the elder Mrs. Foxmour slept in one while the lady's son and his wife occupied the other. Four rolled mats in the corner spoke of where the children slept. "Well," Kitty asked a bit tentatively, "would you children care to tell me your names?"

"Mavis," with real admiration, the tallest of the three girls uttered. Her eyes took in Kitty's fine dress. "And this be Nell," she said of the little one tightly holding her hand. The child sucked a dirty thumb clean.

"And your name?" Kitty knelt before a sweet-faced blonde of five or six.

The child confidently raised her chin, but her voice still trembled. "Tavia."

Kitty stroked the girl's hair. "As I said, I brought paper so we might draw together. You could draw a picture for your grandmother if you like."

Mr. Foxmour picked up the boy. "Let's move the table closer to the fire to keep ye ladies warmer. I be puttin' the wee one to bed in the missus' room. Then I'll fetch in more wood."

Jarvis easily moved the table, and Kitty settled on a bench with Tavia beside her. The other two girls sat across from her. She handed each child a sheet of paper. "Have you ever drawn a picture before?"

"No, Miss Catherine," Mavis remained the spokesperson for the group. "We draw in the dirt sometimes."

Kitty had never felt rich. In fact, she often had bemoaned the Bennets' lack of funds when she and Lydia had wanted to buy every ribbon and feather in Meryton, but these children had never experienced drawing with crayons on paper. "Well, we'll remedy that right away," she said happily. "I thought I might draw a house with a garden and a sun. What about you?"

"I don't know," Mavis said unsurely. "What can I draw?"

"Whatever your heart wishes. Have you ever dreamed of a knight or a princess or of Robin of Locksley or Moses from the Bible? Whatever story or dream you've concocted can become your picture. I like to draw dresses and cloaks and fancy hats."

Mavis's eyes grew larger. "Fancy dresses? I mean, fancier than the one ye be wearin'?"

Again, Kitty felt the disparity between her wardrobe and that of the Foxmours. "Very fancy," she confided. "Fancy enough for Queen Charlotte herself."

"I be," Mavis gasped. "Would ye draw a fancy dress for me Gram? She be always sayin' she jist once wanted a fancy dress of her own."

Kitty's eyes gleamed with a teary mist. "Happily so." She reached for a pencil. "Let me see. How should it look?"

"Long sleeves," Nell piped up. "Gram always be wearin' long sleeves even in the hot months."

Kitty began to sketch the outline of a matronly gown while three little girls crawled closer to watch each scratch of her pencil along the paper's rough texture.

"Lace," Nell whispered. "Gram likes lace. She be lookin' at it every time we be goin' to Lambton."

"Then lace it is." Kitty added the intricate details about the neck and cuffs. "It'll be the grandest dress," she said as little Tavia pointed to a place Kitty had missed. "Your grandmother shall love it because you've designed it especially for her."

❧ ❧ ❧

Darcy sat alone in a corner of the common room. Mr. Joseph had joined some of the other men in a friendly card game, and Darcy relished the few moments of solitude. Leaving for Pemberley tomorrow would be heavenly in more than one way. He anticipated enjoying his wife's happiness when she, at last, saw her family at Pemberley, but having moments with Elizabeth without an audience would be better. For some eight and twenty hours, he and his wife had shared their quarters with the Josephs, and even though the situation had produced some awkward moments, overall, it had been an amiable solution.

"Here be the paper and pen you requested, Mr. Darcy."

"Thank you, Nan." Thinking of the quality paper at Pemberley, Darcy reached for the cheap foolscap the inn provided. With the maid's departure, he took up the pen to tell his wife of his continual devotion.

22 December
My darling Elizabeth,

> *By this time tomorrow, we will be on our way to Pemberley, but a bit of Harrogate and Prestwick's Portal will remain with us always. Within these walls, I have discovered another facet of the remarkable woman I have married. You are the portrait of everything of which I have ever dreamed. When I look in your eyes, I see the man I pray to someday be.*

> *Yet, I sometimes wonder what you see in mine. Can you read what is there? In your opinion, am I more than I seem to be? I want you to know the man that I am—the one who would abandon everything for you. I would leave behind my honor. I would pay any price to have you as my wife. As we move forward with our lives, I offer you solace in my arms—my beautiful Elizabeth—the woman with a soul as beautiful as her face.*

> *Our child grows within you, and I believe that God has given us a glimpse of our future happiness when we look into the Josephs' faces. It is our time. That may be prideful, but I feel it is so. God placed you in my life to bring my faith home to Him.*

Like Moses wandering in the wilderness, I kept my faith in check.
I would have returned to Egypt, keeping it as security in case the
desert held too many dangers, but I have learned that I cannot
love anything partially: not you, not Georgiana, and not our God.
I must place all my faith in those I love, and then God will give
me what I need. He showed me that fact when He placed you
within my life. Yet, I doubted that God knew what was best, and
in my pride, I disdainfully declared myself the wiser; and my heart
suffered much for it.

Now, I do not fear that God will snatch happiness from my
grasp. I have given Him the part of my heart that I can spare from
loving you, and He has accepted my foolish soul as his own. So,
yes, I am confident that our child will come to us in the spring. We
will know no more sacrifice.

D

~@~ ~@~ ~@~

"Mr. Foxmour, your mother wants to see you and the children,"
Mr. Winkler said softly from the draped doorway. Kitty stiffened.
She and the girls had drawn pictures and had laughed, but now it
was time to say their farewells to their grandmother, and Kitty saw
the instant anguish on each of their faces. These children understood death better than she. Kitty did not remember her grand-
parents—being but a babe when the last of them passed.

"Choose the pictures you'll share with Mrs. Foxmour," she
said to the children as she picked up the multi-colored pages.
"Hurry, Girls."

Mr. Foxmour stood stiffly. "Mavis, you three go first." His voice
held traces of his grief. "I'll fetch Hugh."

"Hugh be asleep, Papa," Nell protested.

"I know, Sweet One." Kitty and the girls watched Mr. Foxmour
mechanically walk toward the other bedroom.

"Come, Children," Mr. Winkler motioned them through the
opening.

Tentatively, they entered the room, and Kitty could no longer control the tears streaming down her cheeks. As Mr. Foxmour carried the sleepy toddler through the room, Kitty reached for the boy's arm, as she was unable to console the child's father.

With the family in the small room, Mr. Winkler remained at the opening, and Kitty simply moved into his comforting embrace. Winkler kissed her forehead, and Kitty buried her tears in his waistcoat. "I'm sorry," she sniffed when he handed her his handkerchief.

"I'm not disappointed," he bent his head to whisper in her ear.

Kitty snuggled closer before turning her head to watch the family.

"Bring the children closer," Mrs. Foxmour rasped in a hacking breath.

The three girls scrambled to the straw-stuffed mattress covering a wooden frame. "We brung pictures, Grandmother," Mavis said slowly. The girl was obviously accustomed to tending the older woman. She positioned the other girls where the elder Mrs. Foxmour could see them in the dim candlelight. "Miss Catherine taught us." The girl thrust the drawings into the gnarled hand.

"What be this?" the old woman's gravelly words held tenderness.

"It be a horse," Nell said proudly. "Good enough to win the Ascot. Miss Catherine say that be a fine race."

"His name?" the old woman whispered.

The child shot a quick glance to Kitty, and Kitty gave the first name to come to mind. "Galahad. A real champion."

"Galahad," the child repeated. "A horse with a strong heart."

"It be a fine animal. And this one?" Mrs. Foxmour shuffled the papers.

Tavia crawled closer. "Mine, Grandmother. A princess in a red dress."

"She be pretty like ye, Child." A rheumatic finger traced Tavia's cheek.

"This one Miss Catherine drew, but we be tellin' her what to add." Mavis repositioned the papers in her grandmother's grasp.

The woman's hands began to tremble, and her nearly translucent eyes seeped with tears. "It be the most beautiful dress I's ever seed," she said softly.

Mavis leaned across the woman to kiss the wrinkled cheek. "It be yer dream dress, Grandmother."

"That be true, Child." All three girls surrounded the family's matriarch.

"Here is Hugh, Mama." Mr. Foxmour held the sleeping child.

She briefly touched the child's head. "Ye have good children, Arthur."

"Yes, Mama."

The younger Mrs. Foxmour hefted the boy from her husband's arms and motioned the girls to lead the way to the other room.

Kitty watched solemnly as each girl kissed her grandmother before walking proudly from the room. Then Mr. Foxmour moved to sit beside his mother. He took her hand and began to sob his farewells.

Immediately, Mr. Winkler turned Kitty toward the cottage's main room. "Come," he whispered softly. "The family needs time to grieve. Mrs. Foxmour is at peace."

"But," she began, but Winkler's arm came about her shoulder.

"We can do nothing else. Let us leave them their dignity," he cautioned gently.

Kitty nodded her understanding. Slowly, she gathered her belongings and motioned the Pemberley men to retrieve the sleigh from the lean-to.

"Must ye go?" Tavia tugged at Kitty's skirt.

She bent to kiss the top of the child's head. "Your family requires time together, Sweetheart. I'll return in a couple of days with more paper and colors."

"Yes, Miss," the child said reluctantly.

Kitty cupped the girl's chin. "I promise."

Standing slowly, she allowed Mr. Winkler to place her cloak on her shoulders and then to lead her from the house. Gravely, she waited for the groom to bring the sleigh around. "Shall they suffer? The children?" she said softly when Mr. Winkler stepped beside her.

"These families understand hardship better than the genteel set, but death spares no one its head. Wealth cannot protect a person."

Kitty turned her head quickly to look at the clergyman's face. "What can protect us?"

"Nothing," he said grimly. "All we can do is meet death with God in our hearts."

"Does it ever get easier?" she asked.

Winkler smiled affectionately. "It was tonight with you by my side."

Kitty returned his smile. "It was magnificent. Even though the family faced the worst, I adored every moment with the children."

"And they adored you in return, Miss Catherine, as I knew they would." He caught Kitty's hand in his as the sleigh approached. "As do I." He squeezed her hand gently.

His words sent a rush of warmth between them. "Do you really, Mr. Winkler?"

"More than I have words to explain," he said sincerely as he helped her to the seat.

Kitty couldn't stop her heart's flutter or the shortness of her breath, but neither was a bad feeling. In fact, she quite enjoyed both. "I'm in need of some warm tea," she said as Mr. Winkler seated himself beside her.

"Do you realize the time, Miss Catherine?" he said teasingly.

Kitty looked about the frozen landscape draped in the moon's light and its reflected glory. "Not really," she murmured.

"Nearly one," he announced in triumph.

"You jest."

Again, he possessively caught her hand under the blanket. "Not in the least, my dear."

Kitty allowed herself to lean against his shoulder. "No tea tonight," she whispered. "What shall I do to warm myself then?"

"I might think of something," he hoarsely rasped.

"I certainly hope so," Kitty said on a quick intake of air.

They had arrived at the back door of Pemberley, and Jarvis jumped down from the sleigh. "Mr. Nathan will have retired, Sir. We can use the kitchen door and not disturb the others."

"Of course." Winkler hopped down and lifted Kitty to the ground. "It's most thoughtful of you to consider the household." He gestured to the groomsman. "Thanks to Mr. Arden for the arrangement and to you for a safe passage."

"Good night, Sir." The man touched his hat in respect and drove away.

Jarvis led them through the lower garden and the unlatched kitchen door. "There be candles on the shelf," the footman said. He caught one when it fell into his hand and moved to light it from the banked fireplace. "Do you need me to see you to your quarters, Sir?"

Winkler took the candle from the footman. "That will not be necessary. I'll escort Miss Catherine to her chambers. You are excused, Jarvis. Thank you for your attendance."

"Good night, Sir." The footman took another candle to light his way.

A stirring from beyond the open interior door told Kitty and Winkler that several of the scullery maids heard them. "Come," Kitty said as she caught his hand. "You bring the candle."

Winkler stepped in behind her as they wove their way through the servants' passage. "Your hands are cold," he said upon impulse and stopped suddenly.

Kitty turned quickly to face him. "I told you I needed some warm tea," she said coyly.

Winkler moved closer and slid his free hand about Kitty's waist. He set the candlestick on the edge of a nearby table before cupping her chin in his palm. "And I promised to find an alternate way to drive the cold away."

"And do you know of such a miracle?" she teased. Kitty edged a bit closer.

Winkler smiled secretively. "I'm warmer. Are you not, Miss Catherine?" he said in a husky whisper.

Kitty's eyes sparked with mischief. "Perhaps if I hid my hands under here." She slid her fingers beneath Mr. Winkler's jacket. "They might become warmer." She felt him shiver, and the power of it swelled Kitty's heart.

Winkler's fingers rested on her lower back, and he pressed her to him. "Miss Catherine, I would very much like to kiss you if you'd permit it."

Kitty's eyes closed in anticipation as she raised her chin. Winkler's fingers held her in place, and she could feel his breath warm her cheek as his head bent to taste her lips. Kitty's breathing stopped as she waited for the first touch. His lips brushed hers. Gently. Chastely at first. Then he said, "Open for me, Catherine." It was nothing more than a breath, but Kitty's lips parted, and Winkler's mouth became more demanding. His lips pressed hard against hers as his tongue touched the soft tissue of her mouth. By instinct, Kitty's arms encircled his waist, and she leaned into him.

Finally, Winkler broke the contact and gasped, "You are a temptation indeed." He kissed the top of her head before he pulled Kitty into his embrace. "But it's a most welcomed one."

Kitty said nothing at first, simply enjoying his closeness. "I did not know it could be that way." Her voice sounded deeper than she expected.

"I knew it the moment I laid eyes upon you, Catherine. My heart told me so."

She looked in awe at the man as she edged away from his embrace. "You knew you cared for me that first Sunday when Elizabeth introduced us after services?"

"I know all this is new to you, but you engaged my heart immediately. I looked out over the congregation that morning, and there you sat beside Mrs. Darcy. I couldn't withdraw my eyes from your countenance. I fear my sermon that day was less than coherent." His smile teased her good-naturedly.

"It wasn't your best effort," Kitty said blandly.

"In my defense, I plead being dumbstruck by your beauty." Winkler caught her hand and brought it to his lips. His mouth lingered on her skin, and Kitty felt the heat of his touch radiate up her arm. "Come, my dear," he said and reached for the candle. "You need your rest. We'll skate together tomorrow, and then I must return to Lambton."

Kitty followed him into the main hall. "I wish you didn't have to depart."

"I have duties to the community, Catherine," he reminded her. They turned toward the stairs, but another light brought them up short.

Mr. Bennet stepped from Mr. Darcy's library. "There you are," he said.

"Papa! What are you doing up?" Kitty rushed forward to take his arm.

"I promised Mrs. Bennet that I would see you safely returned to the house." Mr. Bennet's eyes traced both their appearances and found them presentable. "The colonel explained your need to leave so quickly, Mr. Winkler. I hope you were able to give the woman solace."

"Thorne was so responsive to the family's needs. I was so proud of him."

Mr. Bennet's eyebrow rose in interest. "Mr. Winkler has a true calling, not like my cousin's, then?"

Kitty wrinkled her nose in disgust. "Mr. Collins lacks empathy for others. Our cousin is very much like his patroness."

"Miss Catherine was most valuable in entertaining the children." Mr. Winkler smiled again at Kitty.

Mr. Bennet chuckled. "I'm sure she was. All my girls, except maybe Lydia, can prove themselves worthy, but we'll discuss Kitty's value on the morrow. It's late, and we each should seek our beds."

"I am tired," Kitty admitted. She leaned easily against her father's arm. "Miss Darcy shall have to deal with the guests without me early on. I assume we heard nothing from Lizzy while Mr. Winkler and I were out."

"No, and your sister's absence worries me so," Mr. Bennet confessed.

Kitty guided her father's weary steps toward the main stairs. "I wouldn't worry, Papa. If I know Mr. Darcy, he and Elizabeth are waiting out the storm in the best accommodations money can buy."

✒ ✒ ✒

Darcy slid in behind his wife on the newly wrapped mat. After a heated discussion, the Josephs had accepted the bed. Now, Darcy spooned Elizabeth's body. His arm snaked around her rapidly expanding waist, and his fingers gently stroked her abdomen. As she was likely to do, his wife rewarded him by grinding her hips against him.

Slowly, Darcy raised his hand to her back. Gently, he brushed the hair from her cheek and neck before trailing light kisses along her neck's nape and behind her ear. With a breath's whisper, Darcy brushed her ear's lobe with his lips. "I love you."

Elizabeth's right arm reached up and behind his neck. Turning her head sharply to the right, she pulled Darcy's head and mouth toward hers.

He kissed her thoroughly—Darcy's mouth asking for her devotion and receiving it. "Love me?" he asked as his mouth hovered above her lips.

"Always," Elizabeth murmured.

Darcy settled once more behind her and pulled Elizabeth to him. He brushed her hair to the side. Then his hand traced heat down her arm. Finally, it splayed across her extended abdomen. Kissing her shoulder, he whispered, "Mine."

"Ours." Her hand clasped his. "Our family."

CHAPTER 12

~ॐ~ ~ॐ~ ~ॐ~

"WE'LL PRAY FOR YOUR SAFE JOURNEY," Mr. Joseph said. He and his wife and child had come downstairs to say another farewell to the Darcys.

"Thank you." Darcy helped Elizabeth with her cloak. He banked his irritation: They were getting a later start than he wanted. Elizabeth and Mrs. Joseph had said their good-byes three times previously. "Mr. Washington has assured me that the roads are passable."

"Most of the other guests have departed." Mr. Joseph smiled at the two women. "You may need to carry Mrs. Darcy to your carriage."

Darcy watched his wife caress the child's cheek again. "Women and babies," he said with a wry chuckle. "We men cannot always understand the attraction."

"I have a better grasp now that I've held my son."

Darcy sighed. "I pray for the same pleasure."

"In the spring, Mr. Darcy. My Mary believes it to be so." He extended his hand in parting. "Mary and I owe our child's life to you and Mrs. Darcy. Young William will know of the Darcys of Pemberley."

Elizabeth caressed the child's dark hair and then bent to kiss the baby's forehead. "Babies always smell like a cloud," she said softly before sniffing again.

"Not always." Mrs. Joseph laughed as she took the child from

Elizabeth's arms. "Dirty baby cloths, you know."

Elizabeth laughed softly. "Thunderclouds."

Mrs. Joseph's eyes sparkled in delight. "One way to look at it." Companionable silence returned. "I'll never forget you, Elizabeth Darcy. My William shall learn of the woman who calmly escorted him into the world. If there is ever anything the Josephs..." her voice trailed off. "All you must do is ask."

Elizabeth took one last look at the boy. "Just extra prayers for my own child."

"You'll send me word of your safe delivery. Until then, my prayers will drown in your praise."

"Come, Mrs. Darcy." Her husband stepped behind her. "The winter days are short, and we wish to be at Pemberley by tomorrow."

"Of course," she replied. "It's time."

Mr. Joseph placed Elizabeth's hand on his arm and led her from the room.

After watching her depart, Darcy impulsively turned and touched the child's cheek. "You'll send Mrs. Darcy news of young William."

"Elizabeth shall know of my son's many accomplishments."

Darcy bowed to the lady. "I'm certain it will please my wife to learn of my namesake's achievements."

"And you, Mr. Darcy. Shall you celebrate William's many firsts?"

Darcy gave her a knowing smile. "I celebrate anything that makes Mrs. Darcy happy."

～⌐ ～⌐ ～⌐

"Did you see much of battle, Lieutenant?" Mr. Grange asked. Grange and Mary had joined Southland, Anne, and Mrs. Jenkinson in a small drawing room. The ladies watched the gentlemen play chess. "It must be a grand adventure," the young man added. "A chance to become a true hero."

Roman sat quietly for a few moments. He stared intently at the board as if planning his next move, but instead he chose his words. "Despite my eagerness to serve my country and to protect the colonel, there were moments I regretted my decision to follow my commanding officer to America." A long silence ensued. "The colonel would've allowed me to remain in England, to switch posts, but I'd have none of it. Like young Grange here, I thought of heroism."

"But surely, even in the Americas, a man can find the glory of war," Grange protested.

Roman touched his knight, but he did not move it. "There's no glory in war, Mr. Grange." The lieutenant sat back casually in his chair. "There's fear and necessity and cowardice and the overwhelming need to survive, but there's no glory."

"You speak so harshly, Lieutenant," Mary observed.

"I apologize if my tone offends, Miss Bennet. I did not mean for it to do so."

Anne's soft voice brought Roman from his darker thoughts. "And the colonel? Does my cousin express the same feelings regarding war?"

"A hero's image is etched in Edward Fitzwilliam's face. The colonel inspires his men with his own bravery. Your cousin, Miss De Bourgh, is not an officer hiding at the rear. He leads with his own resolve to correct the world's wrongs."

"I would expect nothing less from Edward. He was built to protect. Plus, he was the one who always accepted a dare. The Countess spent many sleepless nights nursing Edward's injuries."

Roman smiled wryly. "I cannot doubt it. The colonel is not one to withdraw. But he's also not one to take foolish chances. Everything is calculated for success. If I were to have to face an enemy again, I would choose Colonel Fitzwilliam as my commanding officer."

"That's high praise indeed," Mrs. Jenkinson challenged.

"And every word is true, Ma'am. The man you know as a cousin and an Earl's son is a military genius."

"Really?" Anne seemed surprised. "I'd expect Edward to be brave, but I had never thought of his tactical intellect."

"Then it's with pleasure that I share something of the man I admire."

～∞～ ～∞～ ～∞～

"Shall they be well?" Elizabeth asked as their carriage reached the main road and turned toward Derbyshire.

From the rear-facing seat, Darcy had watched the emotional turns of his wife's countenance for over a half hour. The desire to stay with the Josephs and the desire to return to Pemberley had warred within her. "Mr. Joseph has assured me that he'd not allow his wife to travel until Boxing Day. They'll spend Christmas at the inn. The man is cognizant of the fact that it'll take more than two days to reach Newcastle with a newborn babe; therefore, he must reasonably arrange his family's passage."

"What of Mr. Joseph's mother?"

"His future lies with Mrs. Joseph and young William. Joseph won't risk their lives to say his farewells. As a clergyman, the man knows that honoring one's parents doesn't override 'cling to her only' in the marriage vows. He obviously cannot leave Harrogate today."

Elizabeth nodded her agreement. "It's too soon for Mary."

"And they cannot travel on Christmas," he added.

"Of course, I'd forgotten the implications of the religious celebration."

Darcy removed his gloves and placed them beside him. "Joseph and I had several conversations about the proper thing to do."

Elizabeth smiled easily. "In other words, Matthew Joseph asked for your counsel, and you explained the man's family duty," she teased.

Darcy's eyebrow rose. "Would you expect anything less of me?"

"My husband, I've never misjudged your consequence."

"As opposed to my finer qualities," he countered.

Elizabeth chuckled lightly. "It was part of my grand plan, Mr. Darcy. A man only wants what he cannot have."

"Ah, now I see," he said sagely. "Your flirtation with Mr. Wickham was only to pique my interest—as was your denial of your cousin's proposal. Therefore, it only follows that your constant disdain was to prove that I didn't understand what I most needed."

Elizabeth's eyes misted with tears. "I never meant to cause you pain, Fitzwilliam."

Immediately, Darcy switched seats. Taking Elizabeth into his arms, he said, "And I never meant to criticize. You must realize I no longer care about the past. It was what it was. As long as we have found each other, nothing else matters."

Elizabeth wiped away the tears. "I don't know what came over me. I was enjoying our conversation, and then I thought of the utter pain displayed on your face when I refused you at Hunsford. I did you such a disservice."

"Could you not instead imagine my countenance at your eventual acceptance?" he teased. With his thumbs, Darcy flicked the tears from her cheeks before kissing her nose's tip.

Elizabeth swallowed a sob with a giggle. "It would be pleasanter." She shrugged her shoulders in good-natured self-chastisement. "Of late, I've been a watering pot over the most insignificant things."

"Perhaps the baby," he said gravely.

"Perhaps."

Darcy shifted her in his arms. "*Perhaps* if I share what I did for the Josephs, it'll bring a smile to those luscious lips." Unable to resist her, Darcy bent his head for a taste.

Elizabeth stroked his chin line. "Tell me," she said in a rasp.

Darcy first had to bring his breathing under control before he said, "I secured the room and board until Boxing Day, paid Mrs. Washington for the ruined linens, and left a small gift for William for Christmas Day."

"How small?"

He removed one of her gloves and kissed her knuckles. "Ten pounds."

Elizabeth smiled broadly. "You're the most generous man," she exclaimed. "Thank you, Fitzwilliam."

"I also paid the innkeeper for extra blankets for Mr. Simpson and Jasper."

"And extras for us, as well," she observed.

Darcy kissed the inside of her wrist. "Yes, I worried for your lack of proper rest. Sleeping in the carriage isn't ideal, but I wished to see to your comfort as much as possible."

～⌖～ ～⌖～ ～⌖～

"Shall you join us, Edward?" Georgiana had discovered him in Darcy's study. "We'll take advantage of the ice you've seen fit to design."

"It was all Southland's doing," he insisted. He sat back in the chair and smiled at her. "Has someone claimed your hand, Cousin? If not, I'll seek your company."

A powerful desire to rush into his arms took Georgiana by surprise. "I can think of nothing that I'd enjoy more. We gather in the main foyer on the half hour."

Edward shot a quick glance at the mantel clock. "Perfect. The roads are clearing, and I've sent word to the Earl of my return, as well as having my report ready for my superiors. However, I've one more letter to address."

"Anyone I know?" she asked teasingly, all the while praying that he didn't correspond with another woman.

"Not unless you're familiar with the Prince Regent's inner circle."

Georgiana experienced disappointment's twinge. He hadn't denied writing to another—perhaps a romantic liaison upon his return to town. Within his entourage, the Prince kept company with many beautiful women. "I'll see you in a few minutes." With a quick curtsy, Georgiana quit the room.

Edward watched her go and wondered what he'd said that brought the frown to her forehead. "Maybe it's something I didn't say. A man's always on tentative ground with a woman," he said aloud.

Two things had brought him to Darcy's study on this day. The first was his continued suspicion that Mr. Manneville wasn't what he pretended to be. Edward had followed his superiors' orders in escorting the man to England, but it made no sense that the British government would take an interest in this particular American. So, today he had written a newsy letter to Mercer Elphinstone's stepmother and father. Admiral George Elphinstone, Viscount Keith, was a friend and distant relative of Edward's father. He had announced his safe return to England and had mentioned Mr. Manneville. He just hoped that the Elphinstones were in residence in London rather than in Scotland. With luck, Lady Elphinstone would inform her stepdaughter of his letter and word would spread among those who attended the Prince—this simple letter could answer some nagging questions.

The other worrisome issue was his uncharacteristic response to Georgiana. Last evening, he'd dreamed of their waltz in this very study—waking totally befuddled by his reaction to her. *"What would happen if I approached my cousin?"* he wondered, not for the first time. *"Would Georgiana accept me? Moreover, would Darcy allow it?"* Edward tossed his letter onto the edge of the desk. *"I'm an Earl's son and have my own fortune,"* he argued with an imaginary opponent.

"But you are twelve years her senior."

"That's not unusual in marriages among our class."

"Georgiana doesn't know her heart. She has had no worldly experience."

"You know I'll protect her with my life. Nothing will harm her again. You can trust Georgiana with me."

Would Darcy entrust him with Georgiana's future? His cousin would have no fear of her husband ever learning of her foolish attempt at an elopement with George Wickham at age fifteen. Edward already knew of how Darcy had unexpectedly joined Georgiana a day or two before the intended elopement and had foiled Wickham's plans. She could enjoy her future rather than live in the past. Georgiana's affectionate heart could grow under his tutelage.

"First, allow me to see if I can win the lady's promise before I consider facing her brother, a task I may not survive. Perhaps another year on the American front might be less dangerous." Edward laughed as he stood and reached for the letter. "'Battle-scarred' may describe my domestic interactions instead of my military ones."

～☜～ ～☜～ ～☜～

Her husband had expected Elizabeth to sleep, but it was he who nodded off. Elizabeth watched as his head rocked gently back and forth with the coach's sway. Darcy was a magnificent man, handsome and fit, but more importantly, he was a kind and generous person. He had raised Georgiana, had assumed the responsibility of Pemberley, had protected her family even when he'd thought she and he had no future, and he had loved her enough to set aside his former prejudices to give them a chance to find happiness.

First checking Darcy's sleep again, Elizabeth reached for her reticule. She'd awakened this morning to find another of Darcy's letters beside her pillow. With the Josephs in the room, she had had no opportunity to read her husband's words, and had quickly stuffed the missive into her bag. Now, Elizabeth removed it and broke the wax seal. Unfolding it, she adjusted her seat so she could use the afternoon's sunlight streaming through the coach's window. With a deep, contented sigh, she began to read.

As they often did when she read his letters, her tears returned, but they were happy tears. By some miracle, she had earned this man's love and devotion. Instinctively, her fingers lightly massaged her stomach's swell. Darcy's child grew within her, and she could think of nothing as precious as the possibilities. She'd soon hold their child. No longer did she doubt that fact.

Noting Darcy's stirring, Elizabeth quickly dashed away her tears and returned the letter to her bag. It would join the others in her portmanteau to be savored in private moments over and over again.

"Did you sleep?" Darcy asked as he righted his clothing.

"Not yet. I'm too excited about returning home—returning to Pemberley. When shall we arrive?"

Darcy glanced out the coach's window at the melting landscape. "With no obstacles, midafternoon tomorrow."

"Tomorrow is Christmas Eve. Do you suppose that Georgiana has hung the holly and has addressed the decorations for the Tenants' Ball?"

Darcy's eyes flashed in amusement. "You've tutored my sister, and she'll perform to your expectations; but even if Georgiana were not to address her duties, Mrs. Reynolds would see to the task."

"I forget how dispensable I am as Pemberley's mistress," Elizabeth said wryly.

"Your value lies not in the day-to-day running of the estate, Elizabeth. I could hire someone to do that. You're Pemberley's heart and soul—as was my mother."

Tears misted her eyes—*watering pot, again*, she thought. Darcy had given her the ultimate compliment: He'd compared her influence on Pemberley to that of Lady Anne Darcy. "Thank you, Fitzwilliam," she murmured. She focused on the changes in Darcy's countenance from the expression of concern to that of love. "Then we'll arrive in time for services."

"Yes, Sweetheart. In plenty of time, as long as you're not too tired."

"As Pemberley's mistress, I must appear at church. People would judge the Darcy name poorly if I shirked my duties."

Darcy raised an eyebrow. "Your resolve is admirable, but you'll make your health a priority," he ordered.

"Yes, Mr. Darcy," she said contritely. Elizabeth knew she'd attend the services despite what her husband had just said, and her husband knew that as well. They wouldn't fight over it. It would just happen. Darcy would grumble, especially if Elizabeth appeared travel worn, but he'd allow her to attend Mr. Winkler's Christmas services. During Mrs. Joseph's delivery, Elizabeth had thought long and hard on what Mary Joseph had called "Fate." Elizabeth had never considered the role of fate and prayer. She believed in God's existence, but not His hand in her daily life. Yet, Mary, a clergyman's wife, seemed so assured of God's choices. "Have you thought of God's role in our earlier losses, Fitzwilliam?" she said softly.

Darcy shifted uncomfortably on the bench seat. "We've never spoken of our personal beliefs, have we? I mean, of our thoughts about God's presence."

"I don't know how I can think on it," Elizabeth admitted. "How can I consider that God in His infinite wisdom chose for us to remain childless? If so, then that means we have been unworthy in His estimation, and as I know your goodness, my husband, it must be I who's been unworthy."

"Oh, Elizabeth, do not speak as such. God will see us as parents in due time."

His voice's emptiness didn't escape Elizabeth's notice. "I want to hear Mr. Winkler's sermon on the Christ child's birth. It's important to me, Fitzwilliam. It's important to witness God's hand at work."

⤳ ⤳ ⤳

"Were you able to find what you needed in the attic trunk?" Georgiana asked Kitty as they gathered in the foyer. Everyone had donned winter wear.

"I did. Thank you for your generosity."

"What did you seek, Kitten?" Mr. Bennet asked from beside his daughter.

Kitty's expression foretold her pleasure in sharing. "Something special for the Foxmour family."

Mr. Winkler joined them. "What of the Foxmours?"

Georgiana noted the man's new possessiveness with Kitty. "A simple day dress—one discarded after my time at Ramsgate."

Mr. Bennet's eyebrow rose in curiosity. "Surely Miss Darcy's dress has nothing to do with her brother's tenant."

Kitty blushed, but she said, "The Foxmour children drew the perfect dress for their grandmother. I took one of Miss Darcy's former dresses and with Hannah's and Meg's help, I added lace and a bit of embroidery. Then I had Thomas deliver it to the Foxmours. I thought the lady could wear it for all eternity."

"Miss Catherine, that is all kindness, but the Foxmours aren't used to such finery," Winkler warned.

"Thorne, please trust me," Kitty whispered. To her father, she said, "I chose a plain dark blue day dress—one from Miss Darcy's schoolroom days. I cut away the beads and trim and added bits of lace to the neckline and cuffs. It's no longer a dress a fine lady might wear. It is one in which a household's matriarch might meet God."

Mr. Bennet squeezed Kitty's hand. "You were always most clever with a needle. I am certain that you've done the Foxmours a great honor."

"I just wanted Nell and Mavis and Tavia to see their creation come to life. Life, even in Death." She turned again to Winkler, needing his approval. "Was I so wrong?"

His countenance softened immediately. "No. No, you were the most generous of God's creatures in this matter."

"Now that that's settled," Georgiana observed, "we should join the others at the pond."

"Am I forgiven?" Kitty whispered as she accepted Winkler's arm.

"There's nothing to forgive, my dear. A man of God couldn't find fault with a compassionate soul, and as I'm inclined to favor you above all others, I am content simply to have you at my side."

"Please don't placate me, Thorne. I must understand where the objection lies. I only wanted to make the girls happy," she puzzled.

Winkler cupped her hand with his free one. "You will," he said softly. After a brief pause, he added, "It's a fine balance a person must walk. One cannot simply rush in to save the world. Instead, a man must extend his hand while not stealing another man's dignity in the same instance."

"Did I steal Mr. Foxmour's worth?" she asked in concern.

Winkler smiled lovingly. "Absolutely not. You gave from the heart. You're exactly the type of person this community needs—the type of person I need, Catherine." He allowed the others to out-distance them. "If I were to offer a caution, it would be to remind you that you cannot place one of Mr. Darcy's cottagers above the others without causing your brother in marriage additional difficulties. Mr. Darcy often must settle disputes between his tenants. If he would rule with Foxmour over another, it would seem that he did so to please his wife's sister."

"But Mr. Darcy would never do anything so dishonorable," Kitty protested.

"I agree, but when a man loses a contested dispute, he often blames others for his failure," Winkler countered.

Kitty blushed. "I was foolish, was I not? All I wished to do was please you—to prove myself worthy of your attentions."

Winkler leaned closer to speak to her alone. "I was vain enough to realize that fact when you confessed your secret." He squeezed her hand. "And you do please me, Catherine, more than you realize."

"Do I, Thorne? Do I truly?"

Winkler laughed lightly. "Are you searching for compliments, my dear?"

Kitty started to argue but quickly switched to a flirtatious attitude. "I shouldn't have to seek compliments if I'm of a pleasing nature. You should shower me with them without my prompting."

Winkler barked a laugh. "You're too precious. You'll bring life to my household."

"I'm happy you decided to join us." Mr. Bennet escorted his wife toward the pond.

Mrs. Bennet clung tightly to her husband's arm. "It's a great sacrifice to spend time in the cold, but a mother must chaperone her children."

"Jane and Mr. Bingley might serve as chaperones for Mary and Kitty if you should wish to return to Pemberley's warmth," he said in that teasing manner in which he'd always spoken to her. Actually, he'd once favored the woman. Captivated by youth and beauty and that appearance of good humor, which youth and beauty generally give, he had fallen for the woman immediately, but early in their marriage, respect, esteem, and confidence had vanished forever, and all his views of domestic happiness were overthrown. But he was not of a disposition to seek comfort for the disappointment which his own imprudence had brought on in any of those pleasures which too often console the unfortunate for their folly or their vice. He was fond of the country and of books, and from these tastes had arisen his principal enjoyments. To his wife he was very little indebted than as her folly had contributed to his amusement. Mr. Bennet readily realized this was not the sort of happiness which a man would in general wish to owe to his wife, but he had often told himself, *"Where other powers of entertainment are wanting the true philosopher will derive benefit from such as are given."*

"Dearest Jane is all that's good, but she could easily be called away to tend the twins. Besides, a mother's care cannot be lessened by convenience."

"My only care is your own health. Heaven forbid that you should precede me in death," he said in a taunt. "You cannot expect me to seek husbands for our girls with the same diligence that you demonstrate."

Ignoring his tone, as she was apt to do, Mrs. Bennet whispered, "I wish Mr. Manneville had sought Kitty's company again today. I fear she has done the man a disservice, and he'll not forgive her."

Mr. Bennet mockingly said, "You find Mr. Manneville the superior choice, my dear?"

"The man has deep pockets, Mr. Bennet," she reasoned.

"In America," he reminded her.

Mrs. Bennet shrugged off his objections. "Kitty could have a house as grand as Netherfield Park. Would you not want that for your daughter, Mr. Bennet?"

"I would want Kitty in a relationship in which her husband respected her." He thought again of his own marriage's failure. "Jane and

Elizabeth have achieved such happiness, and I have hopes for Mary."

"And of Lydia?" Mrs. Bennet cared best for their youngest daughter.

"You know my opinion of Mr. Wickham," he warned. "I'll never understand how Wickham and Lydia can be supported in tolerable independence nor how little of permanent happiness can belong to a couple who were only brought together because their passions were stronger than their virtue."

"Mr. Bennet," she exclaimed a little too loudly and had to moderate her objection. "You should not speak so despairingly of your own child."

"I speak the truth," he contended. "I won't give elegance to misfortune."

Again, Mrs. Bennet disregarded his severity. "And you think this Mr. Winkler a better choice for Kitty?" she asked as she observed how the clergyman leaned closer to say something private to their daughter.

"First, it's true Winkler will never have the wealth of Mr. Darcy or Mr. Bingley, but he has a secure situation under Mr. Darcy's watchful eye. Second, observe how the man protects our Kitty. He's quite besotted by our daughter's charms."

Mrs. Bennet directed her attention to Kitty and the clergyman. "Do you believe Kitty returns the man's regard?"

"Not totally, but the seed's been planted. It was Winkler that Kitty chased from the drawing room last evening. It was he that she tried to please with her gift to Mr. Darcy's cottager. He inspires the best in our daughter." They walked on in silence for a few moments. "Surely, you remember how foolish Kitty and Lydia once were. I often considered them as two of the silliest girls in England. Now that Kitty, to her material advantage, has spent the chief of her time with her two elder sisters, her improvement has been great. I always said that Kitty had not so ungovernable a temper as Lydia, and removed from the influence of Lydia's example, she has become, by proper attention and management, less irritable, less ignorant, and less insipid. I find myself quite proud of the young lady that Kitty has become."

He watched as Mrs. Bennet frowned when he disparaged Lydia's good sense, but she didn't argue. They'd had similar conversations on numerous occasions. "Should I encourage the connection? Should Kitty be made aware of Mr. Winkler's attention? It would please me to have all my girls well settled."

"If you can suppress your enthusiasm until after Mr. Darcy's return, I suspect that Mr. Winkler will take matters into his own hands. Elizabeth's husband will have to give his approval to his clergyman taking a wife and having that wife be Kitty," he cautioned.

Mrs. Bennet glanced around for privacy. "Would Mr. Darcy object to Lizzy's sister living at the Lambton cottage? Would the man's pride deny Kitty a proper marriage?" she asked incredulously.

"I doubt it. However, Mr. Darcy may need to preface their joining. Winkler must be aware that Darcy would prefer to be consulted prior to the clergyman approaching Kitty with an offer." They neared the pond. "And if Elizabeth's husband does object, you could always steer Kitty into Mr. Manneville's arms. Who knows? After my demise, when Mr. Collins takes Longbourn, you might discover yourself in the Southern states. I think you'll find yourself swept away by an American." Mr. Bennet winked at her.

"You bam me as you always do. I have no need of another husband. With five daughters, I shall spend my days in contentment, knowing I have done my best by each of them." She accepted a seat on a wooden bench to which Mr. Bennet directed her. When he started away to join the couples, Mrs. Bennet caught his arm. "Mr. Bennet, I know we're often at odds over our daughters, but would you do me the courtesy of explaining your dislike for Mr. Manneville?"

It was rare when they spoke honestly to each other—even rarer when he felt empathy for the woman he'd married. "I cannot pretend to know exactly," he said softly. "Maybe it's the man's posturing. Maybe it's his blatant declaration of his intentions—his descriptions of his wealth. Or…" Mr. Bennet turned to watch Manneville glide onto the ice. "Or maybe it's his attention to Miss Bingley. The woman hurt my Jane, and not once did she apologize or show any contrition. I do not forget."

"Neither do I, Mr. Bennet. Neither do I."

CHAPTER 13

≈∞ ≈∞ ≈∞

DARCY DRAPED A LAP RUG over Elizabeth's shoulders. She'd
curled up in a tight ball on the opposing bench. They'd stopped at a
small inn north of Rotherham for their midafternoon meal. They'd
made better time than Darcy had expected. The eastern counties
had obviously been spared the worst of the storm. Water dripped
from the branches that canopied the road, but the passage remained
relatively smooth—a fact for which Darcy was thankful, especially
as he watched the gentle sway of his wife's body as it rocked in
deep sleep.

Their earlier conversation remained fresh in his mind. He knew
of Elizabeth's grief, but her self-inculpation had taken him by surprise. She blamed herself for their losses. "My sweet Elizabeth,"
he mouthed as he traced her countenance's pure loveliness. *How
could she consider such accusations? How could Elizabeth think herself
unworthy?* It was always he who wasn't worthy of her love.

Elizabeth had often expressed her gratitude for his saving her
from a lifetime of tediousness, but it was she who'd saved him. Early
on in their relationship, they had talked *at* each other—challenging
and misconstruing, but never truly communicating. Now, they
spoke with acceptance. When she first refused him, Darcy had
momentarily rued the day he had ever laid eyes upon her. He'd
practiced hatred for less than half the time it had taken him to
return to Rosings. Then his disdain had turned inward, and he'd
sought a means to turn Elizabeth's opinions of him. He'd written

her that first letter—the one in which he'd explained his involvement in separating Bingley from Jane, and in which he'd taken her into his confidence regarding Georgiana's near ruin. When he'd reflected upon it later, Darcy had wondered about his sanity in sharing such intimate details with a woman who'd vehemently stated, "You could not have made the offer of your hand in any possible way that would have tempted me to accept it."

But that letter had been their relationship's turning point, and although they'd spoken of it only once since that fateful day, he was happy he'd told her the awful truth. It had freed him from the crippling guilt of inaction, and it had laid the basis for his renewed hopes.

The thought of never seeing Elizabeth again had nearly driven him to distraction. He'd destroyed any connection he might've had to Hertfordshire when he shared in Caroline Bingley's scheme to end her brother's affection for Jane Bennet. He'd wondered over those spring and summer months about Elizabeth. Did she ever think of him? Had she met someone new? Would Elizabeth marry another? Would her children possess her fine eyes? The possibility of her loving another created such havoc.

There had been moments when he'd considered riding at breakneck speed to Longbourn and prostrating himself before her, but then Fate had arrived in the form of Elizabeth's Aunt and Uncle Gardiner's visit to his estate. With Elizabeth in tow, they, literally, had arrived on his doorstep, and life had changed for the better.

From the haze of his thoughts, hazel eyes met his in some amusement. A sleepy droop of the lid said Elizabeth had rested well despite the cramped quarters. Unfolding, she struggled to a seated position. Stretching her arm to the side and rotating her neck to loosen the muscles, she said, "Did I sleep long?"

Darcy placed the idea of her self-chastisement away for now. He would observe his wife's actions and words more carefully. Somehow, he thought her parents' visit would resolve some of Elizabeth's anguish. That is, if he and she ever arrived at Pemberley. "Long enough to restore a bit of color to your cheeks."

Elizabeth nodded in satisfaction. "I admit to feeling the exhaustion you described earlier." She glanced out the coach's window. "Where are we exactly?"

"Mr. Simpson has made exceptional progress. He's well versed in the local roads and has taken two shorter routes; we're a bit north of Matlock. I thought we might stay the night at my uncle's. A decent bed would do you well."

"We're that close to Pemberley?" she asked in anticipation.

Darcy cautioned, "Still too far to reach its doors at a reasonable hour. We've traveled eight hours already today, and we've another hour to Matlock."

Elizabeth sighed deeply. "If you insist, Fitzwilliam."

"I insist."

Elizabeth teasingly tossed him an air kiss. "Only because you are the most handsome man I know do I allow you to exercise your will over mine," she taunted.

Darcy barked a laugh. "You lust after your husband, Mrs. Darcy?"

Elizabeth's chin rose in a challenge. "Lust, Mr. Darcy? What an unladylike quality you attribute to me."

Darcy's voice became breathier. "Actually, I find the concept quite enticing. Stimulating, even."

"Stimulating indeed," she quipped. "In that case, I hope that the Earl shan't expect us to entertain him all evening."

"We'll claim the need of an early departure on the morrow," he reasoned. "A full night's sleep is well overdue."

"Yes," Elizabeth rasped. "A full night."

∽✆∽ ∽✆∽ ∽✆∽

"Thank you for joining me, Miss De Bourgh," Roman said as he braced her balance with his arm.

Anne laughed nervously as she watched her footing. "You may be sorry, Lieutenant. I haven't skated since I was a child. I may take you with me when I fall."

He leaned a bit closer and tightened his hold. "I could never be sorry for your company, Miss De Bourgh, and you'll not fall. I refuse to consider the possibility."

Anne smiled in surprise. "You're a most unusual gentleman, Lieutenant. I fear I don't know what to expect with you." They slid to a wobbly stop near one of the small benches encircling the icy surface. "May we sit for a moment while I adjust my skating blade?"

Roman smiled agreeably. "As long as you agree to return to the ice with me."

Anne allowed him to assist her. "These metal blades are so much faster than I remember my old skates being."

He seated himself beside her and turned where he might watch the other skaters. It would not do to see the lady's ankles. "Has it truly been so long since you've partaken of the sport?"

"As you well know, Kent's climate is warmer. Chances to skate are less frequent there, and even when in London, Her Ladyship would never condone my joining those skating on the Thames or on smaller ponds. The last skates I owned were wooden ones with thick iron runners."

"Were they not terrible?" he said with a laugh.

Anne said quietly, "For me, they were freedom. They were happy times with my father."

"You miss Sir Lewis very much."

"I do—sometimes more than I can express. Life was easier when Papa was with us. Her Ladyship had someone upon whom to depend. My mother did all she does now, but Papa was there, and she didn't have to be so visible. People considered my father the consummate landowner."

Roman nodded his understanding. "I see such situations often among the officers' wives. It sounds as if Sir Lewis found a woman who humored, or softened, or concealed his failings, and who promoted his real respectability. One cannot fault a man who recognizes his own shortcomings and finds a partner who complements his life with her strengths."

"If Papa hadn't died so soon, things might've been different," she said wistfully. After a pause, she added, "Let's rejoin the others, Lieutenant. If I'm to make a fool of myself, I'd like to do so early on in hopes that someone else shall create a larger scandal."

Roman stood and extended his hand. "I suppose that I should take advantage of this surface. After all, I spent enough time creating it yesterday."

"We're all in your debt, Sir." Anne edged closer to the concrete border.

Roman stiffened his stance and braced her first step. "I need no one's gratitude, Miss De Bourgh."

"Then what do you require, Lieutenant?" Anne asked boldly as she placed her feet shoulder-width apart and let him pull her along beside him.

Roman paused and switched to her other side. "Today, I simply need the pleasure of your company."

"And beyond today?" Anne frowned.

"A chance. An opportunity to be more than I am."

Manneville guided her around the struggling Anne De Bourgh. "Would you care to confide in me your other manipulations to order your world?" he said with a smirk.

Caroline bristled. "I do not know of what you speak, Sir."

The man laughed easily. "I do not criticize, Miss Bingley. In fact, I find the concept quite alluring."

Caroline's mouth line tightened. "You're very impertinent, Sir."

Manneville skated closer. "Others will gladly share the gossip, Miss Bingley. Would you not wish me to know the truth as you see it?"

"I would not," she declared just as her brother joined them.

Bingley smiled widely at them. "May I steal my sister away for a time, Mr. Manneville? Mrs. Bingley fears falling."

Caroline fought the urge to roll her eyes, but to do so would prove what Manneville had asserted. "I'm certain it was your idea for Mrs. Bingley to sit out the exercise, Charles."

"I must claim purchase," he said jovially. He caught Caroline's hand. "Come. It has been too many years since I pulled you across an icy pond."

Manneville watched the brother and sister move away before turning to take in the rest of the scene. Miss Bennet and Mr. Grange crawled around the pond's edge. Southland still catered to Miss De Bourgh, and the colonel courted his cousin. Then he spotted Kitty Bennet sitting alone on a nearby bench. "Well, well," he said as he headed her way. Coming to a halt before her, Manneville extended his hand. "Would you skate with me, Miss Catherine?"

The girl bit her bottom lip in indecision. "I suppose a few times about the ice might be acceptable." She placed her hand in his.

Together, they slid into a side-by-side turn about the pond. "I was sorry to have you take your leave last evening, Miss Catherine. The company felt your absence."

Kitty rested her hand on his arm, but she propelled her own progress on the ice. "I'm certain that no one found the entertainment lacking."

Manneville noted how she kept Winkler in sight. "Do you favor the clergyman, Miss Catherine?"

Kitty blushed before saying, "I hold Mr. Winkler in the highest regard."

"Is that why you chased him from the room last evening?" Manneville steered them away from the others.

Kitty's brows lowered in a scowl. "I don't believe my feelings for Mr. Winkler are your concern, Mr. Manneville."

"Ah, but they are, Miss Catherine. I'm looking for a wife, and I find you very enticing. Could you not see yourself as the mistress of a fine house? I would drape you in silks and diamonds and little else."

Thorne had dutifully asked Mrs. Bennet to take a turn on the ice with him. He preferred her daughter's company, but he was determined to win over the mother.

"You are very kind, Mr. Winkler, to indulge an old woman, but I'm content to chaperone my daughters."

She clung tightly to his arm—so tightly that he thought she'd cut off the circulation. "I'm honored by your company, Mrs. Bennet. Mrs. Darcy has been most kind to me over the past two years. Without your daughter's benevolence, many in the neighborhood would suffer."

He waited for her response, but instead a gasp of surprise brought him to a halt. Thorne turned his head to see Kitty accept Manneville's hand, and he couldn't help but stiffen. "Would you mind…?" he began, but before he could say more, Mr. Bennet appeared by his wife's side.

"There you are, my dear." Mr. Bennet said as he approached. "I thought we might return to the house for some hot tea."

Mrs. Bennet's eyes remained on Kitty, but she said, "That sounds pleasant, Mr. Bennet." She laid her hand on her husband's arm.

"Let's find a safe place to remove these skates." Mr. Bennet caught her elbow. "Mr. Winkler, why do you not reclaim Kitty's hand?"

Thorne nodded his agreement. "Thank you, Mr. Bennet. I believe I'll do just that."

"Could you not see yourself as the mistress of a fine house? I would drape you in silks and diamonds and little else." Thorne had heard the end of Manneville's conversation, and rage raced through him. "Yours isn't an appropriate conversation," he hissed from behind Manneville.

The American turned slowly toward him. "With whom should I speak?" Manneville moved closer.

Sliding forward to meet the man's challenge, Thorne said, "A gentleman would first speak to the lady's father." He'd always abhorred violence, but at the moment, he wanted to separate Manneville's head from the man's shoulders.

"Did you first speak to Mr. Bennet, Winkler?" Manneville dared.

Thorne's hands fisted at his side. "To whom I've stated my addresses is none of your affair, Sir." He shouldered his way past the American. "Your father asked that I reclaim your hand, Miss Catherine." He offered Kitty his arm. When she slid her hand into the crook of it, Thorne breathed easier.

"So, this is how it's to be, Winkler? Do you believe your little vicarage and bestowal can compete with my wealth?" Manneville dared.

"Miss Catherine knows what I offer that you do not—what you can never give her."

"Edward," Georgiana's voice grew strained as she turned toward her friend. "Something's not right with Kitty."

The colonel's gaze followed hers. "Bloody hell," he growled. "What's Manneville up to now? Stay here, Sweetling?" Edward moved away toward the posturing duo.

Georgiana followed at a distance, needing to protect both him and Kitty. "Be careful," she warned.

Gliding to a stop beside Manneville, Edward eyed the possessive stance Winkler had taken with Mrs. Darcy's sister. "I say, Miss Catherine," he said as if he didn't understand the situation's dynamics. "Miss Darcy and I were wondering if you might see to refreshments for everyone. If you and Mr. Winkler would lead the way to the main drawing room, we'll send the others to follow."

"We'd be proud to be of service, Colonel." Kitty followed Winkler to a nearby bench.

Edward slid closer to the American. "What the hell are you doing?" he challenged.

"Just skating with a beautiful woman." Manneville nonchalantly shrugged.

Edward edged closer. "Please remember, Manneville, that our English women are far more innocent than anyone to whom you've been exposed previously, and even a man of God must protect them."

Manneville snarled, "You act as if I had debauched the lady, Colonel."

"If you'd touched her, it wouldn't be Winkler with whom you would deal, Manneville," Edward threatened. "I suggest that you wait until we arrive in London to pursue your marital aspirations." He used his position to tower over the man. "Have I made myself clear?"

"Perfectly," the American said sullenly.

Edward turned to those gathering around and purposely placed a smile on his face. "Miss Darcy and I have asked Miss Catherine and Mr. Winkler to precede us to the main house. They will arrange for hot tea and refreshments in the main drawing room for those who wish to follow. Of course, you may remain and enjoy the ice pond if you please. My cousin and I will take a few more spins around the birdbath before we return." He extended his hand to Georgiana, and she slid into the comfort of his arm.

Edward and Georgiana completed their second loop around the concrete pond. They'd said nothing to each other, but Georgiana was well aware of the anger coursing through her cousin. "Would you care to confide in someone?" she asked softly as they slowed for the rougher curve.

Edward's head turned sharply toward her. "What makes you believe something is amiss?" he asked with forced evenness.

Georgiana edged closer. "Either something is of concern, Cousin, or you wish to throw me into the nearest snowdrift. Someone with lesser experience on the ice would have difficulty keeping to your agitated pace." She smiled widely to diminish the criticism.

Edward spun her to a halt. "Georgiana, my dearest, forgive me. I'm acting foolishly—taking my unfounded suspicions out on you."

"Who else should share your most inner thoughts than those who most love you? Who else may one trust with his hopes and dreams but those who know him best and see no flaws—only the face of a beloved?"

"Do you see my flaws, Georgiana?" he asked huskily.

She gave him a slight shake of her head before glancing away.

Georgiana couldn't look at him without betraying her feelings. "I see only the face of a man I respect and honor above all others," she said earnestly.

Edward brought her hand to rest over his heart. "Georgiana," he began, "there are so many things I don't understand. Upon my return to England, I had thought everything would revert to the normal: I would resume my duties without questions, Darcy and Elizabeth would welcome me to Pemberley, and you'd be Georgie, my young, precocious cousin. Instead, I'm saddled with a man I've tried to like, but cannot, and I'm expected to deliver him to my commanding officers and not express my concerns. I arrived at Pemberley to find Her Ladyship in residence rather than Mr. and Mrs. Darcy, and you…" He paused to cup her chin in his palm. "You're the most breathtakingly beautiful woman I've ever seen."

Georgiana flushed with happiness. He considered her beautiful. "You'd wish me to remain a little girl?" she teased.

"I would wish to lock you away in a tower so that I can be the only one to enjoy your beauty. How am I to fight off all your suitors? And there will be many of them, Georgiana. Your handsome face and excellent dowry will drive the men to distraction." With a frown of discontent, Edward released her. Frustrated, he turned to the empty pond and skated away.

Georgiana wanted to call to him—to tell him that she wanted no other suitors but him; instead, she watched him go: the familiar slant of his shoulders, the distinctive gait, and the formidable stance. There was little about the man that she didn't find pleasing, except for the fact that he denied their connection. With a sigh of exasperation, Georgiana removed her skates. Gathering her belongings, she stood slowly and followed the colonel's retreating form.

❧ ❧ ❧

"Mr. Darcy." The Matlock butler hid his surprise as he opened the door to Darcy and Elizabeth. "I was unaware of your arrival, Sir." He took their wraps and handed them to an equally bewildered footman.

Darcy glanced about the shadowed hallway. "My uncle knew nothing of my visit, Mr. Eldon. Might you inform the Earl and Lady Matlock of our arrival?"

Mr. Eldon stammered, "His…His Lordship and the Countess are at William's Wood, Sir. Lady Lindale has taken to her bed."

"I see. Then there's no one to receive us?"

"No, Sir. His Lordship released much of the staff to celebrate the opening of Christmastide with their families."

Darcy frowned. He didn't want to return to the road so soon. "Can you accommodate Mrs. Darcy and me for the evening? We left Harrogate earlier this morning, and Pemberley is still too far for travel after dark. The road conditions are too unpredictable." He didn't mention the possibility of highwaymen. As the neighboring community had suffered with governmental regulations, a larger number of men had turned to thievery. "A clean bed and a meal will suffice. Mrs. Darcy and I mean to be on the road early in the morning."

Mr. Eldon bowed. Upper-class English servants always responded with efficiency. "Of course, Sir. Lord Matlock will be sorry he missed you and Mrs. Darcy. Would you care to take your evening meal in the dining room?"

Darcy glanced at Elizabeth and noted her weariness. "We'd be happy with a simple meal in our room. It's been a harrowing journey. There is thick ice in the North."

Mr. Eldon appeared relieved. "If you'd care to escort Mrs. Darcy to your usual chambers, Sir, I'll send up the maids to turn down the bed and to light the fire. Meanwhile, I will speak to cook about a tray."

"Might I also request some tea while we wait?" Elizabeth added as she removed her bonnet. "And Mr. Darcy would prefer a decanter of port."

"Certainly, Mrs. Darcy. I'll see to it immediately, as well as sending word to the stables regarding your carriage."

～☙〜 ～☙〜 ～☙〜

"Walk me out," Thorne whispered as Kitty offered him another sandwich. Everyone, including Lady Catherine, had gathered in the main drawing room to recapture his afternoon to each person's delight.

Kitty's eyes grew in size, but she responded with a simple nod and then moved on to share the plate with others.

"It was a superb afternoon," Mr. Bingley declared, "and I'm thankful that the colonel had such entertaining foresight."

"We should be thankful to Lieutenant Southland and Mr. Manneville who took my suggestion and made it a reality," Edward corrected.

Manneville sipped on his preferred coffee. "The lieutenant deserves the lion's share of the gratitude. He executed the colonel's plans with typical military efficiency," he said smugly.

Thorne, who had watched the exchange with interest, noted the flick of the colonel's wrist, which stifled the lieutenant's stiffened response. "It has nothing to do with military effectiveness," Edward corrected. "Southland is an honorable man." The implication lay clearly between them, but Manneville didn't accept the bait.

Winkler used the slight pause to come quickly to his feet. "I'm afraid that I must return to Lambton." He bowed to Georgiana. "Miss Darcy, your graciousness is commendable."

"We'll see you for services tomorrow," the colonel returned the bow. "Thank you for seeing Mrs. Darcy's cousin safely to Pemberley."

Winkler bowed to the room. "It'll be my pleasure to attend you for Christmas Eve. Unfortunately, my day will start with less secular activities. Mr. Foxmour's sent word that the ground has been prepared for his mother. A terrible event for such a glorious day."

"Celebrating a life is never terrible," Kitty added from where she stood near the door.

Thorne couldn't hide his affection. "As always, you see the obvious, Miss Catherine—what the rest of us overlooked."

"Thank you, Kitty." After a brief pause, Georgiana said conspiratorially, "I understand it shall be a joyous service tomorrow evening, Mr. Winkler. I'm looking forward to it."

"A bit non-traditional," Winkler said truthfully. "Few Anglican churches celebrate on Christmas Eve, whereas the Catholics flock to their masses. We'll combine the best of both. There are many practicing Catholics still in the area, so I'll deliver a short sermon, and then the children's choir will share a few hymns. It'll be a simple way of welcoming the Christ child."

Lady Catherine harrumphed her disapproval, and Mr. Collins thought to vocalize his own objections, but Mr. Bingley said, "It sounds a delightful way to usher in a solemn recognition—much better than wassailing and carousing."

"I agree," Edward added. "I never understood why St. Stephen's Day takes precedence."

"Our celebration was Mrs. Darcy's idea. The lady recognized my desire to involve the village children more in the church service. Mr. Lancaster, my curate, has taken on organizing the group and bringing them together for practice."

"Calvinism," Lady Catherine intoned in disapprobation.

Winkler simply inclined his head. "I've neglected my duties long enough. Again, Miss Darcy, I thoroughly enjoyed the entertainment."

"You'll join us after services on Christmas, Mr. Winkler. I'm certain my brother would insist."

With a quick glance to Kitty, he said, "I can think of nothing I would enjoy more, Miss Darcy."

"Stay seated, Miss Darcy. I'll see Mr. Winkler out," Kitty announced to the room.

Winkler followed Kitty through the main corridor until they reached the top of the staircase; then he caught her hand and pulled her to him.

"Mr. Winkler," she gasped, but relaxed against him.

"Say my name, Kitty," he whispered hoarsely.

She leaned closer. "You'll be missed, Thorne," she said coyly.

"I shouldn't wish my life away, but I'll count the minutes until I see you again." He kissed her forehead. "It will be your angelic face I seek among the congregation tomorrow."

"Would it be inappropriate for me to attend Mrs. Foxmour's service?" she asked.

He advised, "Take your cue from Miss Darcy. She'll know her family's wishes."

Kitty silently agreed. "I should return to the drawing room," she said reluctantly. Impulsively, she touched his cheek. "You're such a good man, and I'm in awe that you believe me a proper mate."

"You're more than that, Catherine. I cannot speak everything in my heart without overwhelming you with my desires, and you need time to know your own feelings before we commit ourselves to one another."

Kitty swallowed hard before saying, "It's so much so soon."

"I know," Thorne said reassuringly. "But you must take your time. Marriage is forever. Being apart until tomorrow may be for the best. Without my presence, you'll have time to consider what I ask of you. I'll never be rich, Catherine—not like what Manneville or others can offer you. All I can promise is my complete devotion and a life of comfort."

"I don't want Mr. Manneville," she protested.

Thorne smiled happily. "I needed to hear your denial, and I thank you for it. I don't like to leave you in this house with that man."

"There are many to protect me, and I'll make an effort to avoid Mr. Manneville. He and the colonel shall leave for London soon."

"Not soon enough for my taste," Thorne grumbled.

〜☙〜 〜☙〜 〜☙〜

"We'll be at Pemberley in time for a late breakfast," Darcy told her as Elizabeth brushed her hair. The Earl's staff had done an admirable job of meeting their needs on such short notice.

"At the moment, all I care about is a full night's sleep." She had relaxed in a tub of hot water and now languidly prepared for bed.

Darcy thought of those who waited for them. "Yet, being home will be exhilarating, will it not?"

"It shall." She smiled with a stir of regret. "However, I wouldn't mind a week with my husband in quiet solitude."

A flicker of alarm caused him to avoid her eyes. "As delightful as that sounds, we must first see to our Twelfth Night duties."

"Afterward, you promise to sequester us away for an extended holiday?" she pleaded.

"If that's your wish, Elizabeth, then I'll make it so."

Elizabeth shrugged away her embarrassment. "It's not as if we don't possess enough quiet at Pemberley. It's just as I acknowledged at Harrogate: the only thing I need to make me happy is you." She stood and walked into his welcoming embrace.

Chapter 14

❦ ❦ ❦

AS HE HAD PREDICTED, Darcy's coach rolled past the Pemberley gatehouse just before breakfast. Elizabeth, as if she knew what awaited her, had awakened with the dawn and had insisted that they leave immediately. "Do you believe Georgiana is awake?" she had asked anxiously as they stared at the familiar landscape.

"I hope so," Darcy said flatly, wondering again if the Bennets had arrived safely.

"So do I," Elizabeth said softly. "I've missed her terribly. You've no idea, Fitzwilliam, how thankful I am to share Pemberley with Georgiana."

"Last evening you spoke of wanting solitude," he teased.

"Fitzwilliam Darcy," she warned. "Do not twist my words. I'm a woman and can change my mind on a whim."

Darcy chuckled. "So you may, my love."

They both turned to behold the first appearance of Pemberley Woods as the sun danced across the bare branches in spring's promise rather than winter's demise. "I never cease to feel awe at moments such as this," Elizabeth whispered.

They gradually ascended for half a mile, and then found themselves at the top of a considerable eminence, where the wood ceased, and the eye was instantly caught by Pemberley House, situated on the opposite side of the valley, into which the road, with some abruptness, wound. It was a large, handsome stone building, standing well on high ground, and backed up a ridge of high woody hills; and in front a stream of some natural importance was swelled into greater, but without any artificial appearance. Its banks were neither formal nor falsely adorned. There was never a house for which nature had done more, or where natural beauty had been so little counteracted by an awkward taste. "Our child's heritage," Darcy murmured from beside her.

Elizabeth's hand automatically splayed against her stomach's swell. "The master of Pemberley." Her other hand reached for Darcy's. Never taking her eyes from the imposing structure, she interlaced her fingers with his and gave his hand a gentle squeeze.

Darcy brought her ungloved knuckles to his lips. He leaned closer to whisper in her ear. "I know you sometimes feel everything's out of your control, but you must trust in God and trust your heart. Only your own doubts limit your abilities, Elizabeth."

She turned her head and looked lovingly into his eyes. "I know, Fitzwilliam. Something else I discovered in those hours while I waited for William Joseph to make his worldly appearance: God has given me the authority to impact the lives of others, and I plan to do just that. I don't know exactly how, but some way—someday."

Noting over her shoulder the group gathering on Pemberley's steps, Darcy lowered his head to kiss her lips. The movement distracted Elizabeth long enough for the carriage to roll to a halt and for Darcy to scramble from the coach before she had time to realize who was among the throng awaiting her. However, the number and the group's makeup surprised even him.

He reached up to catch her waist when Elizabeth appeared in the open carriage doorway. "We are home, my dear," he said with a soft laugh. Who waited for her still had not registered with his wife, but he knew the instant that she raised her head to see her family.

"Fitz...oh, my," she gasped with glee. "Oh, Fitzwilliam," she repeated as he sat her on the ground, and she broke away from him and ran into her father's open arms. "You're here at last," she sobbed as she cupped her father's face. "I cannot believe it. You're the most magnificent sight I've ever seen. But how?" she looked around frantically for the others.

"It was Mr. Darcy's idea," Mr. Bennet rasped through a tear-choked throat.

Elizabeth glanced over her shoulder at a beaming Darcy. "You'll pay for keeping secrets, Sir," she warned good-naturedly, but she immediately returned to the comforting face of her father. "Where is Mama?"

"As we speak, Mrs. Bennet is dressing for the day. She'll greet you as quickly as her maid can apply her laces."

Elizabeth just half acknowledged what he said. Instead, she was reaching for Mary. Never had she hugged her sister so violently. "I've missed you so," she said as she grabbed Mary's hand, only to have Mary pull her close again.

"And I, you, Lizzy."

Mary's unexpected display of emotion sent Elizabeth's happy tears flowing again. "Mr. Grange, I am pleased that you accompanied Mary to Pemberley. Later, I'll bombard you with news of my Aunt and Uncle Philips," she said as she extended her hand to the young man she barely knew.

Mr. Grange bowed stiffly over it. "It's my honor, Mrs. Darcy, to be welcomed into your home."

So many faces greeted her that Elizabeth turned in circles several times to take it all in. Then her gaze fell on Charlotte Collins. For a brief second, she just stared at her old friend and then launched herself into the woman's embrace. "You're here also," she said as she caught Charlotte in a congenial hug of friendship. "How did Mr. Darcy arrange all this?"

"Perhaps, Elizabeth, we might take this homecoming inside and out of the cold," she heard Darcy say from behind her. Happily, Elizabeth released Charlotte and turned toward the still-open door and Mr. Nathan. She laced her arm about Georgiana's waist and pulled Darcy's sister along beside her. "This is the best Christmastide I've ever known."

∿ ∿ ∿

Darcy had watched with delight as his wife rushed into her father's open arms. "This is what she needed," he congratulated himself, but then his eyes fell on the others who trailed from the door to greet them. "What the hell is Collins doing here?" he asked the waiting footman, who answered with a shrug.

Then he saw the one person who could answer all his questions. "Edward!" he called as he skirted the group encircling Elizabeth. "Thank God, you've returned safely." He encompassed his cousin in an affectionate hug. "You're a most agreeable sight."

"Was on my way to Matlock, but the storm, and Georgiana's being beset with so many guests, forced me to tarry until your return."

Darcy said privately, "I'm afraid the Earl is at Lincolnshire with Lindale. Elizabeth and I stayed at Matley last evening."

Edward nodded. "So I heard. First from Georgiana and then from Her Ladyship."

"Lady Catherine? I don't understand," Darcy whispered urgently.

"Her Ladyship has taken refuge at Pemberley, along with Anne and the Collinses," Edward disclosed.

"Lady Catherine is here?" Darcy said incredulously. "Now? How dare she!"

"She dares, Darcy." Edward said cautiously. "I'll explain in greater detail later." They both shot a glance to the welcoming party. "For now, let's escort Mrs. Darcy safely into the house."

Darcy accepted his cousin's advice. He turned to where his wife hugged Mrs. Collins. "Perhaps, Elizabeth, we might take this homecoming inside and out of the cold," he suggested.

Her brightest smile graced his wife's face, and Darcy's heart leapt in pleasure. She caught Georgiana about the waist and headed toward the open doorway, but a brief word from his sister sent Elizabeth spinning around to meet the colonel's eyes. "Edward," she called and hurried down the steps toward him. "How did I miss seeing you?"

Impulsively, Edward caught Elizabeth and spun her around in the air before planting a kiss on her cheek.

"Easy," Darcy warned with a bit of jealousy. "Do not damage my most precious possession, Cousin."

Edward didn't look at Darcy when he teasingly said, "Mrs. Darcy liked me first, Fitz."

Darcy reached for his wife. "But the lady liked me best," he said flatly.

"I love you both," Elizabeth declared as she laced an arm through each man's offered elbow. "Just in different ways."

They followed the group who had greeted them to the morning room, where Elizabeth found her other sisters and Mr. Bingley. "You've been at Pemberley throughout the storm?" she asked as a footman poured tea for everyone.

"Miss Darcy was gracious and found everyone more than adequate shelter," Bingley declared.

Elizabeth caught Georgiana's gaze. "My dear, Georgie," she said in admiration. "I'm so proud of you."

Georgiana blushed. "Edward made it easier."

"Georgiana required no assistance. She's the perfect hostess," Edward insisted.

"Ah, Mr. Darcy," Caroline intoned as she entered the room. "My maid assured me of your return, but I had to see it for myself. It was naughty of you to leave Miss Darcy to serve in your stead."

"Miss Bingley, I wasn't aware you had plans to join Charles for the festive days. If I had, I would've sent a separate invitation in your name." Darcy hated how the woman continued to ignore Elizabeth's presence in his life, and he took perverted pleasure in his veiled insult.

"Miss Bingley is my sister of a sort," Elizabeth said with her own twisted smile, something Darcy immediately recognized. "As such, she needs no invitation to join us at Pemberley. Miss Bingley is as welcome as say, Mr. Collins, for example." Elizabeth gestured to her weak-chinned cousin, who had returned with gusto to his breakfast.

The clergyman swallowed quickly and washed down too large a mouthful with a quick gulp of ale. "Mrs. Darcy is all benevolence, Miss Bingley. My cousin does her husband credit."

Darcy loved the interchange. It was the old Elizabeth, the one who delighted in the absurd, sitting casually between her eldest sister and her father. "For once, we agree, Mr. Collins," Darcy said as he leaned back in his chair. "My wife is phenomenal."

Mr. Manneville entered on that note, and Darcy rose with Edward for the introductions, and then welcomed the stranger into the group. However, he didn't miss Edward's steely stare to Darcy's questioning glance. "My aide, Lieutenant Southland, is also with us," Edward explained.

"And where is this lieutenant?" Elizabeth asked.

Although Elizabeth directed the question to the colonel, Manneville answered. "Probably waiting attendance on Miss De Bourgh," he said flatly.

Darcy noted his wife's momentary alarm. "Edward has just informed me, my dear, that my cousin Anne and my aunt have unexpectedly joined us for Christmastide," Darcy said evenly.

He realized that until that moment, Elizabeth had thought he'd arranged for the Collinses' visit. "How delightful," Elizabeth said with a forced smile. "It's been ages since we've seen Her Ladyship."

As if on cue and followed by Mrs. Jenkinson, Anne entered on the lieutenant's arm. Glancing at the full table, her eyes fell on Darcy. "Fitzwilliam," she gasped in joyous greeting. "I heard you had returned. I'm so pleased to see you again."

Darcy swallowed his astonishment. His cousin's greeting was more words than he could ever remember Anne saying in one setting. Usually, a nod of the head or a weak smile was the extent of Anne's conversation. "As I am you." He started to bow, but she rushed into his arms, and so Darcy hugged her and kissed Anne's forehead. "I've missed you," he said before shooting Edward a raised eyebrow of amusement. He set Anne from him and said, "You're looking well, Cousin." Anne had color in her cheeks and a sparkle in her eyes.

"I am well, Fitzwilliam," she said softly. "We all went skating yesterday."

"Skating?" Darcy questioned, and Edward confirmed with a nod. "I see that my sister had the foresight to take advantage of the weather."

Georgiana looked cautiously at the colonel. "It was Edward's idea and Lieutenant Southland's execution. Mr. Manneville was also most helpful."

Before Darcy could respond, Anne said, "Let me present Lieutenant Southland." She gestured the man forward. "The lieutenant is Edward's aide. Lieutenant Southland, this is my cousin, Mr. Darcy."

The men exchanged bows. "It's my honor to be among the colonel's family," the lieutenant said.

"The colonel is beyond family in our estimation," Darcy responded before he directed the man to Elizabeth. "Lieutenant, may I present my wife, Mrs. Darcy."

"I've heard the colonel speak so fondly of the Darcys, I must claim a prior acquaintance." Southland bowed to his hosts.

"As Mr. Darcy has indicated," Elizabeth said graciously, "Colonel Fitzwilliam is more than family." She then bowed to Anne. "As is Miss De Bourgh. Welcome to Pemberley."

Darcy noted Anne's blush, but she managed to say, "Thank you for your hospitality, Mrs. Darcy. Georgiana has served you and my cousin well in your absence."

Elizabeth smiled broadly at Georgiana. "I would've expected nothing less. Mr. Darcy's sister comes from the best stock."

"That she does," a strong, authoritative voice declared from the open doorway. "Georgiana is Lady Anne Darcy's daughter. My sister served this estate in an exemplary manner."

Everyone scrambled to his feet in acknowledgement of Lady Catherine's presence. Darcy waited the span of three heartbeats before responding, "It's true that Lady Anne has left a great legacy, but the current Mrs. Darcy reigns graciously as Pemberley's mistress, and it's under her tutelage that my sister has blossomed. They give honor to my mother's memory." He didn't remove his eyes from his aunt's face. His words warned her that he would brook no disparagement of Elizabeth during Her Ladyship's stay.

Lady Catherine remained framed by the door until Edward led her to the table, but all the while she maintained Darcy's gaze, only looking away when the colonel held the chair for her. It was the place that Elizabeth should've claimed, and Darcy saw the pleasure of his acceptance twist his aunt's mouth. "The household hasn't suffered in your absence, Darcy. The colonel has advised Georgiana in her duties," she announced.

"I beg to differ, Your Ladyship," Edward interrupted. "My cousin is quite capable. Georgiana and Miss Catherine had everything well in hand before Southland, Manneville, and I arrived."

Elizabeth smiled brightly. "Georgiana and Kitty have become great friends—a fact that pleases me."

"As well as me," Darcy said to curtail any objection from his aunt.

"When you didn't arrive as expected," Georgiana said, "we were most concerned, especially with the weather."

"If there had been some way to send word, I would've done so readily, but thick ice coated the northern shires. Luckily, we found shelter at a small inn outside of Harrogate. I apologize for causing you any form of anguish, my dear."

"As with Edward," Georgiana said softly, "as you have returned safely, I am content."

"Prestwick's Portal was quite an adventure in itself," Darcy smirked.

The table's curiosity exploded, and his guests bombarded him with requests for details. However, his wife's frown caused Darcy to hesitate, and in the breadth of that hesitation, Mrs. Bennet swept into the room. "Oh, my dear Lizzy," she exclaimed.

Immediately, Elizabeth was out of her chair and catching her mother to her. "Oh, Mama," she sobbed. "I've longed for this moment." Elizabeth choked out the words and held tightly to the woman.

"It's all well, my girl," her mother coaxed. "Letting one's child go is never easy," she whispered hoarsely. "Come, let us sit." And in a rare understanding, very much as she must've done when Elizabeth was a small child, Mrs. Bennet caught Elizabeth's hand and led her daughter to the table. "Let us refresh your tea." And just like that small child, Elizabeth allowed her mother to tend to her.

Darcy watched the woman he'd never respected give Elizabeth a loving dose of maternal care, and in that moment, he ached for his own mother's touch. Mrs. Bennet won his devotion with that simple gesture. "Your visit has surprised Mrs. Darcy," he said. "And I thank you for making the journey from Hertfordshire."

"Well, we would've come before if Mr. Bennet would have agreed to the trip, but the man prefers his study," Mrs. Bennet said vituperatively.

"You've no more concerns about that matter, Mrs. Bennet," her husband teased. "Now that I've seen Mr. Darcy's library, I'll return to Pemberley more times than my son may care to entertain me."

Darcy didn't understand Mr. Bennet's indolent defense in dealing with his family, but he'd developed a fondness for the man. Mr. Bennet possessed a quick mind and a biting wit: two characteristics that Darcy admired in Elizabeth. "Pemberley's door is open to you at all times, Father Bennet. No invitation is needed." He shot a quick glance at his aunt, but, miraculously, Her Ladyship offered no comment.

"So, once again," Edward said, leaning forward, "tell us what happened at the Prestwick's inn. You have piqued my interest, Cousin."

Another glance to Elizabeth displayed her uncomfortable stance, and it occurred to Darcy that his tale might embarrass her before his aunt, but the others would find Elizabeth's courage remarkable. He wouldn't allow Lady Catherine's opinions to define his marriage. With a pause to draw Elizabeth's attention, he began his tale of ice, of overcrowding, of community, of a couple denied a room and then facing the impossible, and of his incomparable wife who brought order from chaos.

"I cannot imagine sharing my room with complete strangers," Caroline said censoriously. "What a quaint concept. Very far from Mayfair."

"Sir Jonathan and Mr. Horvak shared a room," Bingley reminded her.

"But they held a previous acquaintance," Caroline insisted. "A stranger." She shivered in disgust. "How did you know the Josephs weren't thieves?"

Darcy eyed Bingley's sister with renewed displeasure. "As we were all unable to travel because of the weather, a thief would've had difficulty escaping," he said flatly. "Besides, the man holds a living outside Stoke-upon-Trent."

"And they named the child after my cousin?" Edward taunted. "If I were you, Mrs. Darcy, I would demand satisfaction. You did all the work, and Darcy took the credit."

Elizabeth chuckled. "I'm certain it would have done the boy irreparable harm had the Josephs named him 'Elizabeth.'"

"Or made him a world-class pugilist," the colonel observed.

"Or that," Elizabeth responded.

Georgiana stood and acknowledged the others about the table. "If you would excuse Kitty and me, we'll make a brief trip into Lambton."

Darcy frowned. "What's so important, Georgiana? Would not your time be better spent in helping the others hang the holly?"

"Mrs. Foxmour, Fitzwilliam. She lost her long battle with her illness. Kitty and Mr. Winkler aided the family in the lady's last hours. I thought it best that Pemberley is represented at the service," she said. "I'll not be long. Mr. Winkler arranged an early service because of Christmas Eve."

Darcy stood. "I'll go. You remain with our guests."

"But you have just spent hours on the road," his sister protested.

Elizabeth caught his eye and gave a slight shake of her head. "Allow Georgiana and Kitty to handle it, Mr. Darcy. There are more than enough hands to decorate the house, and our sisters have performed admirably. You might call on the Foxmours later today."

Darcy swallowed his need to control every estate detail. "Of course, Georgiana and Kitty are quite capable. Please inform Mr. Foxmour of my intent to call on his family before this evening's service." Georgiana nodded, and she and Kitty slipped from the room.

"Do you wish for me to accompany them?" Edward asked.

Darcy sighed in defeat. "My sister and Miss Catherine are no longer green girls. They'll represent Pemberley properly." It hurt him to let Georgiana become a woman; he would miss the young girl he'd raised after their parents' deaths.

Elizabeth sighed also. "Fitzwilliam, I suspect we should change our clothes and then see to turning Pemberley green with holly."

Darcy nodded his agreement. Turning to his butler, he said, "Have we found a Yule log, Mr. Nathan?"

"It's in the kitchen waiting for Mrs. Reynolds's orders."

"Then tell the good lady to bring on the troops. I expect Pemberley to glisten with the Christmastide spirit."

~๑~ ~๑~ ~๑~

"Mr. Darcy, you be honoring me family, Sir." Mr. Foxmour led Darcy to a place close to the hearth. Discussing the late lady's exemplary life, several of his other tenants stood about the room. Darcy had accepted their reverence as part of his way of life.

"I apologize for missing the service. Mrs. Darcy and I were stranded in the North because of the weather."

Foxmour nodded his acceptance with a quick jerk of his head. "Miss Darcy be sayin' so, Sir. She and Mrs. Darcy's sister be treatin' me family well. Miss Catherine taught me wee ones to draw, and she be sendin' a fine dress for me mother for the buryin'."

Darcy hadn't known those specifics, but he had no objection to his family interjecting themselves into his cottagers' lives. He was in a battle to save his estate. The city's draw had taken renters away, and he appreciated any "debt" which kept a family on the land.

"I'll not keep you, Foxmour. I wanted to pay my respects and to see if you needed anything."

"We be fine, Sir. Me wife has seen to me mother's things."

Darcy accepted the man's reassurances. It was a matter of pride on Foxmour's part. "If something arises, please call on me at the main house."

"Thank you, Mr. Darcy."

～ఴ~ ～ఴ~ ～ఴ~

He had left the decorations to his guests and his staff and had retreated to his study to review newly arrived correspondence and to escape the inevitable confrontation with his aunt. He had addressed a letter to his solicitor and another to his steward, Mr. Lynden, before the room's door opened and his cousin slipped in and slid into the chair across from Darcy.

"I'm busy, Edward," he murmured without looking up from the instructions he was writing.

"And I'm the cousin with whom you've shared everything since we were boys," the colonel argued as he propped his booted feet on the corner of Darcy's desk.

Darcy placed the pen to the side. "Then tell me what the hell Her Ladyship is doing at Pemberley," Darcy grumbled.

"I wish I knew. She swears the weather left her no choice, but before Her Ladyship left Matlock, Lady Catherine sent word to the Collinses to meet her at Pemberley."

"I thought the Collinses traveled with her."

"They will return to Kent in the second coach, but Mr. Winkler brought them to Pemberley when the Collinses arrived on the mail coach in Lambton."

Darcy growled, "Damn! I swear if our aunt ruins the Christmastide for Elizabeth..." Before the colonel could respond, a tap on the door took their attention. "Enter!" Darcy called.

The door opened to a hesitant Lieutenant Southland. "Excuse me, Colonel." The man bowed. "Mr. Nathan told me where I might find you. Will you and Mr. Darcy allow me a moment of your time, Sir?"

Edward shot a quick glance at Darcy, who reluctantly agreed. "Come in, Southland."

"Thank you, Sir." The lieutenant quickly closed the door and came forward to stand politely beside the imposing desk.

"What may we do for you, Southland?" Darcy's eyebrow rose in amusement. He gestured the man to a chair, one of the lessons he'd learned from his late father—never permit a man the advantage of standing over him.

"I seek your advice, Mr. Darcy, as well as that of the colonel. On a private matter." Southland had, obviously, added the idea of privacy as an afterthought.

"If it deals with your service, Southland, perhaps we should discuss this at another time."

"It concerns Miss De Bourgh," the lieutenant said evenly.

Darcy sat forward with interest. "What of our cousin?"

"I wish to pay my addresses to Miss De Bourgh, and I seek your advice on how to approach Lady Catherine."

Darcy shot Edward a conspiratorial smile. "This is a speedy arrangement, Southland." Both men moderated their expressions. "Her Ladyship will question your motives, Lieutenant. Our aunt is quite protective of our cousin."

The lieutenant stiffened, but his facial expression remained noncommittal. "I expected as much. I possess no title and have only limited connections. Lady Catherine would prefer that her daughter find a more compatible match."

"You appear to be arguing Her Ladyship's side of the issue," Edward said wryly. "Trust me, Southland, my aunt will require no assistance in disparaging your suit, and although it is admirable that you anticipate Lady Catherine's objections, your time would be better spent in convincing Her Ladyship of your worth."

"Why do you not share with the colonel and me the reasons you believe you'd make Anne an acceptable mate?" Darcy coaxed.

This time Southland's discomfort showed. "I'm not certain I can explain—not logically." The man paused in contemplation. "The colonel will recall that the late Mr. Knight was my father's cousin. I grew up with tales of Rosings Park and of the De Bourghs. I feel as if I have known the family all my life. As if my relationship with Miss De Bourgh is a matter of fate."

"Her Ladyship will never accept Fate as reason," Edward declared.

"Absolutely not," Darcy agreed. "Southland, to win Lady Catherine's approval you must think more ruthlessly. Her Ladyship has functioned admirably in a man's world. Our aunt won't mince words, and you can warrant her ability to poke holes in a weak syllogism."

The lieutenant shifted uncomfortably. "Then what should I say?"

Edward laced his fingers behind his head and leaned back nonchalantly. "Be brutal. Point out the fact that Anne has never had a suitor and is not likely to ever have one. Present yourself as Anne's last opportunity. Do not hesitate to remind Lady Catherine of Anne's advanced age."

Southland blustered, "I…I couldn't defame Miss De Bourgh thus. She deserves better than such pettiness."

Darcy corrected, "Anne deserves a family and a home of her own. She'll never know such happiness unless you're willing to fight for her. Be the swain in our cousin's presence, but with Lady Catherine, treat your suit as a business proposition. What are the advantages of Anne aligning herself with you?"

"Unfortunately, by no fault of hers, Anne has long since lost her bloom. She can recover some of her youth. Her bubbly conversation upon Darcy's arrival this morning proves that."

"I've never known my cousin to be so animate," Darcy confirmed.

Edward continued, "Besides providing Anne the opportunity to know marriage, stress your connection to Mr. Knight. Lady Catherine bemoaned her loss when the clergyman passed."

"Of course, your allegiance to the colonel should serve you well. Her Ladyship will turn to the Earl for advice. I'm assuming,

Edward, that you'd have no qualms in recommending Lieutenant Southland." Darcy enjoyed this interplay. It had been too long since he and Edward had worked in tandem to solve a problem. Without complex explanations required, they'd always understood each other. It had been Edward who'd first offered compassion and then advice after Elizabeth's initial denial of Darcy's love.

"I'm more than pleased with the lieutenant's service," Edward announced, as if he recited the lines for the Earl's benefit.

Southland took them to heart, nonetheless. "Thank you, Sir."

"You've served your country. Don't forget to stress that fact for Her Ladyship. Our aunt enjoys reflected glory. She'll want to 'steal' your accomplishments," Darcy explained.

Southland looked from one to another. "Do you believe it so?" he asked the colonel.

"Darcy knows our aunt well. Explain how you've served both on the Continent and on the American front. That'll be a key issue for the Earl."

Darcy said, "It's important that you speak to Lady Catherine before she returns to Kent. I assume she'll travel on Tuesday, as Mr. Collins will have missed three Sundays. Her Ladyship won't tolerate the man's shirking his duties. It would be unseemly for you to call at Rosings without permission."

"So, I should speak to Her Ladyship tomorrow?"

"At the latest," Edward assured.

Southland stood. "Thank you, Gentlemen. You've given me much to consider." The lieutenant bowed and excused himself from the room.

With the sound of the door's latch closing behind the man, Darcy released the breath he had held. "Was that wise?" he asked with self-chastisement.

Edward returned his booted feet to the desk. "Southland homed in on Anne immediately. At first, I warned him away, but the more I thought on it, the more I realized this might be Anne's last chance."

"And the man will have to face Lady Catherine eventually," Darcy reasoned.

"And the fact that Southland's request will occupy Her Ladyship's interest until our aunt's departure had nothing to do with our encouraging the man." Edward's lips twisted in a smirk.

"At least, the advice we gave him is the same that I would've issued even if I didn't wish to distract Lady Catherine from Mrs. Darcy."

They sat in silence—each analyzing his part in sending Southland off to face Lady Catherine alone. "I believe it's time that the lieutenant receive a captainship," Edward observed.

"Feeling guilty?" Darcy taunted.

"I just sent my aide into battle poorly armed. Yes, I'm feeling damned guilty."

CHAPTER 15

~~~

DARCY FOUND HER IN HER CHAMBERS. Hannah assisted her mistress with a clothing change. They'd attend the services that she'd suggested to Mr. Winkler last summer. Elizabeth thought it a unique opportunity at the time, but now she wasn't so certain. Christmas would fall on Sunday, and she'd thought the day's significance would be lost to the usual Sunday service. The thought had occurred shortly after she'd discovered that for a third time she carried Darcy's child, and her fear and her maternal instinct had both arisen at the same time. Elizabeth had thought it a good omen to recognize the birth of the Christ child in a joyous manner.

"Could we not have a celebration of the children?" she had asked Mr. Winkler over afternoon tea. Her hand had instinctively rested on her abdomen.

Winkler had responded enthusiastically, "It's a wonderful idea. Mr. Lancaster's been working with some of the village and estate children. How about a children's choir?"

The idea had grown from there, and tonight would be the first such celebration. Elizabeth was a bit worried over the community's reception.

Upon his entrance, Darcy motioned Hannah away and took up the lacing of his wife's gown. They actually each served as the other's dresser on a regular basis. It was part of their natural closeness. "You look lovely," he said as he examined her appearance. The deep forest green dress brightened her hazel-colored eyes and contrasted with Elizabeth's pale skin.

Elizabeth glanced over her shoulder at him. "I feel lovely." Her smile followed. "Thank you for today. Returning to Pemberley to find my sisters and parents was a gift I'll cherish always." She turned into Darcy's arms and lifted her chin for his kiss.

"The contented look in your eyes when you were in Father Bennet's embrace was worth the trouble of arranging everything. It's been too long since you had the Bennets as company." He pulled her closer and buried his face in Elizabeth's hair. "I want you to be happy, Elizabeth."

She turned her head to kiss his temple. "I am happy, Fitzwilliam. I cannot imagine being any place but Pemberley, but seeing my dear family again has been a balm to my grieving heart. You've given me so much of yourself in your gesture."

Darcy kissed her deeply. His wife smelled of the lavender oil that she preferred in her bath, and she was warm and soft in his arms. "I want you safe—want to protect you. I love you, Elizabeth." He kissed her fiercely with all the love they shared.

Elizabeth laughed easily when his lips released her. She rested her head on his chest. "We've everything we need as long as we're together."

He kissed the top of her head before he stepped away and sat on the side of her bed. "Did you have a pleasant time with your family this afternoon?"

"The house has so much greenery. Every room has garlands of holly and rosemary and laurel." He watched as her excitement grew. "Kitty hung mistletoe in every room." She turned quickly to Darcy. "By the way, Georgiana reports that Mr. Winkler has spoken to Papa and plans to speak to you about Kitty. It appears that my suspicions regarding his interest in my sister may prove correct, after all."

Darcy's eyebrow rose in amusement. "Mr. Foxmour praised Kitty's empathy during his mother's final hours. She accompanied

Winkler when Foxmour summoned the clergyman to his cottage. It makes sense that your sister saw a need to attend the services with Georgiana," he observed.

"I'm certain Mr. Winkler's the basis of Kitty's motivations, but maybe not as you expect. According to our sister, she asked Kitty to accompany her today rather than the other way around. In addition, the Foxmours' situation has enthralled Kitty. She taught the young girls something about art and helped them create a drawing—several drawings, in fact—that Mr. Foxmour placed in his mother's casket. One drawing was of the late lady's dream dress. When my sister returned to Pemberley, she spent hours reworking a gown she found in the attic for Mrs. Foxmour's burial. Kitty has shown herself to possess all the compassion she'll need as Mr. Winkler's wife."

Darcy evaluated his wife's words and doubted her conclusion. Although he'd noted Kitty's improvement, he still retained images of a flighty, giggling Kitty tagging behind Lydia Bennet Wickham at the Netherfield Ball. "Mr. Winkler will be a good influence on Kitty."

"You'll give Mr. Winkler your approval, shall you not?" Elizabeth asked apprehensively. "It would be a good match, and I'd enjoy having her so close to Pemberley."

Darcy frowned. Although Winkler would be an excellent match both socially and emotionally for Kitty, the idea of his wife's sister marrying a clergyman—one depending on him for a living—needed to be considered. What would the community think? What of the *ton*? "Georgiana's Come Out could be affected by the connection," he said softly.

Elizabeth, who'd been braiding her hair as they spoke, turned quickly to look sharply at him. "Surely you won't consider denying Kitty's match because of Georgiana's Society entrance. You'd punish my sister to benefit yours? Would not the Earl's influence counter Kitty's alliance with Winkler? The man is a gentleman's son. He's not a tradesman or a simple farmer."

Darcy knew there had been a time when his wife would have said more—would have argued unreasonably. "As this is the first I've heard of Winkler's attentions beyond your speculations, please allow me to hear the man out. I'll protect Kitty's interest, as well as Georgiana's. I'll deal with each honestly and honorably."

Elizabeth's ire faded. "That's all I can ask, Fitzwilliam," she said grudgingly.

"Trust me, Elizabeth," Darcy insisted.

"I do," she responded. "I just want the best for both our sisters." Darcy added, "As do I."

Elizabeth returned to dressing her hair. He knew they'd have this conversation again, but not until he met with the clergyman. "Would you mind if I kept Kitty with me when my parents return to Hertfordshire?"

"If that's your wish, I have no objections. Kitty is good company for both you and Georgiana," he observed.

Elizabeth twisted her long braid and wrapped it tightly in a simple loop at her nape. "What are we to do with Lady Catherine?" she asked.

"Her Ladyship's presence is something for which I have no contingencies."

"That is obvious. Why now? After all the times that Lady Catherine has ignored your gestures for a reconciliation? Why now, Fitzwilliam?"

Darcy came to stand behind her so they might converse through their reflections in her dressing mirror. It was important for her to see his facial expressions when he spoke. "I know not why my aunt has chosen this time to return to Pemberley. I'll speak to her privately once we return from services. If she expresses her usual disdain, I'll see her on her way on Boxing Day. If not, it is my understanding that she plans to depart on Tuesday."

Elizabeth smiled humorously. "I'll have to write to both Mrs. Washington and Mrs. Joseph and express my gratitude for their detaining us in Harrogate. At the most, I'll have to tolerate Lady

Catherine's venom for three days more. It could've been for a full week."

Darcy's eyebrow rose in answer. "There's that blessing." He bent to kiss Elizabeth's exposed shoulder. "Please remember, my love. In this house, you're the mistress. You take precedence over all others, including my aunt."

~∘~ ~∘~ ~∘~

She and Darcy sat shoulder to shoulder in the family pew. All their guests, except Lady Catherine, who claimed a megrim, had joined them for the services. As she looked about the church, Elizabeth was pleased to see many from the community in attendance. Kitty's eyes glistened with pride as she watched Mr. Winkler, but, surprisingly, Georgiana's eyes glowed equally as bright, and Elizabeth wondered privately if her husband's plans for a Season for his sister might be taking a divergent path. She also chastised herself for not seeing the obvious. *I've been so consumed with my own misery that I've forgotten that life goes on. It all makes sense when I see Georgiana look upon the colonel's face. This evening I'll find time to speak to Georgiana privately. I've neglected her too long. My thoughts shall no longer dwell with those who have never seen the light of day; I must return to the world of the living.*

As the children finished an interesting rendition of "Come, Thou Almighty King," the gathering fell silent and Mr. Winkler took his position in the pulpit box. Elizabeth relaxed into the comfort of Darcy's shoulder. His warmth brought her contentment, and she sighed deeply.

Then Winkler began to speak from the heart. "This is the Eve— the eve above all others. It represents the ultimate of sacrifices on God's part. Before He sent His Son into the world, our Heavenly Father knew what Jesus would face. Christmas also represents a personal sacrifice on the part of Mary and Joseph. In all practical terms, God asked the impossible. Of real people. There would be very few in this room who would willingly accept what God asked of this couple.

"Mary made an unbelievable claim, and Joseph accepted it, but please think of the censure they must've faced from family, friends, and neighbors. Mary's apparent infidelity would've driven a wedge into the best of marriages. Add to that the financial strain of a long journey to pay their tax debt. However, although it was emotionally bizarre, Mary and Joseph accepted God's plan for them, and they learned that accepting God brings its own disputations. God's presence in a person's life does *not* necessarily make his life easier; instead, it makes his life more fulfilling."

Elizabeth shifted her weight uncomfortably. Is that what she had done? Had she expected that if she prayed to God that He'd make her life perfect? And had she not always disdained *perfection*? She had blamed God for turning his back on her.

"God has His own agenda in our lives. As He did with Mary and Joseph, God tells us what He expects of us: He doesn't ask us if those plans match ours. God sent His angel to Mary and Joseph; He didn't ask their permission. What does this mean for us? It means that His will shall prevail over our preferences. One cannot change it.

"God could've made things easier for Mary and Joseph, but He didn't because each person grows from the adversity he faces. If that's so, Mary and Joseph must've grown to gargantuan size. They traveled by foot and by donkey to pay taxes. Despite being enceinte, Mary found no room at the inn."

Elizabeth immediately thought of the Josephs and young William. God's will had prevailed over Prestwick's Portal.

"Mary and Joseph had to flee King Herod's vengeance," Winkler continued. "This too must have been a difficult journey. All in all, we must realize that God could've changed each of these difficulties, but He wanted Mary and Joseph to rise above such adversity. What's God's will for you? It may not be an easy journey upon which you embark, but our Lord will be with you as you make your way.

"On Christmas, the Christ child received the gifts of gold, frankincense, and myrrh. Gold declared the child as a king among men. Sweet smelling frankincense represented Jesus' pure spirit. Bitter myrrh predicted Christ's death. As we finish our program for the evening, I charge you to consider what you would give the Christ child on his birthday? What is God's plan for you? And what are you willing to sacrifice to make it so?"

As they stood to depart, Elizabeth caught Darcy's hand. "What did you think of Mr. Winkler's message?" she whispered.

Darcy leaned close so he might speak to her privately. "My esteemed father used to warn of two faults. The first of those was to be wary of the prayer that the Devil answers, and the second was never to share one's plans with God for our Maker would find it offensive. I believe God holds His vision, and He understands what we need and when we need it."

Elizabeth acknowledged his advice with a nod of her head. "I'd like to speak to Mr. Winkler further on this concept. I'll ask him to join us this evening."

"Is this for you or for Kitty?" Darcy asked suspiciously.

Elizabeth shot him a steely glare. "The man is already to be Pemberley's guest for both Christmas and our Boxing Day celebration. One more evening shan't progress his and Kitty's affections any faster. If Georgiana's evaluation is correct, Mr. Winkler's affections are fully engaged already," she said tersely. "You may delay their joining with your objections, but you should know by now, Fitzwilliam, that the heart finds its own rhythm."

Darcy gave her a curt nod. "I said I'd allow Winkler his due, but his interest in your sister creates a situation. When I fund the man's ideas, the community will wonder if I do so because I believe them to benefit the local population or because he holds a *tendre* for my wife's sister."

"I hadn't considered how such an alliance must appear. I apologize for my gruffness, Fitzwilliam."

"You offered no offense, my love. I cannot fault you for protecting your family. It was a characteristic which attracted me to you."

~⊚~ ~⊚~ ~⊚~

"Would you care to explain to me what brought you to Pemberley, Your Ladyship, and do not waste my time with tales of weather woes?" Upon his return to the house, Darcy had demanded that Lady Catherine attend him in his study.

"And why would I offer you a prevarication?" Lady Catherine asked haughtily.

Darcy realized his refusing to accept her excuse of a megrim would thoroughly irritate his aunt, but he'd have the truth from her. "I should've added diversion to my list of exceptions. I'm well aware of your ability to twist a confrontation to your advantage. Do not play verbal games with me, Aunt. I want to know your reasons for coming to my home—especially, at this time."

"You've offered the olive branch," she reasoned. "Suppose that I decided to accept it."

Darcy frowned. "I issued the last offer during the summer. Why not travel under pristine conditions rather than in winter's worst?" He raised his hand to stop her response before he finished. "Over the past two years, *at my wife's insistence*, I've sent you three requests to resolve our differences, and you've ignored each, not even acknowledging them with a refusal. I'm aware of two visits to Matlock during those times, but you chose to shun Pemberley's hospitality on both your ventures into Derbyshire."

"Mrs. Darcy insisted on your offers of reconciliation?" she asked incredulously.

"As far as I was concerned, Your Ladyship, your interference in my life crossed the line of good intentions. With the genuine frankness of your character, your reply to the letter, which announced my arrangement, was loaded with language so very abusive, especially of Elizabeth that my initial reaction was that all intercourse between us was at an end. But at length, by Elizabeth's persuasion, I was prevailed upon to overlook the offense and seek a reconciliation. My wife has a generous heart, and I've honored her magnanimity."

The thought of being beholden to Mrs. Darcy, obviously, disturbed his aunt. She stammered, "I…I have…I've long considered what Lady Anne would've expected of me. On your mother's deathbed, she asked that I take an interest in your and Georgiana's lives. If I'm not at Pemberley, I cannot serve your mother's memory."

Darcy eyed her suspiciously. "My mother's memory is cherished at Pemberley."

"Even with Mrs. Darcy in Lady Anne's position?" she questioned curtly.

"Elizabeth is not my mother, but, likewise, I'm not George Marcus Lucien Darcy, and the Pemberley of today is not the one my esteemed father knew. You deal with Rosings Park on a daily basis, so I'll not bore you with the details of keeping such a large estate solvent, but you realize as well as any that I make investments in modernization, and I look for concessions that'll sustain this way of life. Pemberley survives where others fail because I accept that change is necessary. Elizabeth succeeds as Pemberley's mistress because of her intuitiveness and her benevolence.

"My wife honors her predecessor by maintaining the traditions my mother established. Occasionally, she adapts them for a different audience—you'll observe as much when you see the Tenants' Ball—but she gives honor to Lady Anne Fitzwilliam's legacy."

"And what of her obligation to deliver an heir?" Lady Catherine insisted.

Darcy sighed deeply in exasperation. "Listen to my words, and believe them as the truth, Aunt. I'd love Elizabeth with or without a child. She's my life." Again, he noted the shocked expression on Lady Catherine's countenance, but she quickly recovered her composure. "If my marriage is not blessed with an heir, then the estate will go to Georgiana's children. Either way, Pemberley will remain in the family. I'll *never* turn my back on my wife. Secondly,

I'd vehemently use all the power I possess against anyone who purposely hurt her. If you cannot keep a civil tongue, you'll find yourself on the road on Christmas Day. I'll personally escort you to your waiting carriage."

"It's against the law to travel thusly," she stated the obvious.

"I'd care not for your legal obligations, Aunt. My wife will not suffer because of your disapproval. Never in her own home. I hope I make myself clear, Your Ladyship."

～☜☞～ ～☜☞～ ～☜☞～

"I have a basket," Georgiana announced to the group gathered in a circle at one end of the drawing room.

Edward, seated on her right, responded accordingly. "What is inside?"

"A hat," Georgiana said and then smiled brilliantly at Edward. "Your turn, Cousin."

Edward obligingly said, "I have a basket." The group boo-hooed his having to carry about an imaginary receptacle, but he good-naturedly pantomimed selecting an object and placing it inside.

"What is inside?" Charlotte dutifully replied. She had abandoned her husband to Lady Catherine's company and had happily joined the group.

"Ice," Edward declared.

Charlotte frowned. "Must it be *ice*? Is there not another word beginning with the letter 'I'?"

"No commentary, Mrs. Collins," Edward laughingly chastised. "The word is *ice*. It is your turn to use the letter 'J.'"

"All right," she chuckled. "I have a basket."

"What is inside?" Manneville took his turn.

"A jar," Charlotte said.

Manneville didn't wait for the obligatory group teasing. "I have a basket."

Caroline, who sat beside him, coyly asked, "What is inside?"

But Manneville ignored her flirtation and set his gaze on Kitty. "A kitten," he announced.

Kitty blushed, but otherwise shrugged off his pointed remark. However, Mr. Winkler sat forward in his chair as if to challenge the American.

Edward jumped into the mix, trying to defuse the situation. "No fair, Manneville," he said a bit louder than necessary. "It isn't courteous to use other players to create your responses."

Darcy joined his wife and her parents. "You didn't wish to play parlor games?" he asked as he took possession of Elizabeth's hand.

"No, thank you. I'm quite content to spend time here before the fire."

Darcy understood; she'd missed her parents desperately. "You're exceptional at word games, my dear," he observed.

"I'll enjoy the frustration when the letter 'X' becomes impossible to fulfill."

"Edward will serve as chaperone for the group," Darcy said.

Mr. Bennet added, "Your cousin seems a right fine gentleman. I wish I had realized so at Lizzy's wedding."

"It was an exciting time," Mrs. Bennet said. "Our Elizabeth becoming Mrs. Darcy so shortly after Jane had married Mr. Bingley."

"My friend letting Netherfield was a fortuitous event for us both." Darcy brought the back of Elizabeth's hand to his lips. "But you're correct, Mr. Bennet. The colonel possesses all the qualities of a true gentleman. Edward has been my best friend, as well as my cousin."

"I believe the colonel serves as Miss Darcy's guardian," Mr. Bennet noted.

"We share guardianship," Darcy corrected. "My father thought it best in case something happened to me before my sister came of age."

Mrs. Bennet said, "Miss Darcy must be quite excited about the possibility of her first Season."

Darcy responded, "We may have to consider a shortened stay in London."

"Why ever for?" Mrs. Bennet inquired.

"My confinement, Mama," Elizabeth explained the obvious. "The Season begins before my delivery."

Darcy took on a serious expression. "Neither my sister nor I would consider London if Elizabeth couldn't join us."

"But surely the Countess could sponsor Miss Darcy," Mrs. Bennet pressed.

"Mama," Elizabeth warned.

"The Darcys are a family, Mrs. Bennet, and Elizabeth is an integral part."

Mr. Bennet quickly added, "It doesn't damage a girl's presentation to be a bit older. Most serious suitors would prefer that the young lady not be straight from the schoolroom. Miss Darcy is beautiful, talented, and quite personable. With her connections, she'll be a prime contender for debutante of the year, no matter in which Season she makes her entrance."

"There is no word for 'X,'" Bingley protested.

Edward corrected, "There is a *xebec*."

Southland explained to a perplexed-looking Bingley, "A small, three-masted Mediterranean vessel."

From where he sat, Darcy added "*Xylem*, Bingley. It's a woody plant."

"*Xiphi*. A *sword*," Elizabeth challenged. "It is one of my favorite Greek roots."

"*Xyster*," Mr. Bennet placed another word into play.

"One could always use *Xanthippe*," Georgiana said softly.

Bingley laughed lightly. "Point well taken, everyone. I shouldn't play word games with those who devour books."

～ॐ~ ～ॐ~ ～ॐ~

"Miss Catherine." Winkler approached Kitty near the instrument as she straightened the music sheets employed by both Mary and Georgiana earlier in the evening. "I would take my leave from you."

Kitty turned her back to the room to ensure privacy. "I wish you might stay longer, Sir."

"Do you?" he asked suspiciously.

Kitty's mouth set in a straight line. "When might I have spoken an untruth to you?" she asked tersely.

Winkler, likewise, stiffened with her tone. "I know of no prevarication on your part, but I'm a man who wonders why a stranger expresses intimate thoughts about a beautiful woman."

"You consider me beautiful?" Kitty asked, ignoring Winkler's other remarks.

He closed his eyes in frustration. "Miss Catherine, you're well aware of my feelings."

"I'm aware, Mr. Winkler, but a woman doesn't tire of hearing a gentleman say so. Promise me that you'll shower me with compliments. I'm quite vain," she said teasingly.

Winkler started to reach for her but quickly dropped his arms to his side. "Catherine, I'd give you anything within my power," he hissed. "But I need to know of Manneville's attentions. It's uncharitable of me to speak, but I fear with you, my reason is lacking."

"There's no Mr. Manneville," she whispered reassuringly. "My mother thought the gentleman a possible suitor and has thrust me into the man's path, but I've given him no encouragement."

Winkler grudgingly noted, "I do not wish to press the point, but the gentleman could offer more than I. My living cannot compare to Manneville's wealth. We've no official engagement, Catherine. If you wished me to step aside, I'd do so. I want only your happiness."

"If you truly wish my happiness, Mr. Winkler, you'll speak to Mr. Darcy in a speedy manner," Kitty declared.

Winkler's smile widened. "Tomorrow, Catherine."

∼⊘∼　∼⊘∼　∼⊘∼

Elizabeth tapped lightly on Georgiana's door. Within seconds of her entreaty, Georgiana's maid answered the door. "Is my sister available?" It was an impulsive act. With fondness Elizabeth remembered how when she'd first arrived at Pemberley, she and Georgiana had daily shared sisterly secrets. Elizabeth had desperately missed her nightly talks with Jane, and Georgiana had needed someone to share the anxieties of a young woman, one finishing her time in the schoolroom.

The maid bobbed a curtsy and opened the door wider. "Please come in." Georgiana motioned to the hearth. "Molly has just freshened the fire." Turning to the maid, she added, "That shall be all, Molly. I'll ring if I need anything else." The maid disappeared through the side entrance. "It's pleasant to have your company, Elizabeth. It's been too long."

"My thoughts exactly." Elizabeth pulled her chair closer to the one Georgiana occupied. "I wanted to thank you again for assuming the hostess responsibilities for my family."

"They're my family also," Georgiana corrected.

Elizabeth smiled warmly. "Of course they are."

"Your parents have expressed their concern for you," Georgiana ventured after an awkward pause.

Elizabeth laced her fingers. "I know." She paused also. "Everyone is worried, and I'm profoundly sorrowful for having given any alarm. I didn't know how to justify what happened with what I expected from life, but the last week has brought new perspectives. My helping Mrs. Joseph find her happiness convinced me that Fitzwilliam and I will soon know our own. Even Mr. Winkler's message today added depth to what I've discovered."

"I noticed the two of you speaking privately earlier this evening."

Elizabeth's eyes widened. "There was a time my philosophical musings would've been of no concern to anyone."

"You're loved unconditionally, Elizabeth."

Elizabeth ironically chuckled. "A blessing to be sure. Sometimes, I feel I don't deserve such devotion, but I'm thankful for it."

"Shall you like having Mr. Winkler as part of the family?" Georgiana pointedly changed the subject.

Elizabeth accepted the fact that her fears of remaining childless made others uncomfortable. Only Darcy fully understood. "Mr. Winkler shall be a moderating influence on Kitty, and she'll bring some spontaneity to his existence."

"It sounds as if you describe your and Fitzwilliam's joining," Georgiana observed.

Elizabeth nodded her agreement. "To a lesser degree, but in many ways, it's true." She suddenly remembered all those joyous moments when she'd tease Darcy from his habitual "doom and gloom" outlook. She'd not done so in a while. "I need to make a conscious effort to return a bit of mayhem to Fitzwilliam's life. The man has known enough sorrow of late."

"I'm pleased to hear it," Georgiana said with a light laugh.

"And what of you, Georgiana? Is your heart engaged?" Elizabeth asked.

She watched as Darcy's sister blushed thoroughly. For a moment, she expected the girl would deny her very noticeable attentiveness to the colonel. "Am I that obvious?" Georgiana said softly.

"Not too obvious," Elizabeth teased. "Your brother has taken no note."

Georgiana's agitation increased. "You shan't tell Fitzwilliam, will you? Please, Elizabeth, my brother mustn't know."

"I'll keep your secret," Elizabeth assured. "And what of the colonel? Does Edward return your affections?"

Georgiana's relief at being able to speak of her feelings became apparent as the conversation progressed. "Oh, how I wished I knew for certain. There are moments—one in the study a few days ago, for example—when it appears my cousin shares my interest. Then there are those when I doubt my sanity."

Elizabeth reached for her sister's hand. "I don't doubt it. Men are usually the last to realize their affections are engaged. I imagine the colonel is having difficulty explaining his feelings to his rational mind." She paused briefly. "Would you like to tell me of this moment in Mr. Darcy's study?"

"Oh, yes," Georgiana gushed. "May I truly?" Before Elizabeth could answer, the girl continued. "We spoke of my Come Out, and then Edward took me in his arms, and we waltzed. Without music. We swayed so close together, and I thought for a brief span that he would kiss me."

"Would you have allowed his kiss?" Elizabeth squeezed Georgiana's hand in a gesture of camaraderie.

"Is it wanton to say that I'd like my first kiss to come from Edward?" Georgiana anxiously bit her bottom lip.

Elizabeth leaned forward. "It's not wanton. It's the natural progression of a relationship. Edward is a gentleman, and he'll not take advantage. Again, he probably is experiencing some questions as to how your relationship has changed. May I make an observation?"

"Please do," Georgiana encouraged.

"Tomorrow is Christmas, and Pemberley seems to have sprouted a large number of mistletoe berries." Elizabeth's eyes sparkled with mischief. "Surely, an intelligent young lady could find herself under said berries when the colonel passed."

Georgiana giggled. "I love the way you think, Sister."

CHAPTER 16

~~~

"IT'S A RARITY," Mr. Winkler said to the nodding congregation, "that Christmas and Sunday coincide." He paused briefly for that fact to register. "Last evening, we spoke of the sacrifice each must make to know God's glory. Today, I wish to address the wonderful sacrifice of the women in our lives. Specifically, I wish to speak of the undying love of our mothers."

Darcy felt Elizabeth shift closer to him, and he brought her hand into his lap. He prayed that Winkler's sermon wouldn't upset her.

"In Exodus 2," Winkler continued, "Jochobed made the ultimate sacrifice to save Moses from the Egyptians by placing him among the bulrushes. When Solomon would have divided the child between the two claimants, the true mother offered the boy to the other woman in order to save her child. Unselfish sacrifice is a part of motherhood. A woman's legacy is the faith she passes on to her children. It's the faith that sustains those children through hardships. It is a mother's Godly sway that defines her dotation."

Darcy noted a single tear crawling down Elizabeth's cheek. Without thinking, he slipped his handkerchief from his inner pocket and into her hand.

"And what makes a good woman?" Winkler asked. "In Proverbs 31, we learn the words of King Lemuel, the prophecy that his mother taught him. In these verses, God describes a woman's trustworthiness and her strength. 'She layeth her hands to the spindle, and her hands hold the distaff. She stretcheth out her hand to the poor; yea, she reacheth forth her hands to the needy. Strength and honor *are* her clothing. She openeth her mouth with wisdom; and in her tongue *is* the law of kindness. Her children arise up, and call her blessed; her husband *also*, and he praiseth her. Favour is deceitful, and beauty *is* vain: *but* a woman *that* feareth the Lord, she shall be praised.' Children are God's gift. We know that in certainty on this most precious of days. Trust in God and your household will know the Lord's reflection."

Darcy escorted Elizabeth outside. "Are you well?" he whispered into her hair.

Elizabeth turned her head sharply to him. "Why should I not be?" She too whispered as the Christmas congregation streamed from the church.

"Mr. Winkler's sermon," Darcy explained.

Elizabeth understood immediately. "I enjoyed the clergyman's words. In fact, last evening, Mr. Winkler and I spoke openly of motherhood. I believe that the gentleman changed portions of his message based on our discussion. You should have no more fears for my disposition, Fitzwilliam. God shall give us a child when He's ready, not when we are."

"Are you certain?" Darcy pressed.

"I'm certain of my love for you. Everything else shall fall away as insignificant."

It was another of those moments when his wife innocently expressed her affections, and his desire rose immediately. He stood on the Lambton church's steps and wished to take Elizabeth into his arms and make love to her. Surely, such thoughts would doom him to hell, but Darcy could no more ignore his overwhelming devotion to his wife than he could take flight. It was his destiny to love her.

"I'm forever your servant, Mrs. Darcy." He brought the back of her hand to his lips. He nodded toward the gathering carriages. "Allow me to see Her Ladyship and Anne safely in their coach."

With that, he stepped away from Elizabeth, leaving her to the approaching Mr. Bennet.

Her father placed Elizabeth's hand on his arm, and they began an ambulatory circuit of the area. Many villagers stopped to offer their greetings, and Elizabeth took great pleasure in introducing her father to each. "Having you at Pemberley is an answered prayer," she told him.

"Being able to assuage my concerns for you has made my journey worthwhile."

Elizabeth came to a sudden halt. "Is everyone obsessed with my mental stability?"

Mr. Bennet started their walking again. "Your husband and your parents are naturally sensitive to your changed temperament. Even you must admit, Lizzy, that you've not been yourself of late."

"I suppose," she said reluctantly.

"We all love you," he assured.

Elizabeth accepted his compassion. "I never meant to worry you."

"We know." He patted her hand. "Just come back to us, Lizzy. We all depend on your good sense."

〜◦〜 〜◦〜 〜◦〜

"Miss De Bourgh," Southland bowed to Anne. He'd waited in the vicinity of her private quarters in hopes that she might appear. "May I escort you to the morning room?"

Anne actually smiled at him. "Thank you, Lieutenant." She took his proffered arm.

"I suppose you realize that I purposely sought you out," he said softly as they descended the main staircase.

"I suppose I did," she said with a blush.

"May I speak honestly?" he blurted out.

Her color deepened, but Anne managed, "I'd prefer you did so, Lieutenant."

Southland paused on the stairs. "Although we've known each other only a few days, I feel an acquaintance of many months—years even."

"As do I," Anne said anxiously.

"Miss De Bourgh," he continued nervously. "With your permission, I would speak to your mother and begin a courtship." Roman thought his heart might explode as he waited for her response.

"You wish to court me?" she asked in a barely audible whisper.

"Very much so," Roman assured her.

Anne swayed in place and caught at the railing. He watched as she first paled and then flushed with color. "I…I would be honored," she stammered.

Roman's grin widened. "That pleases me more than you know." Securing her arm to his side, he turned her toward the morning room.

"Might we step into a drawing room?" Anne asked. "I need a moment to recover my composure before I face everyone."

"Certainly." Leaving the door open behind them, Roman led her to the green room. "I never meant to upset you," he said with concern.

Anne turned to face him. "I'm not upset, Lieutenant, but I admit you took me unawares," she impulsively added.

"You must've recognized my interest," he said softly.

"You mistake me for a woman of confidence," Anne said ironically.

Roman took her by the shoulders and brought her closer to him. "Then you must become accustomed to my company. Once your mother grants her permission, I plan to make a nuisance of myself, at least, until you agree to accept my hand in marriage."

"Her Ladyship's permission?" Anne asked in disbelief. "Is it even possible?"

Roman held the same doubts, but he said, "Of course, it's possible. I've already sought the advice of both your cousins."

"You've spoken to the colonel and Mr. Darcy?" Her voice rose in disbelief. "Oh, my," she gasped. "And my cousins believed Her Ladyship would agree?"

Southland's frown lines deepened. "I would understand if you wished to withdraw your consent, Miss De Bourgh. I am without a title."

"I never needed a title."

"But you deserve one," he countered.

"I cannot say what I deserve, but I'd wish for a joining of mutual companionship."

"I'll not speak words of love," Roman said seriously. "We've known each other for but a few days; however, I'll promise my fidelity."

Anne nodded her acceptance. Like most women, she had always dreamed of finding love, but at the moment, she was willing to settle for a lot less. Roman Southland offered her a stable relationship. Although the lieutenant held an anomalous belief in their common fate, he presented an opportunity for a compatible joining. She could have a respectable, attractive husband and maybe even a family—children of her own. It was a dream recently rekindled with her meeting her cousin's aide. "And I would promise you the same," she said softly. She'd hold onto that dream. Now, she *must* find a way to convince her mother to accept the request of an ordinary gentleman. "Did my cousins offer suggestions of ways to earn Her Ladyship's approval?"

"They made specific statements." The way he chose his words told Anne that even Darcy and Colonel Fitzwilliam had their doubts. Panic filled her. In all likelihood, her mother would deny her chance for marriage and a family. Anne would remain on the shelf and die a slow lonely death in obscurity. "I have upset you again," Southland said with renewed concern.

Anne's heart pounded in her ears as her thoughts raced. She had to think of something. Then a familiar scuff on the carpet outside sent her into action. She launched herself into the lieutenant's arms, pulling his head down to hers. She'd never been kissed, nor did she have any idea how to go about it, but that didn't matter at the moment.

Roman had anticipated Anne's agitation. In fact, he shared many of the lady's qualms. He'd no idea what he'd say to the autocratic Lady Catherine. He wouldn't tell the great lady that he represented her daughter's last marriage prospect. His honor wouldn't permit him to do so. With wariness, he said, "I have upset you again."

Anne's countenance betrayed the array of emotions coursing through her, and Roman was considering what he must do to allay her fears when suddenly she cast herself into his arms and pulled his head toward hers. Roman didn't think: he simply responded.

She pressed her lips together and shoved hard against his mouth, but Roman had actually expected as much. From what he knew of the lady, Miss De Bourgh had led a very sheltered life. Only last evening, he had imagined that he would have to teach her about the marriage bed's pleasures.

At least, she is willing to kiss me, he thought as he eased the pressure and softened the intensity of their joining. Shifting Anne in his arms, *he* kissed her and gloried in how she allowed him to lead. He angled his mouth to take hers completely. Surprisingly, she didn't stiffen in his embrace. Instead, the lady sagged, leaning heavily against him. Roman slid his tongue along the seam of her lips, and she rewarded him with a small gasp, but before he could deepen the kiss, a cold dose of reality entered the equation.

"Anne Catherine Margaret De Bourgh, what do you think you're doing?" Lady Catherine exclaimed loudly. Several servants rushed to her aid, thinking Mr. Darcy's aunt required assistance.

Descending the main staircase, Lady Catherine had anticipated her entrance into the morning room: She'd returned to Pemberley without benefit of an apology or a concession to the new Mrs. Darcy. It was more than for which she could've hoped. With

Darcy's last appeal, she'd considered how a reconciliation might be accomplished without her admitting guilt in their argument. Lady Catherine hated expressing regret. It was her plan to stay through the Boxing Day celebration and then take her leave. "Do not overstay the welcome," she had murmured to the portrait gallery lining the wall. "Allow Darcy to wonder why I came. I can reclaim my sister's family without losing face and without everyone knowing my real reason for being here."

On the second floor, Lady Catherine paused to take in Pemberley's glory and consider her family's lasting influence. Her sister Lady Anne Darcy and her brother the Earl of Matlock had done well. She relished their combined impact on English society; they had created a legacy for the next generation. Matlock had Lindale and Fitzwilliam to which to leave the Earldom. Her sister's son had taken Pemberley's realm and had increased his esteemed father's holdings. Only she had failed. Anne had never blossomed into a woman that a man would desire. Lady Catherine predicted an end to Rosings Park with her passing. Anne would never be able to handle it on her own. Early on, Catherine had feared Sir Lewis's shyness would prevail in her daughter. It was why she'd insisted on making a match between Anne and Darcy. It had been a foolish idea between loving sisters when their children were but babes; however, the idea had grown into an obsession as Anne's timidity had become more evident. The De Bourghs would lose Rosings without Darcy overseeing it, and so she'd counseled on behalf of the match.

Whispering came from what should've been an empty room, and she had stepped into the open doorway to investigate. Servants often took advantage of generous masters, especially on a solemn day such as this one. She'd put a stop to such insolence. However, what she beheld enflamed Lady Catherine's temper. "Anne Catherine Margaret De Bourgh, what do you think you're doing?" she barked.

Without preamble, Lady Catherine stormed into the room as the couple jumped apart. Never in all her years had she expected to find her daughter in an intimate embrace with a gentleman. Catherine didn't know whether to celebrate or stand in horror. As was typical, she chose something less sedate than a celebratory moment, centering her disdain on the man who had just compromised Anne. "Lieutenant." she snarled. "Have you no principles? You'll unhand my daughter immediately." Anne took a half step toward her in the lieutenant's defense, but Lady Catherine's cold glare warned her daughter to not interfere. "I ask again, Lieutenant. Have you no defense for your actions?"

❧ ❧ ❧

"Perhaps, Lady Catherine, we could all have a seat and discuss this calmly," she said with authority from the open doorway. With a flick of her wrist, Pemberley's mistress sent the two maids and a footman on their separate ways and closed the door behind her. She quickly assayed the dilemma and discovered a very flushed Anne De Bourgh standing between her mother and Edward's aide-de-camp. Immediately, she moved to defuse the situation. "Come, let me assist you, Your Ladyship." She caught Lady Catherine about the waist and directed Darcy's aunt to a chair. "Allow me to pour you some sherry," she said as she shot a pleading glance to the lieutenant to move.

Southland reacted immediately. He scurried to a nearby tray and poured a glass and handed it to Elizabeth. "Drink some of this," Elizabeth encouraged. "It shall calm your nerves."

Lady Catherine intoned aristocratically, "I'm not the type to succumb to nerves, Mrs. Darcy."

"No one believes you are, Your Ladyship," Elizabeth said softly, "but it'll give us a moment to compose our thoughts. Please do it for me." Elizabeth knelt obediently beside Lady Catherine's chair.

Giving the lieutenant a deathly glare, Lady Catherine reluctantly took a small sip of the potent drink.

"Thank you, Your Ladyship." Elizabeth caught the woman's hand and gave it a weak squeeze. Lady Catherine's gaze fell on her, and for a brief moment, Elizabeth saw vulnerability.

Yet, a soft knock on the door drew their attention, and Darcy slipped into the room. Elizabeth observed the recognition in his eyes. "Mr. Nathan seemed to think Her Ladyship had suffered some sort of shock," he said cautiously.

Darcy's eyes rested on her face. He spoke of his aunt's health, but he would take his cues from Elizabeth. "A bit of an exaggeration, I fear," Elizabeth automatically rose and took a step toward him. It was a response of which she had become conscious upon Darcy's return to Longbourn—when he had brought Bingley to Jane in order to right a wrong, Elizabeth had found herself physically drawn to him. No matter when she saw him, the moment Darcy stepped into a room, she moved closer. "Her Ladyship simply needs a moment. Perhaps you might escort your cousin and the lieutenant into the room next door while I see to your aunt."

Darcy didn't protest. Over the past three years, they'd learned to trust each other exclusively. With a nod of understanding, he asked, "Anne, would you and Lieutenant Southland join me in the yellow sitting room?" He moved to lead the way.

Anne turned to her mother. "I'm sorry, Your Ladyship," she whispered through silent sobs. "You must try to understand." After a brief bow to both Elizabeth and Lady Catherine, Southland caught Anne's elbow and escorted her from the room.

Elizabeth waited for their departure before turning to Darcy's aunt. With a deep sigh, she pivoted, expecting to find an irate aristocrat whom she would have to appease, but was greeted by the distraught tear-stained face of Lady Catherine, and instantly, Elizabeth felt compassion for what she suspected to be a very lonely woman. "Your Ladyship," she empathized and pulled a footstool over to sit at Lady Catherine's feet.

"Might I?" Lady Catherine held the glass for Elizabeth's view.

She took it immediately. "Of course." Walking to the serving tray, Elizabeth glanced over her shoulder at the sunken figure resting back into the chair's cushions. *What happened to the imperious Lady Catherine? Where did all her fight go?* Returning to the footstool, she

276 <a>Christmas at Pemberley</a>

sat and then eased the drink into the woman's gnarled grasp. They sat in silence for a few minutes before Elizabeth asked, "Would you like to speak of it, Your Ladyship? I realize I'm probably the last person with whom you would consult, but I'm at your disposal. You're my husband's aunt, and I desire only the best for you."

Lady Catherine's gaze returned to Elizabeth's face. "Why would you treat me with respect? With compassion?" she murmured. "I've never treated you kindly."

Elizabeth frowned. "We've known our contentious moments, but I understand your intensity. You wished the best for your child, and Mr. Darcy is truly the best of men. If I were to have my own child, I'd fight with a similar ferocity to secure his future."

Admiration played across the lady's face. "I expect you would, Mrs. Darcy. You give as good as you receive. I doubt if Mr. Darcy had any idea of your tongue's viciousness." Lady Catherine half smiled.

"I beg to differ, Your Ladyship. Your nephew was on the receiving end of more than one of my barbs. I like to think my sauciness was part of my charm," Elizabeth impishly said.

The line of Lady Catherine's mouth tightened to hide her smile. "A certain *sauciness* on my sister's part attracted his father, and I am positive that Sir Lewis found it appealing."

"I suspect you're correct," Elizabeth said judiciously. "Therefore, although your words stung, after careful analysis, I accepted your intent. I can place those sentiments behind us if you agree."

Lady Catherine's eyebrow rose in question. "I suppose we might make the effort for Darcy's sake."

"Then for Mr. Darcy's familial benefit we'll persevere," Elizabeth said contritely. "Now, with that settled may we address your concerns for Miss De Bourgh?"

"What is there to address? Anne must marry Edward's aide. She's been compromised."

~⌒~ ~⌒~ ~⌒~

From what Mr. Nathan had shared, Darcy possessed an idea of what had occurred in the room occupied by his aunt and his wife. The fact that Elizabeth had directed him to a nearby room told him that his aunt's possible reaction worried his wife also. Luckily, he detected no raised voices. "Would you care to enlighten me, Lieutenant, as to what occurred?" he asked in hushed tones. Darcy refused to close the door. He might need to rush to his wife's defense.

The lieutenant swallowed hard, but he didn't retreat from Darcy's glare. Darcy supposed the man had become immune to its possible intensity, as the colonel often sported a similar intimidating tactic. "After speaking to you and the colonel last evening," Southland began, "I sought Miss De Bourgh to secure her consent prior to speaking to Her Ladyship. Unfortunately, my suit surprised your cousin, and she required a moment to reorder her thoughts prior to our entrance in the morning room. We never considered the consequences of doing so. I grieve for the depth of alarm our actions have engendered, but my resolve remains the same."

Darcy ignored the man's posturing. The lieutenant had compromised Anne, but if his cousin didn't wish the match, there were ways around the scandal. "Tell me the truth, Anne. Do you wish this joining? If not, the lieutenant will kindly withdraw his suit. Will you not, Sir?"

"If that's what the lady wishes." Southland nervously shifted his weight.

"I've injured my mother," Anne said as she choked back sobs.

"Not beyond repair," Darcy said soothingly. "Her Ladyship can be assuaged no matter what you choose, Cousin, but it must be your choice. Do you welcome this match?"

His cousin appeared nervous, but she met his gaze, something Darcy found unexpectedly pleasant. "It was not the lieutenant's fault that my mother…found us in a private moment. It was purely of my own making. You see…I knew of Her Ladyship's presence. I recognized her tread on the stairs. I thought if my mother saw us…

thus engaged…that she couldn't refuse the lieutenant's suit. I would be Roman's wife. It's my grandest desire."

～ల ～ల ～ల

"Although Miss De Bourgh's reputation is in danger, if it is Your Ladyship's desire, the impropriety can be hushed up. The servants involved are loyal to Mr. Darcy, and others in the house are family, except for Mr. Manneville. It could be easily managed. Mr. Darcy and I shall see to it if that's your wish."

Lady Catherine hesitated, obviously considering the possibility. "It's shameful," she said, "to want to agree to gamble on my daughter's reputation."

Elizabeth quickly noted that the perfect, icy control, so characteristic of Darcy's aunt, had returned. "Is the lieutenant's suit so repugnant?"

"Although the man's attentions might delight some families, I'd hoped for higher connections for Anne."

Elizabeth objected to the cynical amusement in Lady Catherine's tone, but she stilled her retort. What untruth had Darcy's aunt offered? Elizabeth's mother would celebrate such a connection. Keeping that in mind, she began to construct a version of the truth—actually, to "sell" the lieutenant to Her Ladyship. An ungodly thought: to think similarly to her mother. "Perhaps we should examine the lieutenant's assets."

Lady Catherine said with a contemptuous snort, "The man has no assets."

Ignoring the remark, Elizabeth countered, "There's his position in the military, and army officers are quite popular."

"But he holds only a lieutenancy."

Elizabeth disclosed, "Mr. Darcy indicated that the colonel planned to recommend the lieutenant for a promotion." Luckily, last evening, Darcy had shared his conversation with Edward.

Considering Elizabeth's point, Her Ladyship acknowledged

the benefit of an advanced commission. "Being under Edward's command is to the lieutenant's advantage."

"Unlike many in our country's service, Southland has seen action on two fronts: the Continent and the American hostilities. Few men can make such claims. And the lieutenant saved Edward's life at Bladensburg."

"With Napoleon on Elba, the Prince is most enthralled with those who have served honorably."

Elizabeth thanked her lucky stars that Darcy's aunt, at least, was considering the possible joining. With fortitude, Lady Catherine faced what must be a frightening emptiness. "And who's to say that additional commissions might not be forthcoming. The lieutenant will likely remain in his position for the foreseeable future."

"And what would Anne do if she accepts the lieutenant? Would the man expect her to remain at Rosings?"

"As Miss De Bourgh is your heir, it might be a time to instruct her regarding Anne's responsibility to the land."

Lady Catherine hastily said, "Anne has never shown any inclination that she cares to know of that which I see daily."

"Miss De Bourgh shall have additional impetus for learning. Instructing the lieutenant could also be a choice," Elizabeth ventured.

"It would be some time before either would be ready to assume Rosings's helm," Her Ladyship reasoned.

A deep voice from the doorway asked, "Would you ladies care for tea?" Darcy's curiosity laced his tone.

Elizabeth's eyebrow rose in amusement. "Were you not to see to Miss De Bourgh?"

"Mrs. Annesley has kindly agreed to sit with them. They await your company," he said tentatively.

"Go away, Darcy," Lady Catherine ordered. "Mrs. Darcy and I are conferring on the matter. I'll inform you of our decision when one is reached."

He did a poor job of hiding his surprise that his wife had garnered his aunt's favor, but Elizabeth relished the fact that he'd braved

Her Ladyship's wrath to protect her. "We're quite comfortable, Fitzwilliam. Mayhap, you'd see to the rest of our guests."

"I thought my cousin could be of assistance," he explained.

"When I'm ready, I'll send for the whole family. Now, Darcy, leave us." Lady Catherine shooed him several times. "Go!"

Darcy bowed stiffly. "As you wish, Aunt." Elizabeth, however, caught his wink as he closed the door.

As if never interrupted, Lady Catherine said, "It would be necessary for me to instruct Anne and the lieutenant."

"It would show your benevolence," Elizabeth summarized.

"Do not placate me, Mrs. Darcy," Her Ladyship warned. "It wouldn't be the ideal situation for Anne—having me teaching her of the account books and who are the honest tradesmen."

Elizabeth silently admired the woman. There was a time she'd thought that she could never agree with anything Lady Catherine said. "In all honesty, it'll be difficult for you both. Miss De Bourgh must place herself in an uncomfortable position, and you must relinquish some of your control. Change can cause fears, but that doesn't make it nonsensical. The lieutenant is accustomed to dealing with hard decisions, with people from all walks of life. With the changes coming to the English estates, the lieutenant may adapt faster than a titled gentleman."

Lady Catherine's gaze sharpened. "What other *assets* does the man possess?"

"It is my understanding that the lieutenant holds a connection to a former favorite, Mr. Knight."

"I was unaware of the relationship. At least, Southland comes from the gentry," Her Ladyship conceded.

Elizabeth leaned forward and caught Lady Catherine's hands, holding them both tightly. "I expect Anne would not have accepted the lieutenant's attentions if she'd not thought herself well satisfied. Anne is of age, Your Ladyship."

"Meaning if I refuse, I *could* lose my daughter, and if I agree, I *shall* lose her." Elizabeth observed the gamut of emotions displayed on the lady's face. It was a telling moment that Darcy's aunt showed any weakness whatsoever.

"If you permit their joining, Miss De Bourgh and the lieutenant would remain at Rosings," Elizabeth reminded her.

As she pulled at her hands, Lady Catherine said defensively, "I wouldn't be alone. Is that the implication, Mrs. Darcy?"

Elizabeth shot a doubtful glance toward the door. *Should she ask Darcy to return?* "None of us wishes to be alone, becoming tied to the earth. Being counted successful, but knowing a personal deprivation." She released Lady Catherine's fingertips. "It would be my choice in your situation to keep my family close—not because I was an object of pity, but because I have much knowledge to pass on to my child, leaving her secure in her future."

"What makes you so certain, Mrs. Darcy, that if Anne aligns herself with Southland that I'll have a care for her future?"

"Because, Your Ladyship, you honor *family.* You never wanted me at Pemberley because you wanted to align your branch of the *family* with that of your dear sister's. You've returned to my husband's house because you desire a connection to your *family*—to your niece and nephew."

"Yet, neither wants me here," Lady Catherine said unguardedly.

Elizabeth's voice rose in her husband's defense. "Mr. Darcy's allegiance to family is as deep as yours, Ma'am. He'll not turn his back on his cousin if Anne chooses Southland."

"So, Darcy would circumvent my position if I object to Anne's engagement?" Lady Catherine asked incredulously.

"You know Mr. Darcy's sense of duty as well as any. Can you imagine his turning away from Miss De Bourgh?" After a few moments' silence, Elizabeth said, "You didn't appear earlier to have a strong disdain for Anne's choice. Why is it that you have retreated from the possibility? With your familial deference, I cannot imagine your not wanting to experience the thrill of recognizing your own grandchildren. And what of your grand nieces and nephews? Tell me, Your Ladyship, that you have no desire to see your flesh give birth," Elizabeth demanded.

"I never said I've no desire to know Anne's children or Lindale's or Fitzwilliam's or those of Georgiana!"

Elizabeth took offense that Darcy's aunt omitted knowing her children. "Then what are you saying, Your Ladyship?" Elizabeth was on her feet—no longer content to sit in subjugation to Darcy's aunt.

"I'm saying, Mrs. Darcy, that I may not know any of these children beyond Lindale's. I have little time: I'm dying, Madam!"

CHAPTER 17

~∞~ ~∞~ ~∞~

ELIZABETH FROZE IN MID-STEP. "That's not amusing, Your Ladyship."

"It's not a topic I would take lightly, Mrs. Darcy," Lady Catherine said sadly.

Elizabeth returned to the footstool and recaptured Her Ladyship's hands. "How do you know this?"

"Doctor Lipton—in London." Lady Catherine's eyes misted with tears, and Elizabeth noted the defeat in the woman's shoulders. "I've an enlarged area in my stomach. It's too great for the surgeon."

Elizabeth's own eyes blinked back tears. "How long?"

"Six months—a year—maybe two. As the illness progresses, Lipton shall gave me laudanum, but that shall be the extent of his assistance."

Elizabeth fished a handkerchief from her sleeve and slipped it into Lady Catherine's trembling hand. "Are you in much pain?" She choked back her grief.

"Constant discomfort, but not pain. Not yet."

Elizabeth's mind raced with a thousand questions. "Does Miss De Bourgh know?" If so, it might explain Anne's speedy acceptance of the lieutenant's attentions—someone to protect her.

Lady Catherine discreetly dabbed at her eyes. "No. No one knows but you."

Elizabeth couldn't fathom such a disclosure. "Why me? Why tell me?"

"Because I must tell someone," Lady Catherine said flatly. "And if nothing else, Mrs. Darcy, you are circumspect. You would take a secret to your grave, and that's exactly what I expect you to do."

"Surely, you'll allow me to tell Fitzwilliam."

Her Ladyship frowned. "No one, Mrs. Darcy," she said emphatically. "I want no one's pity. If Darcy accepts my gestures, I wish it to be because he finds a need for his aunt in his life, not because he holds regret."

Elizabeth swallowed hard. "It'll be as you wish, Your Ladyship." They sat in silence for several minutes, each contemplating what had just occurred between them. "The strength of your resolve is beyond my comprehension, Ma'am," Elizabeth said softly.

"No pity from you either, Mrs. Darcy. I shan't tolerate your allowing me free reign just because Lipton has pronounced me ill. If you do, I'll make your life miserable—purposely run roughshod over your household."

"That shan't happen, Lady Catherine," Elizabeth reassured.

The corners of Lady Catherine's mouth turned up in approval. "Good. We'll deal well with each other."

"It would seem that we should make arrangements for Anne's marriage as soon as possible. That she has been compromised plays well to the speed of Miss De Bourgh's joining." Elizabeth began to organize her thoughts.

"Why would I wish this so?" Lady Catherine asked suspiciously.

Elizabeth ignored the woman's tone. "Because you want to see Anne safely in the care of an honest gentleman. And if we wait, Miss De Bourgh may have to spend a year in mourning with no one to assist her with Rosings or with personal decisions. We'll let it be known that you don't approve, but you'll accept Anne's decision. It'll deflect emphasis from your illness. You'll have time to transition the estate into Southland's able hands. When you arrive in Kent, charge Mr. Collins with calling the banns. That would put the marriage a month off, which gives Viscountess Lindale time to recover before traveling from Lincolnshire."

"What of your own confinement?" Lady Catherine asked curiously.

A bitter smile touched Elizabeth's mouth. "I should've known that you would be aware of my condition."

"We are family, Mrs. Darcy."

"We are, Your Ladyship." Elizabeth's voice softened. "I'll be well into my sixth month. The trip may take longer than expected, but Fitzwilliam and I shall attend." Another moment of silence occurred. "Let me ring for Mr. Nathan and order some tea, as well as some toast and jam. I suppose the negotiations must begin." Elizabeth rose to tug on the bell cord. "Mr. Darcy's idea of Edward's presence seems a logical solution. It'll appear that the colonel initiated the match." Elizabeth sat in a nearby chair. "Should I remain, Your Ladyship? If you prefer, I'll withdraw after serving the tea."

"You *must* stay, Mrs. Darcy," Lady Catherine insisted. "For but one, I've no secrets from you."

Elizabeth couldn't resist the taunt. It was her nature. "You may as well share that one also, Your Ladyship."

Lady Catherine leveled a sympathetic gaze on Elizabeth. "I'll tell you because it may bring you hope. Anne was my third child. The first two didn't survive."

❧ ❧ ❧

"There you are," Georgiana said as she entered the library.

Edward spun around in surprise. "I apologize, Georgie," he said tentatively. "I was unaware that you sought me."

"My brother had asked me of your whereabouts." For a moment, Georgiana paused on the threshold, but with a steadying breath, she set her plan into action. With satisfaction, she noted the approval in Edward's eyes as she approached.

"Are you aware of your brother's reason for my immediate presence?" He took a step closer as if drawn to her, and Georgiana's heart did a flip.

She frowned minimally. "Something to do with Her Ladyship and Mrs. Darcy."

Edward smiled conspiratorially. "I've heard no shouting, nor have I observed the servants rushing to tend either lady."

Georgiana purposely paused under the mistletoe ornament. "It's a miracle of sorts."

"Am I to stand guard or to serve as a negotiator?" he asked casually as he stepped into the circle she had imagined as being part of the mistletoe's magic.

Georgiana smiled widely at him, but her resolve wavered with Edward's closeness. "Knowing Fitzwilliam," she said with a breathy catch, "all contingencies are possible."

Surprisingly, Edward moved closer still, and Georgiana quit breathing. "Well, in the absence of hysterics, I don't see a need to rush to your brother's side," he rasped.

"What shall you do instead?" she managed to murmur. Instinctively, Georgiana's chin rose in anticipation.

Edward's palm cupped her chin, and his thumb stroked her lips. "I'd thought to keep a Christmas tradition," he said softly. "To kiss under the mistletoe the prettiest woman I know. That is, if she'll have me."

Georgiana's heart sang. "Claim the berry, Colonel," she whispered as she closed her eyes and waited.

Edward didn't understand what had come over him. He'd awakened this morning with thoughts of Georgiana, and those images had grown into full-fledged desire. He'd made a quick reconnaissance of the house to locate all the mistletoe balls that the ladies had hung yesterday. Then he fantasized throughout Winkler's sermon about sliding his lips down the slender column of Georgiana's neck. Now he refused to let this opportunity slip away. He didn't know when everything had changed between them, but it had, and he had to accept it and move forward.

He'd obsessed over the past few hours about Georgiana's lips' softness, and Edward meant to taste them. Her warm breath brushed his cheek as he lowered his head to touch her lips with his. He recognized her innocence, and so, he made himself go slowly. A slight brush. Small kisses planted at the corners. A soft nibble on her bottom lip. The problem with this slow seduction was it was taking away all his self-control.

Edward slid his arms about her and pulled Georgiana closer. With one hand, he lifted her chin to position his mouth over hers. He rested his lips on hers, allowing Georgiana to experience his mouth's pressure before deepening the kiss. As she leaned into him, Edward slid his tongue along her lips' seam. When she gasped, he claimed her mouth's soft tissues.

After a few more seconds of pure pleasure, he forced himself to lift his lips from hers, but Edward's mouth hovered a breath away from hers. "Georgie, I would kiss you again, but if you do not wish it, you should leave this room now," he rasped.

"I shall stay," she managed to say. Georgiana slid her arms about Edward's neck and rose on her toes to meet his lips with hers.

Edward groaned, and his mouth returned to hers. This time she met his mouth with parted lips. It was so intimate; more intimate than he'd have thought possible. He was not without experience, but Georgiana's kiss felt perfect—even with her inexperience. His tongue entwined with hers, and she responded tentatively. The kiss deepened as she arched into his embrace.

His practical mind demanded that he cease kissing her, but for the life of him, Edward couldn't release her. Years of war had branded him as part of the unclean, but Georgiana's goodness wiped all his dissipation away.

The sound of people moving about the hallway penetrated his desire-driven brain, and he reluctantly raised his head. "You're so beautiful," he murmured as he kissed Georgiana's head as it rested against his chest. He simply held her then as each recovered his breath. If someone would walk in on them, he would simply be Cousin Edward, Miss Darcy's guardian. Oh, how he wanted to shed that designation and to assume another role in Georgiana's life.

"Georgie, we cannot stay here any longer," he said reluctantly.

Slowly, she drew her arms from around his waist. "It was perfect," she whispered.

Edward smiled lovingly. "Yes, it was." He caressed her cheek. "Meet me later in the conservatory," he said. "We should speak privately, but that conversation will be delayed until I see what Darcy requires of me, and then there will be the usual gift exchange and an early supper. Will you wait for me that long, Georgiana—that long before we can speak of what has just happened?"

"I've waited for this for over three years. A few more hours shall seem miniscule."

Edward kissed her nose's tip, before reaching up and claiming five berries from the overhanging ball. "Extra berries for when we meet privately," he said teasingly.

"I'll bring a few of my own," she said with a husky laugh. "In case we use all of yours and find additional ideas to discuss."

❧ ❧ ❧

Darcy's agitation had increased after his short meeting with Mr. Winkler. The clergyman hadn't taken well to Darcy's request to postpone indefinitely his joining with Kitty Bennet. Winkler hadn't seen the necessity of Kitty waiting until after Georgiana's Society debut.

"Are you ashamed of Mrs. Darcy's family?" the clergyman had demanded.

Of course, he had denied the man's accusation, but as he waited outside the drawing room where his wife and Lady Catherine held court, he wondered once again about his motives. He'd received instructions from his father—repeatedly—on his duty to Georgiana. He couldn't change his natural inclination to protect his sister, but Mr. Winkler had remained adamant.

"I did not deny the match," he reasoned. "Simply asked for a long engagement."

"How long might that be, Mr. Darcy? What if Miss Darcy

doesn't make a match during her first Season? What then? Your sister is beautiful and is wealthy, but she's of a gentle nature, and I cannot believe you would force Miss Darcy into a match she didn't desire. If she makes no match, must Miss Catherine and I wait additional Seasons?"

"How am I to know?" Darcy had felt the inadequacy of his response.

The clergyman had stood upon that note. "Mr. Darcy, I respect you, but I'll not allow you to dictate my every action. As my patron, I sought your approval, but I'll marry Miss Catherine with or without it. I'll seek another living, if necessary."

"Do nothing foolish, Mr. Winkler," he had warned.

"Unfortunately, Mr. Darcy, love makes a man very foolish."

Love truly had made him foolish; otherwise, why would the Master of Pemberley be lurking outside the door of one of his own drawing rooms waiting to be invited inside? Darcy glanced warily at the closed door. His wife and aunt had been ensconced behind the damn thing for over an hour. He'd wait another quarter hour; then he'd insist that his wife join him. After all, they had responsibilities to the rest of their guests and to his household.

ᢟᢞ ᢟᢞ ᢟᢞ

Of course, he'd not stormed the room, as he'd wanted to do. Nor had he demanded that his wife and aunt inform him of what had transpired. Instead, he'd reluctantly joined the other guests in the main drawing room. Everyone had had a late breakfast following the morning services. That is, everyone except those involved in the negotiations regarding Anne's ruination.

"It was a poignant service, Mr. Darcy. Not typical for a Christmas message, but very apropos," Bingley said as Darcy joined his friends and Mr. Manneville.

"I'm certain Winkler would appreciate hearing you say so," Darcy said flatly. He turned his head to see the clergyman approach Kitty, as she sat beside Georgiana.

Caroline edged closer to Darcy, something he wished that she'd not do, but something she'd continued, even after his marriage. "It's insightful, Mr. Darcy, to employ a clergyman who takes a more progressive stance. So many Catholics and Calvinists refuse to accept the teachings of the Anglican Church. Mr. Winkler has reached out in a non-denominational way."

Darcy would have preferred to speak of something other than his clergyman. He already felt remorse about how he had handled his conference with the man. He would have to find a way to broach the subject of the man's request to marry Kitty. "Many of my tenants are of Irish Catholic descent, and as such, have kept their beliefs. Mr. Winkler's is the only church within seven miles. He's addressed the community's needs in his sermons and in his ministration to the neighborhood."

"You're fortunate to find such a man," Jane said quietly, but her eyes rested on the pompous Mr. Collins, who had cornered Mary and Mr. Grange and was delivering his own version of a Christmas message.

Darcy smiled easily. "I am indeed, Mrs. Bingley."

At that moment, arm in arm, Elizabeth and Anne entered the room. "Oh, Mrs. Darcy," Bingley called upon recognizing them. "You were missed."

Elizabeth rushed to Darcy's side and claimed his arm. Instantly, he felt whole. Issues would resolve themselves as long as she remained beside him. "You shall excuse me, Mr. Bingley," she said as she curtsied. "Lady Catherine, Miss De Bourgh, and I planned for the festivities celebrating Lord Lindale's heir. I regret my tardiness."

"Where is Her Ladyship?" Caroline asked suspiciously.

"My mother would freshen her things before joining us," Anne said defensively.

Manneville asked, "And Lieutenant Southland?"

Darcy hated that everyone noticed the delayed appearance of the De Bourghs and Southland. "The last I saw of the lieutenant, he and my cousin had their heads together. Probably discussing military protocol." At least, part of what he said was true. He'd sent for his cousin to speak to the lieutenant.

As if on cue, Edward and Southland entered. His cousin turned to where Darcy stood, while the lieutenant purposely joined Georgiana's grouping. "See," Elizabeth said. "We knew we could find the colonel and the lieutenant together."

Edward pointedly placed Anne on his arm. "Was I needed?" he asked jovially.

"Your absence was noted, Colonel," Jane observed.

"Southland and I've decided to leave Tuesday morning. We had details to settle." Darcy wondered how much of what his cousin said was true. Obviously, Elizabeth's claim to have planned for Lindale's heir was an agreed-upon story.

"Might we address gifts for the staff, Fitzwilliam?" Elizabeth asked softly. "I would excuse the servants after the midday meal. They'll be engaged well into the evening tomorrow."

"Of course, my dear. I'll ring for Mr. Nathan."

~ @~ ~ @~ ~ @~

"May we speak privately?" Winkler whispered to Kitty.

Kitty shot a quick glance to where Georgiana spoke to Southland. "Perhaps we might walk about the room, Mr. Winkler? I could stand a bit of exercise."

"It would be my pleasure, Miss Catherine."

He placed her on his arm, and they ambled slowly about the room. "I would seek your advice, Catherine," he said in a voice just barely above a whisper. "My conference with Mr. Darcy didn't proceed as I'd hoped."

Kitty frowned. "Did Mr. Darcy refuse us?" She, too, muffled her words.

"Not exactly. Mr. Darcy asked that we not marry until after Miss Darcy makes a match."

Kitty nodded her understanding. "That makes sense. My sister and Mr. Darcy have spoken repeatedly of Miss Darcy's presentation. It'll consume much of their time."

"My concern is what happens if Miss Darcy's betrothal is delayed. We've spoken of a period of time for us to learn more of each other, but I'd envisioned a half year at most. The London Season doesn't even begin until March and runs until autumn. What if Miss Darcy makes no match and requires additional Seasons?"

Kitty defended her friend. "That's not likely. Miss Darcy's delightful."

"I agree," Winkler directed their walk away from the others. "But around strangers, she is also excessively shy, and we're both aware that Mr. Darcy would never force his sister into an engagement. Are we to wait through multiple Seasons?"

Kitty began to see the uncertainty of their arrangement. "And what if Georgiana's Season is delayed? Shall not Elizabeth be busy with her confinement?"

Winkler edged closer to Kitty. "I'd not considered Mrs. Darcy's delivery. What is her date?"

Kitty glanced about to assure privacy. "Some time in mid to late March."

The clergyman fought for composure. "Then how will Miss Darcy make her Come Out? She cannot possibly make an appearance before the Short Season. Mrs. Darcy won't be fit to travel before the autumn. How long must we postpone our joining?"

"I see no cause for delay. If Miss Darcy must wait, we could consider a summer match if all goes as we've spoken," she reasoned.

"Unless you are Mrs. Darcy's sister, and you have chosen a man without a title as your husband," he said matter-of-factly.

Kitty stumbled, and Winkler steadied her arm. "Do you mean to say, Sir, that our joining would reflect poorly on Miss Darcy's prospects?" she hissed.

"The *ton* judges a woman's suitability by her family's connections. How might I say this without offering an offense? Other than Mrs. Darcy's, your sisters' husbands would be rejected by the *ton*. Mr. Bingley has a fortune, but he holds no title."

"And his fortune comes from trade," she finished for him. Kitty paused to process Winkler's reasoning.

"But you're a gentleman," she protested.

"I am. I don't believe that Mr. Darcy feels our joining is a bad one. He would simply want it to occur after Miss Darcy makes a match." He paused as they passed her parents. "What I wish to know, Catherine, is how long you wish to wait. I've told Mr. Darcy that I mean to marry you even if I must find another living. Would you follow me, Kitty, to a new position?"

⤜ ⤜ ⤜

"Come, Georgiana," Elizabeth said. "Mr. Nathan has the staff assembled in the ballroom. Mr. Darcy would have you attend his annual Christmas offering to his servants."

"Of course." Georgiana caught Elizabeth about the waist, and they started for the door, but Mr. Bennet's clearing his throat stopped them cold.

"Yes, Papa?" Elizabeth asked with concern, but the mischief in his eye eased her thoughts.

Mr. Bennet winked at Georgiana. "It seems no one else will take advantage of the ladies. Well, I have no qualms in doing so." He reached up and plucked two berries from the mistletoe ornament. Then he leaned forward to place a brief kiss on Georgiana's forehead. "Happy Christmas, Miss Darcy." Then he turned to Elizabeth. "To you, Child, I wish infinite happiness." He raised Elizabeth's chin and kissed her cheek.

She laughingly accepted his touch. "You staked out the mistletoe and waited for our approach," she teasingly accused.

"I confess. It's an old man's ploy." He cupped Elizabeth's chin. "You are loved, my Lizzy," he said softly.

"As are you, Papa." Elizabeth teared. "Miss Darcy and I shall return in a few minutes. We must address the staff. Save me a place by your side."

"I'll anticipate the pleasure."

Elizabeth watched him casually walk away. She'd not imagined that her father would ever age, but he'd done so over the past two years. His step was a bit less stable, and lines showed around his eyes.

Reluctantly, she turned to Georgiana. "We should hurry. Fitzwilliam must be waiting for us."

They managed to escape before anyone else could delay them. Working their way through Pemberley's hallways, Elizabeth good-humoredly said, "It wasn't the kiss you sought, but Papa meant well."

"I didn't mind Mr. Bennet's chaste kiss," Georgiana said mischievously as she scampered along beside Elizabeth. "Your father's was actually my third kiss this morning."

Elizabeth came to an abrupt halt, and Georgiana skidded to a stop beside her. "Edward kissed you?" Elizabeth whispered. "A real kiss?"

Georgiana blushed, but she met Elizabeth's gaze. "Yes, a very real kiss. Oh, Elizabeth, it was everything I ever imagined."

Impulsively, Elizabeth caught Georgiana up in a hug. "I'm so happy for you. Later, you must tell me everything. Shall he ask your brother for your hand?"

"That's just it. The kiss held no professions of love." Georgiana frowned. "My brother had summoned Edward to assist with Her Ladyship. We had no time to discuss what comes next, but he did ask me to meet him later in the conservatory."

"The colonel is a man of honor. He wouldn't have kissed you if he'd no intentions of an offer of his hand," Elizabeth assured. Hastily, she hugged Georgiana again. "This is wonderful, but we don't wish to make an explanation to your brother. He is still waiting for us."

They clasped hands and hurried briskly along. As they entered the ballroom, Darcy gave them a questioning look, but Georgiana simply said, "Mistletoe delay. We apologize, Fitzwilliam."

Darcy's frown lines met. "Papa," Elizabeth assured. "My father claimed the first kisses." She stepped beside Darcy and prepared to greet the Pemberley staff. Georgiana took her position on Darcy's other side. This could very well be Georgiana's last Christmas at Pemberley. The possibility struck both Elizabeth and Georgiana at the same time, and their sisterly gazes found each other. Many questions remained. *If the colonel proposed, would he leave the service early? Would Edward take a buyout? Where would Edward and Georgiana choose to live? Would it be far away from Pemberley? Would Darcy even allow the match?* Above all these questions, one truth held true: The deepest regard bound them as "sisters."

Her husband turned to his patient servants. "The Darcys are honored to have you as part of the Pemberley family," he began.

⤳ ⤳ ⤳

Edward's mind still reeled from the excitement of Georgiana's kiss. He could taste her sweetness and a bit of cinnamon tea, and it was all he could do to maintain the conversation with Bingley's family. He wanted to speak with Georgiana again—to determine her feelings. *She kissed you*, his mind repeated with a rhythmic drumming.

He wanted to follow her when Georgiana accompanied Elizabeth to the ballroom. He wanted to meet with Darcy immediately and claim Georgiana as his own, but he needed to secure her agreement first. *What would the family say? Would they approve of the joining?*

⤳ ⤳ ⤳

"I need to speak to you," Kitty caught Georgiana in an upper hallway.

"Can it wait until after the meal?" Georgiana kept walking. "Fitzwilliam has sent me to fetch Her Ladyship. He wants to release the staff after supper, and the meal cannot begin without Lady Catherine."

Kitty followed along beside her friend. "You shan't forget. This is important, Georgiana."

"I swear on my mother's grave, Kitty. We'll speak for as long as you need. I promise, but Fitzwilliam shall be unhappy if Lady Catherine isn't downstairs shortly."

As Georgiana rushed on, Kitty called out, "I'll count on you, Georgiana."

～◎◇ ～◎◇ ～◎◇

Darcy stood at the table's head with a glass held high. "Mrs. Darcy and I are pleased to have you share this Christmas with us. It's been too many years since we have shared Pemberley's table with our family and friends. So, to each of you, Happy Christmastide! To my sister Georgiana, you remain my life's center; and to my wife Elizabeth, my eternal devotion!"

A rousing "Happy Christmas" followed as glasses clinked and were lifted to waiting lips.

"There's a small gift on your plate from Mrs. Darcy and me," he announced. He had scrambled upon his arrival yesterday to see that everyone had something appropriate to his station. He had sent Jarvis into Lambton to ask the local jeweler for specific items. Jarvis had had to rouse the man from his home, but Mr. Clifford had responded with suitable choices for the uninvited guests. Darcy had chosen items for the others prior to his trip north. On his next journey into Lambton, Darcy would personally see that the man received a bonus for his excellent service. He took his seat and re-laxed into the chair. He contentedly watched as squeals of delight followed ripped paper.

"This is capital," Bingley declared from the table's far end.

"Look, Mama," Mary held a small cameo on a velvet ribbon.

From beside him, Elizabeth slipped a small package into Darcy's lap. "You'll receive the rest in our chambers this evening." She had abdicated her rightful place to his aunt and had chosen to sit at his right hand.

"As will you, my love," he whispered. He squeezed her hand. Darcy tore the paper away. "What is this, Lizzy?"

"Open it and see," she said with a mischievous grin.

Darcy unwrapped the box and removed a long leather strap. He fingered it, but he couldn't determine its significance. "Is there more to this present?" he asked as his hand recaptured hers.

"Are you not the greedy one?" she taunted. She reached out and caressed his cheek. "There's a very large gift in the stables by the name of Saladin."

"You talked Lord Warwick into selling Saladin to you?" he marveled. Impulsively, he kissed her lips.

Elizabeth laughed easily. "Actually, he sold the gelding to you. I simply used my pin money to solidify the deal. By the way, I'll need an advance on my household funds."

"And you'll have it. I'll double your allowance," he said happily. "I cannot wait to escape to the stables. But how? When?"

"I convinced Lady Warwick first," she said simply, "and His Lordship delivered the horse the day we left for Newcastle."

Bingley noted their exchange. "What have you there, Darcy?"

"A very long leading strap for a gelding." Darcy held the leather strap aloft.

"Not Saladin," Bingley said excitedly.

Darcy declared, "One and the same."

"Are you not a lucky dog?" Bingley rejoined.

Darcy smiled widely. "My luck lies in marrying a phenomenal woman." He kissed the back of Elizabeth's hand.

"And what did Mr. Darcy give you, Lizzy?" Jane asked from beside her father.

Elizabeth held up emerald hairpins. "Something to keep my tresses in place."

"And to match Mrs. Darcy's eyes," Darcy added quickly.

Lady Catherine cleared her throat. "May I have your attention?" She paused and waited for everyone to quiet down. "As we are in a celebratory mood, I wish to announce the betrothal of my daughter Anne to Lieutenant Roman Southland."

Darcy admired how his aunt had kept any disdain from her tone. Lady Catherine actually sounded pleased with the engagement. "Congratulations to the happy pair." He raised his glass again. "To Anne and Roman."

Complete chaos erupted—everyone talking over each other. Words of disbelief and happiness spilled over, and Darcy heard his aunt say, "Anne and Lieutenant Southland have met many times over the years. He's the cousin of my dear Mr. Knight, Mr. Collins's predecessor. They have always favored each other, but his career has kept them apart."

So, that would be the story his aunt would tell the world. Well, he cared not how Lady Catherine turned the tale, as long as Anne was satisfied, and at the moment, Anne beamed with happiness. "Is this your doing?" he whispered to Elizabeth.

"A long-standing affection is a nice touch, do you not think? Like something from a novel."

～☙～ ～☙～ ～☙～

"You must be mistaken," Georgiana insisted. "Fitzwilliam would never manipulate your lives so." They'd found their way to a deserted music room.

Kitty explained, "Mr. Winkler wouldn't lie, Georgiana. Mr. Darcy asks that we postpone our joining until you've found a match. I'm afraid that my family connections shame yours."

Georgiana groaned. "But I don't want a Season."

"If Mr. Darcy has his way, you'll choose a husband when you reach London."

Georgiana's heart sank. "What may I do to change Fitzwilliam's mind?"

"We must tell Lizzy," Kitty insisted. "Only Elizabeth holds sway with Mr. Darcy."

CHAPTER 18

~∾ ~∾ ~∾

ELIZABETH MADE SMALL TALK as she circled the room. Darcy had begged a few minutes to address some urgent correspondence that had arrived during their absence, but she would have preferred that he'd stayed with her. As much as she adored having her dear family with her, Elizabeth required time to privately analyze what had occurred between her and Lady Catherine. Unfortunately, that analysis would have to wait until she retired for the evening, but Darcy's presence would make the wait tolerable. "Yes, Miss De Bourgh's engagement was a bit of a surprise, but a pleasant one, nevertheless," she said in response to Jane's inquiry regarding the afternoon's announcement. "I wasn't aware of Miss De Bourgh's prior acquaintance with the lieutenant, but Fitzwilliam was." Although they'd not discussed it, Elizabeth knew her husband would repeat the skewed tale to protect his cousin's reputation.

"The lieutenant doesn't possess Mr. Darcy's consequence, but I'm certain it'll be a companionable match," Jane added.

"The colonel says the man is in line for a promotion," Bingley said privately.

Elizabeth smiled easily, "Lady Catherine sees the advantage of having a son who has honorably served his country." Georgiana's and Kitty's entrances immediately caught her eye. Their agitation couldn't be hidden. "Excuse me," she said to the others and met her sisters in the room's middle.

"What is it?" she whispered anxiously as she caught Georgiana's hand.

"It's Mr. Darcy," Kitty hissed. "He's refused Mr. Winkler's suit."

Elizabeth grimaced. "Are you certain, Kitty? Mr. Darcy assured me that he'd see to your future."

Georgiana sighed deeply. "My brother asked Mr. Winkler to wait indefinitely—until I find a match. Elizabeth, I've no desire for a Season. How do I make my brother understand?"

Elizabeth shot a glance about the room. "Georgiana, you'll come with me to speak to your brother. Kitty, you'll remain here and assist the colonel in entertaining our guests."

"But I wish to come also," Kitty protested.

"I need you to stay here," Elizabeth insisted. "I cannot have everyone knowing what we discuss, or Mr. Darcy shan't budge."

～෧෧～ ～෧෧～ ～෧෧～

Without knocking, Elizabeth slid the door to Darcy's study open and entered. She tugged a reluctant Georgiana along behind her. Pointedly, she closed the door before turning to say, "You promised you wouldn't pit your sister against mine, but that's exactly what you've done."

Darcy glanced up with a smile at his wife's entrance, but a second glance at Elizabeth's countenance told him she was upset. Then, she delivered her accusation, and he knew immediately that this would be a heated exchange. "Could this not wait until Pemberley no longer holds outside guests?"

"As those guests are of whom you object, my husband, I don't think that's possible." She now stood before his desk.

Darcy remained seated. He'd realized his error in dealing with Winkler, but he'd not found an opportunity to correct it. "What has your sister disclosed?" he tried to keep his tone disengaged.

"That you refused Kitty's match until Georgiana marries," Elizabeth declared. "Can you deny that you have done it?"

Hers was an accurate summary, but his wife didn't understand the *ton*'s snobbishness. Georgiana would be judged by Elizabeth's connections. "I have no wish of denying that I did everything in my power to protect my sister's future."

"By destroying Kitty's?"

Darcy stood and slowly circled his desk. "Kitty's future is far from destroyed. I simply asked Winkler to lengthen his engagement."

"I didn't hear you disparage Mary's joining with Mr. Grange," she accused. "Is my sister's repugnance so strong as to taint Georgiana? If so, how can you consider my presence to be to your sister's benefit? Shall I hide in the country while you entertain in London?"

How could Darcy explain that their marriage eliminated any objection the aristocracy would have to his wife? He was a plain "Mister," but he came from those with titles, and he was one of the country's wealthiest men. All those realities would protect Elizabeth, but not her family. He had considered how Mary Bennet was locked away in an insignificant part of Hertfordshire, but even his association with Bingley could be called into question. "When Georgiana goes to London, you'll be in attendance as my wife."

"But shall I be her sponsor? Shan't my presence shame your sister's entrance into Society? After all, I've the same connections as Kitty." Elizabeth's hands fisted at her waist.

Darcy needed to reason with her, but when she took that stance, reason would be a hard purchase. Her connections were the same as Kitty's, but there was no reason to remind Lady Jersey and the other *ton* leaders of that fact. "I admit I didn't handle Winkler's request well, but I'm familiar with how the *ton* thinks. Although Winkler is a minor son, he has no significant inheritance, and Kitty's joining would ultimately reflect on Georgiana. Plus, we've spoken previously of the delicacy of my future dealings with Winkler if he marries Kitty." Darcy moved closer. "You must realize the depth of my responsibilities to this estate and to the neighborhood."

"It sounds very much as if your prejudice has returned, Fitzwilliam," she said softly.

Darcy took her into his arms and pulled his wife closer. Thankfully, she didn't resist the gesture. "That's not so, but I'm charged with Georgiana's future. As such, I must consider how the *beau monde* will accept her. The situation is not of my making. What would you have me do? The *ton*'s influence is too strong." He kissed her forehead. "I regret that I've given the appearance of improper pride. I seek a solution that will benefit both our sisters."

"I don't want Kitty to be denied because of me," Georgiana protested from where she had remained beside the door.

Darcy turned to his sister. "Georgiana, you're some years out of the schoolroom. People believe I've denied you your inheritance long enough. Most young ladies enter the Season at seventeen. You're already nineteen and will be twenty before your Come Out. It's unprecedented to wait so long," he explained. "I'm charged with meeting my obligation to you."

"But I do not wish a presentation." She raised her chin in defiance.

～&～ ～&～ ～&～

Edward had noted the distraught look on Georgiana's face when she entered the room earlier. Immediately, he would've gone to her, but Mrs. Darcy's mother and Miss Bingley both quizzed him on Anne's engagement. "Yes, the lieutenant saved my life during one of the American skirmishes," he'd said. "I'm pleased that a man I admire has agreed to protect my cousin."

"It was a speedy joining," Miss Bingley said coyly.

Edward wanted to lambaste her gossipy nature, but he said, "Southland has expressed his regard for my Kent family on numerous occasions, so, of course, he was happy to renew his acquaintance with my cousin. I suspect, as they're both more mature, that the time seemed appropriate to express their common regard rather than to let Fate separate them again." As he spoke, he observed how Mrs. Darcy led Georgiana from the room.

Determined to know what had brought on Georgiana's pique,

Edward excused himself and began to circle the room. He would question Kitty, who seemed as agitated as did Georgiana. He paused periodically and spoke to one grouping or another, but he continued on his quest. The Bingleys had taken it upon themselves to organize several parlor games while they waited for the Darcys' return. Finally, he reached her. "Walk with me, Miss Catherine," he said as he steered Kitty away from her sister's betrothed.

Once they were out of earshot, Edward asked softly, "What disturbs Georgiana?"

Kitty didn't hesitate. "Mr. Darcy has decided that Miss Darcy should have a Season."

Edward's chest constricted. "Why should that be an issue for my cousin?" he asked evenly.

Kitty sought a private corner before she responded. "Mr. Winkler has asked Mr. Darcy for permission to court me. My sister's husband has permanently delayed Mr. Winkler's suit until Miss Darcy makes a match. Mr. Darcy seems to feel the connection wouldn't benefit Georgiana."

Edward grimaced. "My cousin wishes to protect his sister." Although he disdained his cousin's tactics, he understood Darcy's objection. In fact, if Georgiana's presence didn't rattle his brain so completely, he might've considered Darcy's diplomacy reasonable.

"Yet, Georgiana eschews her brother's plans," Kitty protested.

"Why would Miss Darcy not want to experience a Season?" He'd his own reasons for not wishing to see a bunch of young bucks fawning at Georgiana's feet, but he'd thought a Season would be necessary before he could declare himself. At least, a few days ago, those had been his thoughts.

Kitty paused and turned to him. "Surely, Colonel, you know what Miss Darcy wants above anything else."

∽❧∾ ∽❧∾ ∽❧∾

Edward strode through Pemberley's halls toward his cousin's study. Mr. Nathan had told him all the Darcys were together in Darcy's private room. Just as he opened the door, unannounced, he heard Georgiana say, "But I do not wish a presentation."

Quietly, Edward eased the door closed and waited. "Edward, thank Goodness." Darcy's recognition brought an immediate blush to Georgiana's cheek. "Perhaps you can reason with your ward."

Edward stepped around her in order to place himself between Darcy and his sister. He suspected his cousin wouldn't be happy with what he'd have to say, and Edward would protect Georgiana from Darcy's rage. "How is Georgiana acting unreasonably?"

Darcy stepped away from his wife. "I've decided that Georgiana will make her debut this Season, probably in the fall, after Mrs. Darcy's confinement, but Georgiana prefers to ignore her obligations."

Edward turned to glance at a downcast-eyed Georgiana. "Is what your brother said true, Georgiana? Do you shun a Season's experience?"

"Tell the colonel the truth, Georgiana," Elizabeth encouraged.

Edward noted how Darcy eyed his wife suspiciously, but his cousin remained silent. "Well, Georgiana," he prompted.

Barely audible, she said, "I do not wish it."

"Tell me your reason," he said softly.

He watched her struggle with her composure, but Georgiana managed, "I want a match of my own choosing."

"Is that all?" Darcy interrupted. "I'd never force you to marry someone you didn't favor. You must know that, Georgiana."

Elizabeth stepped past her husband to rush to Georgiana's side. "Of course, your sister knows you wouldn't force her to marry someone not of her choosing."

"Then what does Georgiana mean? Would someone care to enlighten me?" Darcy fumed.

Edward returned his gaze to Darcy. "I agree with Georgiana. She shouldn't be given a Season."

"I agree also," Elizabeth added.

"This is madness," Darcy asserted. "We cannot coddle Georgiana forever."

Edward took an intercepting step toward his cousin. "No one indulges one of your sister's whims." He paused before saying, "Georgiana's been compromised."

His words, obviously, shook his cousin's composure, and Darcy's hands fisted. "Who?" he growled. "How is it possible? My sister's been at Pemberley."

"Not compromised in the strictest sense, but compromised nevertheless," Edward explained. He heard Georgiana's labored breathing, but Edward didn't turn around. Elizabeth would protect her.

Darcy turned red with anger and began to pace. "I want to know who. I'll kill him!"

Edward removed his sword from its sheath and handed the blade to Darcy. "It was I," he said calmly. "I compromised Georgiana by kissing her repeatedly."

With incredulity, Darcy accepted the sword and turned it on his cousin. "How could you?" he asked in disbelief. "I trusted you with my sister. My father trusted you."

The sword pointed in Edward's direction caused Georgiana to react. "It's not Edward's fault. I encouraged him," she protested.

"And I encouraged her to encourage him." Elizabeth stepped forward and moved the blade aside. "Fitzwilliam, truly look at them. Could you wish a better choice for Georgiana? Edward has guarded your sister throughout her life, and he'll continue to do so." She removed the sword from Darcy's grasp and returned it to Edward's outstretched hand. "Georgiana has carried a serious affection for the colonel for as long as I've known her. Your sister's affection was not the work of a day, but has stood the test of many months' suspense."

"And you didn't inform me," Darcy accused.

Elizabeth eased closer to him. "I was unsure of my suspicions until last evening, but I could say nothing until Georgiana was ready to act."

"And you?" Darcy turned to Edward. "When did you return Georgiana's affections?"

His cousin struggled to understand what had occurred. Edward recognized the confusion. His mind hadn't caught up with his foolish heart. "I returned to Pemberley to discover a vibrant woman. I've thought of little else since my arrival. If she'll have me, and with your approval, I would make Georgiana my wife." He glanced over his shoulder at Georgiana. The glow of happiness on her face could be addicting. He hoped he could keep that radiance there forever. He extended his hand to Georgiana, and she slid her hand into his.

Edward watched as Elizabeth mimicked the movement with Darcy. "What say you, Fitz? Will you accept my suit? It's not as if you need to learn more of my potential. You already know all my most intimate secrets." Although Darcy, obviously, hadn't known all his secrets until a few moments ago, Edward attempted to lighten the mood, but Darcy remained silent for an elongated moment.

Then he asked seriously, "This is your wish, Georgiana?"

She confidently said, "More than anything, Fitzwilliam." The fingers of her free hand wrapped around Edward's arm, and he flexed his muscle in response to her touch.

Finally, Darcy nodded his agreement. "I can think of nothing I would like more than to give Georgiana to someone who truly cherishes her."

"My only qualm," Edward added quickly, "is I'd like a day or two before we make the announcement official. My father would have my head on a platter if he thought Her Ladyship had learned of this before he did." He caught Georgiana's hand and brought it to his lips. "I would also like the opportunity to court you properly. You deserve better than this melodrama. Unfortunately, I must leave on Tuesday, but I'll return before Twelfth Night, and you and I will settle things between us. Hopefully, that'll not be too disappointing."

"I've waited for this for years," Georgiana said. "A few more days will be of little significance."

~శ~ ~శ~ ~శ~

Compared to their mornings, the Darcys' Christmas evening was quiet—not quiet in the literal sense, but without incident. He'd released his staff, and he and his guests had dined on cold meats, cheese, fresh fruit, and more Christmas pudding. They had played snapdragon, hoodman blind, hot cockles, and taboo. As Georgiana accompanied him on the pianoforte, Mr. Winkler had led the others in several hymns. All in all, the guests had simply enjoyed each other's company.

Darcy had taken the opportunity to speak privately to his clergy-man. "I mean to apologize, Winkler," he'd said. "I didn't consider your suit with the proper dignity. You're a valuable member of this community, and no one, especially me, wishes to lose you. Please trust me to deal honorably with your request. Despite how it may have sounded, I would protect both my sister and Mrs. Darcy's."

He wasn't content with Mr. Winkler's acceptance. He supposed the man had taken a wait-and-see attitude. When Darcy had mentioned it in passing to Elizabeth, she'd suggested that he place himself in Winkler's stead and consider the violence of the man's affections. "What would you have done if I had been the one in this situation?" she had whispered.

Darcy hadn't enjoyed Elizabeth's reminder of his own desperation at being denied her hand. "But it was you who kept us apart," he had said tersely.

"It doesn't change the focus of Mr. Winkler's heart," she'd said humbly.

"Is everything in place for tomorrow's Tenants' Ball?" Darcy asked as they prepared for bed.

Elizabeth placed her hairbrush on the vanity. "Mrs. Reynolds assures me there is nothing else to do. Perhaps I'll make a pre-Christmas trip a tradition. I've missed all the last-minute details."

"I'll schedule a new adventure each year," he said as he removed his boots and stockings.

Behind him, he was aware of Elizabeth as she slid her dressing gown from her shoulders and placed it on a chair back. "Mr. Darcy," she said softly. She waited for his full attention, but she need not have. Darcy was completely attuned to the change in her voice. Then she stood and turned to him. "I believe I owe you a proper thank-you for bringing my family to Pemberley."

Darcy swallowed hard. She was absolutely radiant. Elizabeth's luminous eyes spoke of devotion. She wore a pale yellow gown of silk and lace, cut in a Grecian style. It draped across the increased girth from her breasts' swell. Her ivory skin glistened in the candlelight. "Lizzy, you grow more beautiful with each passing day." His eyes focused on her lips. "I'm the wisest of men to have recognized your gifts," he rasped.

She laughed in a throaty manner. "Are you prepared to accept my gratitude, Mr. Darcy?" Elizabeth walked into his arms. As he pulled her closer, she slid her hands around his waist and under his shirt. Going on her tiptoes, she kissed the hollow of his throat.

Caught by her allure, Darcy kissed her passionately before scooping his wife into his arms and carrying her to his bed. "I love you, Elizabeth," he declared as he followed her down.

Silently wrapped in contentment, Darcy kissed the top of her head. "It's been a most unusual day," he drawled lazily.

Elizabeth leisurely rolled over in his arms, and lovingly spooned her body with his. "Two engagements on Christmas Day. It's unprecedented." She caught his hand and placed it on her stomach where he might experience their child's movements. "What do you think of the lieutenant?"

"I spoke with Edward at some length to better understand the situation. His aide has an idealized view of the life at Rosings."

"The ideal and reality must find a common ground," Elizabeth murmured. She liked talking to Darcy this way. They couldn't see each other's countenances so the words outweighed the facial expressions: Truth. "Lady Catherine appears willing to teach her daughter and new son of Rosings's inner workings."

"How did you manage to convince Her Ladyship to do so? I expected to have to physically separate the two of you?" he taunted.

Elizabeth shifted her backside closer to his chest. "I have my charms," she teased.

Darcy kissed her nape. "I succumb easily to your charms, my dear, but my aunt hasn't always been your advocate."

"Everyone changes, Fitzwilliam," Elizabeth countered. "I suspect Lady Catherine is feeling the self-imposed deprivation of her family. Mayhap, Her Ladyship belatedly realized she had done you a disservice."

Darcy chortled. "Perhaps Saladin will sprout wings like Pegasus."

"Only time shall tell," she said reticently, and Darcy wondered if she kept something from him. "Let us accept what Lady Catherine is willing to give us. I'd like for our child to know her, as well as the Earl."

"At least, Anne's marriage may give Her Ladyship an opportunity for grandchildren."

Elizabeth's tone remain guarded, and Darcy became more alert to what she didn't say; however, before he could ask, she changed the subject. "How do you honestly feel about Georgiana's choice?"

"I am thankful that Edward thought to give my sister time to change her mind. Despite his posturing regarding Matlock, I suspect that he, too, doesn't understand what has happened."

Elizabeth snuggled her buttocks into his body, and Darcy's desire increased. "Very few men do," she observed.

Darcy breathed in the smell of lemon in her hair and of lavender oil on her skin. Half-enthralled by his wife's closeness, he had trouble considering her earlier question. "I suppose you're correct," he hoarsely confessed. "I certainly couldn't comprehend why my heart lurched to life every time you walked into a room."

Elizabeth chuckled, but she wasn't finished with the conversation. "I cannot imagine a better husband for Georgiana. The colonel shall value your sister's independence. Besides, who knows her better? Georgiana shall become a confident force in the colonel's life because she shall not fear that her husband might discover her darkest secrets. Edward knows her flaws and sees beyond them."

Darcy sighed in defeat: first, for his quickly dying desire, and secondly, for the loss of his sister. "How do I allow my sister to leave Pemberley—even though the man is Edward?"

"You must find a way, Fitzwilliam. You cannot send Georgiana off with the burden of your doubts."

"I know," he said heavily.

Elizabeth rolled over to cup his face in her hands. "Georgiana carries you with her—every breath your sister exhales contains your spirit. You've been a brother, a guardian, a parent, and a friend. She's everything you esteem in this world; you've treated Georgiana with respect and tenderness."

"It'll be as if I'm losing our mother again. Each day, Georgiana resembles Lady Anne in more definition."

Elizabeth stroked his cheek. "Why not consider Georgiana's leaving as a way to keep your mother's essence alive? Sending it out to meet the world. With Edward, Georgiana shall have a man who accepts your sister's wit and intelligence over her beauty and her wealth. With the colonel, Georgiana shall not have to subjugate herself to her husband. And it's my belief that Georgiana is in love with Edward. Is that not what you want? For our sister to marry for affection and respect?"

"I want her happiness above all else."

Elizabeth wrapped her arm about his neck and pulled herself closer. "Allowing Georgiana the freedom of choice shall secure her happiness. I guarantee it."

❧ ❧ ❧

A light tapping on his chamber door brought Edward from a deep sleep. He dreamed of Georgiana and their wedding night, and he was sore to leave his bed to answer the door. *It is probably Darcy with another sword*, he thought as he groggily staggered to answer the entreaty. In America, his sleep was forever being disturbed with relayed news of the war's progress, but he hadn't expected the circumstance to follow him to Pemberley.

He had properly proposed to Georgiana, and she had accepted. That thought had played through his mind all evening, and in his dream he'd gathered her into his arms and had taken a long, leisurely drink of her lips. His lips had skirted her neck's slender column, and he had kissed along the shoulder blade. But then the tapping had started in the back of his brain and had rattled him out of that exquisite moment. "Coming," he grumbled as he reached for the door's handle. "What the…" he cursed as he jerked open the door. His sleep-induced brain half-expected to find Southland or another officer on his threshold, or even to face his cousin's angry countenance. The appearance of Darcy's butler jolted Edward alert. "Mr. Nathan?"

"Forgive me, Colonel, this just came for you by special courier, Sir. The messenger was from Carlton House." Mr. Nathan extended the silver salver upon which the note rested. He reverently bowed as Edward reached for the heavily waxed paper.

Edward lifted the enveloped "orders" from the tray. Shaken by the possibilities, he warned the butler, "Tell no one of this, Mr. Nathan. I'll inform Mr. Darcy of its contents in the morning."

"As you wish, Colonel." The butler bowed out and closed the door.

Edward took the message to the desk to break the seal. He found a taper and lit it from the fireplace embers. Then he stirred the coal and added more to warm the room before lighting a branch from that first single candle. "What are you avoiding?" he chastised himself as he straightened the bed's linens. He knew exactly what he eschewed: News from Carlton House meant his letter to Elphinstone had drawn the Prince Regent's notice. "It might be something worth knowing," he reasoned aloud.

Accepting the inevitable, Edward brought the folded pages to the bed. First plumping up the pillows and crawling under the blankets, he took the opener he had retrieved from the desk drawer and broke the seal. Silently, his lips read the words that could change everything. "I knew something didn't make sense," he grumbled. "Damn! Darcy will kill me."

CHAPTER 19

❧ ❧ ❧

THE DARCY HOUSEHOLD AWOKE to the preparations for the evening's scheduled event. The decorations had transformed the stables and the attached barn into a country assembly hall. Garlands and wreaths hung from the rafters, creating a winter marvel, smelling of aromatic greenery. Although Christmas Day had passed, the community overlooked the still-evident mistletoe balls. They would be put to good use by many of the local tenants and the village girls. Trestle tables held food platters and lemonade bowls. Ale kegs ensured that refreshments would flow freely.

"Good morning, Mr. Nathan," Darcy said as he strolled through the main hallway. "Is everything in place for this evening?"

"Mrs. Reynolds reports no problems, Sir. I'll have Thomas move the small desk to the stable entrance after breakfast."

Darcy smiled with satisfaction. He would continue a tradition begun by his father: Two hours before the celebration started, he would "hold court." He would listen to disputes and petitions by his tenants and the local shopkeepers. Some asked for small loans; others asked for justice. He would hear all comers and exact reasonableness as he saw fit. He gave some requests credence; others he denied. "Excellent," he said. "I'll join Mrs. Darcy in the morning room."

He strode into breakfast feeling the contentment of having Elizabeth truly happy for a change. Even the stress of Mrs. Joseph's early delivery and of returning home to an eclectic guest mix hadn't lessened her sparkle. She'd always risen to the occasion. In reflection, he wondered if he and his staff had erred by giving Elizabeth too much time to recover from her losses. *Perhaps, she simply needed to involve herself in life rather than to dwell on death.*

"Good morning, Mrs. Darcy." He caught her hand and brought the back of it to his lips. "I hope you slept well."

Elizabeth smiled brightly at him. It was part of the flirtatious nature of their relationship. He knew exactly how his wife had slept. Other than the few occasions upon which he had spent a day or two away from the estate on business, Elizabeth had shared his bed since their wedding night. "Exquisitely so, my husband. And you?" she asked coyly.

"Excellent, my dear." They had made love twice last evening. Once when she had tempted him with her new gown and once after he presented her with the last of her Christmas gifts. Darcy winked at her. "Mr. Nathan reports everything is on schedule."

"As does Mrs. Reynolds," his wife informed him. "The good lady and Georgiana organized some of the guests to assist in the decorating. Mrs. Bingley, my father, Mr. Grange, and Mary were of use in achieving tonight's success."

"I will express my gratitude," he assured. A slight movement to his left caught his attention, and Darcy turned his head to find his cousin standing solemnly by the door. "Edward?" He recognized the colonel's agitation. Darcy prayed his cousin hadn't had second thoughts: It would break Georgiana's heart, and Darcy wouldn't have it. He hadn't resigned himself to the match, but he wouldn't stand by idly and see his sister hurt.

"If you've had your breakfast, Fitz," Edward said gravely, "I would speak to you privately."

Darcy felt Elizabeth tense. "I'll send a tray to your study," she said softly.

Darcy offered a curt nod and turned to where his cousin waited. Neither man spoke as they wove their way through the bustling hallways. Not until the door closed solidly behind them did either even breathe. "If you wish to withdraw your suit, Edward," Darcy began, but an incredulous look from his cousin cut Darcy's threat short.

"My regard for your sister remains, but you may have second thoughts in giving your approval when you discover my news." Edward maintained a serious mien.

Darcy gestured to their usual chairs. "Let us discuss your news."

Edward sighed. "I've delivered possible scandal to your doorstep, Cousin. I ask your forgiveness in advance." Edward sank heavily into his favorite chair.

Darcy took his seat behind the desk and sat forward. "Suppose you start at the beginning."

For the next few minutes, the colonel explained what had occurred, including the previous night's delivery.

"From the Regent himself, you say?" Darcy questioned.

"Evidently Prince George trusted no one else," Edward said. A light tap at the door signaled the arrival of their breakfasts. "I'll see to the tray; you read the letter." Edward rose and handed Darcy the refolded missive.

The footman placed the tray on a table and then bowed from the room. "My Goodness—what a tangled web we weave," Darcy murmured as he set the letter to the side. "The question is what we choose to do next."

"We have to find what the Regent seeks. If we delay, Prince George will send armed men to Pemberley's door," Edward observed.

"That's just what we need," Darcy grumbled. "A few more unaccounted-for guests."

Edward handed Darcy a filled plate. "Can we solve this before Matlock is tainted by association?"

Darcy smiled cynically. "Of course, we can do what is necessary, but I'd prefer not to use force when we have a houseful of ladies." He leaned back in his chair and steepled his fingers on his lap. "Obviously, Lady Catherine won't be happy when she discovers the truth, and she'll quickly inform the Earl. We need to devise a way to solve the Regent's dilemma before everything escapes Pemberley's control." He tapped his fingers against his chin. "I planned the perfect Christmastide for my wife. Little did I know that God and Country had their own plans."

~ぬ~ ~ぬ~ ~ぬ~

Darcy found Southland and Manneville in the billiards room. "May I join you?" he asked as he casually shed his jacket and reached for his favorite cue stick.

"We play for sixpence," Southland warned as he lined up his next shot.

Darcy smiled easily. "I can afford a half shilling." He stepped out of their way as the men finished their game. While Southland ran the table, Darcy carefully watched both men. The lieutenant was not a man he would've chosen for Anne, but he was pleased that his cousin had found someone, at last. "I didn't properly welcome you to the family, Southland," he drawled.

The lieutenant looked up after completing his shot. "Thank you, Mr. Darcy. I'll do my best to bring honor to the De Bourgh connection."

"That won't be easy," Manneville taunted.

The man's attitude set Darcy's senses on edge. "Why do you say that?" He forced evenness into his tone.

Manneville said matter-of-factly, "Her Ladyship is accustomed to having her own way."

Darcy's eyebrow rose in curiosity. "What woman is not?" he asked as a challenge.

Manneville rested his cue stick against his side. "I beg your pardon, Darcy, but your aunt is more formidable than most women."

"Miss De Bourgh says Her Ladyship has always been resilient. That Lady Catherine needed to complement Sir Lewis's weaknesses," Southland defended his future family.

Darcy would prefer to turn the conversation. He would need to speak privately with Southland regarding what to divulge in public, but for now, Darcy needed time to interact with both men. "Lady Catherine hasn't had the leisure of having a husband to address a man's world. I have great hopes that Southland can assume some of those responsibilities."

"Thank you for your confidence, Mr. Darcy."

Manneville chortled. "Do not flatter Southland, Darcy. He needs to enter this marriage with his eyes fully open."

"Unlike you, Manneville, I would offer, instead of ominous predictions of Southland's ultimate failure, my expertise as a landowner. Why do we not give the lieutenant the benefit of our knowledge? You have a large country house. Is that not correct?"

"It is."

"Then let's join forces. As part of the Boxing Day celebration, I'll hear disputes and petitions from the locals who depend on Pemberley for their livelihoods. Why don't you two join me? With each request, we can point out the merits and the deficits. That way Southland can practice the responsibility without damaging others."

The lieutenant looked from one man to the other. "Is this a common practice? Hearing disputes?"

Manneville grumbled, "All the time."

"Then I would appreciate your insights, Mr. Darcy. You too, Manneville," Southland said excitedly.

Darcy took his turn at the table. Smiling amicably to win over their agreement, he said, "Afterward, we can enjoy the celebration." He added hastily, "But I'll swear you both to secrecy: I've asked mummers to perform tonight."

~ ~ ~

Edward traced a path through the deserted Pemberley hallway. Darcy had distracted Edward's traveling companions, and the colonel needed to take advantage of the moment. Except for the possibility of being caught, he and his cousin had planned for every contingency. Being discovered would mean that everyone would know what the Prince would prefer to keep secret. Easing the door open, he slid into the dimly lit room. The afternoon's winter sun had started its descent, but enough light remained for his mission. Shoving away from the door, Edward went in search of something damaging to a person's reputation.

~ᴓ~ ~ᴓ~ ~ᴓ~

Kitty had no idea why the colonel had entered Mr. Manneville's room, but his actions said something was amiss. In the U-shaped wing, she could see into the American's room from her dressing room. But today the view held a determined-looking colonel. Curiously, she watched Mr. Darcy's cousin do a thorough search of Manneville's dresser and traveling chest. "I wonder what he seeks," she said aloud, but there was no one in the room but her. "What could be so important that the colonel would risk being discovered in an awkward situation?" Standing behind the draped narrow portal, she watched in fascination as the colonel continued to seek a mysterious treasure. He ran his hand under pillows and behind paintings. Evidently, he must have felt her intense gaze because he looked up suddenly.

Kitty tried to jump back, but he'd seen her. The colonel strode to the window and stared directly at her. For a moment, she thought he'd madly storm to her room and demand her secrecy. Instead, he put a finger to his lips as if to shush her and then brought his palms together to plead for her cooperation.

Instantly, Kitty nodded her agreement. The colonel smiled brilliantly and blew her a kiss. She blushed, but gave a small curtsy. He returned to the room, and Kitty caught up her pelisse and headed for her room's door. She thought, *He has a wonderful smile—the kind of smile that could light up a woman's heart. No wonder Georgiana has fallen for him.*

~ᴓ~ ~ᴓ~ ~ᴓ~

"If you, Gentlemen, will excuse me, I wish to return to the house and freshen my waistcoat," Manneville announced as he stood and stretched. "I hope you've a better understanding of the type of situations you might encounter. At home, I hold such meetings once monthly when I'm in residence at my country house."

"It's been enlightening," Southland agreed.

Darcy took out his pocket watch to check the time. He'd hoped that Edward would've made an appearance. They'd planned for his cousin to search the American's belongings while Darcy distracted the man, but Edward was to come to them when he'd discovered what the Regent sought. However, the colonel hadn't appeared, and Darcy feared the worst. "You've no reason to change," Darcy assured. "I try to present the image of a country gentleman for these events."

"That's kind of you, Darcy, but I'll still make my way to the main house. I promised Miss Bingley my escort tonight."

Unable to say anything else to dissuade Manneville, Darcy offered a simple bow and prayed that Edward had completed his task. "I've one more petition to hear before I can leave. Please tell Mrs. Darcy I'll return as soon as possible."

"Of course, Mr. Darcy."

With some trepidation, Darcy watched the man depart. Reluctantly, he motioned to the footman to allow in the next petitioner. "This will be a simple request," he explained to Southland. "Mr. Forrest wishes a loan to expand his business."

"What might the good man do with the money?" the lieutenant inquired.

"That is what we'll hear."

～ঞ৴ ～ঞ৴ ～ঞ৴

He'd have to concoct some sort of explanation for Mrs. Darcy's sister of his search of Manneville's room. At least, his presence in the American's room hadn't sent the chit into hysterics. She'd actually encouraged him with her nonchalance. "Where to look now?" he grumbled. He didn't have time to search the suite's every corner. "I need to think like a conniving blackguard," he mumbled. Checking the door briefly for security, he said, "I knew the man was too good to be true."

His eyes searched the shadows. It was too dangerous to light a brace of candles. "Where, oh, where," he recited as he walked quickly about the room. Then he spotted it: a small box on the wardrobe's top. Only the box's edge appeared above the ornate trim that topped the press.

Scooping his find from its hiding place, Edward sat the small, thin box on the bed and lifted the lid. He'd found them: Princess Charlotte's letters to Captain Hesse. Reaching into the box, Edward removed the incriminating evidence and stuffed the tight bundle under his coat and beneath his arm. "Great," he sneered as he also secured a locket, a twist of hair, and a miniature of Her Royal Highness. As he searched for other items, a crash outside the door drew his attention. "Damn!" Hurriedly, he replaced the lid and tried to secure the box in its proper place. Then he looked frantically around for an escape.

～⌖～ ～⌖～ ～⌖～

Thinking it would be pleasurable to tease the colonel about his escapades, Kitty left her chambers, with her pelisse in hand. She still wondered why Mr. Darcy's cousin had chosen to invade Manneville's chambers. Evidently, just like her father, Colonel Fitzwilliam thought the American had something to hide.

Deep in thought, she turned the corner, and her heart sank. Manneville topped the stairs. "Mr. Manneville," she gasped. "I...I didn't expect...to encounter you, Sir. I thought...I thought you to be with Mr. Darcy."

The man took a leisurely assessment of her. "I came to freshen my things, Miss Catherine." He took a step toward her, and Kitty automatically countered with a backward retreat.

From behind him, she noted that the American's chamber door opened slightly and then quickly closed. "As…as did I." She would like to avoid the man, but Kitty wouldn't allow the colonel to be discovered. "Did Mr. Darcy finish his business?" she asked as part of her ruse.

"I believe he speaks to the last petitioner." Manneville closed the distance between them. "I was wondering, Miss Catherine, if you've promised all your dances to the clergyman?" He moved closer still.

Kitty swallowed hard. She desperately wished Georgiana had placed the colonel's traveling companions in a different wing. She glanced around, hoping that someone else would appear, but she was on her own. "Mr. Winkler would prefer that I save the majority for him."

"Does Mr. Winkler control you, Miss Catherine?" He had backed her into a corner with his advance. "Why do you not allow me to show you what a man of the world knows?" He leaned closer as if to kiss her.

Kitty turned her head sharply to avoid him. "I'm perfectly content with Mr. Winkler's knowledge," she defiantly declared.

Manneville stroked her cheek with his fingertip. "How do you know you do not like molasses if all you've ever had is honey?" He caught her chin and turned her face to his. In a heartbeat, his mouth took hers in a demanding kiss of challenge.

Kitty thought this the most disgusting moment of her short life. Even more disgusting than the stale ale on Mr. Denny's breath when he kissed her under the mistletoe at Aunt Philips's Christmas dinner. Without considering the consequences, Kitty jerked her knee up and made contact.

With a profane curse, Manneville staggered backward. In doing so, a vase crashed to the floor. "How dare you?" he roared as he caught her wrist and jerked Kitty toward him.

Kitty whimpered from the shock of his rage, but she fought to free herself. "Let me go," she cried.

"Remove your hand, Manneville," Edward's lethal voice came from their left. They both turned to find the colonel's unsheathed sword aimed at Manneville's chest.

The American pointedly released Kitty's arm, and she scrambled behind the colonel.

"I'll give my cousin your regrets for the evening." The colonel barely controlled his ire.

"Why should I withdraw?" Manneville straightened, but pain remained written on his countenance.

The colonel nudged Manneville with the sword. "Because I desire it. If I choose to tell Darcy of your perfidy, you'll not be accorded even that much compassion," he warned. "We'll leave for London at daybreak."

Manneville snarled, "Is that how it's to be?"

"That's exactly how it is." The colonel gestured with the sword toward the American's room. "I'll have a tray sent up."

Manneville paused when he reached the spot where Kitty still hid behind Colonel Fitzwilliam's back. "You're a fascinating possibility, Miss Catherine." With an abbreviated bow, he turned toward his room.

As soon as the American's door closed, Kitty caught at the colonel's arm. "Thank God," she moaned and leaned into him.

"I'm sorry," he whispered as he caught her to him. "Let me take you away from here."

Kitty's limp legs actually moved—a fact, which surprised her. "Thank you, Colonel."

"It's I who should thank you," he whispered close to her ear when he turned her toward the stairs. As they slowly descended, he cajoled, "You kept my confidence while fighting off a blighter of the worst kind. I'm in your debt."

Despite being shaken by the experience, Kitty looked pleadingly at him. "Would you tell me why you searched Mr. Manneville's quarters?"

The colonel gave his head a slight shake. "I cannot. It's part of my duty to Country. That's the most I may share." They paused on the landing. "Unfortunately, I must ask your forbearance. If we inform the others, scandal could rock Mr. Darcy's household. I require your silence. You cannot tell *anyone* of Mr. Manneville's assault or of my mission."

"Is it that important, Colonel?"

"Maybe not to you or to me, but very much so to those most high in our government."

Kitty realized immediately that not only had this man protected her today, but also he paid her a great compliment: He thought her a woman he could trust. She had found *family* among her sister's new connections. She smiled in relief. "On these two conditions," she teased, "shall I give you my oath of silence."

"Two conditions?" He, too, smiled in an emotional release. "You're a greedy one."

Kitty ignored his taunt. "First, you partner me during this festivity's dances. I do love to dance, and I imagine you are very adept."

"Will Mr. Winkler allow another gentleman the pleasure of your hand tonight?"

She thought of how much of her heart she'd already conceded to the clergyman. "The key word is *gentleman*," she rejoined.

The colonel chuckled. "And your second condition, my dear?"

"A lady likes a bit of gossip. You, Sir, have stolen my greatest glory. Give me something worthwhile to replace my lost treasure. Tell me you return Miss Darcy's affections."

The colonel's countenance registered his obvious surprise. "Miss Darcy's regard? What do you know of my cousin?"

"Only that Georgiana tenderly holds you in her thoughts."

The colonel barked out a laugh. "Poor Mr. Winkler has no idea what a delightful enigma he has claimed." He smiled easily. "I'll ask your forbearance again, Miss Catherine. I wish to speak to the Earl before anyone else knows, but I intend to make Georgiana my wife."

Kitty squealed. "Oh, I knew it!" Impulsively, she hugged him. "Next to my own marriage, this shall be one that most thoroughly pleases me." With happiness restored, she took his arm again. "This second secret may not be of national importance, but I much prefer it to the first."

৵৯ ৵৯ ৵৯

With a signal to those in wait, Darcy stepped to the temporary platform constructed at one end of the large open area. Everything had been removed and scrubbed clean. His staff had outperformed themselves. His wife and family had taken their places on the benches arranged across the front of the open area, and he was ready to begin this annual celebration. His cousin had seen to the only impediment: Mr. Manneville. The colonel had placed two footmen, with orders to guard the American's room, outside Manneville's door. "Good evening," he said loudly, and everyone quieted immediately. "Mrs. Darcy and I wish to welcome you to Pemberley. We'll begin tonight's festivities with a special performance." He gestured to his left. "So let us begin." Darcy returned to the benches to sit beside Elizabeth. Capturing her hand, he brought it to his lap. "This should be entertaining."

She returned his whisper. "I cannot believe you went to all this trouble."

"I wanted this to be a Christmastide like no other."

Elizabeth squeezed his hand. "Do you not think you have succeeded, my husband?"

Darcy chuckled. "I suppose I have."

"Our tale tonight begins with Saint George," one of the mummers announced. The performer wore a high paper cap and a beribboned jacket. "But he's not our only hero."

Thirty minutes later, Darcy's houseguests and his cottagers cheered for the motley actors. "I never thought to see Marco Polo and Napoleon in a play with Saint George and Admiral Nelson," Bingley laughed as he leaned toward Darcy. "But somehow it worked."

"The absurdity should've screamed *ridiculous*, but the juxta-position was entertaining," Elizabeth responded.

Darcy looked around to note the musicians' arrival. "Excuse me," he said to Bingley. "I'll have Mr. Nathan pay the performers." As he stepped away, Miss Bingley shadowed him for several steps before he turned to address her. "Do you require something, Miss Bingley?" She glanced around at his cottagers and unconsciously wrinkled her nose. The gesture made Darcy infinitely glad that he hadn't chosen her as his wife.

"I was wondering whether to expect Mr. Manneville to join us?"

In concern, Darcy studied her face. He couldn't divulge what he knew of Manneville, and even though her pretentiousness often displeased him, he wouldn't have Caroline Bingley injured by the man's duplicity. He quickly decided to speak privately to Bingley on the morrow regarding his sister's interest in Manneville. "I understand that Mr. Manneville hasn't taken well to our good English fare—too foreign for the American's tastes."

"After so many days?" she questioned. "It seems most strange."

"Mayhap it's that blasted coffee he drinks so much of," Darcy remarked. "English tea is better for the constitution. Now, if you'll excuse me, I've duties to perform."

A few minutes later, the musicians tuned their instruments in prepa-ration for the evening's dancing. "Mrs. Darcy," he extended his hand to Elizabeth. "Would you do me the honor of the first dance?"

Elizabeth rose to take his hand, but she said, "I would be *tolerably* pleased, Mr. Darcy."

His heart leapt with pride. "Am I tolerable enough to tempt you, Madam?" he teased.

"I am of a humor to give consequence to the right gentleman."

He adored the way she twisted his words from the Meryton assembly. "Then I am blessed, Mrs. Darcy, to have chosen a woman of discriminating tastes."

"That you are, Mr. Darcy."

He laughed at her light-hearted manner. That was the Elizabeth with whom he'd fallen in love. At Netherfield, when she argued with him, *his* Elizabeth's fine eyes sparkled in challenge, and he'd filled his consciousness exclusively with her countenance's memory. Several others within his party partnered for this opening set: Mary and Mr. Grange; Anne and Southland; Mr. and Mrs. Bingley; Kitty and Winkler, Georgiana and Edward; and Mr. and Mrs. Bennet. His friends and family honored him and his estate with their attendance, and Darcy would fondly remember this moment. Normally, he, Elizabeth, and Georgiana would stay an hour and then depart. The more ale his cottagers drank, the cruder their language, and he'd not expose his ladies to the boisterousness, but perhaps they might stay a bit longer this evening. He was in the mood to dance with his wife.

As he and Elizabeth occupied a position at the floor's center, a rather loud whisper took hold. "Kiss her." The chant began on their left and soon spread to those milling about the open space. Darcy looked up to find an elaborate mistletoe wreath about their heads. "What say you, Mrs. Darcy?" He grinned mischievously at her—offering Elizabeth a dare.

Elizabeth lifted her chin, and Darcy bent to kiss her cheek. Immediately, a groan of disapproval arose. "Kiss her," the chant became louder.

"Will you accept my return, my dear?" He saw immediately how much she was enjoying this mockery. What Elizabeth didn't realize was that he wanted to kiss her before everyone who mattered to him: to claim her before his world.

"Please, Elizabeth." Georgiana giggled.

Elizabeth's voice was honey sweet. "My lips shall make the sacrifice, Mr. Darcy." She puckered good-naturedly.

Darcy removed two berries from the wreath before he caught her chin and lifted it gently. Her placid taunt faded quickly. Gentlemen didn't kiss their ladies in public, but he intended to kiss her, to tell the world of his love. Darcy's mouth touched hers—not a brush of his lips—but a tender acknowledgment of their devotion. Without an audience, the kiss would've led to a more intimate encounter, and everyone realized it, especially Elizabeth, who blushed thoroughly. "Very nice," he murmured as a cheer arose among the onlookers.

~ᬚᬞ~ ~ᬚᬞ~ ~ᬚᬞ~

Throughout the evening, Darcy noted how often Edward had stolen a kiss from Georgiana. Although he knew his cousin's suit sincere, the reality caused his heart to lurch uncontrollably. "May I claim the next dance?" he asked as he stepped beside his sister.

"I thought you'd never ask." Georgiana slid her hand into his, and he placed it on his arm. Before Elizabeth, they'd attended the Tenants' balls together.

He placed her at the line's head—a place of honor such as she would always hold in his heart. "I've missed you, Sweetheart. I feel you've grown up overnight," he whispered close to her ear before stepping backward to assume his place in the line.

"But I have not, Fitzwilliam," she said softly. "I've suffered all the humiliations of a green girl. Now, I wish to claim a different life." They'd come together for the dance's first pass.

As they circled one another, Darcy asked, "And Edward can provide that life?"

"The colonel is what I seek," Georgiana said with a tilt of defiance to her chin. He recognized it as one of Elizabeth's traits. *Did his sister mimic his wife or was it an innate female trait?*

They wove their separate ways through the opposing line. When they came together again, he said, "Elizabeth says you'll carry our mother's quintessence into the world, and Edward will nourish that lifeblood in you. I know that's true, but as your brother, I'm forlorn with the possibility of losing you."

"You'll never lose me, Fitzwilliam. Your influence and love have molded me into the person I've become." On the next pass, she added, "As much as I wish to remain at Pemberley forever…" They parted again, and it was several more dance turns before she could finish. "…a woman must leave behind her parents and her loved ones to join her husband."

With resignation, Darcy murmured, "At least, Edward means you're still close."

CHAPTER 20

❧ ❧ ❧

"EXPLAIN THE LETTERS." Edward and Southland questioned Manneville. Darcy's party had returned to the main house an hour earlier, but the colonel, taking his aide aside, had excused himself immediately.

Manneville lounged casually against the pillows propped behind his head. "What letters?"

Edward paced the area at the foot of the man's bed. "Damn you! You know what letters. Those found in this box." He tossed the slender box onto the bed beside Manneville's leg.

"Is it now a crime to possess letters in England? What a country this has become!" Manneville said sarcastically.

Edward braced his hands on the ornate footboard. "It's not a crime unless those said letters belong to Princess Charlotte, and one plans to use them against her." He watched as his accusation registered on the man's face.

Shifting uncomfortably, the American said, "The letters don't belong to the princess. A gift has an owner different from the giver."

"Then you refuse to explain how you came in possession of the letters and the other items given to Captain Hesse?" Edward demanded.

"I found the box when we landed in Liverpool," Manneville asserted. "I had no idea it would cause such strife. If so, I would've left the items where they rested in the snow."

Edward threatened, "You have no idea what trouble truly is. Come, Southland. Let Manneville consider his choices overnight." The colonel strode from the room. In the corridor, he turned to the lieutenant. "I want you to stand guard. I'll relieve you in a bit. We'll allow Darcy's staff some time to enjoy the Boxing Day celebration. No sense in punishing them. It's not their faults that the princess's advisors duped us."

Southland looked about nervously. "Will our escorting Manneville to England be held against our future service?"

"Recovering the letters and other gifts might save our careers," Edward confided. "I've had a bad feeling about this man from the beginning. I wish I'd listened to my instincts. I would just like to know who cut our orders. We were specifically given the task to see to Manneville's safety."

"Then your intention is to escort Manneville to London and turn him over to the Regent's agents?" Southland took another step away from the American's door.

Edward drew his aide yet further away. "The message I received from the Regent indicated that recovering Hesse's letters would free the princess to form a proper alliance with Saxe-Coburg."

"Mercy!" Southland shook his head in disbelief. "How did we become so entangled in State affairs?"

"God only knows," Edward moaned. "Women in love control the pulse of a country, and we men are only along for the ride."

~❧~ ~❧~ ~❧~

"I wish you didn't have to leave tomorrow," Georgiana whispered. She and the colonel stood apart from the others in the main drawing room. Most of those in attendance played the usual assortment of parlor games.

Edward smiled at her. "As do I. Even though we've known each other your entire life, I suddenly feel we're strangers."

"We've moved into a different phase of our relationship," she observed. Georgiana paused before adding, "I must ask again if this is what you want. No one knows other than my brother and Elizabeth. We can continue as before."

With tenderness that caused her heart to beat erratically, Edward said, "We could never return to 'as before.' We are joined, Georgiana, but I do need for you to think on what picture you have for our future. Do you wish to take up residence at Yadkin Manor? Would you prefer to remain at Pemberley while I finish my service? There are many details we must settle between us, but I wish our joining most ardently. When I returned to England and you, my heart finally knew contentment."

"I do so wish we could tell the others."

"Soon, my love."

~~ ~~ ~~

"Will the colonel propose to Miss Darcy?" Winkler sat beside Kitty on a small settee.

Kitty glanced to where Georgiana stood with her cousin. "I think they'll know happiness before long, but how did you know?"

"I recognize the same bewilderment on the colonel's face as I find in my own mirror's reflection. He's quite besotted with Miss Darcy and does not understand how it happened."

So utterly happy, Kitty wanted to giggle like a schoolgirl, but she said, "I'm most eager for us to define our future relationship now that Mr. Darcy has withdrawn his objection."

Winkler frowned. He still didn't like being a puppet on Pemberley's string. He would think more clearly on his staying at Lambton once he had settled this matter with Kitty Bennet. For now, an odd sense of joy rushed through him. Winkler said, "As am I, Catherine."

~~ ~~ ~~

"I brought you a glass of port," Anne said as she approached Southland.

Roman looked up with pleasure. He'd never expected that his future wife would worry in his absence. Their worlds were so different that he'd had begun to have second thoughts on the alliance. He didn't love this woman who now stood before him, but he'd long carried the highest regard for her family. It wasn't she that he questioned, but rather whether he could transition into her world. "Thank you," he said with a smile. "That's most kind of you."

Anne looked about nervously. "Why do you sit in this empty hallway? Edward was very enigmatic about your absence from the party below."

"I'm afraid that I'm under orders and cannot speak of it." He awkwardly added, "Would you sit with me for awhile? I'd enjoy your company."

Anne blushed. "Since we are officially engaged, I suppose it wouldn't be improper."

Roman found another straight-backed chair in an empty bedchamber and carried it to the hallway. He placed it along the wall, beside the one he had previously occupied. Seating Anne, he returned to his chair. "Thank you for seeking me out. The colonel and I will leave for London at dawn, and I was sore to know how I might have a few minutes of private time with you before my departure. We've several things we should discuss."

"Go on, Lieutenant," she said softly.

Roman swallowed hard. "We should decide when we wish to marry."

Anne looked away in embarrassment, but she said, "Not too long. Long enough for the suddenness of our joining not to lead to gossip, but not so long if we wish to start a family. At least, that's what my companion counsels."

"Mrs. Jenkinson?" Roman questioned in surprise. "Not Lady Catherine?"

"My mother is accepting, but she hasn't totally acclimated to the idea. Her Ladyship shall never rescind the engagement announcement, but I do believe she'd thought never to see the day."

Roman captured her hand in his. "Then what say you? Choose a date. In London, I will purchase a license."

"My mother had suggested Mr. Collins's calling the banns upon our return, but I had considered the end of February." Anne calculated the dates in her head. "The twenty-third or twenty-fourth of February? Those are at the end of the week. Why don't you clear whichever day you prefer with your superiors and then send me the date in a letter. I assume we'll correspond regularly."

When he had proposed, Roman had never considered how they'd handle the particulars of their relationship. He'd just gotten caught up in the possibilities. Now, the idea of receiving mail from his betrothed fascinated him. His was a small family, and he rarely received the amount of mail the other officers did. He relished the idea of someone special writing to him. "Of course, we'll write regularly, and I'll ride to Kent when I have days off duty."

"I'll make you a good wife, Roman," Anne blurted out. "At least, I'll try."

"I know you will," he said compassionately. "Ours may not have been an instant love match, but few of the gentry marry for love. I promise you my fidelity and my respect. You own my admiration already. From those three, we'll build ourselves a foundation upon which we can live comfortably. I'd like to make you happy. Mayhap, a strong affection will grow between us."

"You've made me happy," she assured. "I've the hopes of a young woman again. I'll do whatever is necessary to make us a comfortable home. For you to know contentment."

Roman smiled easily. Possibly, he'd made the correct choice, after all. His future wife was an heiress. As such, upon Lady Catherine's death, Rosings Park would belong to Anne, and, ultimately, as her husband, to him. Their children would inherit a great estate. He'd accomplished much with his choice. With Anne's acceptance, he'd moved up in society. "We'll do well together," he promised.

They stared into each other's countenances for a prolonged minute. "Anne," he said with a rasp. "Would you allow me to kiss you?"

She blushed thoroughly. "I'd like that very much, Roman."

~&~ ~&~ ~&~

It was well after midnight when he entered her bedchamber. He had scaled an icy terrace and the metal claws of the ivy wall to reach an empty chamber in the U-shaped wing. Earlier, he had lowered his trunk to the ground with strips of cloth he'd made from torn bedding. From the empty bedroom, he'd made his way to her suite. Slowly, he opened her door and slid into the darkness. Using the fireplace's faint light, he moved stealthily across the room. Reaching her bed, he placed a knee on the edge and reached for her shoulder. Giving it a slight shake, he prepared for her awakening startlement.

With a gasp, her eyes sprang open. Searching the darkness, she frantically identified him as she clutched the bed linens to her chest. "What are you doing here?" she haughtily demanded.

"Saying my farewells," he replied. "I'm leaving tonight."

She scooted up higher in the bed. "Can you not wait until tomorrow?"

"It must be now," he said softly. "I'd like you to accompany me."

~&~ ~&~ ~&~

Darcy couldn't remember a more confusing night. As his cousin had predicted, the Regent's soldiers had arrived at Pemberley a little short of six in the morning. Mr. Nathan had roused him from his sleep, and Darcy had immediately sent for his cousin, only to discover that they'd lost their "prisoner." Although, in Darcy's estimation, the man they'd known as Beauford Manneville had committed no actual crime, the colonel and the lieutenant had accompanied the Regent's men in their attempt to recover Manneville. True, the American had once held in his possession the intimate letters of Princess Charlotte to her supposed lover, and it had also been true that said lover had intended to use those letters for his own benefit; but *intention* and *execution* were different issues. However, it wasn't likely that the Prince would see it that way. At least, Edward had secured the letters and the princess's mementos in Darcy's household safe.

"And Mr. Manneville climbed down his bedding to make his escape?" Lady Catherine asked incredulously. She and the Collinses and Anne would depart for Kent after breakfast.

He'd not wanted to share the details with the others, but Manneville's trickery and the presence of the Prince's men couldn't be kept secret. Darcy filled his plate from the morning's offerings. "Evidently. With the staff still enjoying the evening's celebration, Manneville hitched up one of the smaller coaches and drove away into the night."

"He's a cad and a thief," Lady Catherine declared.

Anne poured fresh tea for her mother. "Can you imagine living constantly with such scandal? I'm thankful at moments such as these that I never mastered the *ton*'s attentions."

Elizabeth explained, "According to Edward, on Christmas, Her Royal Highness Princess Charlotte finally decided to quit fighting the Regent. Prince George convinced his daughter that his wife would replace Charlotte on the throne with Princess Caroline's adopted son William Austin if our Prince should meet an untimely demise."

Darcy smiled cautiously. "We don't know those to be the facts, Elizabeth. You gossip about His Royal Highness."

"Everyone gossips about the Prince," she retorted. "What else are we to do in the trenches of Derbyshire?"

Lady Catherine added, "Or in Kent?"

This new agreement between his wife and his aunt still perplexed Darcy, but he knew Elizabeth would explain it eventually. Something of significance had brought these two different women into accord. "Then gossip on," he said wryly. "It's not as if I can stop you."

"As my husband, you could forbid it," Elizabeth countered.

"I could, but you have an uncanny way of defying me and then convincing me that it was my idea."

Lady Catherine snorted. "Your dear father used to claim the same about my sister."

Darcy's eyebrow rose in curiosity, but Elizabeth went on with her tale. "Anyway, Edward suspected something troublesome with Mr. Manneville so he sent a *casual* letter to Viscount Keith marking Edward's return."

"Mercer Elphinstone's father?" The story held Lady Catherine's attention. "How very daring of the colonel!"

"The viscount was in Scotland, but the Regent's men intercepted our cousin's letter," Elizabeth continued. "The Prince sent Edward orders to detain Manneville."

Georgiana gasped, "You knew of this, Fitzwilliam, and you told no one?"

"Of course, I knew. When Mr. Nathan answers Pemberley's door in the night's middle to find the Prince's courier, he had better report to me first or lose his position." His masked warning had landed squarely on his butler's shoulders. "Of course, Mr. Nathan is a superior servant. He understands the need to protect Pemberley first."

Elizabeth took up her tale again. "It's long been assumed that Lady Elphinstone holds great sway over Princess Charlotte."

"For a woman who spends little time in London, you seem well versed in the Prince's court," Darcy challenged.

"I have an aunt who devours the gossip pages," she reminded him.

Darcy chuckled. "I hadn't considered your Aunt Gardiner's influence."

"Why do you suppose her letters are so thick?" Elizabeth taunted. "One can only describe a child's latest sniffle or accomplishment so many times without being bland."

"Then finish your story, my dear." Elizabeth smiled prettily at him, and Darcy's heart took flight. He loved seeing her animated and challenging once again.

"Lady Elphinstone reportedly encouraged Princess Charlotte's relationship with Captain Hesse. The princess's correspondence with the captain is what Edward recovered from Manneville's room."

Her Ladyship chortled. "How delightful for Edward. He'll earn a promotion for his efforts."

Darcy warned, "As long as the Prince isn't upset that Manneville escaped."

"Maybe the Regent can finally convince Charlotte to accept Orange," Lady Catherine observed. With that, she stood to take her leave. "The Collinses have seen to my coaches."

The Darcys followed her to their feet. "We'll see you out, Your Ladyship." Darcy came around the table to place his aunt's hand on his arm. Only then did he notice how Her Ladyship's hand trembled uncontrollably. He started to say something, but a staying glare and a slight shake of his wife's head stopped him. Instead, he locked her hand into place with his free one. Slowly, he walked his aunt to the main door where Mr. Nathan awaited with her outerwear. Lady Catherine's domineering spirit overshadowed how frail she appeared. *Why had he not noticed this before?* "You'll no longer be a stranger to Pemberley," he said dutifully.

"And you and Mrs. Darcy shall witness Anne's marriage," Lady Catherine announced.

"Depending on Mrs. Darcy's lying-in," he reminded her.

A quarter hour later, the Rosings coaches departed for Kent. "Come, Mrs. Darcy. You may retell your tale," he said. "The Bingleys and your parents have yet to hear the latest. I expect they slept through the fracas."

When they reentered the morning room, the Bennets, Mr. and Mrs. Bingley, and Mr. Grange were helping themselves to breakfast. "Her Ladyship found safe roads?" Mr. Bennet asked as he scooped jam onto his toast.

"We certainly hope so," Darcy said as he resumed his breakfast.

Mrs. Bennet took the chair beside Elizabeth. "I cannot imagine Mr. Collins's consequence once he pronounces Miss De Bourgh's vows. You'll suffer another of the man's odious letters, Mr. Bennet," she declared.

"You're mistaken, my dear," her husband corrected. "I find Mr. Collins's letters most entertaining. They're very much like the man himself."

"Where is Kitty, by the way?" Elizabeth asked as she sipped her second cup of tea.

Jane sat across from her mother. "Charles asked Kitty to summon Caroline. We were all up so late last evening, he couldn't seem to make Miss Bingley hear his entreaty."

Darcy hid his true reaction to the idea that Caroline Bingley remained abed at the current hour. He'd escaped having his friend's sister as the mistress of his household. "Having so many of our friends and family at last evening's celebration did honor to my tenants. My steward, Mr. Lynden, reports that the cottagers returned home singing Pemberley's praises. I thank you for your participation," he announced to the table.

"We were pleased to be present for your Boxing Day celebration, Mr. Darcy. It speaks well of you and of the man in whose hands I've placed my daughter's future," Mr. Bennet solemnly replied.

Upon that note, Kitty burst into the room. "What is it?" Georgiana asked as she rushed to Kitty's side.

"Miss Bingley." Kitty paled. "Her room is empty. Not a dress or a brush. Nothing."

Bingley was up and moving immediately. "Are you certain, Kitty?" he asked as he darted past her and headed toward the stairs. Jane followed closely behind him.

Elizabeth caught Kitty about the waist to steady her sister. "She left this note." Kitty handed it to Elizabeth.

Elizabeth read it quickly and passed it on to Darcy, who scanned it before saying, "I'll share this with Bingley." Darcy dashed from the room to find his friend.

"What did the note say, Lizzy?" Mrs. Bennet asked excitedly.

"Miss Bingley has eloped with Mr. Manneville," Elizabeth announced.

"I suspected as much," Mrs. Bennet said coyly. "The man offered Miss Bingley a chance at a prominent marriage."

Elizabeth shook her head in denial. "You don't understand, Mama. The colonel and Lieutenant Southland, along with members of the Regent's personal guard, hunt Mr. Manneville. Miss Bingley has made a terrible mistake."

Epilogue

༺ ༒ ༒ ༒

20 MARCH 1815

Edward had arrived at Pemberley two days prior with the specific purpose of speaking to Georgiana. They were to marry in ten days, but he he'd received new orders to report directly to Wellington. On 13 March, the Congress of Vienna had declared Napoleon an outlaw. Four days later, the British government, along with Russia, Prussia, and Austria, had vowed to end Napoleon's hopes by placing 150,000 men in the "emperor's" way. Ever since Napoleon's landing on Antibes on 1 March, the newly minted Major General had spent his days couriering information between the Home Office and various leaders of Britain's military forces.

"You look magnificent in the new uniform." Georgiana's soft voice stayed the anxiety building in his chest.

Edward turned slowly to take in her beauty's complete perfection. He smiled with satisfaction. "I was a colonel for so many years, I sometimes forget to respond to my new title." He allowed his eyes to trace her figure. "I never tire of looking at you," he said seductively. "I'm the most blessed of men to have won your regard."

Georgiana remained framed in the open doorway. "I'm pleased you've returned early to Pemberley. We can finalize our wedding plans together."

Edward's frown lines deepened. "That's why I needed to speak to you, Georgiana. Please come and join me."

Georgiana's countenance betrayed her concern. "Is something awry?" She allowed Edward to take her hand and to lead her to a nearby settee.

Edward didn't answer immediately. Instead, he waited until she was properly settled. He had retained her hand and brought it to his lips for a soft caress. "I feel it's been a lifetime since I last looked upon your countenance."

"Edward, please," she pleaded. "I cannot concentrate on the niceties until you tell me what troubles you."

He grasped her small hands in his, but Edward couldn't make himself look directly at her. "Georgie," he said in his most comforting voice, "I'll not be in England on our scheduled wedding day. With Napoleon marching toward Paris, the government has assembled all able forces. I'm to report to Hull for departure in one week."

He raised his eyes to see his beautiful bride-to-be fighting back the tears. "So soon?" she questioned. "I'd hoped that you would have escaped seeing more action. You…you've already…already served on two fronts." Georgiana swallowed her panic.

"I've no choice, Georgiana. We agreed that I'd not accept a buyout."

Georgiana intertwined her fingers with his. "I know," she said with finality. They sat together for several silent minutes, thinking their way through the dilemma. Finally, she said, "We'll marry on Monday."

Edward removed his eyes from the close examination of her long delicate fingers. He had planned to carry all these memories with him. Now, he was ready to argue with her declaration. "Georgie, I've been thinking. Maybe it's best if we wait until after this campaign. There's the strong possibility that I could return no longer whole, or worse yet, make you a widow. I would not have your mourning my passing wearing your bridal gown."

"Edward, please tell me that you don't believe me so shallow?"

"Georgie, I just want to protect you."

"I'm not made of fine porcelain," she protested. "If my husband is injured, I'll tend him."

Edward caressed her cheek. "You deserve better than a broken man."

"May I not decide for myself what I deserve?"

"But…" he began; however, Georgiana's scowl turned his counterpoint null.

"Edward Fitzwilliam," she chastised. "You're one of the most articulate men I know, but now isn't the time to speak. Instead, listen well to my words. When you leave to join Wellington's forces, you'll do so with the knowledge that I belong to you forever. We shall marry on Monday. His Lordship and the Countess shall be at Pemberley tomorrow, as shall your brother, the Viscountess, and Lindale's heir. With Fitzwilliam and Elizabeth here also, we need share with no one else."

Edward smiled lovingly at her. "What happened to that sweet naive young girl who feared the world?"

Georgiana's mouth set in a straight line. "That simpering miss learned from her hard lessons. Surely, you don't prefer the Georgiana who you cradled in your arms after Mr. Wickham's dejection and possessing the realization of her own stupidity."

"That Georgiana still needed me," Edward taunted. "The woman I see before me now is an echo of her brother's wife."

"Elizabeth has shown me resolve's strength, but what you see is the Georgiana who has always wished to be an independent woman. However, that independence allows me to choose your protection and your love."

Edward chuckled. "I'm not sure I'll ever understand the depth of your graciousness and the reasons you love me, but I'm content to wallow in your goodness." He leaned forward and kissed her lips. "We'll marry on Monday, and I'll leave on Thursday. Do you suppose your brother could ready the dower house? I'd planned for us to visit the Fitzwilliam holdings in Scotland, but that will wait until my return. I'll leave for the Continent with the memory of your kiss on my lips."

⤜⤝ ⤜⤝ ⤜⤝

"What will you do, Bingley?" Darcy asked. His friend had returned recently from a harrowing journey across the Atlantic where he tried to recover his sister.

Bingley heaved a deep sigh. "What can I do? Caroline is Mr. Buckley's wife. I've seen the marriage license. The man married her aboard ship and then a second time when they landed in Baltimore. He claims he wanted to alleviate my anxiety, but I question the legality of their first joining. It wasn't a reputable ship upon which they sailed to America."

"Did not Miss Bingley realize her mistake when *Manneville* became *Buckley?*" Edward asked.

Bingley looked heartbroken. "Caroline had no choice: Buckley had thoroughly compromised her. Luckily, the man was not entirely without scruples. He does own a house in Charleston and a decent-sized estate south of there. But I don't think my new brother is totally solvent. He was most anxious to finally receive Caroline's dowry."

"And you'll comply?" Darcy shook his head in disbelief.

"I cannot deny Caroline her inheritance. My father's will specifies that she'd receive it without my consent when she reaches the age of five and twenty. That's in another two months; whether I wish to delay it or not, I have no alternative." Bingley took a deep drink from his wine. It was too early for any others to imbibe, but Bingley had suffered much from his sister's actions. "My new brother holds high ambitions. Maybe he and Caroline will do well together. I can only hope it will be so."

Edward placed his teacup on the tray. "I wish I'd known Buckley had taken your sister's carriage, and that she was with him. We looked for a single man, not a couple."

"Bingley and I assumed that was part of Buckley's motivation in convincing Miss Bingley to accompany him. He had no coach of his own nor did he know the best places from which to ship out. Miss Bingley served as a source of information and provided the perfect cover for the man's escape."

"It's a shame, Bingley, that the man used your sister so poorly," Edward remarked. "We were late in discovering Buckley's real name and his familial connection to Hesse."

A light tap on the door ended their conversation. Elizabeth appeared, and Darcy's whole composure changed. "It's time to leave, Mr. Darcy."

"We'll be there momentarily, my dear."

She gave them a quick curtsy and departed.

"Mrs. Darcy glows," Edward noted.

"She celebrates the third calling of your banns," Darcy teased.

"I suspect it's more than that." Edward said smugly. "But either way, we shouldn't tarry."

~❧~ ~❧~ ~❧~

"Miss Catherine," Edward said as he touched Kitty's elbow. He'd expected her to be one of the first down for the church services. Her relationship with Winkler was common knowledge, and a summer wedding was expected. "May we have a few moments together?" He nodded toward an empty drawing room.

"Of course." She sounded suspicious. "Is there something faulty, Sir?" she asked when he closed the door behind them.

"Nothing is out of kilter," he assured. "I wanted to speak to you privately because the others don't know of the service you did me when I searched Buckley's room."

"It was truly nothing," she began, but his scowl cut off the words.

"Neither the Prince Regent nor I consider it to be nothing. Because you forestalled Buckley's return to his room, I managed to find Princess Charlotte's letters. Now, the princess is free to accept Prince Leopold's attentions. This pleases the Regent very much. He's sent you a gift to show his approval."

Kitty gasped, "A gift from the Prince. Surely, you must be mistaken!"

"No mistake, Miss Catherine." He produced a small teardrop diamond on a gold chain. "Our Prince wished to send something grander, but I convinced our sovereign that you'd have trouble explaining anything larger to your family."

"Oh, my!" She looked amazed. "It's exquisite. I've never owned anything half as fine."

"The Prince wasn't satisfied with just the necklace," Edward continued. "He's dowered you with two thousand pounds in your name. I'll deliver the papers when we have the opportunity to speak again privately." He hooked the necklace about her neck. The teardrop fell between her breasts and was hidden from view.

"This is too much," Kitty declared, but she fingered the diamond lovingly. "How might I thank the Prince?"

"I'll see to it for you. Possibly, you might write a note of gratitude."

"Most certainly." Kitty stood in complete shock.

Edward smiled happily. "My tale of how Buckley manhandled you and how you persevered entertained His Highness most thoroughly. So, there's one last thing." Kitty's eyes widened in disbelief. "His Royal Majesty cannot bestow a title on you, but he thought that once you and Mr. Winkler joined that he might concoct a reason to give your new husband a knighthood. Sir Thorne and Lady Winkler sounds quite delicious, does it not? You'll have something even Mrs. Darcy doesn't have. The Prince will make arrangements to bring you to St. James."

Kitty's mouth remained agape. "Just like Lady Lucas. I'll be Lady Winkler. Mama will be so pleased, and Lydia will be eaten up with envy." She impulsively hugged Edward. "Oh, how do I thank you?"

"As before, your silence is required," he cautioned. "For that, you'll reap the benefits."

"Tell His Royal Highness that I can be as silent as a tomb."

～☜～ ～☜～ ～☜～

Mr. Winkler's voice rang clear. "Dearly beloved, forasmuch as all men are conceived and born in sin, and our Saviour Christ saith None can enter into the kingdom of God except he be regenerate and born anew of Water and of the Holy Ghost; I beseech you to call upon God the Father, through our Lord Jesus Christ, that of His bounteous mercy He will grant to *this Child* that which by nature *he* cannot have that *he* may be baptized with Water and the Holy Ghost, and received into Christ's holy Church, and be made *a living member* of the same."

He had taken the boy in his arms at the beginning of the service, and his son had immediately fallen asleep. It was his role in tending to their child, and Darcy never tired of it. When Elizabeth could not quiet the boy, Darcy would cradle him and whisper words of protection—a vow of love—and young Master Darcy would go silent.

Now, he and Elizabeth presented the boy to the community. His child secured Pemberley's future, and he couldn't contain his happiness. Looking over at his wife, Darcy observed the same completeness—not so much that she had delivered a male heir for the estate, but that God had found her "worthy," after all. Darcy had no doubts that Pemberley would know such happiness again and again.

The ceremony had progressed to the point where the boy's godparents would perform their duties. Requiring three god-parents, Darcy had asked Edward, Bingley, and Georgiana to serve in his and Elizabeth's stead. His cousin and sister were to marry and would see to the boy, as would Bingley and Elizabeth's sister Jane. His son would never suffer. He would have the best of everything.

"Dearly beloved, ye have brought *this Child* here to be baptized; ye have prayed that our Lord Jesus Christ would vouchsafe to receive *him*, to release *him* from sin, to sanctify *him* with the Holy Ghost, to give *him* the kingdom of heaven, and everlasting life. Ye have heard also that our Lord Jesus Christ hath promised in His Gospel to grant all those things that ye have prayed for: which promise He, for his part, will most surely keep and perform. Wherefore after this promise made by Christ, *this Infant* must also faithfully, for *his* part, promise by you that are *his* sureties (until *he* come of age to take it upon *himself*) that *he* will renounce the devil and all his works, and constantly believe God's holy Word, and obediently keep His commandments. I demand therefore, Dost thou, in the name of this Child, renounce the devil and all his works, the vain pomp and glory of the world, with all covetous desires of the same, and the sinful desires of the flesh, so that thou wilt not follow, nor be led by them?"

The three godparents responded together, "I renounce them all; and, by God's help, will endeavour not to follow, nor be led by them."

Winkler continued, "Dost thou believe all the Articles of the Christian Faith, as contained in the Apostles' Creed?"

Together again, they answered, "I do."

"Wilt thou be baptized in this Faith?"

"That is my desire." Two strong male voices and his sister's sweetness answered.

"Wilt thou then obediently keep God's holy will and commandments, and walk in the same all the days of thy life?"

"I will; by God's help."

Darcy shifted the boy in his arms. He rolled back the blanket and traced the soft cheek with his fingertip. His heir wouldn't approve of what was to follow. The baptism would interrupt the boy's sleep.

"Almighty, ever-living God, whose most dearly beloved Son Jesus Christ, for the forgiveness of our sins, did shed out of His most precious side both water and blood; and gave commandment to His disciples, that they should go teach all nations, and baptize them in the Name of the Father, and of the Son, and of the Holy Ghost; Regard, we beseech thee, the supplications of thy congregation; sanctify this Water to the mystical washing away of sin; and grant that *this Child*, now to be baptized therein, may receive the fullness of thy grace, and ever remain in the number of thy faithful children; through Jesus Christ our Lord."

Mr. Winkler's prompting led the congregation, and the on-lookers responded, "Amen."

Then the clergyman took the boy into his hands, and Darcy fought the urge to snatch the child away and take him home to Pemberley. He felt bereft of his son's warmth. "I charge you as this child's godparents to name the boy."

As planned, Georgiana answered for them. "Bennet Fitzwilliam George Darcy."

Over his wife's shoulder, Darcy could see a lone tear sliding across Mr. Bennet's wrinkled cheek. Darcy thought of his own dear father's countenance and imagined the pure joy that would have been displayed upon his parents' faces at this moment. Elizabeth's father had escorted Georgiana and Kitty to Pemberley after Anne's wedding. Besides wishing to see Elizabeth safely delivered of her child, Mr. Bennet had wanted to escape the chaos surrounding the preparations for Mary's nuptials. Therefore, when Darcy and Elizabeth could not attend Anne's wedding, Mr. Bennet had volunteered to see Georgiana and Kitty to Pemberley from Kent.

Keeping with the Darcy family tradition, early on, he and Elizabeth had agreed to bestow their firstborn son with his mother's family surname. He was *Fitzwilliam Darcy* because Lady Anne was a *Fitzwilliam*. Young *Bennet* would maintain the tradition. Elizabeth's family name would live on after her father's passing.

Repeating the name, Winkler officially certified it. "Bennet Fitzwilliam George Darcy, I baptize thee in the Name of the Father, and of the Son, and of the Holy Ghost." And the clergyman immersed the child in the water, and the congregation said the requisite "Amen," over the boy's verbal protests of being jarred awake.

Elizabeth took young Bennet from Winkler and quickly wrapped him in a large thick cloth, which Georgiana handed her. "I have you," she whispered to the boy and pulled him closer. "You are God's child, now." She kissed the dark curls on the boy's head, and he quieted immediately.

Darcy looked on in satisfaction as Winkler recited the next passage from *The Book of Common Prayer*. "We receive this Child into the Congregation of Christ's flock, and do sign him with the sign of the Cross. In token hereafter he shall not be ashamed to confess the Faith of Christ crucified, and manfully to fight under his banner against sin, the world, and the devil, and to continue Christ's faithful soldier and servant unto his life's end."

After that, Darcy heard little of what remained of the service. His mind remained on the Madonna-like image of his wife and child. Yesterday, they had received a detailed letter from Mary Joseph describing the three-month-old William. Elizabeth had read it twice, and even he'd delighted in her oral recitation. Soon, she would mimic Mrs. Joseph's epistolary style and send volumes of newsy letters of their son's accomplishments: the boy's first tooth, first word, his first steps. Just as Mrs. Joseph had predicted, many momentous occasions would follow this day.

The most surprising part of Mary Joseph's letter wasn't the final passing of her husband's mother, but the news of Mary's reconciliation with her father, who was none other than Edgar Parnell.

"Did you know of Mrs. Joseph's connection to Parnell?" he had asked Elizabeth after reading the businessman's letter, in which Parnell had agreed to partner with Darcy in a shipping venture.

"Of course, I didn't know," she had protested. Then Elizabeth smiled widely before saying, "If so, I might have withheld my services until the dear lady promised to speak to her father on your behalf."

Darcy had laughed at her and then chased his wife about his study. It was the first time they had made love since she had delivered their child some three-plus weeks prior. Afterwards, as they had lain, wrapped in each other's arms, on the animal rug before the hearth, he had nuzzled into her hair and whispered, "Thank you, Lizzy. You've given me a perfect world."

"My heart has been transformed by your love and by God's grace."

Darcy had brushed the hair from her face. "Our last Christmas changed our lives. We befriended the Josephs and will be forever connected to them. Georgiana and Kitty have chosen men to complete them. Anne knows family, at last. You and my aunt have resolved your differences, and we've both come to know the grace of God in our child's face."

Elizabeth kissed him briefly. "I had looked for God in all the wrong places. He's not found among the dead, not in the cemetery. I looked so hard for Godly things that I nearly missed God's grace when it presented itself. I've come to understand that a person needs God's love the most when he sees the need the least."

"An infant is a speck of Heaven that God allows us to experience. I wish to fill this house with Heaven's smallest specks. Will you join me, Lizzy?"

"I can think of no better paradise on this earth. I love you, Fitzwilliam Darcy—with all my heart."

"And I love you, my dearest Elizabeth. Forever and ever."

AFTERWORD

~⊘~ ~⊘~ ~⊘~

WHEN MOST PEOPLE CONSIDER a Regency Christmas, they are really envisioning a Victorian Christmas. The Regency Christmastide began with Christmas Day and ran through Twelfth Night. There are few references to Christmas celebrations in Regency literature other than the occasional wish for a "Happy Christmas" among story characters and real-life accounts.

English Christmases of the time were entrenched in religious observances. One must remember that in the 16th Century, to prevent subversion, the government banned Christmas celebrations. According to the *Jane Austen Centre Magazine*, "We have accounts from early 19th Century journals of Christmas days where the writer mentions the holiday but makes absolutely no fuss about it. Likewise, there are records of newspapers, published on December 25th that do not even contain the word *Christmas*." (http://www .janeausten.co.uk/magazine/index.ihtml?pid=387&step=4; June 17, 2011).

The gathering of greenery—rosemary, holly, laurel, and mistletoe—to decorate the household appears often in period literature. As for the mistletoe/kissing ball, it became quite elaborate during the Victorian Period. However, many believe the tradition remained below stairs in the servants' quarters during the Regency Period, but who is to say?

A Yule log to burn throughout the festive days would have been common, as well as the "Christmas candle." Groups of performers—mummers—date back to the Middle Ages. They sang and performed short plays, and because of their lower class, they often mixed bits of history with the British Napoleonic heroes. Of course, Saint George remained a staple of these plays.

Parlor games entertained houseguests, but there were no caroling or stockings or Christmas trees. Gifts were limited and often took the form of charitable acts by the aristocracy.

With all this in mind, in this story line, I tried to capture the "Christmas story's lesson," without all the hoopla of which we nowadays partake. Plus, I took the liberty to add a bit of romance, hope, and intrigue.

✒ ✒ ✒

In this tale, I have taken some factual liberties in Beauford Manneville's story. Here are the actual facts of Princess Charlotte's "indiscretions." In the spring of 1812, George IV tried to pique his daughter's interest in William, Prince of Orange—a move which would have strengthened England's alliance with the Netherlands. William had lived in exile in England and had even been educated in Oxfordshire. At first, Princess Charlotte refused the connection, but the Regent persisted, and at an arranged Carlton House dinner party on December 11, 1813, Charlotte accepted her father's wishes.

However, the Princess had second thoughts upon discovering that William would expect her to live half of the year in Holland. Part of the problem was that Charlotte feared her mother might follow her to Europe and then Prince George would use his wife's desertion as grounds for divorce. If so, the Regent would be free to remarry and possibly produce a male heir to the throne. Thus, Charlotte would lose her position as the future queen.

During this time, Mercer Elphinstone was Charlotte's chief confidante and aided the willful princess with her liaisons.

Charlotte's next *tendre* was for Prince Frederick, the King of Prussia's nephew. In Frederick's case, Miss Cornelia Knight, one of the princess's ladies in waiting, arranged several discreet meetings and acts of correspondence. Charlotte's relationship with Frederick ended in January 1815, when he returned her portrait and informed Charlotte that he had found another.

In July 1814, the Regent became "fed up" with his daughter's defiance, and he dismissed all her servants and her lady attendants. Charlotte sought protection with her mother Princess Caroline, but still being under the Prince's domain until age one and twenty, Charlotte was returned to Carlton House.

On Christmas Day 1814, Charlotte sought reconciliation with her father. In doing so, she admitted her recent relationship with Captain Hesse. Princess Caroline had encouraged the connection between her daughter and the captain, and Mercer Elphinstone had arranged the meetings and the correspondence between the lovers.

Charlotte had previously requested a return of her letters from Hesse, who had served as an equerry in Princess Caroline's service for a time. However, Hesse made no move to respond to Charlotte's demand, and the foolish princess had anticipated being blackmailed.

Over the next four days, Charlotte ingratiated herself with her father, and the Regent discovered details regarding his wife's duplicity. During those conversations, Charlotte admitted an interest in Prince Leopold, the third son of the Duke of Saxe-Coburg-Saalfeld, the man whom she would eventually marry.

Those are the facts. This is the fiction: Beauford Manneville was *not* Captain Hesse's American relative, and Hesse *did not* send Princess Charlotte's letters and personal items to Manneville for safekeeping. Manneville is a plot device and a pure creation of my imagination. He is used to add a "what if" to the story.

OTHER ULYSSES PRESS BOOKS

~◈~ ~◈~ ~◈~

Darcy's Passions: Pride and Prejudice Retold Through His Eyes

Regina Jeffers, $14.95

This novel captures the style and humor of Jane Austen's novel while turning the entire story upside down. It presents Darcy as a man in turmoil. His duty to his family and estate demand he choose a woman of high social standing. But what his mind tells him to do and what his heart knows to be true are two different things. After rejecting Elizabeth, he soon discovers he's in love with her. But the independent Elizabeth rejects his marriage proposal. Devastated, he must search his soul and transform himself into the man she can love and respect.

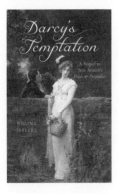

Darcy's Temptation: A Sequel to Jane Austen's Pride & Prejudice

Regina Jeffers, $14.95

By changing the narrator to Mr. Darcy, *Darcy's Temptation* presents new plot twists and fresh insights into the characters' personalities and motivations. Four months into the new marriage, all seems well when Elizabeth discovers she's pregnant. However, a family conflict that requires Darcy's personal attention arises because of Georgiana's involvement with an activist abolitionist. On his return journey from a meeting to address this issue, a much greater danger arises. Darcy is attacked on the road and, when left helpless from his injuries, he finds himself in the care of another woman.

Mr. Darcy Presents His Bride: A Sequel to Jane Austen's Pride & Prejudice
Helen Halstead, $14.95

When Elizabeth Bennet marries Mr. Darcy, she's thrown into the exciting world of London society. Elizabeth is drawn into a powerful clique for which intrigue is the stuff of life and rivalry the motive. Her success, it seems, can only come at the expense of good relations with her husband.

Mr. Darcy's Decision: A Sequel to Jane Austen's Pride & Prejudice
Juliette Shapiro $14.95

Mr. and Mrs. Fitzwilliam Darcy begin their married life blissfully, but it is not long before their tranquility is undermined by social enemies. Concern mounts with the sudden return of Elizabeth's sister Lydia. Alarming reports of seduction, blackmail and attempts to keep secret the news of another's confinement dampens even Elizabeth's high spirits.

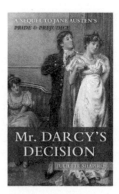

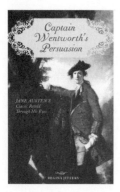

Captain Wentworth's Persuasion: Jane Austen's Classic Retold Through His Eyes
Regina Jeffers, $14.95

Insightful and dramatic, this novel re-creates the original style, themes, and sardonic humor of Jane Austen's novel while turning the entire tale on its head in a most engaging fashion. Readers hear Captain Wentworth's side of this tangled story in the revelation of his thoughts and emotions.

The Phantom of Pemberley: A Pride and Prejudice Murder Mystery

Regina Jeffers, $14.95

Happily married, Darcy and Elizabeth can't imagine anything interrupting their bliss-filled days. Then an intense snowstorm strands a group of travelers at Pemberley, and mysterious deaths begin to plague the manor. Everyone seems convinced that it is the work of a phantom who is haunting the estate. But Darcy and Elizabeth believe that someone is trying to murder them. Unraveling the mystery of the murderer's identity forces the newlyweds to trust each other's strengths and work together.

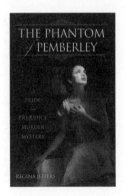

Vampire Darcy's Desire: A Pride and Prejudice Adaptation

Regina Jeffers, $14.95

Tormented by a 200-year-old curse and his fate as a half-human/half-vampire dhampir, Mr. Darcy vows to live forever alone rather than inflict the horrors of life as a vampire on an innocent wife. But when he comes to Netherfield Park, he meets the captivating Elizabeth Bennet. As a man, Darcy yearns for Elizabeth, but as a vampire, he is also driven to possess her. Uncontrollably drawn to each other, they are forced to confront a "pride and prejudice" never before imagined— while wrestling with the seductive power of forbidden love.

To order these books call 800-377-2542 or 510-601-8301, fax 510-601-8307, e-mail ulysses@ulyssespress.com, or write to Ulysses Press, P.O. Box 3440, Berkeley, CA 94703. All retail orders are shipped free of charge. California residents must include sales tax. Allow two to three weeks for delivery.

ABOUT THE AUTHOR

❦ ❦ ❦

REGINA JEFFERS, an English teacher for thirty-nine years, considers herself a Jane Austen enthusiast. She is the author of several novels, including *The Phantom of Pemberley*, *Darcy's Passions*, *Darcy's Temptation*, *Captain Wentworth's Persuasion,* and *Vampire Darcy's Desire*. A Time Warner Star Teacher and Martha Holden Jennings Scholar, Jeffers often serves as a consultant in language arts and media literacy. Currently living outside Charlotte, North Carolina, she spends her time with her writing.